EARTH REBORN

EARTH REBORN

EARTHRISE, BOOK VII

DANIEL ARENSON

CHAPTER ONE

Fiona St-Pierre was drinking wine on the patio, trying to forget her past, when a light kindled in the night sky.

She stared, frowning. The distant light grew brighter, streamed back and forth, then hovered above the forest. It was barely larger than a star. A flare? Perhaps an airplane or comet? It hung like a will-o'-the-wisp from a fairy tale, a luminous eye. Fiona shuddered. The orb, she could swear, was staring at her.

Cold wind blew. The trees creaked, the grass rustled, and her wind chimes sang. Fiona shivered and tightened her hand around her glass of wine.

There had been a lot of wine since the war. There had been a lot of this struggle to forget, to drown the memories. She was not a drunk, of course. Drunks drank cheap beer or hard liquor. They beat their wives. They crashed their cars. They lay on street corners, drinking from paper bags. No. Fiona drank only wine. It was cheap wine, of course—all she could afford—but a sophisticated drink nonetheless. She was an oenophile, she told herself, a connoisseur of the grape, not at all alcoholic. She was French, for God's sake; wine every day was expected of her. She was not at all consumed with nightmares. Not at all the broken, traumatized veteran everyone thought she was.

She took another gulp. She rarely sipped anymore; she gulped. She stared at the light that hung over the forest.

A scum pod.

The thought came unbidden into her mind.

Danger. Danger! Aliens. Monsters! Scum pods raining! Scum—

And she was back there.

She no longer sat outside her countryside home, her husband and children sleeping indoors, just a few meters behind her. She was no longer the twenty-nine-year-old mother of twins, the farmer's wife. Once more, she was nineteen, her face pimply, her heart thrumming in her narrow chest, her rifle hot in her hands. Once more, she was a corporal in Fort Djemila in North Africa, serving under Ensign Ben-Ari. Just a scared girl, a year out of high school, commanding her first squad of recruits.

At first Fiona had thought the recruits worse than the aliens. Pinky, a diminutive delinquent, had mocked her mercilessly, calling her Corporal Pizza and disobeying her every command. The other recruits had called her a witch, a bitch, an alien queen. They had respected the other NCOs. They had seen Sergeant Singh and Corporal Diaz, experienced warriors who had slain many scum, as heroes. Fiona had been inexperienced, awkward, angry, still new to the army and already tasked with molding children into warriors. She had felt so afraid. Afraid that the recruits, only a year younger, would learn how vulnerable she truly was.

Then the scum had attacked.

Then she had stopped fearing mere recruits.

The pods had filled the sky. They had fallen like a thousand flaming comets, shattering, spilling out foul miasma and giant centipedes. The screams had filled the fort. Soldiers had died around her. So much blood. Claws in her legs, scars that lingered. Marco pulling her into a troop carrier, and bullets ringing out, and another soldier dead, and—

Fiona forced herself to take a deep breath, to return to the present.

"No more," she whispered to herself. "No more memories. Stop this."

She took another sip of wine—no, not a sip, a deep gulp, but she needed it now.

That light still hung ahead.

The orb rose higher, darted to the side, and again Fiona had the eerie feeling that it was watching her. Was it merely Venus, bright over the horizon, and the swaying trees made it seem to move? Perhaps a helicopter, searching for a missing child in the woods?

Scum. Aliens. War. Monsters! Death and blood and—

No.

She took another deep breath.

It was just a light. A light couldn't hurt her. She had to stop doing this to herself.

Fear has ruled me for too long, she thought. *I can no longer let the scum destroy my life. I'm no longer that teenage girl with trembling hands, bleeding in the desert.*

She forced herself to turn away from the light. To look back at her house. It was a large country home, built over a century ago, predating the Cataclysm. After the war, Fiona had chosen to live out here in the countryside, to leave the bustle and anxiety of cities behind her. And she had made this a home, full of light and love.

A soft light shone in the upper window. Fiona could make out a night-light, a mobile, and glowing star stickers on the ceiling. Her beautiful twin boys were asleep. Her husband slept in the room next door. The hour was late, but Fiona had found no rest this night. Her husband had fallen asleep after a session of vigorous lovemaking, and Fiona could hear his snores even from here on the patio. But she was not a deep sleeper. Not since that night ten years ago.

She turned back toward the forest.

The light was still there.

The orb rose again. It stared at her. Then the light descended, vanishing among the trees.

Come . . .

The voice spoke inside her.

Help . . .

Fiona inhaled sharply. She rubbed her temples. She was going crazy. She was hearing voices now. She blinked, seeking the light again, but it had vanished into the forest.

A plane crash, she thought. *They need help. They're calling me . .*

.

She shook her head wildly. She felt dazed, confused. Too much wine was all. Too much forgetting.

She gave a short whistle. Hugo, her Dogue de Bordeaux, loped toward her, jowls flapping. She patted the mastiff's wrinkly head.

"Up for a walkie?" she said.

Hugo licked her hand, but he did not wag his tail. That tail stuck out in a straight line. He stared at the forest and growled. Fiona took a deep breath.

"You sense it too," she whispered. "Something . . . wrong."

She put down her glass of wine, and she lifted her rifle. "Come, Hugo."

She always kept a flashlight on her belt. She often needed to use it in the yard at night when Hugo would lose a toy. She shone the beam ahead. She walked across the yard toward the creaky trees, her flashlight in one hand, her rifle in the other. Hugo walked at her side, tail straight, teeth bared.

Fiona reached the end of the yard. The forest loomed before her. It was early winter, and the leaves were gone. The trunks rose like the craggy pillars of ancient temples, and the naked branches stirred above, wooden serpents, creaking, hissing. In the beam from her flashlight, the forest seemed black and gray. White eyes peered, then vanished, and a creature ran into the shadows. Twigs snapped.

Just a deer, Fiona thought. *Maybe a coyote.*

She gripped her rifle a little tighter.

"Hugo, we should turn back."

But the mastiff ignored her. He began racing forward, growling, heading between the trees. Fiona cursed and followed.

"Hugo!" she said. "Come back!"

Come . . .

Fiona froze.

Help . . .

The damn voices in her head again. No. Not voices. Just her imagination. Just the wind in the trees. Just memories.

Light. Light ahead! She saw it again—a dim flicker, moving away, vanishing between the oaks. Somebody was out there. Somebody had crashed into the forest. Somebody needed her help.

Fiona walked faster. She could no longer see Hugo. The thick branches hid the moonlight. Only her flashlight now lit the forest. This was stupid. This was wrong. She should not be out here alone, not even she, a trained soldier with a rifle. There were dangers in the forest. There were dangers in the darkness. She had learned that throughout three devastating wars, one against the scum, one against the marauders, one against the nightmares and memories.

A shadow stirred at her side.

Fiona spun around, aiming her flashlight. She caught just a glimpse—large eyes, pale skin, a shadow scurrying away. Fiona sneered and gripped her rifle. With shaking hands, she loaded a bullet.

That had not been a deer. Not a man. Not an animal.

Monsters.

She inhaled deeply.

"Hugo!" she called.

He was barking ahead. He was far now. She could barely hear him.

"Hugo, to me!"

He barked louder, growled, then squealed.

He fell silent.

Fiona began to run.

Her legs shook. Her breath trembled. Again she felt like a teenage girl caught in a war too big for her. So afraid. But she ran onward. She had failed to save Caveman, Sheriff, Jackass, so many other recruits. She would not abandon Hugo now. She would be brave, braver than she had been a decade ago.

As she ran between the trees, only her flashlight illuminating her path, she was back there again. Running across the dark desert. Running through the inferno of Fort Djemila as the scum rained from the sky, as her friends died. Perhaps she had been running since.

The light shone ahead, at first just an orb, then growing brighter, brighter still, moving through the trees. She chased it. It was fast. She could not catch it.

"Who's there?" Fiona shouted. "Do you need help? Hugo?" She panted. "Hugo, boy, where are you?"

Terror thudded in her chest. Sweat dripped down her back even in the November chill. The branches snagged at her like the fingers of lecherous old men, knobby, stabbing. The oaks seemed to laugh, trolls from old stories. Eyes. Eyes peered from the trees, vanishing when she turned toward them. Laughter sounded, high-pitched, a sound like wooden dolls scurrying in basements, like centipedes in the desert, like cracking bones.

"Hugo!"

Come . . .

"Where are you?"

Help . . .

"Who are you!"

Fiona . . .

Their voices—all around her. Her memories—dancing in the darkness. She tripped. She fell, and her flashlight hit a rock, rolled from her hand, and its light died.

But there was no more darkness.

The light blazed across her now, white and searing, filling the woods. It was bright as day. Naked creatures stood among the branches—pale, tall, skeletal. Yet whenever she turned toward one, it vanished, only to reappear in the corner of her vision.

A whimper sounded ahead.

Hugo.

Fiona rose to her feet, knees bleeding, and ran onward. The light still filled the forest, cruel and pale like fluorescent emptiness in an interrogation room. She tripped over more roots, raced around a twisting oak full of holes and whispers, and she found him there on the ground.

Fiona fell to her knees, and tears filled her eyes.

"Oh, Hugo . . ."

Her dog lay in wet red leaves. Somebody had cut open his belly, navel to neck, and removed his organs. The pulsing heart, liver, stomach, all the other parts of him—they glistened on the forest floor, still connected to the torso by arteries. Somehow, Hugo was still alive. Still breathing raggedly.

Just a nightmare. Just a dream. Just a dream.

Hugo looked at her. He licked her hand. Then his head slumped, and the heart on the leaves ceased beating.

In an instant, the searing white light vanished.

The forest plunged into pure darkness.

Fiona screamed and fired her rifle.

The bullets blasted out, and her ears rang, and across the forest, she heard them laugh. She saw their eyes—black, oval, staring everywhere. She fired again. Again. Only her muzzle lit the forest. In the flashes of light, she saw them. They were everywhere, moving in, seven feet tall and so slender, pale gray and naked.

Fiona fired at one, missed it. She fired her last bullet, then turned to flee.

She ran through darkness. She tripped on a root, hit the ground hard, and leaped back up. Blood filled her mouth, and she kept running. She banged against a tree, whipped around it, and raced blindly. They chased her. She heard them in the forest all around. She saw their eyes. Dead black eyes. The eyes of corpses. Eyes like the space between stars.

"Tom!" she cried to her husband.

The voices laughed. Pale hands reached out to grab her, fingers long, tipped with claws. They cut her.

"Boys!" she cried, voice hoarse, desperate to protect her children.

She kept running. She was lost in the woods. She could not see the light of her home, that soft light in the window, that warmth and love. She was in darkness here. She was cold. She was alone.

Then fight.

Another voice in her mind—but not the voice that had taunted her, that had summoned her to this hell.

It was the voice of her commanding officer.

Of Einav Ben-Ari.

Of strength.

Fiona nodded. She stopped running. She raised her rifle. It was out of bullets, but it was still a weapon.

A clawed hand reached toward her, and she swung her rifle. The barrel slammed into the those long, knobby fingers, and they cracked.

Another hand emerged from the shadows. It had only four fingers. She swung the rifle again, hit a creature, and heard it hiss. It withdrew.

Fiona swung her rifle like a club, panting.

"Back!" she shouted. "I am Sergeant Fiona St-Pierre! I am a soldier of the Human Defense Force! Turn back now!"

And they turned back.

She heard leaves and twigs creak as they retreated. She heard their whispers growing distant.

Fiona stood in the darkness, breathing heavily, drenched in sweat. She allowed herself a sigh of relief. Whatever they had been, she had scared them off. In the morning, she would drive into town, summon help, search this forest. Right now, she had to return home, to protect her children, to—

With a *thud*, a spotlight turned on above.

The blue beam fell upon her, searing, blinding, leaving all else in darkness.

Fiona tried to run. Her legs were frozen.

She tried to scream. No voice left her throat.

Her rifle fell.

All around her, she saw them. Shadows beyond the spotlight. Towering over her. Slender. Naked. Smooth. Staring with those oval eyes.

Her feet left the ground. The beam pulled her up into its brilliance.

A ship, she thought. *A ship above me* . . .

She tried to struggle. Her body was limp. Her eyes rolled back. And the beam kept pulling her upward, taking her above the trees. The forest rolled below her.

A hatch slammed shut beneath her feet.

She fell onto a hard metal floor.

She lay, dazed, struggling to breathe. She coughed and pushed herself to her knees, dizzy. They had done something to her. Drugged her. She tried to rise, fell again. She looked around her, blinking. She was in a shadowy chamber, a hangar on a ship. A cavernous, dank place, cold. So cold.

And from the shadows, figures emerged.

For the first time, Fiona got a good look at them.

Her chest seemed to shatter.

"No," she whispered, tears in her eyes. "You're just a myth. Just legends. You're not real. You can't be real . . ."

For centuries, humans had told tales of these creatures. The grays, people had called them. Just legends! Myths from Roswell and Area 51. Just tales told to frighten children, no more real than ghosts, Bigfoot, or the Loch Ness Monster.

Yet here they stood before her.

In the tales Fiona had heard, the grays were small, delicate beings. Yet these creatures stood seven or eight feet tall. Their heads were massive and bald. Their skin was gray, wrinkled, and covered with liver spots. They had no noses, but thin nostrils sniffed on their triangular faces. Their chins were small, their mouths mere slits. Their eyes were what terrified Fiona the most. Black eyes. Eyes without pupils, without any white to them. Eyes without humanity, without compassion, without mercy. Evil eyes.

"Who are you?" she whispered.

They grabbed her.

Their claws dug into her flesh. Her blood flowed. Fiona screamed.

The grays carried her through their starship. Fiona floundered. She kicked. She scratched. But in their grip, she was like a child.

This can't be happening. This can't be real. I'm back on the patio. I fell asleep. It's just a dream. My family is still with me. Wake up. Wake up!

But her pain, her blood, those searing eyes—they were all too real.

As she struggled, she caught glimpses of the cavernous starship. Shadowy halls. Rusting altars. Hieroglyphs were carved into the walls. Strange creatures lurked in the shadows, small as children, some almost human, others deformed lumps of spines and jaws and eyes. All gazed in fear, daring not approach. As the grays carried her past a porthole, Fiona saw the stars. She saw Earth. Her homeworld. It was already distant.

Fiona wept.

"What do you want?" she said. "Why did you take me?"

A door dilated. The aliens carried her into a chamber. Strange instruments hung from the walls, and tubes and wires dangled from the ceiling. Bloodstains coated the floor and walls. A rusty wooden cross rose in the center of the room. No. Not a cross. An ankh, Fiona realized. A cross topped with a ring. It was ancient Egypt's symbol of life, yet here was a chamber of death, of pain, of blood.

The grays carried her toward the wooden ankh. Fiona struggled against them, but their grip was like iron.

"I am a soldier in the Human Defense Force!" Fiona said, fighting to keep her voice from trembling. "If you do not release me, you will incur the wrath of humanity."

The aliens spoke in a foreign tongue, guttural, clattering. A language like cracking bones, like crumbling temples, like dying children. They shoved her onto the ankh like Jesus onto the cross. The grays surrounded her, looming like vultures over prey. Their black eyes narrowed. Those eyes were inhuman, but Fiona could read them.

There was cruelty in those eyes.

There was bloodlust.

They enjoy my pain, she thought.

She wanted to beg. To weep. To speak of her children, of her husband, to appeal to their mercy. But she was certain that the grays knew no mercy.

But perhaps they knew fear.

"Release me or suffer!" Fiona shouted. "We humans have defeated the scum. We have defeated the marauders! If you do not—"

They twisted her arms and pinned her wrists against the ankh. She stood before them, arms spread out.

One gray lifted a hammer. Another lifted a nail.

Fiona felt the blood drain from her face.

"I am a soldier," she whispered. "I am a soldier. I—"

They drove the nail into her hand, and she screamed.

They nailed her second hand, and she wept.

When they nailed her feet into the ankh, she finally begged.

Her blood dripped, her eyes rolled back, and she plunged into darkness.

For a long time, she floated in the black.

She dreamed.

She dreamed that she was a child again, just a child, that was all, her helmet too big on her head, her gun too heavy for her slender arms. A child in the desert. Running from the scum. Her friends dying around her.

She dreamed that she was a young woman, in love, marrying a kind man, giving birth to a pair of angels. They ran toward her, tiny feet padding, and embraced her. She lifted them, twirled around, kissed their soft cheeks. Her twin hearts. The loves of her life.

She dreamed of stars streaming outside. Of great darkness and knives in her hands.

She dreamed of a cross. Of whips flaying her. Of demons with merciless eyes.

When she looked up, she saw foreign stars. She saw towers. A city spread around her, thrusting up jagged towers like claws. Archways rose over roads like ribs. Obelisks loomed. A dark city, a place of dust, of rust, of dripping metal. Vultures circled above, their rotting wings hiding the starlight.

This was no dream, she realized. She was awake again, still nailed to the ankh. The grays were carrying her through the city. The aliens stared ahead, stooped, eyes narrowed. Their patchy skin clung to their skeletal bodies. They were so thin, yet strong enough to carry the wooden ankh she was nailed to. She saw their muscles coiling like ropes.

They carried Fiona toward a dark pyramid. A temple. An edifice of night, darker than the space between stars, and upon its crest blazed a golden Eye of Horus, all-seeing, never sleeping.

Two guardians stood before the pyramid, mummified, decaying, wrapped in rancid shrouds, and each stood taller than ten men. They held their arms over the pathway, hands fused together, forming a dripping archway of flesh.

Beyond these undead sentries, a staircase stretched up the pyramid's facade. Near the pyramid's crest, beneath the blazing eye, an obsidian platform thrust out like a tongue. The gray aliens carried Fiona up the stairs and onto this craggy platform. From up here, they could see the entire rancid city spread out around them. Beyond the city walls rolled charcoal plains, and black mountains loomed on the horizons, capped with fire.

The grays slammed the ankh down. Fiona hung from this cross, bleeding, fading away.

A throne rose before her, cloaked in shadows, and a figure sat upon it.

Fiona stared, tears in her eyes.

A demon.

A queen.

A goddess.

The figure unfurled from her throne like smoke rising from a corpse. She walked across the platform, rawboned and tall, clad in a dark robe with burnt hems. The robe was opened, revealing naked breasts that dripped bloody milk, ribs that pressed against papery skin, and a scar across the belly shaped like an ankh. The creature's head was massive, twice the size of a human head, the eyes gleaming and black, the nostrils two slits, the thin mouth frowning in a nest of wrinkles. Jagged metal spikes had been nailed into the creature's head, forming a lurid crown. Blood dripped down the creature's brow.

She was shadows and blood. Pain and antiquity. A queen of rot and a goddess of the night. She was like the other grays, and she was endlessly mightier. She was alien, and she was divine. She was torturer and salvation. She was the terror in the night and the comfort of death after agony. Fiona wept to see her.

"Worship her," whispered one of the grays, the creature that had nailed Fiona to the ankh. "She is Nefitis. Worship her glory."

Fiona hung on the ankh, barely clinging to consciousness. The blood still dripped from the nails in her hands and feet. The alien queen came to stand before her. The creature leaned down, bringing her face level with Fiona's, and stared into her eyes. The alien's eyes were as deep as the vastness between galaxies, as cruel as winter's heart. Eyes with all the secrets of the cosmos and not a shred of pity.

And then the alien queen spoke.

"You . . . are . . . Fiona."

Fiona stared through her tears. "I am Sergeant Fiona St-Pierre of the Human Defense Force. Service number EI-1723824." She took a shaky breath. She raised her head. Even hanging on this ankh in this alien world, bleeding, dying, she managed to stare steadily into the alien's eyes. "I am human. I am not afraid."

And the goddess smiled.

"You will be," she hissed.

Her claw thrust into Fiona's chest.

Fiona screamed.

The claws tore off her clothes, tore open her skin, cutting from the collarbone downward.

Her screams echoed through the hall.

"You know Ben-Ari," Nefitis hissed, pulling her claw downward, widening the wound. "You served her. You fought for her. You will tell me where she is."

Fiona wept. She gasped for breath, screamed again.

"Go to hell!" she shouted.

Nefitis's smile widened. "We're already here."

The alien pulled her claw down to the navel, gutting Fiona like a fish. The clawed fingers reached inward, grabbed organs, and pulled them out. When Fiona closed her eyes, trembling, those claws gripped her eyelids, tore them off. Fiona wanted to faint. She wanted to die. She could do neither. Chanting spells, Nefitis arranged the organs in the air, and they hovered, still connected to Fiona with dripping strands. Her heart still beat. Her lungs still breathed. All the organs of her body—hovering before her, veins dripping. With her long fingers, Nefitis moved them around, arranging, rearranging, peering, auguring.

"Let me die," Fiona whispered. "Please."

Nefitis stroked her cheek. "Worship."

"I worship you," she whispered. "I want to see my family. I want to die. Please."

"Tell me of Ben-Ari," Nefitis said. "Tell me of Marco Emery. Tell me of Addy Linden. Tell me of them all. Tell me of Earth. Tell me everything, and I will let you die."

And Fiona told her. She told the goddess everything, all the secrets inside her, all spilling out like her organs, like her hope, like her life. This life she had built with her husband and children. This life of peace she had sought after the fire. This life of love and lingering pain. It all spilled out from her here in this alien hell.

She gave the goddess her all. And when she was done, Nefitis nodded and stroked her cheek.

"I am Nefitis," she said. "I am the goddess of the night. And I am merciful. Your suffering will be short. But the suffering of your friends will last eternally."

I'm sorry, Fiona thought. *I'm sorry, my friends, my world. I'm sorry. I love you, my family. I love you.*

The goddess's claw sliced across Fiona's neck, for she was merciful, and in her eyes was kindness. All light faded, and Fiona fell into the black.

CHAPTER TWO

Marco sat alone on the day of his wedding.

He sat in his living room, wearing a suit, feeling numb.

He gazed blankly at the television before him. A journalist was interviewing a farmer, a man with buckteeth, a flannel coat, and a straw hat. The man spat and looked at the camera.

"I'm telling you, they're real!" he said. "Them aliens are real! First they abducted my chickens, and then they abducted *me*."

The interviewer, a dark-haired woman in a suit, nodded politely. "Can you tell us about your abduction, Mr. Horton?"

The farmer scowled. "I told you. Mr. Horton is my father. They call me Big Hungry Hort."

The interviewer gave the slightest crinkle of the nose. "Can you tell us about your abduction, Mister, um . . . Big Hungry Hort?"

The farmer nodded. "Well, them aliens—the gray ones with the big eyes—they strapped me onto a table. And then . . ." He gave the camera a knowing look. "They probed me."

"Poet!" Addy burst into the room. "For fuck's sake, why are you watching television? You're about to get married!"

He looked up. "I'm watching a show about aliens."

She groaned. "Fuck aliens." She switched off the TV, grabbed his shoulders, and shook him. "Emery, you're getting married today!" She yanked him to his feet and pulled him into a hug. "Can you believe it?"

He extricated himself from her crushing embrace. "You're wrinkling my suit." He narrowed his eyes. "Addy, what are you wearing?"

She gave a twirl. "It's a toga! Your wedding is on a Greek beach, after all, so I figured I'd match the theme."

Marco looked at her. Her garment was white and silky, and a laurel rested in her golden hair. That hair, which the marauders had sheared off two years ago, had grown to shoulder length. Her blue eyes shone.

"Actually, you're wearing a stola," Marco said. "Togas are larger and were worn by men. Stolas are more delicate and were worn by women—Roman women, actually, not Greeks, and—"

Addy raised her fist. "You'll be wearing my fist as a hat if you're not careful." She snarled. "Now tell me I look beautiful."

"You look beautiful," he said softly. "And I mean it."

Addy embraced him again, more gently this time. "How are you feeling, Poet?"

"Nervous," he said. "Scared."

"Cold feet?"

"My feet are frozen," he said.

She mussed his hair and kissed his cheek. "Tomiko is sweet, Marco. She's good for you. Really." She held his hands, and her eyes dampened. "I'm happy for you."

They looked into each other's eyes, silent for a moment, holding hands.

Addy had been his best friend since the fifth grade. It was a friendship he still cherished every day. Yet now, holding her hands, Marco found himself remembering that night ten years ago. They had been only eighteen. They had been scared, haunted by war, lost in a dark space station. That night, they had made love, had slept in each other's arms.

That night had never repeated itself. Addy had remained only a friend.

Could she have become something else? Marco thought. *Could we have ever become more than friends, become . . .*

No. He pushed that thought away. Addy was his friend. His oldest friend. His *best* friend, whom he loved with all his heart. But still just a friend. That night of sex long ago had been only a one-time occurrence; Addy had said so herself. Just a sweet memory that could never repeat. Addy had Steve now, her fiancé, and she loved the man. And Marco was about to marry Tomiko, a kind, gentle girl who loved him, who was good for him.

"Addy, I—"

He hesitated.

"Marco?" she whispered, eyes shining, still holding his hands. And God above, she was beautiful.

I love you, he wanted to say. *I'm sorry for hurting you on Haven. I'm sorry for the pain you suffered in captivity. We've been together for so long, and you understand me more than anyone, more than Tomiko ever could. I love you, Addy, and I don't want to lose you now.*

But he could say none of these things. Not here, wearing a suit, his bride waiting for him outside. Not with Steve upstairs. He said nothing.

Addy laughed and mussed his hair. "Silly Poet! Speechless for once. Go on. Warm up those cold feet of yours. And walk out there and marry your girl." She grinned. "You faced scum and marauders in battle. This can't be any scarier."

Marco laughed nervously. "No. It's not scarier."

Yet when he stepped outside onto the beach, his stomach roiled, and his head felt too light.

The guests were already there. Marco had seen no need for a party, no need for a suit, no need for so many guests. His family and most of his friends were dead. Pain still lingered in him, too great to allow for celebrations, even now. Yet Tomiko had insisted. For months, the girl had scuttled across the islands, planning the wedding: inviting guests, ordering flowers and decor, interviewing caterers, and dragging poor Marco to every engagement.

"This is my *wedding*," she had insisted. "It has to be *amazing*."

"It'll be amazing because I'm marrying you," Marco had said.

A thousand times, she had looked away, tears in her eyes. "You don't understand. You never understand!"

And she had returned to her planning, to her notebooks, to her samples of fabrics, to her catalogs of rings and bridal dresses.

"The girl's gone crazy," Marco had confessed to Addy one night.

Addy nodded. "She's a girl getting married. They all go crazy around this stage. Just wait until she's pregnant and sends you running out at three a.m. to buy her pickles and vanilla ice cream." She tapped her chin. "Actually, that sounds pretty good. Poet, go get me some pickles and vanilla ice cream! Pronto!"

And finally, after months of labor and countless dollars, here it was. A wedding on the beach. Rows of chairs. A flowery arch. Waiters with appetizers and a bar. Marco had never needed a drink more in his life.

He stepped toward the bar. He had a shot.

He felt empty.

He had another shot.

He felt scared.

A third. Enough. Enough! He forced himself away. He had fallen into that pit once before, had drowned in Haven. He did not intend to fall back in.

He walked across the sand, heading toward the wedding arch.

There were barely any guests.

A few people from the islands, barely more than strangers. The owner of the local bookshop. A few fishermen. None of Tomiko's family had arrived. Her Japanese mother had died in the marauders' assault on Osaka. Her French father had vanished years ago; Tomiko barely remembered him. The rest of their families—gone to the fires of war. Most of their friends—gone. A handful of Marco's friends had survived the wars, yet they had not come. Lailani was in the Philippines, building schools for homeless children. Ben-Ari had taken command of the *Lodestar*, humanity's new flagship, and was off exploring distant stars.

Marco wished he were out there with her.

He took a deep breath.

Come on, Marco, he told himself. *Space is full of terror, coldness, loneliness, and giant monsters with fangs like swords. You're about to marry a sweet girl, then spend the rest of your life on the beach, making love to her and writing novels. Why are you so nervous? Why does this feel so wrong? Warm your goddamn feet and walk onward.*

He gave Addy one more look. She nodded at him.

Marco walked toward the wedding arch.

Tomiko was waiting, wearing a white gown, and she was beautiful. At the sight of her, some of Marco's anxiety faded. The girl had only turned twenty last week, eight years his junior. Her black hair was long and flowing, and light filled her almond eyes. She smiled at him shyly.

He had met her only months ago—a homeless girl on the beach, a fan of his books. A girl named Tomiko, the same name as the heroine in *Le Kill*, his second novel. A girl meant to be. Her name a sign.

Marry me, he had told her.

Yes, she had said.

Under their wedding arch, he held her hands. She gazed into his eyes.

I emerged from fire, Marco thought. *I fought through darkness and the searing light of collapsing stars. I saw friends and family die. I suffered the wounds of a thousand battles. I suffer the nightmares of a thousand terrors. I am scarred, inside and out. I am broken. I am a survivor. I emerged from death and despair. Here is new life. Here is new love. Here is Tomiko. Here is my rebirth. Here is a new Earth, the planet I fought to save—an Earth reborn. A place of peace.*

He did not speak these words. Nobody would understand—nobody but Addy. Her words returned to him now: *Tomiko doesn't need to understand, Poet. She needs to make you happy.*

"You make me happy, Tomiko," he whispered, and he kissed her, and he married her.

She had hired a DJ. A ridiculous thing. He needed just another shot, this one of strong *arak,* to dance with her. The faces all swirled around him. Fishermen. A few people from the nearby town, come for the free booze and food. Steve and Addy were dancing; for hockey players, they were surprisingly graceful. A couple of people were fighting. Marco needed just one more drink to make the memories fade. To make the marauders and scum go away. To cloak the memories of Addy—hugging him, holding his hands, making love to him. Just one more shot until there was nothing but Tomiko in his arms, swaying with him on the dance floor, and he was happy. And he was at peace. And he was in a haze.

She doesn't need to understand. She needs to make you happy.

"I am happy," he whispered to himself, the beach swaying. "I am happy, Tomiko."

The sun set, and they made their way to their home on the beach, this house they had built after the war. It was a large house. A dream house. For a year, fighting the marauders, Marco and his friends had dreamed of building this house, of retiring on the beach. The yurei, mystical aliens from another cosmos, had given them a treasure of azoth crystals, valuable enough to fund this home with many rooms.

It was mostly empty.

Lailani had moved back to the Philippines, serving her church, building her schools.

Ben-Ari had flown into space.

Kemi had fallen.

For a long time, Marco had lived here with Addy and Steve, a third wheel.

But now you're here with me, Tomiko, he thought, holding her hand as they stepped toward the door. *Now* . . . He swayed, struggling to find his keys. *Now* . . . His head spun.

Tomiko groaned and unlocked the door.

They walked upstairs and lay on the bed. Marco tugged off his tie and shirt. Tomiko undressed quietly, not meeting his gaze, her movements stiff. When she lay on the bed beside him, he caressed the curve of her hip.

"Tomiko, I—"

"You're drunk," she said.

He blinked. "I'm sorry. I just had a few drinks." He kissed the back of her neck. "I love—"

"Don't touch me." She wriggled away from him. "Goodnight, Marco." And she was weeping.

He wanted to comfort her. To apologize. To explain that it wasn't her, it was the scum, it was the marauders, and he had to silence them. He couldn't let them ruin his wedding. He wanted to make love to her, to make this right. But his head kept spinning, and he had to throw up.

He stumbled out of bed. He made it to the bathroom just in time to vomit into the toilet.

Head reeling, he walked outside. He made his way along the beach to the water.

He fell to his knees before the beach, and the waves dampened his knees. He was still wearing his dress pants.

"What are you doing, Marco?" he whispered, gazing at the sea.

The moon and stars shone above, reflecting on the water. The sea seemed a living being, breathing with every wave. When Marco looked up at the sky, at those distant stars, he did not see beauty. He saw the fire rain. He saw the monsters. He saw his friends die. He saw Malphas, Lord of Marauders, murder his father. He saw Kemi die in his arms. He saw himself on Haven— he could see Haven's star right above now. And he was there again, fading away, addicted to alcohol, to sex, to self-pity. To pain. To memory.

"Marco?"

She spoke softly behind him, and Marco stood up. He turned to see her there. Addy was walking toward him, still wearing her stola, a laurel in her hair.

"What are you doing here, Marco?" she said, concern in her voice. She almost never called him Marco.

He sat down and faced the sea again. He patted the sand beside him, and Addy hiked up her stola and sat down too. They watched the waves together, silent.

Finally Marco spoke.

"Do you remember Anisha?"

Addy nodded. "Of course. Anisha Morgan. Your girlfriend on Haven. I liked her."

Marco sighed, watching the sea breathe, the moonlight dance on the waves, the foam limned with light. "She wanted to marry me. She never officially proposed, but she talked about it. About settling down. Buying a home together as husband and wife. Having kids."

Addy was quiet for a long time. "I didn't know that," she finally said.

"Do you remember that night Anisha and I broke up?" Marco lowered his head. "It was one of the worst nights of my life. Maybe *the* worst night. I went to her family home. I met her parents. I saw artwork on the wall. Lobsters on the plates. A dog in the backyard, wagging his tail. I saw suburban bliss. And I was afraid, Addy." He looked into her eyes. "I was so afraid."

"Of what?" she whispered. She placed a hand on his knee.

"That I didn't belong there," Marco said. "Not anymore. That I didn't know how to be happy. How to laugh at jokes. How to make small talk. How to be a normal human." He laughed bitterly. "I didn't even know how to dance at my own wedding, not without six or seven drinks. So I pushed Anisha away. I fell into self-pity and self-destructiveness. I drove you away too, Addy. One night after you moved out, I went onto the roof of a tall building, and . . . I almost jumped off the edge."

Addy gaped at him, but then her eyes softened. "You never told me."

"After fighting the scum, after surviving a war, I didn't know how to live in peace. So I shattered. And I fought another war, Addy. Against the marauders. A war larger, more terrible than the war against the scum. And I don't want this to happen again. What happened on Haven. Addy, I'm not strong like you."

She scoffed. "You think I'm strong, Poet? You think I don't have nightmares too?" Her eyes dampened. "You think I don't see the scars on my body every time I undress, don't remember the marauders cutting me, branding me, and . . ." She inhaled sharply. "But I don't let them control my life. I don't let them ruin it for me. The fucking scum and marauders. Because we beat them. And they're gone, and we're still here. And I won't let them ruin this. I won't let them steal my happiness."

Marco spoke softly. "Addy, what if I can't be happy? What if I'm too broken for peace?"

"Marco." She grabbed him and looked into his eyes. "Listen to me carefully, all right?"

34

He nodded.

"Are you listening?" she said.

He nodded again.

"Do not fall to pieces again," Addy said. "I won't let you. This isn't Haven. This isn't some fucking cluster of concrete and smog on the ass end of the universe. This is our dream home on a beautiful beach, and your beautiful bride is sleeping inside, and beautiful me—the best part!—is with you. This is what we fought for." Her voice softened. "So enjoy it, Poet."

"And if I can't?" he whispered.

Addy grabbed a fistful of sand and dumped it onto his hair. "Then I'll bury you in sand." She grabbed more sand and tossed it onto him. "I'll bury you up to your neck and let the crabs eat you!" She shoved him down, dumping more sand onto him. "I'm forcing you to be happy. Forcing you! On pain of death—by crabs!"

He groaned, shoving her off. "Addy! God! I got sand in my eyeballs."

She nodded. "Good. You deserve it. So choose, Marco. Happiness or death by crabs."

He sighed. "Happiness, all right?"

"Perfect." She kissed his cheek. "I love you, little dude. You know that, right? That I love you a ton." Suddenly she frowned and spat. "Eww, gross! You taste like sand!"

He tossed sand at her. "I love you too, you big sand monster."

She mussed his hair for the millionth time. "Now go back to your wife. Make her happy. And be happy. Promise me, Marco. Be happy."

He returned home. He had a long shower. When he crawled back into bed, Tomiko was asleep. When he placed a hand on her hip, she moved to the edge of the bed. Marco lay alone, cold, until sleep tugged him into a dreamless darkness.

* * * * *

Be happy.

Addy's voice kept echoing through his mind as the days went by.

Be happy or else!

He had some money stashed away, royalties from *The Dragons of Yesteryear*, his fantasy trilogy. He bought passage on a boat, took Tomiko to nearby Crete, the largest of the Greek islands. They spent a week hiking, eating fresh fish at the tavernas on the beach, making love at night. On the first day, Tomiko was distant, cold, but slowly she forgave him for drinking at their wedding. At the tavernas, he only had Diet Coke. She drank chocolate milk.

They explored ancient ruins from three thousand years ago. They visited the labyrinth where the Minotaur was said to have roamed, and Marco remembered seeing the great HDFS

Minotaur, the flagship of humanity, battling the ravagers over the ruins of Toronto. He pushed that memory aside.

Slowly the smile returned to Tomiko's face. She had a beautiful smile. He told her silly stories and made her laugh, just to see those sparkling teeth, those dimples. At night, when he slept with her, he could forget everything, and the world was only her.

Be happy! Addy had told him.

I am, Addy. I am. I promise.

On their last night in Crete, they visited a boardwalk beyond the ancient temples and labyrinth. They walked hand in hand, admiring the boats and the songs of fishermen. Men pulled in their catches: nets of clams, fresh fish, squids, and Marco even saw several octopuses.

"They look like aliens!" Tomiko said, pointing and wrinkling her nose.

Marco laughed, watching an octopus making its escape along a pier. "Not nearly as bad as aliens."

This is good, he thought. *This is happiness. This is peace. Addy, you won't get to bury me in sand now!*

They approached a taverna, where they ordered a seafood platter. They sat by the water to eat. Marco had bitten into his first calamari when he noticed the men draw knives at the table beside him.

Tomiko saw them too—rough men, seven or eight of them, faces unshaven, eyes dour. Empty bottles of arak littered their table. They were cursing in Greek, shooting glances at Tomiko and Marco.

"Let's go," Tomiko said, lip trembling. But Marco had faced scum and marauders in war. He wouldn't flee from men. He took a closer look at them.

They were grumbling amongst themselves, clutching their knives. But Marco noticed that they were shooting suspicious glares everywhere, at every table, at the sea, at the sky.

One of the men was shaking, his knife swaying his hand. He pointed skyward. "*O diavolos.*" His voice was raspy. "*Ston ourano.*" His eyes reddened, and suddenly he was weeping. "*O diavolos!*"

Marco didn't speak much Greek, but he had learned a little since moving here. He understood this.

The devil. In the sky. The devil!

"They're scared," Marco said softly. "One of them said he saw the devil. A devil from the sky. Gray and—"

"Marco, I want to go." Tomiko stood up. "Take me back to hotel."

His Greek had improved over the past few months. Her English had too, and she only rarely spoke with mistakes now, though her accent was still thick.

"It's all right, Tomiko," he said, reaching to her. She was trembling. "Calm down and—"

"Don't tell me to calm down!" she said—loud enough that several people turned toward them. "I want to go."

Marco cringed.

Never tell a woman to calm down, Addy had once cautioned him, a lesson he vowed to never forget again.

"All right," he said. "All right. We'll go back. I'll just pay and—"

Beside them, the trembling man leaped to his feet and pointed across the water. "*O diavolos!*" He drew a handgun. "*O diavolos ston ourano!*"

Devil in the sky!

Marco looked. There, above the dark sea, he saw them. Three hovering lights, perhaps airplanes flying low, perhaps drones.

Scum.

Marauders.

Marco reached for his rifle, realized he had none. He hadn't carried a rifle for a year now, but he still often reached for his old gun, a phantom limb.

Tomiko clutched his hand, gazing at the lights. "What are they?" She shuddered. "Marauders? Like the ones that killed my mother?"

The lights flew lower, soon skimming the water. They came streaming toward the boardwalk. People shouted. The trembling man fired his gun. Marco had no weapon, but he did have his camera. He raised it.

The lights streamed overhead.

He snapped a photo.

The lights soared skyward at incredible speed and vanished.

Marco looked at his camera. He saw mere smudges.

The man with the gun fell to his knees, trembling, speaking of devils—gray devils from the sky, devils who had hurt him, who would hurt them all.

Marco had lost his appetite. He and Tomiko returned to their hotel, then the next morning, they took the ferry back home.

He tried to work that day. He was still the household's sole provider. Steve and Addy had been searching for work, had found none on these sunny, idyllic isles. It was up to Marco to keep the operation funded. After the success of *The Dragons of Yesteryear*, he had begun a new series.

Under the Stairs was another work of fantasy, but this one was different, no longer epic fantasy about dragons, elves, and knights in armor. The heroine of this novel, a young girl named Anabel Lee, discovered a portal under the stairs in her home—a gateway to a world of dark beauty, of danger and wonder. When her brother vanished into this realm, Anabel Lee followed, seeking him. She traveled through fantastical landscapes, meeting the strange denizens under the stairs: towering, beaked creatures that shuffled forward, canes tapping; old men infected with the sky, small stars and planets growing from their bodies like tumors; fairy creatures who danced in rings of mushrooms, playing flutes, luring children to catch and consume; and a hundred other creatures of dark majesty. Perhaps Marco had merely watched *Labyrinth* and *The Dark Crystal* too many times. Perhaps he was tapping into the terrors deep inside him.

Under the Stairs would be his magnum opus, he had decided when penning the first page a few days earlier. More important than *The Dragons of Yesteryear*. More emotional than *Les Kill* and *Loggerhead*. It would be the first novel in a series he titled *Phantasmagoria*. A series of shadows but of beauty too. His legacy series.

Yet when Marco sat down to write today, still rattled by the encounter in Crete last night, he struggled to find the right words. When finally they flowed, the heroine of *Under the Stairs*— young Anabel Lee—encountered strange gray demons, tall and slender and naked, their heads bald, their eyes black and oval.

Finally Marco tossed out those pages. Nonsense. This was meant to be a series of dark beauty, not science fiction. After a few hours of pointless effort, he left his office and stepped downstairs.

His housemates were on the couch, watching television. Steve sat slumped, legs stretched out, beer in hand. The hockey player had been growing a scraggly beard on the island. Some days he worked at odd jobs, doing handiwork at locals' houses. Most days he just lounged at home, watching television and keeping Addy out of trouble. Addy now sat curled up against him, munching on popcorn. As usual, her feet were bare and sandy, and no amount of scolding from Marco could deter her from trailing sand through the house.

Tomiko sat primly at the opposite side of the couch, and Marco sat beside her. She didn't look his way.

"You didn't come down for lunch," Tomiko said in a low voice, though Marco knew that Addy and Steve—just beside them—could hear.

Marco nodded. "We'll have dinner together."

She stared ahead. "I'm not hungry anymore."

Marco could feel Addy's eyes burning into him. He stared at the television. *Space Galaxy VI* ended with Captain Carter—by now, the actor was desperately hiding his paunch with a girdle—flying into the unknown, seeking another adventure. The news came on.

The dark-haired journalist stood outside in a field, speaking to the camera. "Sightings are occurring across the world. People have seen UFOs. People are speaking of abductions. Some citizens have reported seeing little green men skulking through the woods."

A bearded, wild-haired man leaned into the shot and grabbed the mic.

"They're gray, man!" he cried, round glasses hanging askew. "Not green. They're *gray* aliens. *The* gray aliens! Like in Roswell, man. Like in Area 51, man. Like the government has been hiding from us. Don't let the government read your mind, man!" He slapped a tinfoil hat onto his head. "But I knew all along. The grays are real, man. They're real, and they're going to bring us peace and love." He pulled open his jacket, revealing a T-shirt printed with three smiling aliens beneath a rainbow. "Join the Alien Welcome Commune, friends! Join us, and the grays will take you too to their utopia in heaven!"

The journalist wrestled her microphone back. "As you can see, reaction to the UFO phenomenon has been mixed. Are these truly extraterrestrial visitors? Or are they merely old myths? Judge for yourself. We're going to show you an image now, supposedly of the aliens. Warning: this might be disturbing. If you have young children, you—"

"Boring!" Addy grabbed the remote control and switched the channel.

"Addy!" Marco groaned and tried to grab the remote from her. "I was watching that."

She tossed popcorn at him. "Yeah, well, now I'm watching hockey. The Leafs are playing, so suck it."

As Addy was holding the remote away from Marco, Steve reached over and grabbed it.

"Yoink!" Steve switched the channel to *Robot Wrestling*. "Sorry, babe, but Hammerhead is making a comeback tonight, and he's about to smash Psycho Blade."

On the television, one robot was swinging a hammer at another, sending saw blades flying.

Addy growled and tried to grab the remote back. "But Steve, you love the Leafs!"

He scoffed. "Ads, the Leafs haven't won the Stanley Cup in over two hundred years. But Hammerhead is going to win tonight. Pow! Hammer 'em, Head!"

"I'll show you wrestling!"

Addy leaped onto her boyfriend, sending the bowl of popcorn flying, and soon the couch tilted over. Marco knew it was no use. The two would be engaged in battle for a while, a bout to put *Robot Wrestling* to shame. With a resigned sigh, Marco stepped outside onto the beach.

He stood on the sand, staring at the water.

He thought of the lights over the sea last night.

He thought of Tomiko's cold eyes.

He thought of Addy holding his hands before his wedding.

He thought of his friends—of Lailani, Ben-Ari, Kemi, all the others, living and dead—and how much he missed them.

He thought of the scum. Of the marauders. Of monsters. Of something still broken inside him, coming out onto the page, in nightmares, leaking, eternally spilling, a rot.

Finally he pulled out his tablet, and he pulled up the photo he had taken at Crete. Smudges of light, that was all. Just smudges. He zoomed in. He tapped a few buttons, sharpening the image, reducing the brightness, increasing the contrast. He frowned.

Shapes.

He saw shapes in the light. Disks. Flying saucers.

He zoomed in some more—as far as the image would go—focusing on one of the saucers. It almost looked like a starship. There seemed to be a windshield or porthole. When he zoomed in some more, the image blurred further, but he could just make out a figure in the porthole. A large, shadowy head. Two dark eyes, each a single pixel.

Marco . . .

A voice spoke in his mind.

He sucked in air.

Come to us . . .

A shiver ran through him.

"Marco?"

A hand touched his shoulder, and he jumped. He spun around to see Tomiko standing on the beach. He let out a shaky breath.

"Tomiko."

She gazed down at her toes. "I just want say I sorry. For being rude before. About lunch." She touched his cheek. "I bring you lunch to your office tomorrow, okay? I cook something good."

Relief flowed through Marco, and he felt foolish for ever having cold feet, for doubting his love for his beautiful young wife. He kissed her.

"Thank you, Tomiko."

She smiled. "I good cook. Not like Addy who just makes hot dogs and popcorn."

"And she gets sand on them too!" Marco said.

Tomiko laughed. "Sand dogs. Sandcorn. Come home with me? I have surprise."

They returned to the house, stepped around Addy and Steve—the two were still battling over the remote—and walked upstairs to their bedroom. Tomiko revealed her surprise—new lingerie she had bought, an outfit that had Marco's jaw hitting the floor.

"You're beautiful." He stroked her hair. "You're so beautiful."

She smiled shyly, looking down. "Too skinny."

"You're perfect," he said.

She caressed his cheek. "And you're pretty."

"You mean handsome."

Her brow furrowed. "I say wrong? I'm still learning English. Better but not perfect." She smiled. "You're handsome."

He made love to her, and it was good, and he was happy. He was finally happy. She slept in his arms, the window open, the sheets tossed off in the heat. Marco lay awake for a long while, holding her.

Be happy, he thought. *Stay happy. With her. Here. Forever.*

He closed his eyes, sleep gently tugging.

Marco . . .

His eyes fluttered open.

A shape stood in the window. Through the blur of sleep and darkness, Marco couldn't see much. He could make out a slender figure. A large head, bald, oval. Two black eyes.

Gently, he rose from bed, drawn by a power he could barely understand. He stepped toward the window. Figures. Figures on the beach. Staring. Seeing him. Calling him. And—

"Damn it, Steve!" Addy shouted downstairs. "Will you stop stepping on my popcorn? I'm eating that!"

Tomiko stirred in the bed. Marco blinked, looked at her, then glanced back outside.

The creatures were gone.

Marco let out a shaky breath.

Just a dream, he told himself. *Just my exhaustion.*

Yet when he returned to bed, he kept thinking of the photo he had taken, of the reports on television, of the voices in his head, of the feeling that he could not be happy. That this was not the end. That there was darkness out there, just outside the window, waiting for him. He held Tomiko close.

I don't want to lose you, Tomiko, he thought. *I don't want to lose you like I lost Anisha and Kemi and so many others. I don't want the darkness to fall again. Be happy. Be happy. I promised.*

He slept, and he dreamed of black alien eyes, of figures in the night, and of a dark queen in a distant sky.

CHAPTER THREE

Lailani walked through the tropical brush, pushing a wheelbarrow full of books.

The sun baked her straw hat, and Lailani paused to wipe her forehead. She had been born and raised here in the Philippines, but after so long in the darkness of space, she had trouble readjusting to the heat and humidity. Insects buzzed around her, and the hot wind rustled the papaya trees and bamboo shoots. Tarsiers, tiny primates with huge eyes, curled up among the branches, looking to the world like furry coconuts. To Lailani's right spread the Pacific, a few fishermen's boats sailing the clear waters between many little islands, most only large enough for one or two palm trees. To her left, terraced rice paddies covered the hills like staircases for giants, and farmers toiled in the low water, growing the precious grain.

Lailani pushed the wheelbarrow along the road, paused again, and wiped her forehead. Her dress was thin, but sweat soaked it. She stood for a moment between rows of banana trees.

I miss Canada, she thought. *I miss the snow. I miss Marco and Addy.*

But of course, that was foolishness. Marco and Addy had left Canada too, had settled down in Greece in their dream home, happily retired after the wars. But Lailani could not imagine herself retiring. She was only twenty-eight, still young, still with so much to do, so many to help.

I fought in wars, she thought. *I bombed. I destroyed. I killed.* She winced, the guilt filling her, the terror gripping her, claws inside her. She forced a deep breath. *So now let me build. Let me heal.*

Sensing her grief, Epimetheus moved closer to her and licked her arm. Tipping the scales at over a hundred pounds, the Doberman was larger than her. He was only a year old but already fierce, loyal, and taller than Lailani when he stood on his back feet. Epimetheus could always sense her anxiety, it seemed, was always there to nuzzle her, lick her arm, gaze at her with loving eyes.

She patted his head.

"You understand me, Epi, don't you?"

The Doberman licked her fingers and gave a short *ruff.*

She felt calmer already. She drank from her bottle of water, gave Epi a sip, and kept pushing the wheelbarrow through the banana grove.

The banana trees parted before her, and there ahead she saw it, nestled by the fishing village.

Her school.

She had named Abasi Elementary School after Captain Kemi Abasi, her fallen friend. It was not a large school. It was a simple wooden building, painted with pastel yellows and blues, nestled alongside the Pacific. But it was large enough for a hundred children, a hundred who would otherwise spend their childhoods in the fishing barges or in the rice paddies. A hundred who would now learn to read and write, to do math, to escape the cycle of poverty.

I destroyed. I killed. Now let me heal.

After the marauder war, the yurei had given Lailani a handful of azoth crystals, more valuable than diamonds—crystals that could bend spacetime, allowing starships to travel faster than light. Lailani had given the crystals to the Human Defense Force so that they could rebuild Earth's fleet. She had refused compensation—she cared about Earth, not financial gain—but the HDF had still given her a handsome sum. Not nearly what the crystals were actually worth, but handsome nonetheless. Lailani had given some of the money to Marco and Addy, enough to build their house on the beach. But Lailani had kept the lion's share. With it, she had built Abasi School here in the provinces, and she had built five more schools across the islands of the Philippines.

I grew up poor and homeless, she thought. *I grew up an orphan, eating from landfills, struggling to survive. I will make sure these children have better lives.*

When she drew closer to the school, the doors slammed open, and a gaggle of children came racing toward her.

"Tita Lailani, Tita Lailani!" they cried, smiles bright.

They wore the uniforms she had bought them: plaid skirts for the girls, shorts for the boys, button-down shirts and ties for both. They carried backpacks brimming with notebooks.

Seeing the children, Epimetheus let out a happy bark and ran toward them, tail wagging. The children gathered around the Doberman, patting him, squealing as he licked them.

"Children, children!" Lailani said, laughing. "Back to your classroom. You'll drive Mrs. Reyes up the wall."

As if summoned by her name, the schoolteacher emerged from the school too, waving a ruler, shouting of scoundrels fleeing her geography class. Yet the matronly teacher stifled a smile; she would never use that ruler on the children, and her sternness hid a deep love for her job and her students.

Lailani and Epimetheus helped herd the children back into their classroom. Lailani distributed the new books from her wheelbarrow, passing them between the desks. Even Epimetheus delivered a few, carrying them gently in his jaws.

I wish you could be here with me, Sofia, Lailani thought as she worked, and her eyes stung with tears. *You and I once taught children in the slums of Manila, working with a wheelbarrow of books but no walls around us. I wish you could see this school that I built.*

She winced with sudden pain, memories flashing through her. Sofia, her beloved—falling into the flaming maw of a ravager. Kemi, her dear friend—dying in the ruins of Toronto, sacrificing her life to defeat the marauder king. Thousands of starships— crashing around her in the great, last battle over the ruins.

But deeper still, colder, stronger, lurked the worst memory of all.

The memory of the night the scum had hijacked her mind.

Lailani inhaled sharply and touched her head. Pain flared through her. She had been only eighteen, only a child, only several months into her military service. The alien had controlled her thoughts from afar, had made her grow claws, had made her grab her friend. She had murdered Benny "Elvis" Ray that night, had ripped out his heart. She had learned that she was not fully human, that she was a scum hybrid, that the aliens could control her. Afterward, surgeons had placed a chip in her skull, firewalling the aliens, and the scum were dead now. And yet that chip now burned, blazed inside her, and the scum were scuttling in her skull—she could hear them!—and blood dripped from her hands, and Elvis's dead eyes stared at her, and—

Whimpering, Epimetheus licked her fingers and nuzzled her.

Lailani took a deep breath and patted him, her anxiety fading. She found herself back in the classroom, the children gazing at her curiously.

She patted her Doberman. "Thank you again, Epi," she whispered.

With the books distributed, Lailani lifted the little cage from the wheelbarrow. A blanket draped over it, and she pulled it back to reveal a little creature within: a slumbering tarsier.

The primate was barely larger than a hamster, but its eyes were huge. It opened those eyes, blinked, and looked at Lailani. The children gasped and gathered around the cage.

"A monkey!" one said.

"It's a guinea pig," said another.

"It's a tarsier!" said a third child and nodded knowingly.

Lailani nodded too. "A tarsier, yes, but not an ordinary one. This is Darwin. He's a genetically engineered tarsier. Do you remember what Mrs. Torres taught you about genetic engineering?"

The children nodded. "Yes, Tita Lailani."

She opened the cage. The tarsier climbed up her arm and nested on her shoulder.

"Darwin has been genetically engineered to be docile and friendly," Lailani said. "Unlike tarsiers in the wild, he's domesticated. That means he'll enjoy living in this classroom instead of the wild, and he wants to be your mascot."

The children oohed and aahed and reached out to pat Darwin. The animal purred. These children were orphans. They had seen the marauders murder their parents. Some of these children bore the scars of war themselves.

I have Epi to comfort me, Lailani thought. *May Darwin give them the same comfort.*

She left the school. Epimetheus at her side, she returned to her home on the islands, a hut on the beach. It was a humble abode, just a single room, the roof woven of straw. It was a far cry from the large home Marco and Addy had built in Greece. But it was all Lailani needed. It was the nicest—the only—home she had ever lived in, she who had grown up homeless, who had spent years bouncing from one military base to another.

She looked around her. A bed in the corner. A bed for Epi, which he never used, preferring to sleep on Lailani's bed. A kitchenette with a small fridge and stove. A few books, including *The Dragons of Yesteryear*, the trilogy Marco had written, and a hefty tome of *The Galactic Wars*, Ben-Ari's memoirs of fighting the scum and marauders. She displayed no mementos from the war. Her service ribbons, her medals, the scum claw and marauder tooth she had claimed—Lailani had locked them all in a chest, refusing to look at them. All but her dog tags. She still wore those around her neck every day.

Because I'm still a soldier, she thought. *I just fight a different enemy now.*

Suddenly, looking at this humble home, the loneliness hit her. She missed Sofia. She missed Marco. She missed being with her friends.

She looked at the single picture frame she had hung up. It was a photograph. Ten years old now. A photograph from boot camp. Lailani looked at it, her eyes damp, and a trembling smile touched her lips. The entire Dragons Platoon appeared in the photo, all wearing dusty, tattered fatigues, standing at Fort Djemila. Ben-Ari stood at the head of the platoon, plasma rifle in her hands, stern and strong. Sergeant Singh stood behind her, his turbaned head towering over the officer. Marco was looking solemn as always, while Addy grinned, holding up two fingers behind his head, giving him rabbit ears. Lailani stood beside her— the shortest one in the platoon, not even reaching Addy's shoulders. In the photo, Lailani was making a silly face, her cheeks puffed out, her eyes crossed. She had her arm slung around Elvis's shoulder. Elvis was smiling at the camera, giving a karate chop.

Benny "Elvis" Ray. Her friend. The man she had killed.

"I miss you all," Lailani whispered. "I wish I could be back with you again. I'm lonely here. I'm scared."

She knelt and embraced Epi, and the Doberman licked her face.

"But I have you, Epi." She kissed his cheek and mussed his ears. She had kept his ears floppy, not cropping them like many Doberman owners did. "You keep me safe."

She stepped toward the kitchenette and filled Epi's bowl. As he chowed down, Lailani turned on the stove. She opened the fridge and pulled out the sea bass the fisherman had given her that morning.

"Cook it with some coconut sauce and chili flakes," the fisherman had told her, handing her a pouch. "Here, try these seasonings."

Lailani had tried to refuse the gift. She knew how poor these people were, how precious a fish was, especially after the war which had sent starships crashing into the Pacific, polluting the waters and casting so many dead fish ashore.

"I insist," the fisherman had told her, all but shoving the fish into her hands. Tears had filled the weathered man's eyes. "You teach my daughters to read and write, teach them numbers, so that someday they can do more than catch fish or grow rice. I could never repay you. Not with all the fish in the ocean."

Lailani had kissed his careworn cheek, the skin brown and wrinkled. "*Salamat, Tito.* Thank you."

Standing in her kitchen, she bit into the fresh fish. It squelched between her teeth. The skin was rubbery, the flesh raw and wriggling. The head crunched when she bit down, and the eyeballs popped in her mouth. The fisherman had not gutted the fish. That was good. She let the innards slide into her mouth, and—

Lailani froze.

Terror flowed across her.

She tossed the raw fish onto the frying pan, where it sizzled. Fish entrails, raw and bloody, filled her mouth, and she spat them out.

Fingers bloody and shaking, she turned off the stove. She washed out her mouth, then stumbled toward her bed and sat down hard.

"What's wrong with me?" she whispered.

She scuttled through tunnels, hunting.

She found the small, wet creatures. She crunched them between her jaws. She sucked up the juices.

She screeched in the depths, raising many claws, a creature of shadows and soil.

She trembled.

She panted.

And Epimetheus was at her side, nuzzling her, pulling Lailani back into the present.

She hugged him, trembling. The chip inside her skull blazed, an ember. But as she embraced her Doberman, the pain slowly faded, and she was just a girl again.

But no, she thought. *I'm not just a girl. I'm only ninety-nine percent human. It's that one percent of me. The alien DNA. The part that killed Elvis.*

She held her dog close.

"Keep me safe, Epi," she whispered. "Don't let me become that monster again."

The sun set, and she lay down on her bed, Epimetheus at her side. Strange dreams haunted her that night. She was wandering through tunnels, a centipede the size of a python, lined with clawed legs. She was lost. She was trapped. She was seeking a way out. There were men with guns chasing her, and vats full of molten metal, and prisoners that hung on ceilings, laughing maniacally, bellies stuffed full of honey, obscenely bloated, food for scum. A circus, she realized. Not tunnels but a circus. She stood on a stage, the crowd around her. A carnival barker with a handlebar mustache and top hat cracked a whip.

"Behold the freak!" he cried. "Step right up, step right up, behold Centipede Girl!"

His whip cracked against Lailani. She reared on her back feet. She spun for the crowd, a girl with a centipede body, and they squealed in fright. Women fainted, babies wept, and men pointed at her and laughed.

"Freak!" they cried.

"Monster!"

"Murderer!"

Elvis was in the crowd. Her friend Elvis from boot camp. He was alive, but his chest was cracked open, the heart removed. He pointed at her.

"Murderer!"

The carnival barker dragged her off the stage as the crowd pelted her with apple cores and popcorn. Men with whips hustled her into a circus train. They chugged along the tracks, delving deeper into the tunnels. She languished in her cage with the other freaks, the conjoined twins, the bearded lady, the dwarfs, the strongmen. She, Lailani de la Rosa, a bug with a human head, the famous Centipede Girl.

The train kept plunging through the tunnel, moving faster, faster, roaring downward, and now they were traveling through a wormhole. Stars streamed at their sides. They spun madly, and she was on a starship now, lost, alone.

They burst out from the wormhole into open space.

Stars hung before her. A great map of stars, forming the shape of a rearing bear. One of the stars on the claw pulsed.

Find the hourglass.

The voice spoke in the darkness, and Lailani realized she was hovering in space. She reached out, tried to grab on to something, but she fell, fell, fell through darkness, screaming.

Her eyes snapped open.

She lay back in her bed.

She panted, awash with sweat, bleeding, her sheets in tatters around her.

Epimetheus was running around her, mewling, approaching, retreating. Finally he backed into a corner and growled at her. Moonlight bathed the room, pale and deathlike.

Lailani looked at her bed. The mattress was torn apart, splotched with blood. She looked down at her hands. Claws grew from her fingertips. Scratches covered her thighs.

She had grown claws like this once before.

She had used them to rip out Elvis's heart.

She stumbled out of bed and turned on the lights. When she looked at her hands again, the claws were gone. But she still saw the scratches on her thighs, the shreds of her bed.

She rubbed her eyes, struggling to fully wake up. The dream returned to her: the tunnels, the circus, the constellation shaped like a rearing bear. Had her claws merely been a part of her dream too, and it was Epimetheus who had torn her bed?

No.

This was real. The raw fish. The claws. The nightmares inside her.

"It's happening again, Epi," Lailani whispered. "The scum inside me. You're not safe. The monster is back."

CHAPTER FOUR

The HSS *Lodestar*, flagship of humanity, sailed through the cosmic ocean.

Captain of the ship, representing Earth in the vastness of space, Einav Ben-Ari felt a little like a cat leading a pack of lions. Her claws perhaps were sharp, but she had to growl damn loudly to earn some respect.

I'm all of thirty years old, she thought. *I have no doctorate, no university degree at all. And I'm leading five hundred of Earth's finest scientists, engineers, and explorers into the vastness of space.*

She sighed.

I led soldiers in battle. I fought two wars. I faced two alien kings. And I feel woefully unqualified.

Yet Ben-Ari kept walking through the starship, her navy-blue uniform neatly pressed, her hands clasped behind her back. Whenever she passed by a shipmate—all of them older and wiser than her—she gave a nod and slight smile. Just a slight smile. She had to be polite, yet not ingratiating. At least, she thought so. She didn't know, damn it. She was used to leading soldiers, a bunch of teenage killers. Not scientists who were twice her age. Was she meant to keep her distance? To frown and glower? To smile and chitchat?

Outwardly, Ben-Ari kept that thin smile—a compromise, perhaps. Inwardly, her soul was storming.

What am I doing here? I'm an impostor. I can't lead these people.

One of her crewmates, a geologist with a stony face, walked down the hall toward her. He began to speak to her about rock samples collected on the asteroid last week, of finding fascinating chemical compositions within. Ben-Ari listened politely, nodding, not understanding half of what he said, afraid to admit it. When he began rattling off the names of molecules and asking questions, she had to pat him on the arm.

"Well, what do *you* think, Mr. Higgins?" she asked him.

"It's Herbert, actually," he said.

Damn. Damn damn damn. Fuck!

"Mr. Herbert, of course." She allowed her strained smile to widen just a bit. "Forgive me."

He nodded. "Already forgiven. But don't you think, ma'am, that our collected soil samples should be inoculated with a dilute aqueous nutrient solution to determine the evolution of $14CO_2$ gasses?"

Um . . . yes?

Ben-Ari made do with another pat on his arm. "I trust your judgment, Mister—" She almost said Higgins again. "Herbert."

She walked on down the corridor, leaving him behind, feeling weak. She was not used to feeling weak. Not used to feeling overwhelmed. She felt Herbert's eyes boring into her back as she walked away.

He knows I'm an impostor, she thought. *He knows I'm just a soldier, not a scientist. He knows I'm in over my head. They all know.*

She felt so trapped. She paused by a porthole, gazed outside at the stars, and sighed. She was not used to this. For twelve years in the military, rising from cadet to major, she had felt confident, in control, in command. She knew every way to kill an alien, but what did she know about civilian leadership? True, she had a uniform here, and she had a rank, and the *Lodestar* came equipped with weapons, but this was different from the army. HOPE—the Human Outreach Program of Exploration—was not a military organization. They were tasked with exploration, with finding new civilizations and forging alliances.

My father would know what to do here, Ben-Ari thought. *I know how to kill. How long before I'm exposed? Before the crew mutinies? Why, Petty, did you choose me for this mission? And why did I accept?*

Of course, she had a thousand answers to that. She had been bored on the beach with Marco and Addy. She had respected Petty—once a general, now President of the Alliance of Nations—too much to refuse. She was ambitious. She believed in humanity. She believed in her task. And she felt totally, completely inadequate.

Killing aliens was easier.

With a deep breath, she kept walking down the corridor. Even this corridor was alien, too clean, too well lit, not like the grungy, dim corridors of military warships. Finally she reached the door she sought.

She paused for a moment, steeling herself.

She smoothed her uniform, turned toward a porthole, and examined her reflection, seeking flaws. She wore the navy-blue trousers and button-down shirt of HOPE, the brass buttons polished. Her blond hair was pulled into a sensible ponytail, and a beaked cap topped her head. She was used to wearing dusty battle fatigues, the fabric threadbare at the elbows and knees, the hems fraying. This rich, pressed uniform made her feel even more like an impostor.

Her insignia shone on her shoulders: a blue circle on each strap, denoting her the captain of the ship. Back in the Human Defense Force, the word "captain" denoted a junior officer, the rank she had carried for most of her service. Here in HOPE, a "captain" was a senior officer, comparable to an HDF colonel, high ranking enough to command a ship of this size.

And yet I still look like a girl, she thought. *Even at thirty, even with so many battles and kills under my belt, I still look like a damn ensign.*

But no. That was a lie. That was her vanity speaking. That was just the poor quality of her reflection in the porthole. She did look thirty. She saw that in her bathroom mirror every morning. The first hints of crow's feet tugged at the corners of her eyes. Her metabolism was slowing, and she had to watch her meals now to fit into her uniform. She had even caught a white hair— just one!—a week ago. She had left it in, a reminder of her age, that she wasn't that young ensign anymore.

You are a capable, strong, intelligent woman, she told her reflection. *You led the platoon that slew the scum emperor. You commanded the starship that found the Ghost Fleet and helped defeat the marauders. With a little help, you will do this too.*

She turned away from her reflection, back toward the door, and knocked.

"Come in!"

For the first time, she entered the quarters of the famous Professor Noah Isaac.

Her eyes widened.

Wow, she thought. *It's* . . . She let out a long breath. *It's beautiful.*

Quarters aboard military starships were cramped, barely larger than closets and usually home to multiple officers. But HOPE had spared no expense when building its flagship. Aboard the *Lodestar*, the senior commanders had chambers the size of decent bedrooms back home. *This* room was crammed with wonders. Shelves covered all four walls, holding thousands of books. At a glance, Ben-Ari saw that only about half the books were scientific; the rest were works of literature and poetry spanning from Homer and Gilgamesh to twenty-second-century masterpieces. Other shelves held globes of various planets, seashells from alien shores, at least twenty flutes of different civilizations, statues from various human and alien cultures, and countless other curiosities. No fewer than four desks filled the room, topped with books, notebooks, pens, compasses, and orreries.

The professor also, she noticed with a thin smile, had an impressive collection of bongs.

"Professor?" she said, frowning. She did not see the man. She heard no reply.

She stepped deeper into the chamber. A glint caught her eye. Something golden. She stepped closer, and her eyes widened. It was the professor's Nobel Prize, tucked away in a corner, half hidden behind books and knickknacks. Gently, she lifted it. She hefted the golden medal.

Professor Noah Isaac was a household name, a famous scientist, his lectures and books beloved by millions. Ten years ago, a young scientist of only thirty-five, he had catapulted into public awareness after inventing wormholes. Granted, Isaac's Wormholes were not wide thoroughfares like some alien species could build, tunnels that starships could fly through. Isaac's Wormholes were tiny tubes, only several atoms wide. But they allowed faster-than-light communications between worlds. They had changed humanity forever. For the first time, humans could speak across the light-years in real time. That year, Isaac had won the Nobel Prize, had become as famous as Newton or Einstein.

Ben-Ari remembered the day Isaac's Wormholes had first been activated. She had been a young lieutenant, only twenty years old, and had just arrived at Nightwall. The first wormhole, connecting Earth and Nightwall, had carried terrible news: Vancouver had been destroyed. An invention of such wonder had been christened with blood.

She placed down the Nobel prize. She turned toward a side table, where she saw a model of the *Lodestar*. Ben-Ari had seen the true *Lodestar* from the outside only once, and she spent a moment admiring the model. HOPE's flagship was shaped like an old sailing ship, complete with a figurehead of Eos, the Ancient Greek goddess of dawn. All it was missing were the masts and sails.

My ship, she thought. *My pride and joy. Yet a ship that overwhelms me so much.*

Ben-Ari tore her gaze away from the model. She looked from side to side.

"Professor?" she said, confused. "Are you here?"

His voice rose from behind a pile of books. "Ah, here we go!" He rose, holding a leather-bound tome. He blew on the cover, and dust flew. "I was looking for this."

Ben-Ari sneezed. "You know, Professor, we have many e-readers aboard."

He winced. "Sorry, ma'am. I got dust on your uniform. Oh, and call me Noah. No need for any of that *professor* or *doctor* nonsense."

She brushed the dust off her uniform. "And you can call me Einav. No need for ma'am, at least not when it's just the two of us. You're my First Officer, after all."

Professor Noah Isaac was an unassuming man of forty-five years. His skin was olive-toned, his eyes kind, and his black hair was a little too long for a man in uniform. Not that he was wearing his uniform here in his quarters. Instead, he wore corduroy pants, loafers, and a tweed jacket over a turtleneck sweater. Perhaps he did not want to be called *professor*, but that was exactly how he looked.

"Actually," Isaac said, "I prefer being called Science Officer rather than First Officer. I see myself as more of a scientist than the second-in-command of a starship. I've come here to explore the galaxy." His eyes shone. "Something I've always dreamed of, ever since I was a young boy looking up at the stars." He cleared his throat. "But where are my manners? Tea? Coffee? Something . . . stronger?" He glanced at the bongs on the shelf.

Ben-Ari smiled narrowly. "Just tea would be nice. Chamomile if you've got it."

He nodded. "I'll put on a pot, and then our lessons shall resume! Thank you, Einav, for coming to my quarters this time. Easier than me lugging all these books to your quarters every week."

She stifled another smile. "E-readers, Professor, I keep telling you."

"They are wonderful devices, e-readers. A little tablet that can contain entire libraries! Imagine it, Einav. In our pockets, we can carry the entire Library of Congress, the entire Wikipedia Galactica, indeed all the literature and science of humanity. The full knowledge and wisdom of our species—in a single electronic device, so small I can hide it between my palms. If any invention is truly magical, it is the e-reader." The professor sighed wistfully. "Yet I'm old fashioned. I like to feel the weight of science in my hands." He hefted the book he carried.

Ben-Ari looked around her, cringing. "I can already feel the weight of all these books crushing me."

The professor smiled. "The weight of knowledge, Einav. And the weight of wisdom. From the former springs the latter."

She returned his smile. "Thank you. I know you're busy. Thank you for teaching me."

Professor Isaac gazed out the porthole at the stars, then back at her. His voice and eyes were warm. "The cosmos is filled with beauty. Nebulae of brilliant colors, sprawling for light-years, stellar nurseries that illuminate the darkness with shimmering golds, blues, and greens. Planets lush with promise, where mist wreaths blue mountains that dwarf Everest and clouds of carbon rain the very stuff of life upon deep oceans. Stars of many colors glistening like ornaments, lighting the void, forging in their hearts the elements that comprise us, for we are all starstuff. And yet a simple truth humbles all this glory. Nothing in this cosmos is as wonderful as the open mind of a curious student."

She touched his arm. "My dear professor, you are scientist, teacher, and poet."

"And a wonderful tea maker!" he said.

Soon they sat at one of the desks, two steaming mugs of tea before them, as well as the open book.

"See, what I'm confused about is how our quantum engine behaves," Ben-Ari said. "I hear the engineers speak about how particles pass through slits in the engines, but then Humphries was talking about the wave patterns they create."

Isaac nodded. "Excellent question. You see, in quantum mechanics, at a very small scale, the laws of physics are different.

Electrons can behave like particles or like waves. Here, see this illustration?"

She listened for a long time, nodding, taking notes as Isaac explained. Whenever the other scientists aboard tried to explain things to Ben-Ari, they seemed impatient, even upset, and she could never fully understand them. But Isaac was patient with her, a natural teacher. He had a way of explaining things with drawings, with metaphors, even with little experiments he conducted with his portable lab, that let Ben-Ari understand everything. His voice was always soft, his smile always kind, and his eyes shone with pure joy when he spoke of science.

He loves what he does, Ben-Ari knew. *He loves teaching it, living it, breathing it.*

She wondered what it was like to love something so much. Marco loved books. Lailani loved charity work. Kemi had loved flying. Addy, well . . . Addy loved hot dogs. Ben-Ari only wished that someday she could find something she loved this much—not just duty, not just leadership, but a true passion, a true love.

She found herself glancing at his hands, which were moving animatedly as he spoke.

No wedding ring, she thought, then scolded herself. A stupid thought. She was both his commander and his student, making that thought doubly wrong. Besides, he was too old for her, and she was married to her duty, had no time for such foolishness. She was not Marco, for God's sake!

She realized that she hadn't been paying attention to his words. She forced herself to focus.

"So . . . particles don't have mass without the Higgs Field?" she asked.

"In a sense." Isaac nodded. "The Higgs Field is what gives them mass. In fact, what we think of as mass is simply how particles react with the Higgs Field. Imagine the field as a big pot of soup, and each particle is another vegetable you're dropping in. A carrot will behave differently than a piece of parsley. Similarly, a proton will—"

Yellow lights flashed on the ceiling.

Ben-Ari's intercom, pinned to her lapel, lit up, and a voice emerged.

"Mistress of dark waters, greetings and many colors! These are the colors and lights of Aurora of the Deep Trench, now the Dweller of the Bridge and Navigator of the cosmic ocean. I have deeply seen enemy shells in the dark emptiness, a hundred thousand of your kilometers away from this tribe of starfarers and moving toward us fast."

Ben-Ari had to consider that for a moment. Aurora, the *Lodestar*'s pilot and navigator, was not human. She was a Menorian, heralding from distant Menoria, a planet of lush forests and deep seas. She had a strange way of thinking, of phrasing things. But after a few weeks on the ship, Ben-Ari had begun to understand her navigator.

"Alien starships," Ben-Ari said, glancing at Professor Isaac.

He nodded and closed the science book. "Let's join Aurora on the bridge. Science will have to wait."

Ben-Ari made for the door. "I'll go first. Put on your uniform, then join me." And suddenly she was no longer his student; she was his commander.

As yellow alerts flashed across the ship, Ben-Ari ran down the corridor and into an elevator. The pod rose, emerging directly into the center of the bridge.

The Lodestar's *bridge* was shaped like a planetarium. Viewports covered the walls, the domed ceiling, and even the floor, affording a view of space all around them. To stand on the bridge was like hovering in open space. These were not actual windows. They were monitors connected to cameras mounted outside the ship, able to zoom in, zoom out, and detect a host of magnetic fields, gravitational waves, and photons across the spectrum of light. Letters flashed across these viewports, scrolling through information. Dozens of monitors and control boards glowed everywhere, and officers stood at their stations. Stars spread all around, a dizzying array.

The first time Ben-Ari had stepped into this circular room, she had felt overwhelmed. Her head had spun at the endless barrage of data streaming in from every direction; even the floor was lit up, displaying nuggets of information about what was happening below the ship. But over the past few weeks, she had become accustomed to the room, and Isaac had been teaching her to understand it. Every week, more of the information here made sense to Ben-Ari.

I'm learning to do more than fire guns, she thought. *I'm learning to see the cosmos.*

And in one viewport, she saw that they had visitors.

Several images flashed there, denoting alien starships. They were still too far to see with the naked eye, still too far to reveal their shapes. But one thing was clear. They were not human ships. All human ships broadcast their serial numbers and stats; these ships broadcast nothing. The viewports revealed no information about whatever was flying ahead. These ships were not only alien; they belonged to no species their computers recognized.

"Aurora," Ben-Ari said. "Lay in a course to intercept them."

A chair swiveled toward her, revealing the *Lodestar*'s pilot.

It was still strange to look at Aurora. Her species—the Menorians—were amphibious mollusks, similar in appearance to Earth's octopuses. Their skin constantly shifted colors, changing from indigo to deep purple to burnished gold, often blending patterns as well as hues. It was how they communicated. Without vocal cords, they had developed a complex language based on colors. By changing their colors—originally evolved as a form of camouflage—the Menorians spoke to one another. In fact, their language was so thorough, they had invented poetry and literature that were masterpieces of flashing, swirling colors of every hue, all racing across their abdomens and eight tentacles.

Sitting in her chair, her eight limbs slung around her, Aurora was now shifting between purple to grayish green. A camera was mounted on her seat, reading in the colors, then translating them into English. A robotic female voice emerged from a speaker, delivering the translation to Ben-Ari's ears.

"We must simply float upon our current, mistress of the dark waters, for the alien shells swim toward us through the cosmic ocean, fast as sunlight through clear water, moving with great purpose like those hungry to feed upon growing, fleeing things. They will reach us within a flower's bloom toward the moonlight."

Ben-Ari was thankful for the translation device, but she wished its programmers would not translate the mollusk's colors so literally. She would have to speak to the developers, see if they could install an update, could try to make sense of Aurora's metaphors. Not only Aurora's body was different from humans, what with her foreign organs and lack of bones; her mind too worked differently. A brilliant mind, yes. Perhaps the brightest mind on this ship. But one completely alien.

"You mean the enemy ships are flying toward us?" Ben-Ari said. "And they'll reach us in half an hour—that is, half an Earth's hour?"

A flower's bloom, she thought. The damn device should be translating that into human time.

Aurora changed her color to burnished silver patched with blue lines. "*Enemy* shells, mistress? We do not know their hunger nor their aggression, for perhaps they are curious beings who float like bubbles, seeking merely mooring and play among the waves."

"Perhaps they're friendly, you mean," Ben-Ari said. "My service in the HDF taught me that strange ships rarely are." She turned around toward the security station. "Mr. Marino! Divert power to our forward shields and heat up our cannons. Better be ready for battle. Just in case."

Marino's eyes sparkled. "Yes, Captain!" His face split into a grin, the sort of grin a wolf gave the sheep.

Lieutenant Commander Mario Marino was an imposing man in his midthirties, built like a bull on steroids. He wore the black uniform of HOPE's security branch. His black hair was cropped short, and stubble covered his wide jaw. An assortment of weapons hung from his belt: two pistols, three daggers, and two electric batons. If you asked a random stranger to draw an ideal companion for a walk down a dark alley, the drawing would likely look like Marino.

Ben-Ari had known of him even before taking on this job. Everyone knew the famous Mario Marino, the Jersey Giant. Fifteen years ago, he had become the youngest martial artist to win the Mixed Martial Arts Golden Belt in a fight broadcast to billions. Since then, Marino had starred in superhero movies, launched a line of video games and action figures, and successfully defended his title every year since. At age thirty-six, still undefeated, the Jersey Giant had retired from professional fighting and begun a new career: Chief Security Officer aboard the *Lodestar*.

While Ben-Ari perhaps admired Marino's striking physique, she was skeptical about the appointment. She would have preferred a security chief who had fought the scum and marauders, not a celebrity. But HOPE depended on government funding. And, President Petty had informed her, they needed star power. And so the famous Jersey Giant, whose posters hung in bedrooms and bars across Earth and her colonies, now controlled security—both inward and outward—aboard humanity's flagship.

"Forward shields at maximum capacity, Captain," Marino said, eyes shining. "Cannons are heated up. Can't wait to kick some ass."

Ben-Ari shot him a glare. "Mind your language on my bridge, Lieutenant Commander."

"Sorry, Captain." Marino nodded. "Here's hoping we kick some posterior."

Ben-Ari returned her eyes to the viewport showing the alien vessels. They were moving fast. The elevator returned to the bridge, and Professor Isaac emerged, wearing his navy-blue uniform. He came to stand beside her, a comforting presence.

"A new species," the professor said, curiosity and awe in his voice. "We're about to make contact. What a wonderful day for humanity!"

Yet Ben-Ari could not summon his enthusiasm for science, not now, not here. Nor could she share Marino's eagerness for battle.

Because I met too many aliens, she thought. *And I fought too many battles. I know the evil that's out there. I know the terror of war.*

Instinctively, her hand reached toward her rifle, but of course she no longer carried one. Even now, no longer a soldier in the HDF, she kept reaching for her missing gun. She didn't know if she'd ever get used to living without one.

The bridge crew fell silent. They all stared at the viewport, watching the alien ships approach. The aliens were soon only a hundred thousand kilometers away—still too far for the naked eye, but when it came to space, this was brushing shoulders.

"Open all common hailing frequencies and deliver my words in all common galactic tongues," Ben-Ari said, and her communication officer nodded and tapped a few buttons. Ben-Ari took a deep breath and spoke. "This is Captain Einav Ben-Ari of the Earth starship *Lodestar*. We come on a mission of exploration, peace, and friendship. We would be glad to host your ambassadors aboard our ship, share our knowledge and tales, and—"

A voice emerged from the speakers, interrupting her, grainy and cruel.

"Worship her . . ."

Ben-Ari frowned. Behind her, she heard Marino curse.

"Alien vessels!" Ben-Ari said. "We come in peace. Would you like to accept our invitation to—"

"Worship her," rasped the voice. "Or die."

The ships charged toward them, coming into view. Ben-Ari inhaled sharply.

Flying saucers, was her first thought. She had seen these ships in countless old movies and grainy, twentieth-century photographs. But while those old images had looked more like hubcaps on strings, the ships ahead were very real. They were forged of craggy dark metal. When she zoomed in on one, she saw symbols engraved onto its hull. They reminded her of Ancient Egyptian hieroglyphs.

There were three ships. And Ben-Ari had seen enough enemy starships to recognize a battle formation. They were only moments away now.

"Show yourselves!" Ben-Ari demanded.

On a central monitor, an image crackled to life.

Ben-Ari felt the blood drain from her face.

A hideous visage peered from the screen. The alien was vaguely humanoid. Its head was oval and hairless, the cranium massive compared to its pinched face. The eyes were oval, very large, and pure black—no pupils, no irises, no white to them, just two black pits. There was no nose, only slits for nostrils, and no lips, just another crack for a frowning mouth. The skin was gray, wrinkled, and splotchy. The legs were hidden, but Ben-Ari could see the torso. It was cadaverous, the ribs prominent, the red heart vaguely visible through the papery skin.

A gray, Ben-Ari thought. *A Roswell alien. Like from the old stories.*

"Who are you?" she whispered.

"Your death," the alien said and laughed—a cruel, horrible laughter that sounded like snapping bones.

The image vanished.

The alien ships stormed forth, and their weapons fired.

CHAPTER FIVE

Lailani walked through the banana grove, pushing her wheelbarrow of books.

This time, she did not smile at the fishermen she passed by. She did not wave to the farmers in the rice paddies. She did not even bother swatting aside the insects. Epimetheus walked at her side, loyal as ever, but today the Doberman did not rub against her side or lick her fingers. The dog kept a safe distance.

Because he knows, Lailani thought. *Knows that I'm not fully human.*

She winced, the chip in her skull sizzling hot.

She thrust her claws into Elvis's chest.

Laughing, she tore out his heart.

She crawled through tunnels, hunting, crunching wet things.

She inhaled deeply, rubbed her temples, and walked onward.

"Keep it together, de la Rosa," she mumbled to herself. "Don't let that monster return."

Taking deep breaths, she reached the school. Once more the children ran out to greet her, grinning, calling out to her. "Tita Lailani, Tita Lailani!"

She smiled at them wanly. Sweat trickled down her brow. It was so hot. It was so damn hot here. She was so thirsty. She was so hungry.

Hunt. Hunt! Catch them. Eat them! Drink their blood!

She swallowed. She found herself standing in their classroom. She didn't even remember stepping inside. Epimetheus was distributing the books, carrying them gently in his powerful jaws, but the Doberman kept glancing back at her, concern in his eyes.

"Tita Lailani, look!" A boy raced toward her. "We taught Darwin how to roll over."

The boy was carrying the tarsier. He placed the petite primate on a desk.

"Roll over!" the boy said.

Darwin obeyed.

"Shake!" said the boy, and Darwin reached up a long-fingered hand.

"Play dead!" said the boy, and Darwin fell over and closed his massive eyes.

Lailani lifted the animal. She stroked his fur. Soft. So soft. He smelled so good. She brought the tarsier to her nose and inhaled deeply.

Hunt.

She stroked the fur.

Lost in the tunnels.

She kissed the tarsier.

Find a way out.

She bit through skin and hot flesh. She ripped out chunks and swallowed, drinking the blood, consuming the innards. Hunting. Crunching the soft wet things.

The children screamed.

Lailani stared at them.

She dropped the dead, half-eaten tarsier and stared in horror at her bloody hands.

"Run," she whispered, then raised her voice to a shout. "Run!"

The children fled, and Lailani fell to her knees, trembling, weeping, as it all came back again.

* * * *

"I'm telling you, I'm not crazy!" Lailani sat on the examination table in the hospital's psych ward. "It's not me who killed the trained monkey. It was the giant centipedes controlling me! And the microchip in my brain normally tells them to go away, but it's been telling me to fly into space now." She tapped her head. "Aren't you listening? The microchip in my brain!"

The doctor and nurses glanced at one another, then back at her.

Lailani slumped. "Look. I know how this sounds. But just ask President Petty, okay? You know, the president of Earth? He's a friend of mine! He made me an officer in the army after I killed the marauder king. Really!" She sighed. "This isn't helping, is it?"

Again the medical staff glanced at one another.

"Layla," her doctor said, "it's common for—"

"Lailani," she said. "Lieutenant Lailani Marita de la Rosa."

The doctor nodded. "Lailani. It's common for schizophrenics to suffer delusions during times of stress. In fact, it's—"

"Damn it, man!" She leaped onto her feet and stood on the examination table. "I'm not crazy! I'm an alien hybrid!" She heaved a sigh. "Look, if you don't have a way to contact President Petty, just contact Addy Linden and Marco Emery. You know them, right? The heroes of the war?" From her pocket, she pulled out a photo showing her, Addy, and Marco. "There, see? I know them. Photographic evidence. Call Addy and Marco. Actually, just call Marco. Addy is crazier than I am. Here's his number."

The doctor frowned. "I'm sorry, Lailani, but you must take your medication, and then I'll commit you for a while into the—"

"Talk to Marco!" she shouted, pulling out her phone. "Now!"

She was a tiny girl, only four-foot-ten and didn't even weigh a hundred pounds, but her voice carried authority. The doctor fell silent and took a step back. Lailani dialed Marco and set the phone to hologram mode. A moment later, a hologram of Marco burst out from the screen, hovering in the center of the hospital room.

"Marco, they think I'm crazy!" Lailani said.

Addy's head peeked into the holographic image. "Hey, Lailani!" She waved. "Still going around telling people you're Napoleon?"

Marco shoved her back. "Not now, Addy! God. Go back to roasting hot dogs." He turned toward the doctor. "You have the wrong patient. It's the hot dog monster here you want committed."

Marco spent a while speaking to the doctor, then managed to tap through to President Petty himself. Soon the gruff, grizzled president was speaking to the doctor, confirming Lailani's story. The doctor looked ready to faint.

During the war, General James Petty had commanded the remains of the human fleet. Following Earth's victory, he had run for President of the Alliance of Nations, unseating Maria Katson in a landslide election. The brusque general had become the *de facto* leader of Earth.

Petty had also become a good friend of Ben-Ari's Dragons, the name the media had given Lailani and her friends. The new president had given the surviving Dragons medals and promotions. The sergeants among them had received commissions too, becoming officers. After all, the Dragons had saved Earth. And today Petty saved Lailani.

Or at least, when they took her out of that loony bin, Lailani thought she was being saved. When they slapped handcuffs on her, she realized: *I might be jumping from the frying pan to the fire.*

By the end of the day, she was in a military plane, being transferred from the local nut house to a military hospital in Okinawa.

"Can you at least loosen these handcuffs?" Lailani asked, sitting bound to her seat on the plane.

Her guard, a burly sergeant with enough weapons to overthrow a small country's government, shook his head. "No."

Lailani groaned. The military plane was spacious enough—unlike passenger jets—but the cuffs were digging into her. She tugged on them.

"I'm friends with President Petty, you know," she said.

"His orders," said the guard. "Handcuffs stay on."

Look at the freak! The voice from her dream echoed. *Step right up, step right up!*

"You just need to put on a top hat, grab a whip, and present me to the crowd," Lailani muttered to her guard. He did not reply.

She wanted to make another quip, but her head hurt again. The visions flashed before her. Blood. Racing through the tunnels. Hunting. Feasting.

Find them.

She raced in the darkness.

Control them.

The plane seemed to unfold around her. The sky opened up. She could see the clouds, the turbines moving in the engine, the air flowing over the wings. She could see inside the guard— his organs, his flowing blood, his mind. See them? No. Not sight.

Her eyes were not seeing any of this. She could *smell* it. *Sense* it. The pulsing sweetness of it. His tendrils of thought.

She thrashed in her handcuffs, could not free herself. Her claws grew.

Freak, she heard the guard thinking. *Monster. I should shoot her now.*

Lailani's eyes widened.

She could hear his thoughts! She could caress them. Grab them.

Control him, the voice spoke inside her.

She took a deep breath.

You will release my handcuffs, she thought, shoving the words into his mind. *Reach for the keys in your pocket. And release me. Now.*

At first he resisted. Lailani persisted.

Do it. Free me.

The guard gritted his teeth. Sweat dripped down his brow. Lailani reached to the right part of him, and she moved him. Like a puppeteer, she directed his hand into his pocket. She felt the key touch his fingers. She could feel what he felt. She pulled out the key. The guard was trembling, trying to resist.

I am a daughter of great power, she thought. *You cannot resist me. Free me.*

Hand shaking, he reached out with the key. He placed it into her handcuff. Lailani inhaled in anticipation.

"No!" the guard shouted.

He wrenched his hand back, shouting, and drew his gun. He aimed at her.

"Wait, don't shoot!" she shouted. "Not on a plane, damn it!"

Her higher awareness vanished. Her claws retracted. She was just Lailani, the human, once more.

She took a deep breath.

Fucking hell, she thought. *My scum daddy gave me mind control too?*

It had been a decade since the Scum War, since her alien powers had awoken. She had used those powers for only several months before the HDF had installed a chip in her brain, stoppering her abilities. She had dared not think of that war in years. Especially not the terror she had found on Abaddon, homeworld of the scum.

Yet now those memories flooded back.

She had connected to the scums' great pheromone network. She had led her platoon through their hive. She had found the scum emperor's throne room, a cavern deep underground.

Lailani winced to remember the hybrids she had seen there, twisted monsters forged from the DNA of her dead friends. Beast, Elvis, Sergeant Singh, and the others had risen in the cavern, reborn as centipedes with human faces.

Sitting on the plane, Lailani clenched her fists, the memories chilling her. In that dark chasm, the scum emperor had attacked. He had been so fast. He had dodged every bullet. Lailani's platoon had fired at him again and again, missing every time.

But Lailani could reach the monster with her mind. She had grabbed him with tendrils of her thoughts. She had held him in an invisible grip.

She and her platoon had then opened fire, slaying the immobile beast.

Yes. She had always had this power—the power to seize another, to control their body, to paralyze or move them. But where had this power come from? As far as she knew, normal scum possessed no mind control. Why did Lailani?

Cold sweat trickled down her back. Trembles seized her. She shoved those memories aside, not ready to probe deeper. Not here. Not now.

She spent the rest of the flight covered with cold sweat, handcuffed, the guard pointing his gun at her.

Still nicer than flying coach, she thought.

They landed in Okinawa, an island that had suffered massive casualties in the Galactic Wars, that now held the largest military base in the Pacific. The guard strapped Lailani to a gurney, blindfolded her, muzzled her, and rolled her through the base. Lailani began to feel like the world's most dangerous super villain. With her blindfold on, she kept seeing the old visions. The scum in the tunnels. Her claws ripping out Elvis's heart. Her mind was a storm, a mix of hatred and hunger and grief and guilt. The scum part of her—monstrous, bloodthirsty. The human— drowning, weeping, clinging to goodness. She was only one percent scum, but that evil was strong. And it was dragging her down into its pits.

The next few hours passed in a daze. When they finally removed her blindfold, she was in another hospital. They kept her in handcuffs. They took her from hospital room to hospital room. They interrogated her, one after another—nurses, psychiatrists, surgeons, military intelligence officers. She remembered the last time the scum had controlled her, had controlled her movements, had forced her to sabotage the HDFS *Miyari* and kill Elvis. Back then too, the military had chained her, poked and prodded her. Eventually they had released her, of course, but only to use her as a weapon, to sic her against her scum masters.

And a terrible weapon she had been. She had hacked into the scum's network, had led her platoon through the hives of Abaddon, and finally had managed to mentally wrestle with the scum emperor himself.

But the scum empire is gone, she thought. *The marauders, their offspring, are dead too. Will the military release me, or will I end up in a lab for the rest of my life, studied like a rat?*

"Well, Lailani." Yet another doctor entered the room and sat before her. "How are we doing today?"

The doctor was a middle-aged woman in blue scrubs, a colorful bandanna wrapped around her blond curls.

"You need a top hat, not a bandanna," Lailani said. "And a whip."

The doctor smiled. "I'm a doctor, not a lion tamer." She pointed at Lailani. "And you're not a circus animal."

Lailani gave a shaky smile. "You understood my reference. I think I'm in love with you now."

"Sorry, Ms. de la Rosa, I never form romantic attachments with my patients—unless they're fabulously rich, that is. Or if they look like Cary Grant. My name is Billy."

"Not Doctor Something or Other?" Lailani said. "Just Billy?"

She nodded. "Just Billy is perfect."

Lailani narrowed her eyes. "Are you sure you're a doctor?"

"I hope so," Billy said. "Otherwise the hospital made a dreadful mistake naming me chief of neurosurgery."

"Well, I'd shake your hand, but they've got me in handcuffs. Got the key, Billy? My handshake is worth it."

"No key. But I do have these." Billy pulled out some X-rays. "Now now, an old microchip in the brain. I'm sure the psychiatrists gave you some strange looks when you spoke of it." She winked. "We get many people here claiming to be controlled by microchips. You're the first one whose story has checked out."

"Actually, the chip is what normally holds me together," Lailani said. And she spent a while speaking, telling Billy her terrible secret. How she was a genetic experiment of the scum. How the aliens had tweaked human DNA, engineering her to be a secret agent, a sleeping drone, how they had woken up her monstrous side on the HDFS *Miyari*, forced her to crash the ship.

"They no longer control me," Lailani said. "The scum are dead now. But that alien part of my DNA is still there." She grimaced. "And my chip, which normally holds that side at bay, is not working. I feel like Jekyll and Hyde, and Hyde has just busted out of prison."

Billy nodded. "Your chip is ten years old now. Older than most cars. Did they tell you how it works?"

Lailani nodded. "A bit. That it releases some chemicals into my brain. And has some code in it too."

"The code is still working," Billy said. "But the reservoir of chemicals is running low. That's why it's malfunctioning. When your last surgeon installed it, did they tell you it would need to be replaced?"

Lailani snorted. "That last surgeon was on Nightwall. The whole base is gone. The marauders blew it to smithereens. And to be honest, I don't remember much of what happened ten years ago. Hell, I can barely remember what I ate for breakfast most days, which is weird, because it's always champorado."

Billy raised her eyebrows.

"Chocolate rice porridge," Lailani said. "Try it. It's delicious."

The doctor smiled. "I don't think our cafeteria makes it, but after I replace your chip, I promise to get you some chocolate ice cream."

"For chocolate ice cream, I'd undergo a lobotomy."

Billy's smile widened. "Sorry, lobotomy only earns you an apple. Worst dessert in the cart."

Lailani made a gagging sound. "Apples? What kind of hospital is this?" She chewed her lip for a moment, hesitating. Finally she spoke again. "Doc, I wanted to ask you something. While you're poking around in my brain, replacing the chip, I was wondering if . . . if there's a way you can . . ." She groaned. "All right. It's really stupid, but I'll just ask. Can you erase some of my memories?"

Billy frowned. "Your memories? You want them gone?"

Lailani nodded. "Yeah. Not all of them! Just the bad stuff."

My memory of Sofia dying in the fire, she thought.

My memory of the thousands falling, she thought.

My memory of killing Elvis, she thought. *Most of all that one.*

"Just ones I don't want in my head," she added in a soft voice.

Billy's eyes softened. She touched Lailani's shoulder. "There is a lot we don't know about the human brain, Lailani. We know where memories are stored, but not which memory is stored where. I wouldn't be able to pick out specific memories from the thousands of them."

Lailani nodded and lowered her head. "I figured. Stupid question. I knew it."

"There are no stupid questions. Just questions we don't have answers for yet. But there are ways of dealing with a painful past. Meditation. Even medication." Billy smiled. "Even chocolate ice cream sometimes works."

"I'll need a lot of chocolate ice cream," Lailani said. "I'll grow fat. I might even weigh more than my Doberman at this rate." She sighed. "Poor pup is waiting for me back home. He helps too."

"You'll be back home in no time," Billy said.

Lailani chewed her lip. There was another question gnawing at her. Finally she blurted out, "Why do I have mind control powers?"

Billy frowned. "I'm not sure I understand."

"On the flight here," Lailani said, "I was able to grab my guard with my brain. To move his hand into his pocket. And back on Abaddon, I could control the scum emperor. And . . ." She sighed. "I sound like a crazy person again, don't I?"

Billy stared at her somberly. "Telekinesis is widely considered a myth. Multiple studies have debunked it."

"But it's real!" Lailani said. "The scum were able to control me from afar. It was how they got me to crash the *Miyari*, to kill Elvis." Tears filled her eyes. "Some of the scum had this power. Not the mindless soldiers, no. But some. Their hive-kings. Their emperor. I have that power too. My alien DNA can't just be from any old scum. My father must be a scum king, maybe the emperor himself. I'm scum nobility. I'm a fucking alien princess. And I killed them, Billy. I killed my friends."

She wept. Billy embraced her. Lailani laid her head against her doctor's shoulder, shedding tears.

She spent the next few days in the hospital, speaking to surgeons and programmers. It took a lot of convincing, but they eventually removed her handcuffs. It took even *more* convincing, even a stirring speech about human freedom and her right to choose, to convince the team to install an Off switch in her microchip.

Having these powers might just come in useful, Lailani had decided. She wanted a new chip. She wanted to hold this evil at bay. But having the option to activate her evil, only at the utmost hour of need, was too alluring to resist.

The scum created me to be a weapon, Lailani thought. *The military used me as a weapon too. And I'm not ready to disarm.*

So an Off switch she would get—and that took not only days of insistence but also a handwritten approval from President Petty himself. Of course, Lailani could not reach inside her skull to switch off the chip. But they had given her two keywords. She had only to think of the word *Nightwish* to deactivate the chip. It would reactivate on its own an hour later, sooner if she thought the word *Serenity.*

"All right, boys and girls," she said on the day of the surgery. "Get to sawing!"

Dr. Billy patted her hand. "Lailani, one more thing. We'll have to tie you down."

Lailani cocked an eyebrow. "I thought you weren't interested in romantic relationships with patients."

Billy sighed. "There's a small chance—just one in a hundred—that the surgery won't work. And just in case . . ."

"In case I wake up a monster." Lailani nodded. "All right. Strap me down, Doc. Better use the extra-thick chains. I'm stronger than I look."

They strapped her down. They shaved the back of her head. They gave her the anesthetic, and she drifted off.

She floated through darkness.

In the distance, muffled, she heard the voices of the doctors. She heard saws buzzing. She wanted to scream, to tell them she was still awake. And they were cutting her. And she fled them. She fled down tunnels, scurrying with thirty-six legs, a centipede with a human face, racing through the darkness.

She plunged down the tunnel. It became a wormhole. She fell through space and time. The stars streamed at her sides, and she became a girl again, just a girl, naked, her head shaved, flowing down the wormhole as nebulae spun around her. Finally she fell out into open space, and she hovered in the darkness, gasping for breath.

Silence.

Before her, she saw it again. A constellation shaped like a rearing bear.

Find the hourglass.

The voice spoke in the darkness, androgynous, coming from everywhere.

"Who are you?" Lailani asked.

One who is here to help you.

She looked around. Still she saw nothing but darkness.

"What is the hourglass?" Lailani said.

It is what you seek. A way to change the past. To undo evil. The hourglass can open a portal through time. It can send you back.

Lailani gasped. Strands of light were spreading out from her fingertips and toes, forming many paths like the branches and roots of a tree. Shimmering crystals grew from these strands like leaves, and within each crystal, she saw images. The crystals below her showed the past, the terrors that lurked there: killing Elvis, losing Sofia, losing so many other friends, suffering as a child in the slums of Manila. But the crystals above showed possible futures: futures where her friends were still alive, still with her.

Tears flowed down her cheeks.

"Where can I find the hourglass?" she whispered.

Seek the constellation, the disembodied voice answered. *Seek the rearing bear. But beware, Lailani. Beware the evil from beyond. Beware the Night Queen. Beware the goddess and her children.*

"Who is this goddess?" Lailani said. "Who are you? How do you know my name? I—"

You will know me in time. Now you must only trust me.

Something was sucking her back into the wormhole. Light was flowing around her. She was waking up. Above her, blurred, she saw human faces, heard muffled voices.

"No," Lailani mumbled. "No, not yet! I still need to learn more."

"Lailani!" Hands shook her. "Lailani, wake up! I bought you a hot dog!" A pause. "Oops. I may have spilled relish on you. It's okay, I'll just eat it up."

"Addy!" Another voice. "For God's sake, stop biting Lailani!"

"I'm not biting her, Poet! I'm just eating what I dropped."

"That's what you said when you squirted mustard on me this morning, and I still have teeth marks on my arm."

"It's not my fault you're delicious!"

Lailani opened her eyes.

She could barely believe it.

"Marco?" she whispered. "Addy?"

She rubbed her eyes, and they came into focus. For a moment, Lailani wasn't sure where she was. In the house in Greece? Back in the war, flying across the galaxy? No. When she looked around her, she still saw the Japanese hospital, though she lay in a recovery room now. Marco and Addy sat at her side. Marco held a few books, while Addy held a pile of hot dogs, potato chips, cookies, and other snacks.

"I brought you some books to help you pass the time," Marco said.

"I brought food," Addy said. "Much better."

"She ate half of it on the way over," Marco said.

Addy bristled. "I'm a growing boy!"

"You're a ravenous Tasmanian devil with a black hole in its stomach, that's what you are," Marco said.

Lailani gasped and sat up. She winced and touched the back of her head. She felt a bandage.

"You flew all the way from Greece just to see me?" she said.

Addy nodded. "Yep. We even had to fly coach. Coach! With no legroom! Can you imagine? With my long, lovely legs?"

Marco rolled his eyes. "Please. Your legs were slung across my lap the whole time, with your knees digging into my stomach."

She poked his stomach. "Maybe if you didn't eat so many hot dogs, your stomach would have more room."

"*Me?*" Marco said. "You ate both our lunches on the plane, and you were gnawing on the armrests by the time we landed here in Okinawa."

Addy was too busy tearing into a box of cookies to reply.

Lailani climbed off her bed and embraced them.

"Thank you for coming," she said. "Did Tomiko . . .?"

Addy paused from eating, crumbs falling down her chin. She and Marco shared a dark glance, then looked back at Lailani.

"She couldn't make it," Marco finally said.

Lailani didn't miss the hint of pain in his voice, the shadow in his eyes. She had never met Tomiko, Marco's new wife. She had not attended their wedding. Marco had invited her, but it was too painful.

I still have feelings for him, Lailani realized. *I left him. He wanted to marry me, and I said no. But now it hurts me. Now the guilt fills me.*

So much guilt. For hurting Marco. For killing Elvis. For causing so much pain to others. Perhaps she was a monster and that had nothing to do with her scum DNA.

Addy broke the awkward silence. "So, Lailani, how's the new potato chip?"

"Microchip," Marco said.

Addy frowned. "Are you sure?"

Marco groaned. "For Chrissake, Addy, they didn't implant a potato chip in her brain."

Addy bristled. "How do you know? I once saw a TV show about somebody who went through open-heart surgery, and the doctor dropped a mint into him, and that mint cured an infection!"

"That was a sitcom!" Marco said.

"I know, genius." Addy rolled her eyes. "That's why I asked if it's *potato* chip, not a mint."

Marco rolled his eyes. "Are you sure you didn't undergo neurosurgery too, Addy? A complete brain removal?"

"I think I'd remember *that*," Addy said, but for safe measure, she touched her head, seeking scars.

Lailani reached up to touch her own scar—or at least, the bandage now covering it. She felt nothing but a tingle. The pain of her old chip was gone.

Did it work? she wondered. *Do I now have a new chip with an Off button?*

She was tempted to test it, to think of that word, of Night—

Stop.

She took a deep breath.

She mustn't think that word. Not here, with Marco and Addy nearby. It was too dangerous. She knew her code word, the word that would turn off her new chip, would release the beast within her. She would use it only at the utmost need. Not here. Not now. Hopefully not ever.

She stepped toward the window, clad in her hospital gown. She stared outside into the night. She could see the stars, the moonlight over the Pacific, and a few distant ships.

Find the hourglass.

She turned back toward her friends.

"I'm leaving," she said softly.

Addy pointed. "You might want to lace up your hospital gown first."

Cheeks flushing, Lailani placed her back to the wall and tightened her gown, hiding her *other* cheeks. She found her clothes on a bedside table and began to dress.

"You're going back home so soon?" Marco said. "You won't even stay overnight to recover?"

Her claws tore through Elvis's chest.

His heart dripped in her grip.

She laughed as he died.

She feasted on raw meat.

She watched the spaceship crash, the dozens die.

Find the hourglass.

"I'm not going back home," Lailani whispered. "I'm leaving Earth."

Her friends' eyes widened.

"Where are you going?" Marco stepped toward her. "Lailani! You're crying. What's wrong?"

She pulled on her jeans and shirt. She buckled on her belt.

What's wrong? she thought. *I caused the* Miyari *to crash. I killed half the soldiers aboard. I murdered Elvis. I'm a monster. Even with this chip in my brain, the monster is inside me, waiting to break out. I did not slay the beast, merely caged it. And you ask me what's wrong?*

"*I* am," she merely whispered. "*I'm* what's wrong. But I'm going to make things right. I'm going to find redemption."

They stared at her in silence.

"Does that mean I can eat your food?" Addy finally said.

Marco ignored Addy this time. He touched Lailani's arm. "Redemption? Leaving Earth? What do you mean?"

And suddenly the tears were flowing down Lailani's cheeks, and she was shaking. "For what I did. For killing him, Marco. For killing Elvis. And the others. For what that monster inside me made me do." She was sobbing now. "It came out again. I almost killed again. It's why I'm here, in the hospital, why I'm broken. Why I'm a sinner. And I need to fix this, Marco. I need to . . ."

Her voice faded into her weeping. Marco embraced her.

"Lailani." He wiped away her tears. "You're not to blame for what happened. It wasn't you that day. It was the scum. Just the puppeteers. You can't blame the puppet for its movements."

She shook her head, fresh tears falling. "There is no puppet master, Marco. There is evil and sin inside me. But I saw a vision." She touched his cheeks and stared into his eyes. "When I was asleep, I saw it. A constellation shaped like a bear. An hourglass that could change the past. Somebody spoke to me, somebody I couldn't see. The voice of a friend. He told me I could undo what I did. That I could bring them back."

She felt Addy's eyes on her. She sensed Marco's incredulity.

"Lailani, you can't change the past." Marco held her hands. "I've learned that since the war. I learned that on Haven. I learned that in Greece. I learned that whenever the nightmares haunted me. You can't change the past, but you still have a future on Earth. Of building. Of healing. Of helping others."

Lailani nodded, head lowered.

"Okay," she whispered.

"The new chip will help," Marco said. "And I'll help. I'll stay here for as long as you need me."

"Thank you, Marco." She stood on tiptoes—she was no taller than his shoulders, and he himself wasn't very tall—and kissed his cheek. "But you shouldn't stay for too long. Tomiko is at home, waiting for you." She smiled, wiping away her last tears. "But stay long enough to eat. If Addy left us anything, that is."

They turned to look at Addy. She stared back, a bunch of potato chips and cookies in her mouth, a hot dog in one hand and an ice cream bar in the other. She swallowed. "What?"

They sat together on the bed, and they ate, and they shared old stories. Addy organized a card game, and soon they were all laughing. And this was good. And this felt like old times. Lailani could almost imagine that they were eighteen again, kids at Fort Djemila, eating snacks from the vending machine. That the war was still distant. That no blood stained her hands. That no nightmares haunted her. That no monster lived inside her.

I'm ten years older, Lailani thought, *and I suffered, and I shattered, and I hurt so many. But for today, let us be kids again. Let me have this last memory of them. In case I never come home.* She had to wipe her eyes again. *Because I'm leaving. Because I'm bringing you back, Sofia, Elvis, and all the rest of you. Because I'm saving you and I'm saving my soul.*

"Gin rummy!" Addy announced, doing a victory dance.

Marco groaned. "Addy, we're playing poker."

She nodded. "And I won."

"Addy, for Chrissake!" Marco grabbed her arm and rolled up her sleeve. "How many aces do you have hidden up there?"

Addy gasped. "How dare you accuse a lady of cheating, you scoundrel! I shall have you whipped in the public square."

"And give me back my wallet!" He snatched it from her back pocket, and she squealed and slapped him.

A nurse showed up, frowning, and confiscated the cards. The stern Jamaican woman almost tossed Marco and Addy out. It took plenty of innocent eyelash batting to earn a second chance. But only if they kept the noise down.

"Hey, Lailani, you got cable in this place?" Addy asked. She switched on the television. "The Galactic Asteroid Belt Supreme Adventure Race is about to begin."

Marco rolled his eyes. "You and your NASCAR."

"It's not NASCAR!" Addy crossed her arms. "It's *GABSAR*. You know, GABSAR? It's only the most important drag race in the history of humanity, which I've been talking to you about all year. And Firebolt is competing! You know he's my favorite racer."

Marco frowned. "I thought Mario Marino, the Jersey Giant, is your favorite racer."

"Marco!" Addy punched him. "The Jersey Giant is a *martial artist*. A ten-year champion, in fact. Firebolt is the drag racer." She found the right channel. "Ah, here we go! Now shush, all of you."

Lailani sat quietly, watching the GABSAR race. Several starships, each no larger than a typical race car, flew toward an asteroid belt in a neighboring star system. Floating cameras followed them, broadcasting the event across Earth and her colonies. Thanks to Isaac's Wormholes, drag races outside the solar system could now reach Earth in real time.

The asteroid belt was dense, filled with millions of stones, some as large as towns, others no larger than marbles. The starships whipped around them, blasting out fire. One by one, they slammed into asteroids, exploding, barely leaving time for their pilots to eject. Even Firebolt only made it halfway through the gauntlet, finally slamming into a basketball-sized asteroid that tore his ship apart. The pilot managed to eject, though he lost his leg in the crash. He gave the thumbs-up to the camera, offering sponsors advertising space on his upcoming prosthetic.

"This is barbaric," Marco said.

"This is glorious," Addy said.

They both turned toward Lailani, awaiting her judgment.

"I'm switching back to watching Filipino romantic comedies," she said.

Marco and Addy both groaned.

Lailani spent another day recovering in the hospital. Once her bandage was removed, and the chip in her brain was humming along smoothly, she traveled to the airport with Marco and Addy. They bought tickets back to Greece, and Lailani hugged them.

"Come visit us soon," Addy said, squeezing her. "Promise me, Tiny. We'll have a feast in your honor. And we'll play poker. And we'll laugh as Marco loses and gets angry."

"Maybe if you didn't cheat," Marco muttered, then he too hugged Lailani. His voice softened. "Remember, Lailani. You can't change the past. But you can move forward. You can heal. You can be happy. And should you need us, Addy and I are always just a short flight away. After traveling across the galaxy and back, that's not too bad."

Lailani nodded. "I'll be all right. I promise. Now hurry, you'll miss your flight! Don't let Addy eat your lunch this time."

Marco nodded. "Not to worry. I bought a sandwich at the airport and hid it in my backpack, and—Addy! Addy, how did you get my sandwich? Give it back!"

Lailani stood at the terminal, waving as they boarded their flight, then stood at the window, watching their plane fly back to Europe.

Her tablet beeped. An incoming message.

Lailani pulled it out from her pocket, expecting to see a final goodbye from Marco and Addy, perhaps a photo of them on the plane, making silly faces.

But it was a message from Tomiko.

I know who you are. I know how Marco feels about you. Don't you touch him. I know how you hurt him before. I won't let you hurt him again. I won't let you hurt me. He is mine. STAY AWAY!

Lailani felt something strange, something she didn't recognize at first. Not anger, no. Not anxiety or fear.

It was sadness.

Should I tell Marco? Should I reply?

No. Not her circus. Not her monkeys. She deleted the message.

I hope the circus goes easy for you when you get home, Poet.

She had told Marco and Addy that she would fly back to the Philippines—it was just a hop and a skip away from here in Okinawa. But instead, she left the airport. She stood on the bustling street, backpack slung across her shoulder, and hailed a cab.

"Where to?" asked the driver, a slender man in a buttoned white shirt. Lailani had to use the translation app on her phone to understand his Japanese.

"The nearest used-starship yard," Lailani said. "Actually, no. The cheapest used-starship yard."

The driver nodded. "They're the same one. JEX's Starship and Robotics Emporium. It's an hour drive though. You got money?"

She flashed a credit card glowing with credit points. "A lot, and I'll tip if you change the radio station. Play me some J-Pop."

The rickety cab drove, belching out smoke, making its way through the traffic of cars, lumbering tanks, racing motorcycles, and mechanical horses. The skyscrapers soared at their sides, and atmo-cars flitted above. Shops selling everything from sushi to sexbots lined the roadsides. It was Earth—planet of sin, delight, dirt, beauty, humanity. The planet Lailani had fought for in the wars. The planet she had spent years away from, dreaming to someday return to. The planet she must now leave again.

Once more I fly into the darkness, seeking light. Find the hourglass.

I will. She nodded, wiping her eyes as the cab rumbled along. *I will.*

CHAPTER SIX

The three saucers flew toward the *Lodestar*, lasers firing.

"Divert power to port and starboard shields!" Ben-Ari cried, standing in the center of the bridge.

Lieutenant Commander Mario Marino raised his eyebrows. The retired martial artist, now the security officer of the *Lodestar*, hesitated. "Captain, they're coming from ahead. The forward shield should—"

"Do it!" Ben-Ari shouted. "That's an order! And return fire, damn it!"

Marino obeyed. The front shield drained to a third of its power, leaving the rest of the energy to secure the sides of the ship. An instant later, photon bolts thrummed from the front cannons, flying toward the enemy saucers.

The enemy's lasers slammed into the front of the *Lodestar*.

The ship shook.

The bridge crew clung to their posts, and cracks raced across several monitors.

Their own fire destroyed the central saucer. The two other alien ships streamed alongside the *Lodestar*, firing their lasers onto the port and starboard shields.

The *Lodestar* jolted madly.

Several officers fell.

Monitors detached and shattered.

But the *Lodestar* kept flying.

"God damn!" Marino said. He looked at Ben-Ari. "If you hadn't ordered me to divert energy to the side shields, we—"

"Aurora, turn and face them!" Ben-Ari cried. "Marino, keep firing! Photons from the fore cannons, and release our missiles!"

Aurora, the invertebrate pilot of the *Lodestar*, was flashing a bright yellow with blue lines, a sign of her distress. Her eight tentacles moved in a flurry, adjusting controls. The *Lodestar* spun toward the enemy again—an instant before more lasers slammed into their hull.

"Marino!" Ben-Ari cried.

"Firing, Captain!"

Missiles and photons flew from the *Lodestar*, but the enemy saucers dodged the projectiles, shooting upward.

"Aurora, keep our strongest shields facing them!" Ben-Ari said. "Charge! Don't give them time to fork us!"

"Yes, mistress of dark waters!" the alien octopus said, speaking through her translation device, and the *Lodestar*—a mighty ship the size of an aircraft carrier, home to five hundred souls, charged toward the smaller alien vessels. More weapons fired. The ship shook. Fire blazed through space.

The elevator emerged into the center of the bridge.

"Crikey, I'll be stuffed!" rose a voice. "What's going on here? Have you drongos got kangaroos loose in your top paddocks?"

Ben-Ari cringed.

Commander Richie "Fish" Fishburne, Chief Exobiologist and third in command of the *Lodestar*, stomped onto the bridge.

Fish was forty, a decade older than Ben-Ari, but he barely looked older than her. His hair was long, wavy, and blond. He wore khaki shorts, a khaki shirt opened halfway down his chest, and a necklace of crocodile teeth. Fish had a doctorate in exobiology, but he was more entertainer than scientist; the Australian was famous back on Earth, host of the hit television show *Alien Hunter*. The show had begun humbly, featuring Fish exploring new planets, wrestling alien animals, and explaining their ways to the audience. Since the first season several years ago, *Alien Hunter* had expanded into a franchise, complete with video games, action figures, two feature films, and an alien safari. Now the famous Alien Hunter himself was on a new adventure—crossing the galaxy on the *Lodestar*.

And getting in my way, Ben-Ari thought.

If you asked her, it was ridiculous that HOPE was hiring showmen instead of serious scientists. But the *Lodestar* had cost taxpayers an arm and a leg—it was among Earth's most expensive projects in history—all while Earth was in a deep recession following two galactic wars. To excite the taxpayers, HOPE had hired celebrities. Fish was the famous Alien Hunter from television. Marino was the champion martial artist and fitness guru, his posters hanging in gyms around the world. Professor Isaac was a renowned science communicator and author, his popular science books found in every bookstore on Earth. HOPE was about science. But it was also about pleasing the taxpayers. And that meant a bridge full of famous faces.

Maybe, rose a sneaky voice in her mind, *it's why they hired me too. I am, after all, the famous Einav Ben-Ari, commander of Ben-Ari's Dragons, the group that defeated the scum and marauders.*

She shoved that last thought aside. She never wanted to think it again.

"Fish, get off my bridge!" Ben-Ari said. "And change into your uniform. Marino, fire our lures! Try to confuse their lasers. Aurora, barrel roll! Marino, keep firing our photons, scatter pattern!"

The enemy ships were charging toward the *Lodestar* again. Aurora tugged at half a dozen controls, and the *Lodestar* spun madly. Her photons blasted out.

Fish marched across the bridge toward Ben-Ari. "I've had a gutful of this! This is a scientific expedition, and you drongos are buzzing for war like hornets in a bottle. We're here to study aliens, not wallop the bludgers apart! I'm the expert on aliens here, remember. *Alien Hunter* had ten million viewers per episode last season. We need this battle like a third armpit."

"Fish, shut up. Marino, switch to plasma bolts!"

The security officer nodded. But while the martial artist was renowned for his speed in the ring, his reactions aboard the *Lodestar* were too slow. He hesitated before each control, firing the weapons a second too late each time. The enemy saucers kept dodging the fire. The saucers flanked them again, and lasers flew.

"Incoming!" Marino shouted.

Blasts rocked the ship.

Ben-Ari clung to a rail.

Fish collapsed onto the floor. Cursing, the exobiologist leaped back up.

"You're as mad as a frog in a sock, sheila!" Fish spat at her. "You're destroying my ship, mate, and I'll—"

"Shut up or I'll have security escort you off my bridge!" Ben-Ari said. "Marino, damn it! Pulse your fire!" She raced toward the security station.

"I'm not going to just rack off," Fish said. "This is what happens when we let soldiers command a scientific vessel. This isn't one of your toy gunships, ya grommet. You've chucked a wobbly! *Talk* to the aliens. Have a chinwag!" He grabbed one of the controls. "Alien vessels, do you read me? Do—"

"Somebody get him out of here!" Ben-Ari shouted. She joined Marino at the gunner's station. "Here, with me, Marino. Like this. Aurora, keep us barrel rolling! Marino, you fire the starboard cannons, I'll fire the port."

More lasers flew their way. Aurora dodged projectile after projectile. The alien mollusk was a terrific pilot, Ben-Ari realized, her eight tentacles able to control the *Lodestar* better than any human could, manipulating rolling, yawing, thrusters, main and secondary engines, and brakes all without an instant's hesitation. With all her heart, Ben-Ari still missed Kemi, her old pilot—but right now, she was grateful to have an octopus at the helm.

Ben-Ari aimed the cannons at an enemy saucer. She fired three missiles in rapid fire—one to send the saucer fleeing left, another to divert it right, and a third to finish the job. An old move she had learned in the war.

The third missile slammed into the saucer.

It shattered.

Only one saucer now remained, and the battle became more manageable. Aurora managed to dodge most of the enemy's attacks, and Marino was able to keep redistributing the shields' energy to wherever the saucer flew.

"All right," Ben-Ari said, voice softer now. "Marino, keep firing, but fire over the saucer's bow. Aim to keep it busy, not to destroy it. Understood?"

The martial artist gave her a sidelong glance, eyebrow raised. "Captain? Aren't we to destroy the bastard?"

Ben-Ari shook her head. "No. Reduce our cannon power to five percent. Hit their cannons. Hit their engines. Cripple them. But keep their hull intact. I want them alive."

Marino nodded, teeth bared. "Aye, Captain."

Ben-Ari turned toward Aurora, who was now deep indigo, denoting her concentration. The octopus was still gripping controls with all eight tentacles. "Aurora, keep shadowing that saucer. While Marino is chipping away at the saucer, dodge its assaults. But do not launch offensive maneuvers against it. If it begins to flee, you chase. Understood?"

The octopus flashed bright orange before fading back to indigo. Ben-Ari did not need the translator to understand the emphatic, "Yes, mistress!"

The fighter and octopus busied themselves at their tasks. The *Lodestar* kept shadowing the saucer, and Marino struck it with weak photon blasts, crippling the enemy's weapons and engines but sparing the hull. Soon the saucer was limping through space, too weak to fight back, too wounded to escape.

We got 'em, Ben-Ari thought, satisfaction swelling in her.

While the battle continued, a few ensigns raced across the bridge, extinguishing fires. Damage reports came in from across the ship. The hull had suffered several dents. The bio lab on the third floor had been breached, spilling out its tanks of tardigrades, but those little bastards were virtually indestructible, and they could be collected later. No lives had been lost.

Among the crew, she saw Professor Noah Isaac looking a little rattled. He had probably never seen a battle before. But when he looked at Ben-Ari, he gave her a little nod, the slightest of smiles.

Good job, his eyes said. *I'm proud of you.*

For a brief instant, Ben-Ari was elated. For weeks now, Isaac had been teaching her science, had seen her as a bright, inquisitive, but ultimately ignorant girl. Now she had shown him her worth.

She allowed herself a single deep breath, then got back to business.

"Marino, come with me," she said. "Help me assemble a boarding party—eight security guards, one of them a medic—and we head to the shuttle. We're taking over that enemy craft."

"Mistress of dark waters!" rose Aurora's voice—or at least the voice from her translator. Her body turned black, and red lines squiggled across it. "The rounded shell of metal and life flees upon the currents!"

"Follow it," Ben-Ari said, then turned toward Isaac. "Professor? You have the bridge while I'm away. Marino—come with me."

Ben-Ari and the security chief turned to step off the bridge. But Fish moved to stand in their way.

"Hold on, mates. Stop right there!" The Alien Hunter held out his hands. His seashell bracelet chinked. "Boarding party? Have you got dingoes loose in your drawers? We came in contact with a new alien species. We can't just off like a frog in a sock, attacking them!"

Ben-Ari stared at her exobiologist. When she had first assumed command of the *Lodestar*, she had instantly taken a liking to Doctor Richie "Fish" Fishburne, TV's famous Alien Hunter. He wasn't like the other scientists aboard this ship. With his long hair, crocodile-tooth necklace, and Aussie accent, he had seemed refreshing. Ben-Ari had even forgiven his lack of a uniform; he wore the same outfit here as he did on his television show. Fish was not only young and cool: he was incredibly handsome, incredibly intelligent, and incredibly wealthy.

He was also incredibly single. And Ben-Ari had to admit: At first, she had developed something of a crush.

Yet over the past few weeks, they had been clashing. Many times, she had told Fish to change into a uniform, only for him to scoff, to say he was a scientist, not a soldier, and it was "crazy as a cockeyed koala" for a soldier to command the ship. Other times, she had scolded Fish for his language; he would call her "mate" instead of "ma'am" or "Captain." Often, when she spoke at meetings, Fish would slump in his seat, groan, roll his eyes, even place his bare feet on the table. He actually walked around in bare feet! At the last meeting, while talking to her, Fish had scratched his cheek with his middle finger; she still suspected it had been intentional.

For weeks, Ben-Ari had known they were on a collision course, heading toward a final showdown between a young captain and an older, better-educated, more experienced man. And now, as they chased the fleeing saucer, that collision finally hit.

"Crikey, mates." Fish crossed his arms, blocking Ben-Ari's passage to the elevator. "This is shonky business. We've encountered a new life form! And you blasted two of their ships. Now you're going to barge into the third one like a Tasmanian devil into a chicken coop? That's mad as a cut snake! We're scientists here. Oh wait. *I'm* a scientist. *You're* just a stickybeak soldier."

Across the bridge, everyone turned to stare at them. Many of these officers, Ben-Ari could tell, silently agreed with Fish. She was the youngest one here. The only one without a doctorate— without any university degree at all. Just a soldier, just a young woman, only thirty years old, commanding them all.

They all think it ridiculous, she thought. *And they're right. What am I doing here?*

Only Professor Isaac was giving her a soft look, but Ben-Ari wondered if even he—deep down inside, despite his kindness toward her—agreed with Fish.

Standing before the blocked elevator, Ben-Ari inhaled sharply.

For a moment, she wanted to justify herself. To tell Fish that President Petty himself had chosen her for this mission. To tell Fish—all of them!—that space was full of terrors, that this was a realm for warriors, not scientists. That the saucers had attacked them, needed to be attacked back. That naivety about the evil in space had already allowed the marauders to attack, had cost millions of lives.

She had so much to say. But she would not justify herself to them. Justifying herself meant she was weak. Meant she gave them power. Meant she had to convince them of her worth. That she depended on their approval.

I am a soldier, she thought. *And I must rule this ship as a soldier. Like Petty wanted. Like he knew was necessary.*

"Lieutenant Commander Marino," she said, speaking to the burly martial artist at her side. "Accompany Commander Fishburne to the brig. Set the lock to forty-eight hours. Then join me at the shuttle bay with your crew."

Marino nodded, his eyes narrowing. "Yes, Captain."

At least one person on my crew has some discipline, Ben-Ari thought. *The rest will learn.*

"This is ridiculous!" Fish blurted out, struggling as Marino gripped him. "Unhand me, mate!" He managed to point at Ben-Ari. "She's off her rocker! Mad as a croc in a dunny! You don't have to listen to her. Fight the poddy-dodger soldiers! Fight the—
"

"Get him out of here!" Ben-Ari said, then turned to stare at the rest of the crew. "You are all free to question my orders. But if anyone disobeys me during battle again, you'll join Fishburne in the brig. Is that understood?" She raised her voice as if speaking to mere recruits, not esteemed scientists. "Is that understood!"

And they fell into line.

"Yes, ma'am!"

She nodded. She marched through the ship, chin raised, shoulders squared.

You understood, Petty, she thought. *You knew that space is not like the lab. That space is full of danger. And that nobody is better than me at handling it. Even here, even part of HOPE, even on a mission of science rather than war, you need a soldier.*

Marino met her in the shuttle launch bay, eight security officers with him—all carrying assault rifles. All of them wore armored spacesuits and helmets. They carried an extra suit, helmet, and weapon for Ben-Ari, and she geared up quickly. At Ben-Ari's insistence, they all put on jet packs too. On a spaceship, wearing a jet pack was like wearing a parachute on a plane.

"How's Fish?" Ben-Ari said, hooking up her pack.

"Taken care of," said Marino, and Ben-Ari thought she saw something new in the wrestler's eyes. No longer cocky pride. She saw respect.

He was a champion wrestler, a celebrity, Ben-Ari thought. *Never a soldier. Now he will see true battle.*

The *Lodestar* came with two shuttles: *Romulus* and *Remus*. They were triangular and sleek, able to fly in space or air, their hulls heavily armored and their wings supporting both telescopes and missiles. Each shuttle could hold six passengers. Each could serve as a landing craft, exploration vessel, lifeboat, or starfighter. Today they would fight.

They entered the shuttles. Ben-Ari commanded *Romulus*. Marino took command of *Remus*. The hangar opened, and the two slick vessels burst out into space, engines roaring.

The alien saucer flew ahead. The *Lodestar* grew smaller behind them. From the bridge of the *Lodestar*, using the magnification on the viewports, the saucer had seemed so close. Flying here within this rattling, roaring shuttle, the enemy was just a speck in the distance.

But these shuttles were fast, roaring forth with state-of-the-art EmDrive engines, so fast they could have flown from Earth to the moon—a journey that would take days with conventional engines—within three hours.

The enemy ship grew larger ahead. They were trailing smoke, and blasts of photons from the *Lodestar* kept slamming into their hull, denting the dark metal, knocking the saucer from side to side. The saucer was like a wounded bull, lumbering forth, taking arrow after arrow but still stumbling through the night, still desperate to flee.

Yet they cannot flee us, Ben-Ari thought, gripping the controls of the *Romulus. We are two birds of prey, and we will not rest until we grab our quarry.*

The saucer was soon near. It hovered in space, smoking, its hull badly scarred. Another blast from the *Lodestar* hit it. The shuttle's engines sputtered, then gave a last belch before dying.

Ben-Ari's communicator crackled to life. Marino's voice emerged, speaking from the second shuttle.

"That saucer is dead in the water, Captain."

Ben-Ari spoke into her mic. "Proceed carefully. It might be a feint. Approach from the left, and I'll lead my shuttle from the right. Attach to its hull and saw through. We'll meet aboard."

The two shuttles split apart, charging toward the enemy from each side. Behind Ben-Ari, four security officers in black body armor clutched their guns. Four more were flying with Marino. It was all they could fit in these crafts.

It better be enough, Ben-Ari thought.

When they were only a few kilometers away, Ben-Ari saw the glyphs engraved onto the enemy's hull. The runes were shaped as star systems, as kneeling slaves, as humanoid gods, and as ankhs.

"Who are you?" Ben-Ari whispered, eyes narrowed. They were flying closer, closer, soon only seconds away, about to attach to that dark hull. Those glyphs looked vaguely Egyptian. Was this a mere coincidence, or—

The wounded saucer suddenly lurched, spun, and its cannons extended toward Ben-Ari's shuttle.

She stared.

Her eyes widened.

"Eject!" she shouted.

As the enemy cannons fired, Ben-Ari hit a red button on her controls.

A hatch opened above her.

The enemy lasers slammed into her shuttle.

Light flared.

Fire roared.

Shards of metal flew everywhere.

Ben-Ari blasted through searing heat and jabs of pain and blinding light and roaring sound. She tumbled madly, not sure if she were alive or dead, spinning through fire and metal.

Lasers and missiles flew around her.

The saucer spun, appearing, vanishing, as Ben-Ari tumbled through space, no air to slow her spin. Pieces of corpses flew.

I'm alive. I'm in space. The shuttle is gone. I—

A jagged metal shard, as large as a spear, came flying toward her.

Ben-Ari narrowed her eyes and ignited her jet pack.

She soared, and the shard flew beneath her, slicing the soles of her boots.

She grabbed the controls of her jet pack, steadying her flight, and finally managed to stop spinning. Beside her, the *Romulus* shuttle was gone; nothing but scraps of bloody metal remained. The rest of her crew—four warriors—floated as severed limbs, a couple of heads, and gobbets of flesh.

The second shuttle, the *Remus*, was still flying toward the enemy saucer.

And the saucer's cannons were heating up again.

Ben-Ari unslung her plasma rifle from across her back, aimed, and fired.

The bolt of plasma, no larger than an acorn, blasted toward the saucer at hypersonic speed and slammed into its cannon with a force powerful enough to knock over a tank.

Fire roared across the saucer.

Its cannon tore free and flew through space, spinning like a top, firing laser beams every which way, a disk of light. A blast from the *Lodestar*—still far behind them—shattered the loose cannon.

Where the cannon had been mounted, a gaping hole now loomed on the saucer.

Ben-Ari narrowed her eyes, released a stream of fire from her jet pack, and flew toward the opening.

Meanwhile, the *Remus* reached the saucer. The shuttle attached to its hull like a leech and began sawing its own opening.

"Captain, are you all right?" Marino said through the communicator.

"Get into the ship, Marino!" Ben-Ari said. "Kill anyone inside who resists. But try to take one alive!"

Not waiting for a reply, Ben-Ari blasted closer toward the breached hull. The opening was just wide enough for her body—

barely. She dived through the hole, arms first. The hole's jagged rim scraped across her back, denting her jet pack.

Ben-Ari tumbled into the enemy starship, rolled across the floor, then leaped up, gun firing.

A creature crashed down before her, a smoking hole in its chest.

Three more aliens raced into the chamber, holding weapons that looked like spears with electrical blades.

Ugly fuckers, Ben-Ari thought, cringing.

After a while, she had gotten used to the scum and marauders; they had been just big space bugs to crush under her boot. But these creatures were humanoid, which made them all the more disturbing. They towered above her, easily seven feet tall, maybe taller, but stooped like old men. They wore only loincloths, and their skin was wrinkled, patched with liver spots, and clinging to their bones; she could count their ribs, see their hearts beating within. Dark hearts, rotten, twisted. Their heads were massive, twice the size of human heads, but their faces were pinched and bitter, the mouths mere slits. They had no noses, no ears, but their eyes were the size and shape of avocados, pitch black and filled with malice.

Grays, she thought. *Like in the urban legends. They're real.*

They raised their weapons.

Bolts of electricity flew.

Ben-Ari leaped aside. Two bolts missed her. A third grazed her side, burning her armor, and she screamed. Electricity crackled across her, but she ignored the pain. She fired in automatic, blasting out a stream of fire, a torrent of heat and light and agony and liquid death. The plasma showered over the grays. They burned. They screamed. But still they advanced, reaching out their claws. Their flesh dripping, they lunged toward her.

Ben-Ari swung her rifle, knocking one's claws aside, then slammed the stock against the alien's chin. Its head snapped back, and Ben-Ari leaped, spun, and kicked its chest. A rib snapped, and the gray stumbled backward.

The two other grays reached toward her, skin ablaze. They clawed at her armor, tearing it off. They ripped her skin. Their eyes seared her, cutting into her, and she howled in pain. They were penetrating her brain, driving their consciousness into her, twisting, cutting, raping, seeking, burning, digging out all her secrets.

Einav Ben-Ari. Their voices spoke inside her. *We know you. We will break you. See the pain that will be yours.*

And in a flash of terror, her consciousness expanded.

She leaked out from her skull. She hovered above her body. She saw—everything, the cosmos, space, time, all unfurling around her in a devastating nightmare.

She saw Earth—blackened, burnt, cracked open, all her cities in ruin, all her life extinguished.

She saw herself—screaming, grays flaying her, pulling out her organs, cloning her, torturing thousands of her, each destined to endure more agony.

She saw her friends—Marco, Addy, Lailani—strapped onto altars, weeping, organs hovering above them.

And looming above this nightmare, watching with twisted delight—a dark goddess. A rancid queen. A female gray, breasts leaking bloody milk, teeth like rusty needles, claws clutching the armrests of a decrepit throne. Jagged iron spikes were nailed into her brow, and blood leaked from the wounds. The queen sneered and licked her lips, watching the torture, the ruin.

Then the alien queen raised her eyes.

She stared at Ben-Ari.

And Ben-Ari screamed.

She screamed with more terror than she had ever felt.

She screamed—devoid of thought, devoid of humanity. All that remained of her was her scream. Eternal agony.

Bullets fired.

Blood splattered.

A gray cried out and collapsed.

Ben-Ari took a deep, ragged breath, tears on her cheeks. Her consciousness slammed back into her body. She blinked, realizing that she was back on the alien saucer. Marino was racing down the hallway, bellowing, firing his assault rifle at one of the grays that had grabbed Ben-Ari. The creature crumpled to the floor, head shattered open, brains oozing out.

One alien still lived.

Kneeling, Ben-Ari grabbed her fallen plasma rifle, aimed, and bathed the creature with death. Its flesh melted, revealing bones and a beating heart. Ben-Ari kept firing until that heart crumbled to ashes.

"Captain!" Marino knelt beside her. "Are you all right? You're white as a sheet."

The *Lodestar*'s Chief of Security was pale himself. He bled from a gash on his thigh, and bruises were already spreading across his face.

The wrestling ring is one thing, war quite another, Ben-Ari thought, then frowned. War? Is that what this was? No. Not yet. Not if she could stop it.

"I'm fine." She rose to her feet. "Status of your crew?"

Marino shuddered. He tried to speak, his voice cracked, but then he stiffened and raised his stubbly chin. "Two of my men are dead. The other two are guarding the opening we carved into the hull. We met some resistance—two of these gray fuckers. We took them out."

Ben-Ari nodded and clasped the tall man's shoulder. "Good work, Lieutenant Commander. I'm proud of you."

Marino squared his shoulders. "Thank you, Captain."

You're scared, Ben-Ari thought. *But you're brave. You spent years fighting on the mat as the crowd roared and the cameras rolled, and this is your first taste of true blood. You'll be a soldier yet.*

The two walked down the corridor, stepping over the dead grays. For the first time, Ben-Ari got a good look at the innards of this ship. It was like walking through an ancient tomb. Engravings coated the walls, depicting labyrinths, obelisks, and strange animals: birds with humanoid faces, winged sphinxes, and feline creatures with coiling necks as long as snakes. Other engravings showed alien crafts visiting distant worlds and local species bowing before their gray masters.

They regrouped with the two surviving security guards. The hull was breached here, and through the hole, Ben-Ari saw the *Remus*'s airlock.

The two dead guards lay on the floor, skin burnt black, faces twisted in anguish.

Guilt filled Ben-Ari.

I came to space to explore, to reach out to friendly life. Now six men are dead—two here at my feet, four torn apart outside in space.

She tightened her lips. There was no use for guilt now, no use for weakness. In the professor's study, let her be a student of science. In the privacy of her quarters, let her deal with guilt and ethics. Here let her be the soldier again, her resolve made of steel.

"Follow me," she said to her three remaining fighters. "Guns raised, loaded, safeties off. Marino, you bring up the rear. You see a threat, you fire. Aim at the heads; they're the biggest targets on these creatures. You see any unarmed grays, do not fire. I want one alive."

With that, she turned and began walking down another corridor, heading deeper into the alien ship.

They entered a shadowy round chamber. Corpses hung on the walls, chained and flayed. Their torsos had been cut open, the organs removed. Their faces were still locked in anguish; they had been alive when the surgery had begun.

The corpses were in bad shape, but Ben-Ari could tell these were human corpses.

An operating table lay in the center of the room, engraved with glyphs. It looked almost like an altar. A human lay on the table, naked and nailed into place. He was still alive, screaming into a gag. Several grays loomed over him, hunched over, holding surgical tools. As Ben-Ari and her guards approached, the aliens turned their massive bald heads toward them. Their black eyes narrowed, and their mouths opened with hisses. Blood coated their hands. As they stepped back from the operating table, Ben-Ari saw that the human—God, how was he still alive?—had been carved open, his organs removed and placed onto the tabletop, attached only by veins.

"Take them alive!" Ben-Ari shouted as the guards began to fire.

The grays leaped toward them, thrusting their surgical tools. One guard fell, a bone saw in his throat. Bullets tore into the aliens, but they kept advancing. The creatures grabbed another guard, lashed a scalpel, and tore the man open from collarbone to navel. The man screamed as his innards spilled.

A gray leaped forward and slammed a syringe into Marino's thigh. The burly man screamed and fell to one knee, still firing, and his bullets tore open the alien's head. Then the martial artist toppled over, vomiting, trembling. His leg turned green where the poison infected him.

Ben-Ari stood alone.

She fired her plasma gun in automatic, spraying out a flaming torrent. The room blazed. The prisoner on the table thrashed and screamed as he burned. The grays too blazed. Several fell.

Ben-Ari removed her finger from the trigger.

The grays smoked before her, hunching over, breathing raggedly. Several had died. Three still lived.

Ben-Ari lifted one of the fallen scalpels. It was as long as her forearm.

She had trained with blades, and a thin smile touched her lips.

Bring it, she thought.

The burnt aliens lunged toward her.

With a battle cry, Ben-Ari leaped toward them.

She lashed her blade, slicing one's throat. She landed on the tabletop among the ruin of the burning man. The grays spun toward her. She leaped again, kicked off one's head, and landed behind them. She knelt and swung her blade, sweeping the legs out from under a gray.

The alien fell. She plunged the blade into his chest.

Claws grabbed her.

She screamed as the third gray lifted her.

She kicked in the air, struggling to free herself. The creature dwarfed her—thin but so much taller, so much stronger. His grip was iron, and he twisted her wrist until her scalpel fell. Her rifle followed, clattering against the floor.

"Die now," the gray hissed, tightening his grip. "Die in pain . . ."

Ben-Ari screamed, feeling like he would rip off her limbs, shatter her bones. He was so strong.

She couldn't reach her fallen gun. Couldn't reach the blades.

But she could reach the controls of her jet pack.

She turned it on.

Fire roared out, and Ben-Ari shot upward, tearing free from the alien's grip. She slammed into the ceiling, and her helmet rang. The fire from her jet pack washed the alien. She switched it off, fell to the floor, and saw her gun and scalpel before her. She chose the scalpel and embedded it into the alien's leg.

The charred creature screamed and fell to his knees.

Ben-Ari lifted her rifle and swung it, slamming the stock into the alien's massive head.

The creature fell, burnt, bleeding, unconscious but still alive. The other grays lay around him, immobile; they seemed dead.

With the immediate threat quelled, Ben-Ari rushed toward Marino's side. The security officer was groaning, eyelids fluttering, struggling to remain conscious. He had removed the alien syringe from his leg; it lay shattered at his side.

"Captain," he said. "The . . . medic. His . . . pack."

One of their guards had been a medic. He now lay on the floor, torn open. His pack lay beside him, splattered with blood. Ben-Ari rummaged through it and found a needle full of adrenaline.

"Here goes!" she said and slammed the needle into Marino.

The security chief bolted upright, eyes widening.

"Damn." Marino shook his head wildly. He looked down at his leg and winced. "I feel numb. I can't move my leg. Maybe they just use it to paralyze their victims before the torture." He shoved himself to his feet, swayed, and cursed again. "I can walk. I can still swing the leg. It's like the world's worst case of a leg falling asleep." He took a step and bellowed. "Hurts like a son of a bitch. But I can walk."

Ben-Ari nodded. "Pain is good. It means the leg is waking up." She grabbed chains from a wall and began wrapping them around the unconscious gray. "Let's head back to the shuttle."

Marino limped at the lead, aiming his rifle ahead of him. Ben-Ari walked behind him, dragging the unconscious gray. The creature was heavy, heavier than Ben-Ari, but the floor was slick with blood, and Ben-Ari's natural adrenaline—as powerful as any shot—gave her strength.

They had flown here with two shuttles and eight warriors.

They flew back with one shuttle, just two humans—and one chained, unconscious gray.

"We'll come back with more people," Ben-Ari said, piloting the shuttle back toward the *Lodestar*. "We'll bring aboard a crew of engineers and a couple of pilots. I want us to tow this saucer back to Earth." She nodded, thinking aloud. "These creatures are dangerous. We need to study their technology. We need to—"

Before she could complete her sentence, the saucer exploded behind her.

Shards of the ship peppered them, and the shuttle jolted.

Ben-Ari clutched the controls, gritting her teeth, struggling to steady their flight. One of their engines sputtered and died. They limped forth, teetering toward the *Lodestar*.

"They self-destructed," she muttered. "Of course."

Beside her, the chained gray opened his eyes. The gangly, burnt creature began to laugh. It was a demonic sound, a sound from humanity's deepest nightmares. Ben-Ari shuddered.

"You don't know what you've done," the alien hissed, cackling. "How you will suffer!"

"Gag him!" Ben-Ari said, and her fists clenched. "Gag that fucking thing."

Marino drew tape from the shuttle's toolbox. His eyes blazed. "Gladly."

They flew into the *Lodestar*'s hangar. A team awaited them there, ready to tend to their wounds, to grab the alien, and to drag the creature into a containment chamber. They had succeeded at their mission. They had captured a gray. Yet that night, as Ben-Ari stood in her shower, she couldn't stop seeing the tortured captives aboard the saucer, couldn't stop hearing the screams of her dying guards, and couldn't stop seeing the alien queen from her vision. Whenever Ben-Ari closed her eyes, that dark goddess was there, staring at her, smiling cruelly.

CHAPTER SEVEN

Lailani walked through the used-starship yard, searching for a new ride.

I come and I go, she had told Marco long ago. *I'm like a dandelion seed.*

She had not forgotten. Even now she was a wanderer.

I must find the hourglass that can bend time. I must go back. I must stop myself from killing Elvis. For him. For me.

The dusty lot spread around her. Hundreds of used starships, dented and charred, rusted away in the dirt. A handful were massive, large enough for hundreds of passengers; their prices were massive to match. Most other ships here were much smaller, the size of trucks or buses, even some microships no larger than cars. A handful were ex-military vessels, built by Chrysopoeia Corp; most were built by civilian companies, such as Asmotic Institute. Trading ships. Asteroid mining ships. Pleasure ships that had once serviced the wealthy. They all rusted away here, cracked, scraped, peeling, withering. Lailani doubted any could still fly.

"I'll have better luck attaching feathers to my arms and flying," she muttered.

"Welcome, welcome, to JEX's Starship and Robotics Emporium!" A robot teetered toward her, shedding rust and gears with every step. "Whatever your price, whatever your pleasure, you will find the ride of your dreams here. My starships will take you to the stars—and beyond!"

Lailani frowned at the rusty old robot. He stood a little shorter than her, rotund and leaking oil. He chomped on an electronic cigar, a prop made from a car's cigarette lighter. Letters were painted onto his barrel chest. *JEX: Junkyard EXpert.*

"What's beyond the stars?" Lailani said.

JEX hesitated. "No better deals than you can find here!" he finally said, flashing a metallic grin.

Lailani rolled her eyes. "I have fifteen thousand credits. What can that buy me?"

The robot's smile vanished. "Ah. I see. Well, for fifty thousand credits, you might only be able to afford a modest ride, but I can still suggest a few—"

"Not fifty," she said. "*Fifteen* thousand. One five."

The robot's rusty jaw fell to the ground—literally. He had to lean down and pick it up. He snapped the jaw back on and blinked.

"*Fifteen* thousand, ma'am?" He cleared his throat uncomfortably—probably a programmer's bad joke. "You can't buy anything for that price. Not anything that's spaceworthy, at least."

Lailani groaned. It was all the money she had left. She had been wealthy once—briefly, after selling the azoth crystals. She had spent nearly all that money on building her schools.

"Fine," she said. "So I'll take my business to the Spacecraft Supermart."

She turned to leave.

"Wait, wait, wait!" JEX rushed after her, shedding gears and grommets. He grabbed her and tittered nervously. "No need to go to the Supermart. Those guys are crooks! Horrible quality. Fifteen thousand credits . . ." The portly robot muttered something under his breath. "I'll see what I can find." As he toddled off, he muttered something about poor robots never being able to retire.

Lailani followed. She noticed that several other robots, most of them switched off, stood in the yard. Some were realistic android companions, ranging from friendly servants to alluring sexbots. If not for all the dust and grime, they could have passed for humans. Other robots were hulking work machines, drills and chainsaws attached to their arms instead of hands. A few were robotic canines, and Lailani's heart twisted. She missed her dog so badly.

"Mistress." A deep, mournful voice spoke nearby. "Would you consider buying me, please, mistress?"

Lailani turned to see one of the robots. This one was certainly no android; nobody would mistake him for a human being. He stood over seven feet tall, forged from armored steel plates. That steel was dented and rusty now, charred from old fires. This robot had seen combat. He reminded Lailani of some medieval knight. She could imagine that, in his glory days, he would have appeared terrifying on the battlefield. His face was a blank mask of metal, two blue eyes peering. His breastplate was dusty, but Lailani could just make out letters printed there.

HOBBS: Human Offensive Biometric Battle Soldier.

"I don't have much money," Lailani said.

HOBBS lowered his head. "That is regrettable, mistress. I would much like to find a new home. I can serve all combat functions, from defense to assault to strategy. I cost only thirty thousand credits."

"That's twice what I have," Lailani said. "I'm sorry."

HOBBS slumped. "I am sorry too, mistress." He gave her a sad look. "For fifteen thousand credits, I recommend purchasing the ESS *Ryujin*. She has been sitting on this lot for a year now. JEX has previously confided in me that he would bargain her down to fifteen thousand, and she is a good ship."

JEX, smaller and rounder than HOBBS, came trundling toward them. "What's that? *Et tu*, HOBBS?" He kicked the metal beast. "Silence, you hunk of junk! I should have you sold for scrap metal."

He clicked a remote control, and the towering battle-bot powered down. JEX kicked the larger robot.

Lailani turned toward JEX. "Show me the *Ryujin*."

The little robot grumbled. "The *Ryujin* costs twenty-thousand, no less, and—wait, wait! No Supermart!" He groaned.

"If I had a heart, you'd be breaking it. Fine, human. Come with me."

JEX led her past the other robots, around several grounded trading starships, and toward a bus-sized starship.

Lailani gasped.

She fell instantly in love.

The ship was painted with a dragon flying over a rainbow. The paint was faded and flaking, but the artwork was still beautiful. It was a sign, she knew. She had a dragon tattooed onto one arm, a rainbow on the other. This ship was meant for her.

"I'll take it," she said.

JEX gave her a cockeyed look, and mechanical noises rose from inside his head. "Don't you want to look inside first? To give her a test flight?"

She bit her lip. "Uhm . . . yes. Yes, of course. Better to be prudent. I will—"

"We're looking for a girl."

The raspy, inhuman voice rose from behind. Lailani spun around and took a step back.

Several creatures stood there. She thought of them as creatures, not men, though she couldn't see their faces. They wore black robes embroidered with golden ankhs, and hoods covered their heads. Gas masks covered their faces. Not ordinary gas masks like the one Lailani had owned as a soldier; these were deformed masks, the lenses massive and tainted, the filters shaped like beaks. They reminded Lailani of plague-doctor masks. The creatures were tall, as tall as HOBBS, gawky giants, hunched over like vultures over prey.

Then again, I'm only four foot ten, Lailani thought. *Pretty much anyone other than JEX is a giant to me.*

"Hello, hello!" JEX said, toddling toward the newcomers, already smelling a better deal. "Welcome to JEX's Starship and Robotics Emporium! A girl, you say? We sell a variety of girl androids! From geishas to schoolgirls, from European beauties to exotic—"

The robed creatures raised pistols. Gray, knobby fingers—inhumanly long—pulled the triggers.

Red bolts slammed into JEX.

The little robot exploded. Springs, bolts, and gears flew everywhere. The rusty jaw clattered down at Lailani's feet, gave a pirouette, then collapsed into the dust.

The masked creatures turned toward her, hissing. They raised their long, clawed fingers. They advanced toward her.

Aliens, Lailani thought. *Great. More goddamn aliens.*

"Lailani . . ." they hissed, voices high-pitched, grainy, demonic.

"Hiya, fellas." Lailani cringed and took a step back. She had no weapons. Back home, she had traveled everywhere with a pistol, but the hospital had taken all her guns. "I think you've got the wrong girl. My name is *Leelani.* Totally different chick." She took another step back, hoping to make it into the *Ryujin.* "In fact, I think I saw Lailani head that way, right where you came from, so if you just—"

They leaped toward her. Lailani ran. She tried to reach the *Ryujin*. She jumped toward the ship.

A knobby gray hand grabbed her.

She hit the ground, and the hand tightened around her ankle. The creature dragged her back.

Lailani sneered, grabbed JEX's fallen jaw, and tossed the jagged metal piece. It hit the alien holding her, shattering the lens of its gas mask. That knobbly hand released her leg.

Lailani jumped back up. She turned toward the *Ryujin* again, but one of the robed aliens now stood there, blocking her path. They surrounded her. They closed in, claws raised, breath heavy in their gas masks.

"Lailani de la Rosa," one of them hissed. "We know who you are. We know what you seek. The hourglass is ours. You will fail. You will scream. You will meet our goddess. You will lead us to Ben-Ari . . . and perhaps then we will let you die."

Lailani winced.

Great. So Ben-Ari is in trouble again—and dragging me into it. What else is new?

She turned from side to side, seeking a way to escape, finding none. She leaned down, grabbed a rock, and hurled it. It hit one of the towering creatures and bounced off, doing it no harm.

The aliens stepped closer, a ring of robes and gas masks and claws.

Lailani saw the remote control below—the one JEX had used to power down HOBBS. She grabbed it and hit the On button.

"HOBBS!" she cried. She could see the battle-bot in the distance. "HOBBS, I could use a little help!"

From the distance, the robot gave her a mournful look.

Claws lashed toward Lailani. She swung the remote control like a club, shattering it against the alien's hands. Another creature grabbed her from behind and hoisted her into the air.

"HOBBS, attack!" she cried.

"I am sorry!" HOBBS said. "I cannot attack on behalf of one who does not own me. My programming does not allow it."

Lailani flailed. More hands grabbed her. They began carrying her away. She saw their ship in the distance—a dark saucer engraved with hieroglyphs. One of the aliens' hands gagged her, and she placed a finger between her teeth. She bit down hard, then spat out blood.

"HOBBS, I own you now!" she lied. "I bought you from JEX before he exploded! Attack these bastards!"

And HOBBS sprang into action.

Guns emerged from his forearms.

Bullets sprayed out, tearing into the creatures holding Lailani. Their massive heads shattered.

"Whoa!" Lailani cried as she fell. "HOBBS, careful!"

More of his bullets flew in a hailstorm, slamming into the creatures. Lailani scurried aside. Bullets whistled around her, deafening. She raced toward the starship *Ryujin*, arms pumping.

The aliens abandoned her, turning toward HOBBS. They drew their guns and fired. A blast slammed into HOBBS's shoulder, knocking him back. A second blast shattered the robot's elbow. The forearm and hand fell, still firing bullets.

"Damn it, damn it, damn it!" Lailani shouted. She leaped through the airlock into the *Ryujin*.

Dust and cobwebs covered the inside of the small starship. It obviously hadn't flown in years. A mother possum hung upside down in a corner, her babies clinging to her. Cigarette butts lay everywhere. A couple of teenagers were making out on a cot. They saw Lailani and fled the ship, eyes wide with terror.

She glanced out the airlock. HOBBS was still battling the aliens. He had slain another one, but more of the robed, masked beings were emerging from their saucer. Another blast hit HOBBS, denting his breastplate.

Lailani raced across the hold, scattering paper coffee cups, and onto the *Ryujin*'s bridge. She wasn't a trained pilot, but she had flown the *Marilyn*, Ben-Ari's old starship, enough times to know her way around a cockpit. She kick-started the engine.

It coughed and died.

Lailani groaned. "Come on, baby, don't let me down."

She tried again. Again.

The engine roared to life.

"Yeah, baby!" Lailani whooped. She flipped switches and grabbed a joystick. The old starship began to rise, creaking and shedding rust.

She spun the cockpit toward HOBBS and the robed creatures.

"Cannons, cannons, cannons . . ." Lailani mumbled, surveying the control panels. "There!"

She dusted off the right controls. She picked out her targets. She hit a button, and two cannons emerged from the *Ryujin*'s prow.

Bullets as large as daggers tore into the creatures.

In the middle of the devastation, only HOBBS remained standing.

One of her bullets had knocked the gas mask off one alien. The creature was still alive, twitching in the soil. It came crawling toward the *Ryujin*, blood trailing behind it. Cloak tattered, the alien raised its head and stared at Lailani.

Her heart nearly stopped.

The creature was hideous. Its head was massive, bloated, and covered with wrinkled gray skin. The cheeks were sunken, the mouth just a thin line, but the eyes were as large as hearts, pitch black, dripping hatred. Those eyes stared at Lailani, and they were like daggers cutting through her. She heard the alien's voice in her mind.

Hybrid . . . Freak . . . You will scream for us!

"Yeah, well, this freak has a fucking .50 cal cannon, asshole," she muttered and opened fire. Her bullets riddled the beast.

But she wasn't yet in the clear. Across the field, three more saucers were landing.

Who the fuck are these assholes? Lailani thought.

She rolled down the window. "HOBBS, come on! Into the airlock!"

"You are taking me with you, mistress?" he said.

"Come on, move your metal ass!" she shouted.

HOBBS grabbed his fallen forearm and ran over the corpses. He leaped into the airlock.

The saucers opened fire.

Lailani hit full thrust, and they soared upward, blasting out fire.

The saucers pursued.

Lailani sneered, yanked the joystick, and turned to face the enemies. She blasted all her guns.

A hailstorm of bullets slammed into the three saucers.

Lailani rose higher, roaring over the enemy ships.

A blast hit her hull.

The *Ryujin* jolted madly. Sparks sprayed. The starboard hull cracked open.

"Fuck!"

Lailani soared toward the sun, swerved downward, and swooped toward the saucers. She released a volley of missiles.

The missiles slammed into the saucers, and Lailani leveled off, skimming the explosions.

Pieces of enemy ships rained onto Japan's coast.

When the dust settled, only one saucer remained.

A laser blast hit the *Ryujin*, searing through the starboard hull. Smoke rose from them. Lailani raised the ship, but she couldn't escape this saucer. It was too fast. Too powerful.

"Great," Lailani muttered. "And we're out of missiles."

"No we are not, mistress," HOBBS said. "Excuse me."

He stepped back into the hold.

"Where do you think you're going?" Lailani cried from the cockpit. In the rearview mirror, she saw him stand at the open airlock.

"Mistress, please point me at the enemy ship," HOBBS said.

The saucer flew toward them, firing lasers. Lailani flew madly, dodging the assault, then spun so that the airlock faced the saucer.

A missile launcher emerged from HOBBS's shoulder.

He fired.

The small missile slammed into the saucer.

The enemy ship exploded.

Pieces rained down into the Pacific.

Lailani breathed a deep, shaky breath of relief. The enemy ships were all gone.

"Holy shit." She slumped in her chair. "Not how I expected today to go."

She kept flying, leaving the coast of Japan. With the *Ryujin*'s hull busted, they weren't going into space yet. She still wanted to travel to the bear constellation. To follow her vision. To find the hourglass that could open a portal through time.

The creature's voice echoed in her mind. *We know what you seek. The hourglass is ours . . .*

Lailani shuddered.

"Who the hell were those sneaky fuckers?" she mumbled.

HOBBS joined her on the bridge. "Mistress, I thank you for purchasing me! Are there any more enemies you would like me to defeat?"

She glanced at him. The robot's armored plating was cracked, and with his right hand, he held his severed left arm.

"Do you know how to fix yourself?" she asked.

"Yes, mistress."

She nodded. "Good. Get to it. And then we'll fix this hull. We'll be leaving into space—soon. But we're making a pit stop first in my hometown. We need to pick up one more passenger."

HOBBS nodded. "Yes, mistress!"

An hour later, they landed in the Philippines. As HOBBS worked at repairing the ship's hull, Lailani raced across the fields toward her home.

From her house, he emerged.

He ran toward her, tail wagging.

He leaped into her arms.

Lailani hugged Epimetheus, her dear Doberman.

"Hey, buddy." She patted him. "Ready to become a spacedog?"

He licked her face. She took that as a yes.

Lailani contemplated staying the night, saying goodbye to her students the next morning. But after she had gone all Ozzy

Osbourne on their tarsier, she doubted the children would greet her warmly. Besides, Earth felt too dangerous for even one more night. Memories of those creatures in the junkyard haunted her. Their saucers had seemed too similar to the reports all over the news—reports of aliens abducting humans, torturing them.

They know my name, she thought. *They know Ben-Ari.*

Lailani had a bad feeling about this.

She packed her things. She didn't have much. A few guns. A few knives. Some food and some clothes. The framed photograph of her platoon. It was all she owned. She slipped her military dog tags around her neck, slung a rifle across her back, and entered the ESS *Ryujin*.

By nightfall, they were soaring out of the atmosphere. In a creaky old ship, the hull welded together, they hurled into deep space. A hulking robot. A dog. And a woman with fear and guilt in her heart.

Lailani sat in the cockpit, staring out into the darkness. Her framed photograph stood on the dashboard. And the old memories—from a decade ago—surfaced in her mind. Herself at eighteen. A girl. A creature. A puppet of the scum. Growing claws. Ripping out Elvis's heart.

"I'll find that hourglass, Elvis," she whispered, tears in her eyes. "I'll use it to go back in time. I'll stop myself from killing you. I'll save you, Elvis. And I'll save you, Sofia. I'll save everyone. I swear it."

Epimetheus noticed her tears. The giant Doberman, heavier than her, climbed onto her lap and licked her tears away.

She placed the ship in autopilot and leaned against him. HOBBS approached and stood above them, a silent guardian. Hesitantly, he placed a metal hand on Lailani's shoulder.

They cuddled together as the ship sailed onward, and Earth disappeared in the distance.

CHAPTER EIGHT

"Tomiko, she's just a friend," Marco said. "A friend from the war. She was undergoing neurosurgery. We had to be there for her. We—"

"Do you still love her?" Tomiko stood before him, hands on her hips, tears on her cheeks. "Do you still love Lailani?"

Marco winced. He reached out to his wife, but she took a step back, glaring through her tears.

"Of course I love her," Marco said. "But as a friend. Not like . . . what you think."

They stood in their bedroom. Addy and Steve were just downstairs, and Marco knew they could hear the fight. His cheeks burned. He had hoped to come home and hug Tomiko, give her a gift, spend an evening laughing with her, then a night holding her in bed. Instead, she stood before him, face red, eyes burning.

"Did you fuck her?" Tomiko said. "Don't deny it! I know you did! I heard the stories."

Marco's chest felt tight. "Tomiko, that was a long time ago. Before I met you. Before—"

"So you admit it!" Tomiko lifted a lamp off the nightstand and tossed it at him. Marco ducked, and it shattered against the wall.

"Tomiko!" Marco roared, surprised to hear so much anger in his voice. "Enough!"

"Don't tell me enough!" She slapped him. "You travel to Japan. To my country! Without me! To see a girl you still love, a girl you slept with. Did you fuck her again?"

When she tried to slap him again, Marco caught her wrist. Tomiko glared at him, lips trembling, tears flowing.

"Of course I didn't," Marco said. "I love *you*."

"You liar!" she shouted. She wrenched herself free from him and lifted a vase.

"I'm not going to talk to you when you're like this," Marco said.

She tossed the vase. It shattered, and shards flew and cut Tomiko's hand. She bled but barely seemed to notice.

Marco stared at her, eyes wide.

She's mad, he thought. *It's like she's possessed by an alien.*

He turned to leave the room. "We'll talk when you're calmer."

"Don't you walk away from me!" she shouted after him, weeping, bleeding. "Coward! Cheater!"

He closed the bedroom door behind him. He heard her still screaming inside.

Marco's walk across the living room, as Addy and Steve pointedly tried to ignore him, was the most awkward moment of his life.

He stepped outside onto the beach, walked across the sand, and stood before the dark sea. He took slow, deep breaths, but his mind was a storm. His breath shook.

He was scared.

"Her name is Tomiko," he whispered to the waves. "The name of the heroine from *Le Kill*, my second novel. It was a sign." He looked up at the stars, eyes burning. "It was a sign! Had to be. A sign that I was to choose her. To marry her. To love her."

He lowered his head, and the waves washed over his feet. Since they had married—too much anger, too many battles. He had never fought like this with Kemi or Lailani or Anisha.

He would spend another night sleeping on the beach, he knew. He had not shared a bed with Tomiko in weeks. He wanted to fix this. He wanted to ask Addy for advice, but he felt too awkward.

I must fix this, he thought. *I hurt Anisha. I hurt so many girls in Haven. I treated them badly, neglected them, broke relationships. Let me fix this one. Let this be the one that works. I lost so many. I can't lose Tomiko too.*

In the morning, he pretended that nothing had happened. He made Tomiko breakfast. He found that she had cleaned the mess upstairs. They took a walk on the beach and spoke a lot of small talk.

By the next day, she was smiling again, her beautiful smile. And she cooked him dinner. The next day, when it was his twenty-eighth birthday, she gave him a gift—his medals in a frame to hang on the wall, along with a cake she had baked herself.

We can do this, Marco thought. *We can be happy together. After so long of breaking things—of war, of death, of pain—let us build. Let us be happy.*

He and Tomiko lay in bed one night when he said, "Tomiko, have you thought of having a baby?"

She turned toward him, her eyes widened, but then she frowned. "Marco, we're not ready."

"Why not?" he said. "We have a house. I'm making good progress on *Under the Stairs,* and *The Dragons of Yesteryear* is still making money. Why not add a baby to the mix? It'll be good for us."

Suddenly her eyes were damp. She stared at the ceiling. "Not like this. Not how we are. Not how we've been fighting. First we have to fix this."

He placed a hand on her waist. "We'll fix this. We'll be happy."

"You don't know that!" Her tears were flowing. "You're not ready. I know it. You talk of Lailani and Kemi all the time."

"I don't—"

"When you're with Addy you do!" Tomiko said. "I hear it. I know it. And you don't love me. You love your books. You love Addy and the others. I'm always the last priority for you. Just the silly girl who can't understand anything." She sniffed. "I know what you think of me. That I'm stupid and can't understand what you did, what you know. You just care about the other girls! About your books! About your old army stories! About everything other than me."

"That's not true! I chose *you*, Tomiko. Not any other girl." He embraced her. "I want to be with you, to be happy, to make this work. To be a happy family."

Like normal people, he thought. *Like happy people. Not like broken veterans, haunted with nightmares. Not how I was on Haven. Not how I was with Anisha. I want to be like other people. I want us to be happy.*

"Imagine it," he said softly. "You and I, and a little one running in the house . . . just together. Just at peace. A family." He kissed away her tears. "Okay? Don't you want that?"

She looked at him, eyes red. "Do you? Or do you just want it because that's what other people do?"

"I want it for real," Marco said.

She closed her eyes. "I don't know if you're lying."

"I'm not."

They began to try.

Months of happy attempts, of disappointments.

Days of Tomiko bursting into tears, claiming he did not love her, storming off, breaking things. Nights of apologizing, of making up, of lovemaking in the dark.

As the time went by, as they kept trying for a baby, Marco kept writing. He completed the first draft of *Under the Stairs*, his darkest, yet most beautiful, novel. He had begun the novel with a simple premise. The novel's young heroine, the reflective Anabel Lee, was playing hide-and-seek with her brother. During the game, the boy vanished under the stairs in their Victorian home. When seeking him, Anabel Lee discovered a portal to a land of wonder, danger, and magic. On her journey under the stairs, she encountered a host of dreamlike creatures, some beautiful, most terrifying, all fantastical. At first, Marco had meant it to be a homage to Brian Froud, one of his favorite artists. But as he polished the final draft, he recognized much of himself in the story.

When Anabel Lee fought giant, human-faced insects in a briar patch, she was actually fighting the scum. When she vanished into the Pit of Forgetfulness, a misty realm full of ghosts, she was in truth languishing in Haven. When she battled the giant Tree Spiders, with their long beards and webs woven of human hair, she was facing the marauders.

At the end of the novel, Anabel Lee lost her way. She remained under the stairs and became one of its creatures. She grew twigs and branches, and she wore a dress woven of acorns and leaves from the Memory Tree that grew in the center of the magical realm. She became a tree herself, putting down roots, to spend the rest of her life gazing upon the misty sea and the ships that sailed there. She drew a map so that her brother could find his way back home, but she herself could never more emerge from under the stairs. Yet Anabel Lee was not lonely. The friends she had met along her journey, strange and magical creatures, came to visit her every year, to rest in her shade and to feed upon the fruit she grew.

Because I want to put down roots too, Marco thought. *And I want to offer shade and sustenance to others. To bring forth life.*

He always wrote several drafts of his novels; *Under the Stairs* was still far from completed. Meanwhile, *The Dragons of Yesteryear* was still selling. Not enough to make him rich and famous, but enough to power their home, to put healthy meals on the table, to buy gifts for Tomiko, to save for their future. For the baby he still hoped for.

And then one day, after months of disappointments, it happened.

Tomiko emerged from the bathroom and burst into tears.

"What's wrong?" Marco said.

She tossed a pregnancy test at him, then fled downstairs, weeping.

Marco looked at it.

Positive.

He chased Tomiko, and he found her weeping in the laundry room. He tried to embrace her, but she shoved him away.

"This is good news!" he said. "It's what we've been trying for."

"You don't love me!" she shouted. "You still love Lailani. You don't care about me. You only care about yourself! About your friends and your books and the girls you love. Not me. You just want to go fuck Lailani again! Like you did in Japan! You're fucking Addy too, aren't you? I know you love her! Cheater! Cheater!"

Tomiko howled, enraged, as if possessed. Her hair was wild. Her cheeks were red. She punched the wall. She bloodied her fist.

She stared at the blood, then ran down the hall. She leaped into the closet and closed the door. When Marco pulled the door open, he found her curled up inside, cradling her bleeding hand.

He spent a while calming her down, describing to her all the wonderful ways they'd enjoy life with the baby. Finally Tomiko—his sweet, temperamental Tomiko—was smiling and laughing and hugging him.

She's a storm one moment, then a sunny day, Marco thought. *She's now a devil, now an angel. She's completely mad. She's horrible and she's wonderful. I fear her and I love her. And we're going to have a baby.*

* * * * *

Addy sat on the couch, her bare legs slung across Steve's lap.

"Stevie," she said. "Tell me we're not nutty like Marco and Tomiko."

Steve put down his bottle of beer and raised an eyebrow. "Babe, you're nuttier than a squirrel's balls."

"Ha ha." Addy rolled her eyes. "I'm the good kind of nutty though, right?" She raised her fist. "*Right?*"

Steve groaned. "Babe, I'm trying to watch this educational program."

Addy glanced at the television. He was watching something called *Mud Wrestling Championship*. He had been watching a lot of *Mud Wrestling Championship*. And *Robot Wrestling*. And regular wrestling. And football. And infomercials. And every episode of *Big & Lil Love,* a new reality program about dwarfs who married giants.

"Steve," she said. "Maybe it's time for a bit less television. What about that job hunting? Any progress?"

He groaned and shoved her legs off his lap. "Ads, I told you. I sent out a bunch of resumes last week, all right? I expect a job any day now. So will you get off my back?"

"I'm not on your back." Addy switched off the television.

"Hey, I was watching that!"

She grabbed his head and spun it toward her. "No more television! We need to start contributing. It's not fair that Marco is supporting us."

Steve bristled. His cheeks reddened. He rose to his feet. "So that's what you think? That Marco's funding us and I'm some kind of freeloader in his house?"

Addy stood up too. She was a tall woman, used to intimidating people with her height, but Steve was something of a giant, easily half a foot taller. Refusing to be cowed, Addy placed her hands on her hips and glared at him.

"Marco has a job," she said. "We don't!"

"I work!" Steve said, voice too loud. "I worked last week, remember? When I fixed those boats."

"That was a month ago!" Addy said. "And I did half that work, and we haven't done anything useful since. We just sit around on our asses all day, watching television, eating, drinking beer, growing fat and soft, and I'm starting to feel like we're two useless lumps."

"You mean you feel I'm a useless lump," Steve said. "Because I'm the man, right?"

"That's not what I said! Don't put words in my mouth."

"You were thinking it!" Steve said. "When you compared me to Marco. Well, I'm sorry that I'm not as smart, successful, or rich as Marco, and that you don't love me as much."

Addy let out the loudest groan of her life. "Oh for fuck's sake, are you listening to yourself? You're fucking moping! Some man you are. Whining like a baby."

His face darkened. "Don't you dare."

Addy sighed. "I'm sorry, all right?" Her voice softened. "I don't want to insult you, to demean you. I'm sorry. It's not just you. It's both of us. We need to do something. Why don't we start that construction business?"

"Because we live on a goddamn island!" Steve said, voice rising, so loud now that Addy knew Marco and Tomiko would hear them upstairs. "Because you wanted to live in fucking Greece, like a princess in some fairy tale, cavorting across magical islands. I had job offers back home, Addy. Toronto lay in ruins, and they wanted my help to rebuild. I moved here for *you*. Because you and your Marco wanted this. What construction business am I going to start here? Constructing fucking sandcastles?"

"See?" Addy said. "See how you mope? How you blame me for everything? You never take responsibility for yourself, Steve! It's always my fault, or Marco's fault, or the war's fault. Never your fault!"

"You think everything is my fault!" Steve shouted. "You think everyone else is perfect. That Marco is some genius. That Ben-Ari is a heroine. That Lailani is a fucking lady Jesus or something. But just I'm a useless lump, right? Just the idiot who can't even find a job."

"Steve." She touched his arm. "Baby, I love you. Okay? I love you so fucking much. And I don't want to see you—us!—waste away like this."

"I was fine, Addy." His voice choked. "I was fine back home in Toronto. I was happy. *You* wanted this." He turned away. "So enjoy it."

He stormed out of the house, slamming the door behind him.

Addy stood for a moment alone in the living room.

"Jesus Christ," she muttered. "We *are* as nutty as Marco and Tomiko."

Then she burst outside, chasing Steve.

She caught him by the water. He was standing still, staring at the sea. The sun was setting, casting golden beams over the water. Steve did not turn toward her.

She tapped his shoulder. "Hey, doofus."

He did not turn around, but finally he spoke. "What do you want, butthead?"

She gasped. "My head is not a butt! You pencil neck."

"My neck is enormous!" Steve said, finally turning toward her. "So be quiet, baboon."

She gasped. "Baboon! You're the ape here!" She pointed at his chest. "See? Hairy."

"You're the one with the big red ass."

"It is not red!" Addy shoved him. "So be quiet, you stinky gorilla." She shoved him again, knocking him into the water. "Or I'm going to drown you. Drown you!"

Steve reached up, grabbed her hand, and yanked her down. She squealed, tried to free herself, but he wouldn't release her. Soon the two were wrestling in the shallow water, coating themselves with sand.

"Hey," Steve said, pausing to frown. "This is just like the *Mud Wrestling Championship*."

Addy snorted. "You wish I were a mud wrestler." She sighed and leaned her head against that wide hairy chest of his. "Sorry for being a baboon."

He played with her hair. "Sorry for being a gorilla."

She kissed him. "I love my big furry gorilla."

He thumped his chest, let out a roar, then lifted her in his arms. "Me King Kong, you Jane!"

Addy rolled her eyes. "You're a very confused gorilla, aren't you?"

Steve carried her off the beach to a patch of grass by some cypresses. They made love in the sunset.

Two crazy monkeys, she thought. And when she lay in his arms afterward, she realized how hard this was for him. How this big, strong man felt emasculated here without employment or pride. And guilt filled Addy that she had dragged him away from his home.

We can be happy here, she thought. *We can build a new life here. And it's nice to have normal problems for a change, not fucking aliens everywhere.*

Yet when Addy slept that night, curled up in Steve's arms out there on the grass, she dreamed of those news reports. Of the photograph Marco had taken in Crete. Of those whispers that were flowing across the islands—rumors of strange lights in the sky, of people vanishing, of creatures walking through the forest.

Past midnight, she awoke to the sound of footsteps and whispers. She glanced toward the cypresses, and she saw a figure standing there, watching her. He was tall, slender, and naked, his skin wrinkled and gray. His head was massive and bald, his eyes black ovals. Addy blinked and rubbed her eyes, wondering if it was a dream. When she looked toward the trees again, the figure was gone.

* * * * *

The next few weeks were woven of joy.

Marco worked on the final draft of *Under the Stairs,* barely able to concentrate, thinking instead about the baby. Choosing names. Drawing plans for a nursery. Seeking baby stores on the nearby islands. One night, he lay by Tomiko and placed a hand on her belly. It was still small, but he could imagine the life kindled within.

"You'll have a better life than I did," he said softly. "You'll grow up in peace, with two parents who love you. You won't have to go to war. You'll be happy. You'll have things I never had. And you'll never see the bad things that I saw."

Tomiko leaned her head against him. He had never told her everything about the war—only the good stories, not the terrors.

Let those terrors fade away, he thought. *Let new life rise.*

The next night, he was up late in his office, working on the last few chapters of *Under the Stairs*, tossing out some scenes that didn't work, adding new ones, revising, polishing, almost done with the manuscript. When he finally went into the bedroom, it was nearly two in the morning, and he expected to find Tomiko asleep. But she was sitting on the bedside, staring ahead blankly.

Marco sat beside her. "Can't sleep?"

She looked at him, eyes huge and haunted.

"I didn't know what to do," she whispered.

He frowned. "About what?"

A tear fled her eye. "I didn't know if to call anyone. I thought it was just a little blood. But then I kept bleeding."

He held her hand. "Tomiko. What happened?"

Her eyes were red and damp. "I saw him. I didn't know what to do. So I just pulled. I just pulled because he was stuck. Dangling. And I didn't know what to do. Who to call. So I just took some paper, and flushed the toilet, and—" Another tear fled. "What should I have done, Marco? What did I do?"

He understood. He embraced her gently, but she was still, did not return the embrace.

"It's not your fault," he said. "It happens half the time. Half the time, Tomiko! You didn't do anything wrong. In a few weeks, we can try again."

She lay down and closed her eyes.

Marco lay at her side, a space between them.

Our child is gone. He could barely register the thought. *Our child is dead.*

He shut his eyes tight, and he clenched his fists, and they did not sleep that night. Every few moments, Tomiko rose, stumbled to the bathroom, bled again. No more tears. Endless bleeding. Finally, before dawn, a rushed trip by boat to a hospital, hours in waiting rooms, a quick moment with a doctor, a boat ride home in the rain. More bleeding. Days of silence. Days of solitude.

"Poet, tell me if there's anything you need," Addy said to him one day, pausing as she passed him in the hallway. She placed a hand on his shoulder. "What can I do? How can I help you?"

He stood, looking at her. At his Addy. Her blue eyes were soft with concern. Outside the window, Steve stood in the yard, sawing wood, working at building another cabinet for the house; he had been spending so much time building cabinet after cabinet. The noise of his saw was overwhelming, a roar like starship engines, like falling cities, cutting at Marco's ears.

He looked back at Addy.

He wanted to tell her that he was mourning. That his child had died. That he was afraid it was punishment—for how he had treated women in Haven, for all the lives he had taken. That he was afraid it would happen again. That after the miscarriage, there had been a terrible feeling of relief. That perhaps the universe was telling him that Tomiko was wrong. That Tomiko was fire and ice. That Tomiko was storm and clear waters. That he was confused, afraid, guilty, cracking apart inside. That he was nothing but shards in a shell. That he was staying strong just for Tomiko, that inside he was crumbling, that he had nightmares every night. That his dead child visited him in his dreams. That he saw bloody visions. That he was going crazy. That he was cursed. That he thought there were demons cursing him. That he kept seeing bad numbers and ill omens. That there was evil in this house. That he had brought it here. That he was a monster, that he had bred monsters, had seen them rise in the form of the marauders. That perhaps his child had been a monster. That he felt so lost.

"I'm fine," he whispered.

Addy nodded and touched his cheek. "Anytime you want to talk, Poet. I'm here."

"I know," he whispered, voice tight.

"I love you," Addy said.

"I know," he whispered again, glancing around.

She clasped his hand. "Poet. Look at me. Don't look around for Tomiko. Look into my eyes. I've been your best friend since we were eleven. We survived our childhoods together. We survived boot camp together. We survived two fucking wars together. We've been together for most of our lives, inseparable. That won't change now. It won't change ever. If you need help, talk to me." Addy caressed his hair. "Okay?"

Marco nodded. His throat felt too tight for speech.

"I know," he whispered for a third time, and in those two words, he told Addy that he loved her, that he would always love her, that she was his best friend, that he had not forgotten everything they had gone through, that they would be best friends forever. He did not need to speak more. He needed only to look into her eyes, and he knew that Addy understood.

She embraced him. "My silly poet."

They stood for a long time in the hallway, holding each other.

When I embraced Tomiko, she stiffened up, Marco thought. *She moved away from me.* He held Addy close, and her arms were warm around him. *This is what I needed. This is what I want.*

He opened his mouth, and he was about to finally speak more than two words, when the lights flashed outside, and the sound of the saw died, and they heard a scream.

Marco looked out the window.

The cabinet lay overturned, the saw fallen.

A light ascended in the sky, then flew away.

Steve was gone.

CHAPTER NINE

Ben-Ari sat in her chamber, alone, staring at the monitor.

She ran the numbers again and again. Each time, a chill filled her.

I have a traitor on board.

She inhaled deeply. She ran the simulation once more on her monitor.

The *Lodestar* flew through space, wrapped in a stealth cloak, moving in warped space. They should have been invisible.

And yet the grays had seen them. In interstellar space. In *warped* space. Light-years away from any star. Somehow, the saucers had known their location. That required more accuracy than pinpointing a single sunken coin in all the world's oceans.

Ben-Ari narrowed her eyes. She hit keys. She ran more numbers.

"What are the odds that the saucers randomly stumbled across us?" she asked her computer. "That they just happened to be flying by?"

The answer was one in millions.

The grays knew our location, Ben-Ari thought. *And somebody aboard my ship tipped them off.*

She rose from her chair. She paced her room. The traitor would be somebody knowledgeable. Somebody who understood physics, who understood the ship's computer systems, who could broadcast their exact coordinates and trajectory. That didn't narrow things down a lot. This was a ship full of scientists.

"Could it have been Marino, my security chief?" she whispered to herself. "No. He's just a warrior, not a scientist. The professor?" She shuddered. "No. No! He's far too sweet and kind. Aurora? Could she secretly hate humans? Or could it have been Fish?" She inhaled sharply, and her lip peeled back. "Fish hates me. He's always hated me. If anyone wanted to betray us, it must have been him! It—"

She bit down on her words. She was paranoid. Nobody in her top command would betray her. Why would they? Why would they want to doom this ship?

Unless they work for the grays.

She shivered. Those creatures had evil eyes. And one was on this very ship. Only a few decks away. Kept prisoner, yes. Tied down to a table. Guarded. Yet still here, scheming, breathing their air, planning revenge.

We brought evil aboard this ship, she thought. *Yet was evil always here?*

Her communicator beeped.

"Captain?" It was the professor. "We're all waiting for you in the lounge, Captain."

She let out a shaky breath. "I'll be right there, Professor."

She hung up. Of course. It was Christmas Eve.

Granted, time was relative in space. A day aboard the *Lodestar* could mean several days, even weeks or months, back on Earth. Velocity and gravity all changed how time flowed, and on Earth right now, Christmas had long passed. And yet they kept their own calendar aboard the ship, tracking their own relative flow of time. Here aboard, it was Christmas, and—

Ben-Ari sighed. She was thinking like a physicist already, thanks to the professor's teachings. It took something away from the holiday's magic.

She looked around her chamber. She had placed a menorah by her porthole, and candles flickered in the brass holders. A few holiday cards stood on her table. And yet she had forgotten.

She dressed quickly, putting on her mess dress—a finer uniform than she wore daily. The trousers and shirt were navy blue, a rich fabric. She placed a military cap on her head. Her brass buttons shone. It was the nicest outfit she had ever owned. When she looked in the mirror, she seemed strong. Proud. Wise. A captain of HOPE. Yet inside, she felt cracked.

A traitor aboard. Or just my paranoia.

She left the chamber. She walked toward the lounge, ready to join the others. She would have to make a public toast and speech, of course. That seemed even worse than fighting the damn grays.

On her way down the corridor, she passed by the brig.

She paused.

He was inside.

Specimen A001.

The gray they had captured.

The brig door was thick iron, and guards stood outside it, wearing armor and holding big guns. Yet as Ben-Ari walked by, she felt the evil within. Radiating outside. She felt those dark eyes staring through the door, through her uniform, seeing the cracks inside. All her insecurities, her fears, her weaknesses.

She clenched her fists.

I am not as weak as you think, creature, she thought. *I beat both the scum and the marauders. I will not fear you.*

And in her mind, the vision returned. The dark city spread out. A black pyramid soared, an Eye of Horus upon its crest. The goddess sat on her rotting throne, smiling.

Ben-Ari ground her teeth and walked onward, wishing she were back in her battle fatigues, that she had her rifle, and that her friends—noble and true soldiers—were still with her.

CHAPTER TEN

They floated through the vastness of space: a woman, a dog, and a robot, all rattling inside a small starship painted with a dragon flying over a rainbow.

"Has there ever been a more ridiculous spaceship?" Lailani said, sitting in the cockpit. "And a more ridiculous crew?"

HOBBS sat at her side, metal knees pulled up to his chest. The giant robot, all seven feet of him, barely squeezed into the copilot's seat. Mechanical noises rose from inside his steel skull.

"I do not know, mistress." He tilted his head with a creak. "To provide you with the answer, I would need access to logs of every spaceship in the galaxy, along with a roster of its crew and their biographies. I would also need to assemble a heuristic algorithm to calculate levels of ridiculousness. Perhaps you could provide parameters for this? Though if you wish to limit your question to Earth-origin ships only, perhaps we can retrieve the information more quickly, and—"

"HOBBS." She patted his shoulder. "Rhetorical question, buddy. And you don't need to call me mistress. My name is Lailani."

He nodded, blue eyes shining. "Yes, Mistress Lailani."

"Just Lailani." She leaned forward in her seat, squinting out the viewport. "Now . . . a constellation shaped like a rearing bear. Where will we find it? HOBBS, you must have starcharts coded into your databases. See anything that matches?"

HOBBS was silent.

"HOBBS?" she said.

He looked at her. "Yes, Lailani?"

"Any matching constellations, buddy?"

"Ah!" HOBBS said. "Forgive me, mistress. I mean— Lailani. I thought it was another rhetorical question. Can you draw me a map of the rearing bear constellation as seen from Earth?"

She had no pen and paper, but the windows were incredibly dusty. She hopped out of her seat, leaving the ship in autopilot. She approached a porthole and paused for a moment, trying to remember her vision.

The memory hurt. Again she saw herself as a centipede with a human face, scurrying through tunnels. Again she tumbled through a wormhole, reliving her nightmares. Sofia falling into the fire. Elvis's heart dying in her fist. Her starship falling, burning, crashing.

And then—open space before her. The constellation shining. Stars forming a rearing bear.

She nodded, keeping the vision before her eyes, and drew the constellation onto the dusty porthole of the ESS *Ryujin*.

"There," she said. "That's where we're going, HOBBS, old boy." She patted the robot, leaving a dusty imprint of her hand. "So dig up your starcharts and scan for a match."

"Yes, mistress."

HOBBS stood straight and closed his eyes, his head brushing the ceiling. Clicks and hums rose from inside him as his processor worked away. As Lailani waited, she figured it was Epi's turn for a pat, and she spoiled the Doberman for a few moments. He licked her hand and wagged his tail, as cheery as always.

Finally—it must have been a good fifteen minutes of processing—HOBBS opened his eyes.

"I am sorry, mistress," the battle-bot said. "I have scanned all available constellations as viewed from Earth, both those visible to the naked eye and those only visible through a telescope. None match the pattern you drew on the porthole."

She frowned. "Bullshit. Maybe you're taking my drawing too literally. Maybe I'm off by a millimeter. Nothing that even approximates this shape?"

"No, mistress," HOBBS said. "I accounted for human error in your drawing. I can display the closest candidates I've found, but they aren't very good matches."

Lailani pursed her lips. She thought for a moment. Constellations depended on the location of the observer. Every planet, looking at the same stars, saw those stars form different constellations. Perhaps whoever had sent her this mysterious vision—and she could not guess at its origin—wasn't from Earth.

"All right, Hobbsy buddy," she said. "We're gonna have to expand our search beyond Earth's origin. Find me a constellation that looks like this bear—but from any possible origin."

HOBBS tilted his head. "Mistress, there are billions of possible origin planets in our galaxy. To scan all possible constellations would take me . . ." Clicks rose from his head. "Thirty thousand, seven hundred, and fifteen years and three days, assuming regular service maintenance and power recharges every year."

Epimetheus whimpered.

Lailani sighed. "Never mind." She paced the cluttered starship. The *Ryujin* was filled with junk JEX had stored here: board games, mechanical doohickeys, old dolls with cracked faces, candle stubs, and that family of possums in the corner. The clutter made it hard to think. "Planet of origin, planet of origin . . . where did my vision come from?"

She shuddered to remember the beginning of her vision, herself as a centipede with a human face. She understood the significance. She was part *scolopendra titania*. Part scum. Her new microchip kept the alien at bay, but it was still a part of her, forever inside her, even if its whispers were now silent.

It was that part that was whispering, she thought. *The scum. The alien inside me. I was seeing a vision with my alien eyes.*

"HOBBS." She turned toward him. "Run another scan. This time from Abaddon as the point of origin."

The robot tilted his head. "Mistress? The planet of the *scolopendra titaniae*?"

She nodded. "Dat's da one."

HOBBS closed his eyes and began running calculations again. Lailani spent fifteen minutes playing fetch with Epi, using the severed head of a creepy Victorian doll. Finally HOBBS opened his eyes. She swore that she could see humanlike excitement there.

"Mistress, I have found a match."

Lailani exhaled in relief, though suddenly a new fear replaced it. This was all real now. She was actually doing this. In the chaos of the past few days—her old chip breaking, her descent into madness, her emergency surgery, her battle with the hooded creatures—she had barely found time to think.

Now, finally, it all sank in.

She was out here in space. She had left her schools, her friends, her very world behind. All to chase a vision. To find an hourglass that could bend time. To try to travel back in time, to save all those who had died.

It seemed crazy, yet HOBBS was already drawing a map onto another dusty porthole, labeling the stars on the way.

"The rearing bear constellation," the robot said. "It lies forty-seven light-years from here. With this ship's azoth engine, we can be there in three weeks."

"All right!" Lailani nodded. "Three weeks. Almost a month here in this ship. We can do that. We got a dog. We got board games. I think there's an entertainment system in here somewhere. We'll watch some movies, listen to some tunes, and—"

Warning alarms blared from the cockpit.

Lailani cursed. She ran back into the cockpit and leaped into her seat. She saw them on the scanner, mere specks of light.

She couldn't make out any details, but she knew who they were, who they had to be.

She shouted over her shoulder, "Guys, more of those weird-ass saucers are here!"

Fuck fuck fuck. There were seven or eight of them. Saucers, each larger and deadlier than the *Ryujin*. During her service aboard the HDFS *Saint Brendan* and later the *Marilyn*, Lailani had functioned as navigator and technician. What did she know of battle maneuvers? She wasn't Kemi.

She gripped the controls and soared higher.

The saucers followed and fired their weapons.

A blast hit the *Ryujin*, knocking them into a spin.

"Damn it!" Lailani said. She sneered and pushed down on the throttle, trying to escape. But the enemy was too fast. Another volley fired around her. A shot grazed the *Ryujin*, denting the hull.

She flew in a loop. When she faced the enemy, she released plasma blasts. She hit one saucer, knocking it into a tailspin. Then she completed the loop and kept flying forward again. The enemy pursued, closer now.

"What the hell do you assholes want?" Lailani shouted into her communicator.

A monitor crackled to life. A ghastly visage appeared there. A giant bald head. Wrinkly, ashen skin. Cruel black eyes. A gray, and a particularly vile one. His face was gaunt, his head was warty, and deep grooves framed his slit of a mouth. A cord hung around his neck, slung with human hearts—still beating, still bleeding, a living necklace of his victims.

"Foul human," the creature said, amusement filling his black eyes.

"Who the fuck are you?" Lailani said.

The creature sneered, revealing teeth like needles. "I am Abyzou, Born of Nefitis, Lord of Pain, Baptized in Blood, Head of Legions."

Lailani waved. "Nice to meet you, fuckface. I'm Lailani."

The creature's sneer widened. "Humor. A pathetic, weak trait of apes, used to mask your fear. I know who you are, hybrid. Freak. You slew our brothers on Earth. You will never find the hourglass. You will scream for my mother. She will be your goddess!"

Lailani gulped. "Yeah, well . . . at least I don't look like a ball sack with eyes." She hung up. "Fucking mama's boy."

The saucers fired their cannons. More photon bolts blasted toward the *Ryujin*. Lailani zigzagged through space, knowing she couldn't lose them. She did another loop, fired again, hit a saucer, but could not damage it. She plunged downward, and the saucers swooped in pursuit. The old dolls, board games, and knickknacks clattered across the hold. Epimetheus growled.

"HOBBS!" Lailani said. "Still got ammo?"

The robot nodded. "Yes, mistress. My plasma cannon is fully charged."

"Good. Get into the airlock, hang out the door, and make yourself useful."

"Yes, mistress!" The robot exited the cockpit, entered the airlock, and leaned out into space.

As Lailani flew, focused on fleeing, the robot blasted his bolts back toward the pursuers. For a dented, rusty old machine, HOBBS carried impressive firepower. Blast after blast of plasma flew from his guns, slamming into the saucers, pockmarking and cracking their hulls. Back in his heyday, HOBBS must have been a true terror to behold. Lailani wondered how the machine, probably built during the Scum Wars, had ended up in JEX's junkyard.

But she had no time to contemplate it further. The enemy was still pursuing. One saucer exploded under the barrage of HOBBS's wrath, but the others were flying fast, dodging the assault—and returning fire. Another blast hit the *Ryujin*, tossing them into a tailspin. A second blast grazed HOBBS, knocking the robot back into the airlock.

Terror bloomed in Lailani.

We can't outrun them. We can't defeat them.

She had no idea why they were after her. But she had not survived the scum and marauders to die here in space.

I will not die before I've found redemption. I will bring back Elvis. I will atone for my sins, for the murder I committed. She bared her teeth. *I will not fail!*

She scanned the horizon. She knew this area of space. It should be ahead of her, the place few starships dared to fly.

More blasts flew around her. One hit the bottom of the ship, and the *Ryujin* jolted. Epimetheus barked madly. Charred and dented, HOBBS managed to lean out of the airlock again, to keep firing. His arm had fallen off again. Lailani kept flying, fast as she could, looping every moment to return fire from her main cannons.

Finally—there! She saw it ahead, just a few moments away at this speed.

An asteroid field.

Specifically, the asteroid field from the drag race—the one Addy had forced her to watch.

Many asteroid fields, such as the one back in the solar system, were mostly empty space. But this one, the remnants of a destroyed world, was a dense minefield that stretched for many kilometers.

Lailani vividly recalled watching the drag race here. Not one starship had survived. Not even the one the famous Firebolt had flown.

Lailani headed there now.

She zigzagged along the way, taking more fire, losing one wing. Finally she could see them with the naked eye: the asteroids.

There were thousands, maybe millions. Most were no larger than barrels. Some were the size of cities. Countless rocks were the size of pebbles or grains of sand, but flying at this speed, even grains of sand could rip through the hull like bullets.

Lailani was grateful for all those hours playing *Asteroid Sweep* on her tablet.

Wincing, she flew into the field.

The asteroids tumbled around them. She rose, dropped, swerved left and right. An asteroid rolled overhead, grazing *Ryujin*'s top. Another skimmed their side, scraping off bits of the dragon painting. She bolted upward, dodging several rolling stones the size of basketballs.

Nobody had ever navigated this asteroid field successfully, not even the best pilots. The saucers would have to be mad to follow. Lailani could hide here. Maybe land on a large asteroid. She would—

Lasers blasted from behind her.

The saucers were following.

A blast hit the *Ryujin*, searing the hull, nearly breaking through. They jerked and slammed into a comet the size of a house. The corner of the ship dented. The viewport cracked.

"Damn it!" Lailani shouted, struggling to fly onward, dodging more and more of the asteroids.

HOBBS popped back into the cockpit. "Mistress, would you like me to fly? My instincts are inhumanly fast, and—"

"Get back into the fucking airlock and keep firing!" she shouted.

HOBBS vanished back into the airlock. Through a camera feed, she saw him firing at the enemy.

He hit one saucer. The vessel veered off course and slammed into an asteroid. An explosion filled space.

"Yes!" Lailani shouted, her joy soaring even through the fear. She kept flying.

Kemi would have maneuvered here with ease. But Lailani needed every bit of concentration, and soon she was scraping more paint off the sides. She banged her remaining wing, crippling its tip.

Another laser blast hit them. Lailani screamed. Fire blazed through the ship. The *Ryujin* rattled as it flew onward, puffing out smoke.

"HOBBS, keep them off our tail!" she shouted.

"Their hulls are thick, mistress!" came his reply. "My fire cannot penetrate."

Lailani had an idea.

"Don't shoot at them!" she said. "Shoot the asteroids. Knock the asteroids off course! Slam those asteroids into them like a giant game of billiards!"

HOBBS spoke through the communicator. "Mistress, I am detecting a high likeliness of microbial life upon the asteroids. Would you care to override HOPE regulation 17-B concerning the protection and preservation of new lifeforms on—"

"Blast those fucking asteroids!" she shouted.

"Yes, mistress!" came his reply.

HOBBS began firing at the asteroids instead of the saucers, diverting the giant stones off course.

A plasma bolt hit an asteroid. The stone rolled and crashed through a saucer, shattering it. The alien ship exploded.

"Fuck yeah!" Lailani cried. "Keep hitting those billiard balls!"

His head popped back into the cockpit. "You wish to play a game of—"

"Goddamn it, HOBBS, keep hitting the asteroids!"

Another plasma bolt hit another asteroid, knocking it into a saucer. The alien ship careened, hit a second saucer, and both slammed into an asteroid and exploded. HOBBS diverted a craggy asteroid the size of the White House. The saucers fired on it, shattering it into several pieces, but the debris slammed into them, ripping them apart. Shards flew toward the *Ryujin*, and Lailani barrel-rolled, dodging the stones.

Only two saucers remained.

Teeth bared, Lailani spun around.

She charged toward the enemy, cannons firing.

The saucers fired at her. She flew from asteroid to asteroid, hiding from the barrage. She crested a massive comet the size of Manhattan, and she unleashed an inferno of hellfire.

Her missiles slammed into the last saucers, and they exploded.

Lailani hooted with triumph. Shards flew toward the *Ryujin*. She flew high, swerving around asteroids, and emerged from the field into open space like a whale breaching a murky sea.

She slumped back in her seat and exhaled slowly.

"Who has two thumbs and is a flying ace?" she asked Epimetheus. "This girl."

Her Doberman jumped onto her and licked her cheek.

Lailani realized that she was shaking, that her heart was racing.

"Wish you could have seen this, Kemi," she whispered, missing the fallen pilot. "You'd have been proud of me."

HOBBS stumbled back into the cockpit.

Lailani gasped and leaped from her seat.

"HOBBS!"

The robot looked a fright. His arm had fallen off again, his breastplate was cracked, his jaw hung loose, a dent drove into his head, and cables dangled from a gash in his side. Smoke rose from him.

"Mistress . . ." His voice was staticky.

She placed her hands on him, then winced and pulled her hands back. He was burning hot.

"We'll get you fixed up, Hobster," she said. "I used to fix machines all the time back in the army."

The *Ryujin* itself, Lailani realized, probably looked no better. Dents and burn marks probably covered it, and smoke still rose from the instruments. Thankfully, there was a spacesuit and welding tools in the utility closet. Lailani would need to spend hours outside, fixing the starship—especially the broken wing—if she hoped to ever fly through an atmosphere again.

"Well, boys," she said to her robot and dog, "rain check on the board games and movies. We got a lot of repairs to do. And I think I need to change my underpants."

The *Ryujin* kept sailing through the darkness. Lailani spent the time outside, clinging to the hull, clad in an oversized spacesuit, feeling a little like a girl who had climbed into her father's clothes. With a soldering iron, wrenches, screws, and a dusty user manual, she worked at repairing the battle damage. Meanwhile, inside the ship, HOBBS was working on repairing himself, and Epimetheus was sound asleep.

Things were going well for once. She knew where the constellation was. She had a ship, had a plan, had a hulking killing machine with the firepower of an army. Yet as they flew onward, Lailani couldn't shake that bad feeling.

There were creatures roaming the galaxy, seeking her, seeking her friends. She would encounter them again before the end, she knew.

She returned to the ship. HOBBS was in sleep mode, his body patched together, and Lailani lay down on the mattress at the back of the hold. Epimetheus curled up at her side. She hugged her loyal dog.

"I'm worried about Marco and Addy," she whispered to the Doberman. "I'm worried about Ben-Ari. I don't have a way to contact them from out here. And I'm scared these creatures are chasing them too."

Epi gave a soft snort and licked her cheek.

Lailani thought of them. Of sweet Marco, a man she still loved with all her heart, even though they had gone their separate ways. He was the first man she had ever truly loved, her first and only boyfriend, and he would always be dear to her. And she thought of Addy, of loud, bluff, funny, brave, and wonderful Addy, her best human friend in the world. Of Ben-Ari, her mentor, her anchor, her heroine.

Are you staying safe?

"Maybe we should go home, Epi," she said, lying on the mattress with her dog. "To find Marco and Addy. To find a way to contact Ben-Ari on the *Lodestar*, maybe the next time the flagship opens a communication wormhole. To warn them. To fight with them if war is here again. Am I forsaking the living for the dead?"

Epimetheus tilted his head. He looked at her, then glanced out the porthole to the stars.

"Yes," she whispered. "The hourglass is still out there." She took a shuddering breath. "Elvis is gone; I killed him. Sofia is gone; she died because I let her go, let her fall into the fire. Hundreds of soldiers aboard the *Miyari* died because of me. We have to save them. I have to let Marco, Addy, and Ben-Ari fight this one alone. We have to find the hourglass, Epi, and we have to go back in time. You understand, don't you?"

Her dog nuzzled her. Yes, he understood. He could always understand.

She was drifting off when she heard the creaking, and she opened her eyes to see HOBBS sit down beside her, settling down for a vigil. It was cold, dark, and lonely out here with her memories, but she had new friends, as dear as any humans. Her eyes closed, and she slept with Epimetheus curled up at her feet and HOBBS's warmth at her side.

CHAPTER ELEVEN

Ben-Ari stood in the *Lodestar*'s mess hall, dressed in her gala uniform, her wineglass raised. The officers stood before her, filling the room—five hundred men and women. It was the largest room on the ship, spanning the entire top floor like a sailing ship's deck. It was the only room where the full crew could fit. Viewports on the ceiling displayed the stars above. It felt as if they indeed stood atop an ancient sailing vessel, navigating the cosmic ocean.

Ben-Ari had been speaking to her crew for long moments now, and she was nearing the end of her speech.

"Though we are far from home, and our sun is but a speck in the distance, we do not forget our traditions, our loved ones, our winter spirit." Ben-Ari raised her glass high. "Happy Holidays and Merry Christmas!"

She drank, and across the lounge the others cried out their season's greetings and drank too. Ben-Ari was thankful for the wine. Her cheeks were already flushed from stage fright. She could easily deliver an inspiring speech to troops before a battle. This was harder.

Last night she had spent hours planning her speech. In early drafts, she had talked about the threat of the grays, the danger in space, the sanctity of their mission. She had tossed those drafts out. Tonight didn't need to be about duty. She had dedicated her life to duty, but her crew was different. Her crew had not seen the things she had seen. They needed this evening to celebrate. To feel at home.

But she had added some solemn words too, words she could not neglect to speak.

"Today, while we celebrate our holidays, we remember those who have fallen." She read out the names of the eight crewmen who had died while attacking the gray saucer. "We will remember them always. They are here with us in spirit." She raised her glass again. "To their memory. To their sacrifice. To life!"

She drank from her glass again. Perhaps she was the soldier still. In the crowd, she saw Fish staring at her. The famous Alien Hunter still wore his outback khakis, not even donning a uniform for the holiday gala. In his eyes, she saw his accusation. His grief.

You led them into the saucer, his eyes seemed to tell her. *You led them to death.*

Ben-Ari stared into his eyes until, with a snort, Fish looked away.

Is Fish the traitor? Ben-Ari thought. *He certainly has no love for me. Could somebody here have led the grays to us—an agent of the enemy?*

She passed her eyes over the crowd. Scientists, engineers, explorers. Even Aurora was here; the mollusk clung to a wall. Somebody had revealed the *Lodestar*'s location to the grays. Ben-Ari had grown more and more convinced of this. Yet she kept her

183

suspicions to herself. Anyone she confided in could be the traitor. She could trust nobody here.

I miss you, Marco, she thought. *I miss you, Kemi, Lailani, Addy. I could always trust you guys. I'm alone here, even among five hundred souls.*

She stepped off the stage, and she joined the others in the crowd.

Her crew had bedecked the lounge for the holidays. A Christmas tree rose in the center, glowing with lights, gifts lying around its trunk. A menorah stood on a table, shining with electrical candles. Other religions had their own displays. Among the crew of five hundred, there were explorers of several faiths, representing the diversity of humanity. Marino was Christian; back in his wrestling days, he had often kissed his cross before a fight, was renowned in the media for volunteering at his church. Ben-Ari herself was Jewish, as was Professor Isaac, her science teacher and mentor. The ship also had many fine officers from the Hindu, Buddhist, Sikh, and Muslim faiths.

But here in space, we are all just human, she thought. *All the same. All just meat for our enemies to burn. All just vermin in their eyes. All united against the darkness.*

"Captain!" Professor Isaac approached her, smiling. "Happy holidays! Would you care for some candy cane?" He lifted two of the candies.

Ben-Ari blinked, for a moment confused, caught between the darkness of her thoughts and the light and joy around her. She forced a smile.

Enough with the grimness, she told herself. *Try to enjoy yourself tonight.*

She had always been one for contemplation, for solitude. For her, a good night meant staying in her chamber, ideally in her pajamas, listening to classical music and reading a good novel. She had never cared much for social gatherings, had always felt awkward, out of place. Perhaps she did not know how to feel joy. Contentment, peace—maybe, on the rare occasion. Happiness? She had never felt such a thing. It was a foreign feeling to her, as incomprehensible as color to the blind.

She accepted one of the candy canes. "Thank you, Professor."

Isaac wore his service uniform too, but he had added some holiday cheer to it, pinning a little snowman to his lapel. It was against regulations, but Ben-Ari decided to let it fly tonight. The professor's dark hair was a little too long again too. At least he was finally wearing a uniform; that was progress. When she had first come aboard the *Lodestar,* Isaac kept showing up on the bridge wearing a tweed jacket and corduroy pants.

Perhaps we all have trouble adjusting to life in HOPE, she thought. *I'm still the soldier. He's still the professor. Fish is still the rebel.* A shudder ran through her. *And the alien trapped in our containment cell is still hell-bent on destroying humanity.*

She did not like thinking of that creature aboard her ship. She forced the thought away.

It's a party, Einav, she told herself. *Try to put aside the morbidity. At least for one night.*

"There's real food here too, you know," she said to the professor, smiling again. She pointed at a table topped with ham, turkey, fruits, vegetables, pies, and all the other goodness of the holidays. "Don't ruin your appetite on candy canes."

The professor's eyes sparkled. "We humans are a traveling breed. Since we rose from the oceans, we've been wanderers. Forever have we scaled mountains, crossed seas and forests, and explored the unknown. We've always been curious. We've always been adventurers. And yet sometimes when far on a journey, we get a little homesick. We seek a little comfort in the familiar. An old song, perhaps one from childhood, a tune a parent would sing by the hearth. Perhaps the company of a dog-eared book, an old favorite that has soothed us in the past. And perhaps a little taste of beloved candy, as comforting and as sweet as a loved one's embrace." He took a bite of candy cane. It crunched.

Ben-Ari couldn't help but laugh. *And they call Marco the poet!*

"You're still like a child during the holidays, aren't you?" she said.

The professor nodded. "I've learned something, Einav. It pays for a scientist to retain a little childlike wonder. It's something too many of us lose."

Now Ben-Ari's smile faded. "It's something the cosmos takes away from us."

His face too grew solemn. He nodded. "Yes, of course. I'm sorry, Einav. I know how you fought in the Galactic Wars, how you saw things perhaps you wish to forget. The cosmos can also be dark and dangerous. I grew up shielded, and—"

186

"Professor, it's all right." She forced her smile back. "I'm sorry. I was grim. I have trouble letting go, trouble relaxing, trouble . . . well, trouble being normal." She looked around her and winced. "I feel comfortable on a battlefield, but I don't know how to behave at parties." She looked back at him, and now her smile was real. "Maybe you can spend the evening teaching me the science of Christmas trees, the physics of the menorah's light, and the chemical composition of candy cane?"

"Or," rose a voice from behind her, "you can try some dancing."

Ben-Ari turned to see Marino approach her. The tall, powerful wrestler wore his service uniform, though he had left the top unbuttoned, revealing his golden chain and cross. His cheeks were stubbly. Did nobody here have any discipline? Would they force her to send them to the brig at Christmas?

"I do *not* dance," Ben-Ari said. "And you are not presentable."

Marino smiled. He gestured toward a section of the lounge where the tables had been pushed back, creating a dance floor. Several people were already dancing.

"Nobody looks presentable while dancing," Marino said, "but it's about having fun, Einav."

"Call me Captain."

Marino nodded. "Captain. So? A dance?" He glanced back toward Isaac. "That is, if the good professor does not mind me stealing you away."

Isaac raised his eyebrows and spoke before Ben-Ari could.

187

"I do believe our good captain goes and does as she pleases, and no man can steal her. But—ah! They have just brought out the fondue."

The professor made a beeline toward the refreshment table, though Ben-Ari did not miss the last glance he shot their way. She thought—maybe just imagined—that she saw disappointment in his eyes.

Ben-Ari turned back toward Marino. "Join us for fondue. I've never tried it, and—"

He reached out—quite brazenly—and took her hand. "Actually, Captain, I still demand that dance. Shall we?"

She did not know why she let him pull her toward the dance floor. It was stupid. She had never danced in her life. Perhaps it was the wine, but she soon found herself on the dance floor with this towering, brutish wrestler. His hands held the small of her back. Begrudgingly, she placed her hands on his shoulders.

"Fine, I'm dancing," Ben-Ari said.

He smiled down at her. Ben-Ari was not a short woman—she was at least average—but he still had to look down at her, like an adult at a child. "You seem to be struggling. Would you like to step on my feet and let me guide you?"

She groaned. "The last time I did that, I was six years old, dancing with my Uncle Shmuley at my cousin's bar mitzvah."

Marino grinned. "You soldiers don't know how to have fun! Once we're back on Earth, and once I'm competing again, I'll invite you to one of our parties after a fight. We toss some wild parties in my house."

Ben-Ari snorted. "You'll fight again? You're too old, Marino."

He bristled. "I'm only thirty-six."

"Old man," she said.

A slow song came on. Ben-Ari was thankful; it was easier to dance to without embarrassing herself. But it also meant dancing intimately close to Marino. His hands felt too good on her waist. His height, his scent, his bristly chin against the top of her head—it all felt too comforting, too alluring.

I can't do this, she thought. *I'm the commander of this starship.*

"I'm going back to the food," she said.

"Wait," said Marino. "Before we enjoy the fondue, I wanted to say thank you. For saving my life on the saucer."

She looked up at him, eyebrow raised. "If I recall correctly, you saved my life there too."

"And I was terrified," Marino said. "That's not easy for me to admit. I'm a ten-time Mixed Martial Arts Federation champion. I shouldn't be afraid of anything. But on that ship, seeing those creatures . . ." He shuddered. "You fought bravely, Captain. I see why your soldiers admire you so much. Why Petty chose you to command this ship. Tomorrow morning, I'll hit the gym for some training. Would you join me? We can spar. Maybe I can show you a few moves."

She couldn't help but snort. "I think I'll be the one showing *you* moves. I've trained extensively with Krav Maga, I'll have you know. And not just for show; for actual battle."

He grinned. "Oh, sure, call what I do just showmanship. We'll see who beats who at the gym tomorrow."

She gasped. "First of all, you're easily twice my size! Second, I didn't agree to spar with you. Third, I'll kick your ass." She stiffened and tore away from him, remembering herself. "To the fondue, Commander."

The rest of the party passed awkwardly. She had two more glasses of wine—just enough to steady her nerves, stopping when she began to feel lightheaded. She exchanged pleasantries with the scientists. She shared soft, comforting words with the fallen guards' friends. Whenever she could, she spent time with the professor; his calm voice soothed her, and she asked him to explain about the nebula they saw through the porthole, the chemical process of fermenting wine, and every other science question she could think of. She was nervous. Nervous about this party. Nervous about the alien aboard their ship. Nervous about her new command. Most of all, nervous about this new threat in space. The professor's words, his mere voice, quieted the storm inside her. She could listen to him forever.

People began trickling back to their chambers. As captain, Ben-Ari had to stay to the bitter end. It was two in the morning before the last guest—Fish, a little drunk and teetering—departed. Finally Ben-Ari was able to leave the lounge. The ship's three service robots, cat-sized machines, remained to clean up.

She walked through the dark, empty corridors of the ship. They dimmed the lights at night, mimicking the cycles of day and night back on Earth. During the days, the ship was brightly lit, impeccably clean, modern, and bustling with activity—far nicer than any military ship Ben-Ari had ever served on. Yet at night, especially this night, the shadows seemed foreboding. The Christmas lights they had hung up glowed eerily; they looked to Ben-Ari like splatters of blood.

We carry evil on this ship.

She saw them again in her memories. The grays. Grabbing her. Staring at her.

She winced with sudden pain. The wounds on her body had healed. And yet she could still feel the claws gripping her, piercing her. She still felt the aliens' eyes upon her, digging in.

When she passed along a dark corridor with no Christmas lights, Ben-Ari imagined *her* in the shadows. The dark queen. The creature with a rusting crown nailed into her head.

"Who are you?" Ben-Ari whispered.

She intended to return to her bunk, yet she found herself walking toward the containment chamber.

She paused outside the heavy fortified door. She opened a hatch no larger than her wallet. She stared through the window of thick bulletproof glass.

Inside, the gray lay strapped to a table.

The alien was still unconscious. Ben-Ari had wounded it when boarding the saucer—wounded it too seriously. IVs were attached to the creature, and an oxygen mask was strapped over its face. The *Lodestar*'s doctors had never treated such a creature, had never even seen one up close. CT scans had revealed familiar organs: a heart, lungs, a stomach, intestines. The works. But its

191

blood was strange, so dark it was nearly black. Its brain was far larger than a human's, impossible to decipher with scans.

For now, all they knew was that the creature was in a coma. And they didn't know how to wake it up.

"I need you awake," Ben-Ari said softly. "I need you to answer my questions. I need to know what you bastards are doing."

She had heard the news from Earth, of course. The saucers had been spotted over all major cities. Thousands of people claimed to have been abducted. Many claims were revealed as hoaxes, but some stories checked out. Yet nobody had captured a live gray before. Nobody since Roswell over two centuries ago, at least, if you believed the stories.

And I have one here. And the damn thing won't wake up.

On the table, the alien sat up.

Behind the thick glass, Ben-Ari started.

The creature began ripping off the tubes attached to him. His head turned toward her, and a thin smile stretched across his face. A raspy voice spoke in her mind.

Einav . . .

"Rockin' around the Christmas tree, at the Christmas party hop!"

The sound of singing came from behind her. Ben-Ari spun around to see two drunken ensigns stumbling down the corridor, leaning on each other, bottles of beer in hand. They sang a few more words, then fell silent and gulped when they saw their captain.

"Get to bed, Ensigns," she snapped. "Sleep it off."

"Yes, ma'am!" The two managed clumsy salutes—not even necessary in HOPE—and fled the corridor.

Ben-Ari turned back toward the containment chamber. She stared through the window again. Once more, the gray was lying on the table, eyes closed, tubes reattached. Had he even risen at all?

Just a daydream, she thought. *Just the wine. I'm scared. I'm exhausted. I'm a little drunk.*

With a shaky breath, she walked onward.

By the time she reached her chamber, it was only three hours until simulated dawn. Her room was luxurious compared to her old military dwellings. It was not as nice, perhaps, as Marco's house in Greece, but compared to an army bunk, these quarters seemed a palace. She had decorated sparsely. A shadowbox hung on a wall, containing her ancestors' medals, mementos from a dozen wars. Her own medals hung among them. A framed photograph hung on another wall, showing her with her old platoon. In the photo, she was standing with her best friends: with Marco, Addy, Lailani, Sergeant Singh, Corporal Diaz, all the rest of them. Many of whom were now gone.

She missed them, both the fallen and the living. She missed them so much that it ached.

I wish you were here with me, my friends, Ben-Ari thought. *I feel lost without you.*

She showered, changed into her pajamas, but felt too wound up for sleep. Her mind was racing. She considered meditating, but she feared what visions might arise in that silent solitude.

Instead, she turned on some music: *La Boheme*, her favorite opera. She curled up on the couch with a mug of tea and the novel *Tigana* by Guy Gavriel Kay. Music and words and brewed chamomile. She had so little time for them, yet they could always soothe her mind.

Before she could read two pages, her doorbell rang.

She frowned and leaped up.

The alien must be awake! The ship was under attack! Earth was at war!

"Who is it?" she said, speaking into her intercom. "What's wrong?"

"It's Mario, Captain," rose the voice. "Mario Marino."

Her heart thundered. The last thing a captain wanted was her Chief Security Officer calling at three in the morning. She opened her door, revealing him in the hallway.

"What happened?" she said. "Who's attacking us, how many, and—" She frowned. She tilted her head. "Why are you carrying a bottle of Champagne and two glasses?"

Marino stood at the doorway for a moment. "Are you going to let me in, or will I have to drink these alone in the hallway?"

Frowning, still flummoxed, she let him in. "What's your emergency?"

He placed down the drinks. "Just a bit of insomnia. I figured you'd still be awake. I enjoyed dancing with you, Einav.

After our dance, you rushed off in a hurry, spent the rest of the party with the professor. And I wanted to spend a little more holiday time with you. Alone."

She placed her hands on her hips. "I'm wearing my pajamas!" She glanced down at herself, and her cheeks flushed. She realized how ridiculous she looked. She wore actual pajamas, pink ones, like a little girl. She even had fluffy slippers on.

"They're cute," Marino said. "You're cute."

She glared at him. "I'm your commanding officer."

He looked at the couch. "May I?"

She groaned and raised her arms in resignation. "Fine!"

He sat, popped open the bottle, and poured two glasses. "This is HOPE, Einav. A civilian organization. Not the military. We're allowed to socialize."

"Is that why you came to my bedroom at three in the morning with a bottle of Champagne?" she asked, hands back on her hips. "To socialize?"

He patted the couch. With an eye roll, she sat down beside him.

"Fine. Busted!" Marino smiled. "I care for you, Einav. I like you. A lot."

She sighed. "I was busy reading a book. And I have to be up in three hours."

He glanced at the paperback. "Fascinating, I'm sure. And you don't have to be up tomorrow. It's Christmas. A day off."

"A captain has no days off, Marino."

When he kissed her, she wanted to slap him, to scold him, to fire him. But his hand in her hair felt good. And her heart fluttered against his chest. And she allowed him to kiss her—just for a moment. Just for a lingering moment before she could come to her senses.

This isn't the army, she thought. *I can do this. It's not illegal here. I can seek some romance, some joy.*

He wrapped his arms around her, and she allowed herself to relax, to surrender to him. Maybe just for one night, maybe just for a single, secret night of—

Yellow lights flashed across her chamber.

Her communicator beeped.

She pulled back from Marino, inhaling sharply, and spoke into her communicator.

"Ben-Ari here. Speak."

Aurora's voice emerged from the communicator.

"Mistress of the dark waters! A trumpeting of great fear has reached us through the cosmic ocean! A cry of warning from your pod-kin! Danger! Danger!"

Ben-Ari inhaled sharply. She understood.

An urgent Mayday. From fellow humans. Danger.

She nodded.

"Be right there, Aurora."

She grabbed her uniform from the closet. She rushed toward the bridge, Marino fast on her heels.

CHAPTER TWELVE

"Steve!" Marco cried, walking through the forest. "Steve, where are you?"

"Doofus!" Addy shouted. "Answer me, you gorilla! Where the hell are you? Steve!"

They walked through the dark forest, holding flashlights. They had already scoured the beach—kilometers of it—and seen no footprints, no sign of Steve at all. Addy struggled to curb the tremble in her legs, to stop the terror from overwhelming her.

"Steve!" she shouted. "Where are you?"

They had been searching for two days and nights now. Ever since that scream. Those flashing lights in the sky. That glowing orb that seemed to have descended here into the forested hills in the island's center.

Since then—nothing.

Not a sign.

"Steve!" she cried. "Where are you?"

She and Marco were both hoarse. Eventually, after hours of uninterrupted trudging through the forest, they were forced to rest.

Marco sat on a boulder, breathing heavily. "I never realized how damn big this island is."

Addy wanted to keep going, to keep searching every last meter of this giant island. But even she had to pause to catch her breath. She sat beside Marco.

"He must be somewhere on this island," she said. "No boats left the docks. And the idiot can't swim."

Marco was quiet for a long moment, catching his breath. Finally he spoke in a low voice.

"The light in the sky, Addy. Remember? After we heard him scream, we ran outside, saw a light in the sky, and—"

"Just an airplane!" she said.

In the eerie glow of the flashlights, Marco's face was grim. "It looked like the lights I saw in Crete. The saucers. The ones we saw on the news too." His voice dropped to a whisper. "Alien spaceships."

Addy snorted. "Oh please, Poet. You sound like some farmer on TV, claiming little gray men from space molested his chickens. There's no such thing as grays. They're fairy tales! Just like pixies, poltergeists, and pygmies."

"Actually, Addy, pygmies are—"

"No such thing!" She crossed her arms. "Steve is somewhere on this island. Just lost. We'll find him." She rose and began trudging along the dark hills again. "Steve!"

They traveled along a natural pathway strewn with goat droppings. Many wild goats lived in these hills, carving walkways through the brush. In the daytime, this was a beautiful landscape, the hills draped with pines, cypresses, and olive trees, and from the hilltops one could see the sea. But at night the hills were a nightmarish realm of twisting roots, snagging branches, and dancing shadows.

Addy shivered. She remembered the figure she had seen on the beach a few days ago—a pale humanoid, head large and bald, staring at her with black eyes. Addy had fought both scum and marauders, monsters from the depths of hell, but something about that figure—its inhuman eyes, its long fingers, the malice she felt emanating from it—had disturbed her more than armies of giant bugs.

It was just a dream, she told herself. *Just my subconscious remembering all those stories from television. Humanoid aliens? Grays?* She snorted. *They don't exist. Space is full of giant bugs, dumb critters with sharp claws and tiny brains. Not humanoids. Not those creepy gray fucks.*

A shadow moved in the trees. She pointed her flashlight, heart bursting into a gallop. A creature scurried away, vanishing into the brush. A goat. Just a goat.

"Poet," she said softly.

"Addy?"

She hesitated for a moment, not sure how to proceed. Then she said, "Are we cursed?"

He nodded. "Oh, definitely."

Addy bit her lip. "You know, I was happy for a while. Having normal problems. I complained about washing the dishes. I fought with my boyfriend. I pulled weeds from the yard and cursed every one. But I was happy. Happy to have normal people problems. To struggle with dirty dishes, weeds, domestic disputes. To be ordinary. Poet, I don't want to fight aliens anymore."

They walked for a moment in silence, their flashlights casting back shadows. Finally Marco spoke.

"Addy, I'm not happy."

She looked at him. He was staring ahead blankly.

"Why not?" she said. "Don't you like having normal problems? Don't they beat scum and marauders and whatever creepy fucks might be creeping around here now?"

He thought for a long moment, then finally spoke slowly, as if considering every word. "I defeated the scum and the marauders. I'm not sure I can defeat Tomiko."

Addy burst out laughing. "You're being ridiculous."

He sighed. "I know, I know! It's just that . . . Addy, I don't know how to make her happy. Not for more than a day, at least. I'll make her laugh one day, and the next day she's weeping, tossing things, shouting . . . Then the day after that, she's all smiles again."

Addy nodded. "She's an emotional one. But hey, so am I. And you love me, right?"

"With you it's different," Marco said. "Even when you're beating the shit out of me, I know we're best friends, that we understand each other. I don't know if Tomiko understands me. Understands what we lived through. She'll never have that connection you, me, Lailani, and Ben-Ari have. Before I got married, you told me that it doesn't matter. That it only matters that Tomiko makes me happy. But Addy, what if Tomiko and I are making each other miserable?"

Addy paused from walking. She stared at him. "Poet, if you two make each other miserable, why the fuck are you trying to have a baby together?"

"To fix things," Marco said. "To give us something in common, something to share."

"A baby can't fix things! *You* have to do that." Addy touched his cheek. "Marco, you lived through too much shit to be miserable now. You didn't survive the scum and the marauders to mope. You need to be happy, all right?"

He nodded. "All right. And besides, my problems seem petty compared to what we're going through now. The only thing that matters now is finding Steve." He coned his hand around his mouth and cried out again. "Steve!"

"Steve!" Addy shouted. "Can you hear me, doofus?"

From ahead, they heard twigs snapping.

A whisper shuddered through the forest.

Addy froze.

It's them, she thought. *The grays.*

She glanced at Marco. She saw the fear in his eyes. She drew two pistols from her belt; she had taken to carrying weapons in these hills, a lingering paranoia from the war. She handed Marco one of the weapons.

The whispers sounded again ahead, speaking in a foreign language.

In the distance, an orb shone, soared upward as fast as lightning, then vanished.

Footsteps creaked ahead. More twigs snapped. A tall shadow moved between the trees, naked, gray.

Addy's heart pounded against her ribs. She held her breath and tightened her grip on her gun. She approached slowly, Marco at her side.

The figure moved away from them, vanishing into the shadows.

Addy burst into a run.

"You!" she shouted. "Come back here, you sneaky gray fuck!"

She raced around the trees. The figure turned toward her. Addy aimed her pistol and pulled the trigger.

"No!" Marco shouted, grabbing her arm.

Her gun fired into the sky, hitting the canopy of branches.

The tall, naked figure approached them, stepping into the light.

It was Steve.

He shuffled toward them, ashen, eyes sunken. He was thin—downright cadaverous. He looked like he had lost half his weight during the past two days. His hair had gone white. He stared at them with blank eyes, naked, trembling. A surgical scar stretched across his torso, shaped like a cross, stitched shut.

"Steve!" Addy cried, tears leaping into her eyes, and raced toward him. "Oh God, Steve. Marco! Marco, give him your jacket!"

Steve looked at her, confused, as if he didn't recognize her. Then he fell to his knees, trembling. He spoke in a foreign language, babbling, weeping, and hugged her legs. Addy stood above him, feeling helpless, rocking him back and forth in the dark forest.

* * * * *

As dawn rose, they sat in the living room, Steve with a blanket wrapped around him, the others gazing at him.

"Steve," Addy tried again, voice softer this time. She touched his cheek. "Can you—"

He recoiled from her touch. A whimper fled his lips. The strong man she had known, bluff and powerful and so brave, had been reduced to a cowering wreck. She barely recognized him. His cheeks were so gaunt. The chicken soup they had been feeding him had barely returned color to his ashen cheeks. He had been back for hours now. He still had not spoken.

Addy looked at him, and everything inside her seemed to shatter, to melt. She had to fight not to weep.

What did they do to you, Steve? she thought, gazing at what remained of him.

"All right," she whispered. "No touching. I'll get you more soup. I'll make you strong again. And when you're ready, you can talk. You can tell us what happened."

Tomiko, who stood farther back, said, "I'll get the soup." She hurried into the kitchen.

Marco said, "I'll go get you another blanket, buddy, all right?" He made to walk upstairs.

And for the first time since coming home, Steve spoke.

"Wait!" He began trembling. "Wait. Don't! They'll come back. Stay. Guns! Stay with guns. Stay. Stay. They'll come back . . . They'll hurt us . . ."

Addy embraced him. Steve whimpered again, cowering at her touch, but she refused to release him. She squeezed him in her arms, rocking him until he calmed. Finally Steve's eyes closed, and he sank into sleep. Addy gently laid him across the couch.

She retreated to the back of the living room with Marco. Both still wore pistols on their hips.

"How did this happen to him in only two days?" Addy whispered. "How did he become so thin, so . . . broken? His hair is white. How can a man lose half his weight in just two days?"

"Because it wasn't just two days," Marco said softly. "Not for him. Time dilation."

Addy spoke in a whisper, not wanting to wake Steve. "What's that?"

"Remember when I flew to the Cat's Eye Nebula to fetch the Ghost Fleet?"

Addy nodded. "Of course. I was fighting the marauders here on Earth that entire year."

"Only it wasn't a year for me," Marco said. "It was just six months for me. Time is relative. It flows at different rates depending on where you are in the galaxy. Your velocity and gravity can change how time flows for you. More than two days

204

passed for Steve. For him, it's been weeks, months, maybe even years. It's the only explanation."

Addy's eyes widened. "But how? Where was he? What was changing time for him?"

Marco's eyes were dark. "I don't know. But we saw a flash of light the day he vanished. And another light over the forest when he returned. When *they* returned him." He scowled. "The grays."

Addy shuddered. "Marco, a few days before he vanished, I saw one. A gray. It was between the trees just outside our house. I thought it was a dream. I was half asleep when I saw him. But he was real, wasn't he? All those stories on the news, the photograph you took . . . They're real. And they're here."

Marco nodded, and his fists clenched. "Yes." He gave her a look, his eyes still hard, but she saw the ghosts too. "So much for normal problems."

Addy looked outside the window. She could see the copse of trees from here, the place where she had seen the creature. In daylight, the place seemed innocent enough. But at night, what creatures lurked there?

"At least the goddamn space bugs came out in the open," Addy said. "I prefer a straight fight to these sneaky fucks."

"Me too," Marco said. "We'll implement a guard shift in the house. Tomiko can take some shifts too. We'll all sleep in the same bedroom for now, a guard at the door. Steve won't guard until he's recovered, of course."

Addy nodded. "All right. And we still got those laser pointers, right? The ones from the house construction? We can set up an alarm system, the way Ben-Ari taught us. If any of those sneaky gray fucks creep up, we'll catch 'em." She growled. "They'll regret ever fucking with Addison Elizabeth Linden."

Steve mostly slept for the next twenty-four hours. Sometimes Addy woke him, forced him to drink some soup, and then he slept again. When finally he rose from bed, he ate a proper meal, and some color returned to his cheeks. When Addy helped him into his old jeans and shirt, they hung loosely across his frame, but he began to look a little like the old Steve.

"Steve, I want to take you to a doctor," Addy said. "On the island next door. I want him to look at that scar on your chest, and—"

"No!" Steve blanched. "No doctor. No examination. Please. Please . . ."

Before he could crumble into a trembling, weeping heap again, Addy nodded. "All right. All right! No doctor. I promise."

Seeing him like this, her heart broke. She had been through a lot with Steve. They had fought the marauders together, had seen death and despair, but he had faced it all with a brave heart, a raised chin, squared shoulders.

What had those grays done to him?

Rage flared inside her. Addy wanted to race into the forest right now, to find the grays who had abducted him, to torture them, to break every bone in their skinny gray bodies. And if she could not find them here, she would buy a starship. She would fly into space. She would hunt them all down.

She forced a shaky breath.

But first I need information, she thought. *I need to know where they come from. Otherwise I'll be hunting ghosts.*

"Steve," she said, voice gentle, and touched his hand. "What happened to you? Can you tell me who did this, where they are?"

He cradled his mug of steaming coffee between his hands. "I don't remember."

Addy felt like somebody was pinching her heart. She sat beside him. She placed a hand on his knee.

"Steve. You can tell me. You can talk to me." She touched his cheek, turning his head toward her. He looked so haggard, his cheekbones prominent, his eyes sunken. Tears filled Addy's eyes. "Let me help you. Tell me."

He was quiet for long moments. Shadows passed over his eyes. He closed those eyes, wincing, then looked at her again. He shook his head. "I don't remember. I just . . . Shadows. Fog. Like a dream that's fading. I was in the yard. Working on the cabinet. And then . . ." He cringed, and pain twisted his face. "Then I was in the forest. Lost. How many years has it been?"

Addy glanced at Marco, then back at Steve. "Baby." She caressed his hair. "You've only been gone for two days."

His eyes widened. "Two days! But . . . I was in the fog for so long. Lost. I saw stars . . . I saw shadows . . ." He let out a shaky breath. "I thought it was years. I thought it was years . . ."

And he was shaking, and tears filled his eyes, and Addy held him until he calmed.

"All right." She kissed his cheek. "Enough questions for today. Let's watch some *Mud Wrestling Championships*. You like those, right?"

She switched on the television. Scantily clad girls wrestled in mud, giggling. Steve, who normally cheered them on, sat silent and still, watching them blankly.

That night they all slept in the same bedroom, taking guard shifts outside. Even Tomiko took a shift; Marco had spent the afternoon teaching her how to fire a gun. Throughout the night, Steve suffered from nightmares. Several times, he woke up screaming. Nobody got much sleep.

"It hurts," Steve whimpered in his sleep. "Please. Don't cut me again. Please. No more. Not the knife. No!"

Addy knew something of PTSD; she had seen Marco suffer through it in Haven. But she had never seen anything like this. When she wasn't guarding the door, she lay by Steve, soothing him.

It took a week to convince him to see a doctor.

They took a boat to a larger island and spent the day in waiting rooms. Doctors poked him. Prodded him. Took X-rays.

"He's underweight, seems to lack vitamin D, and suffering from hypertension," a doctor finally told Addy. "But otherwise, there's nothing wrong with him. He just needs to gain a few pounds and spend time in the sun."

"But what about the scars!" Addy said. "The scars on his chest and stomach. Those are surgery scars."

The doctor nodded. "That's the strange thing. Nothing inside him seems out of the ordinary. If anyone performed surgery on him, they restored everything perfectly. I see no signs of trauma on the inside."

For the first time that day, Steve spoke.

"They took out my organs," he said.

They all turned to stare at him. Addy. Marco and Tomiko. The doctor.

Steve stared back, face oddly blank, voice flat.

"I don't know how I remember," Steve said. "I remember nothing else. But I remember that now. They took everything out of me. My heart. My lungs. My stomach. Then they put them back inside and zipped me up."

The doctor pulled Addy into the corridor.

"I'd like to refer you to a top psychiatrist," the doctor said. "Somebody who can treat his schizophrenia."

"My boyfriend isn't crazy!" Addy said.

The doctor nodded. "Of course not. We don't use that word here. Now, I cannot forcibly commit him if he's not a danger to anyone. But I urge you to get him psychiatric help."

"He's telling the truth!" Addy's eyes stung with tears. "I know it sounds crazy. Taking out organs, stuffing them back in? I know how it sounds. But I believe him, damn it."

But did she? As they sailed back home, she kept glancing at Steve, uncertain. He stared ahead at the water, eyes blank.

For the next few weeks, Steve spent his days outside in the yard, building cabinet after cabinet. He sold only one, but he kept building them. When Addy approached him, seeking to joke around, he just nodded curtly. He never smiled. He shaved his head, which made him look even more dour. He began to sleep on the couch downstairs, and when Addy insisted that he needed to be behind the guarded door, he would get mad. One time he tossed a glass at the wall. Another time he smashed a cabinet in his rage. They could no longer watch television; news reports of gray sightings would toss him into a terror.

It's them that did this to him, Addy knew. *Those sneaky gray fucks.* She wanted to fight them, but how could she fight an enemy that lurked in shadows? She didn't know their homeworld, didn't know their species, and when she asked Steve for details of his abduction, he would become mad again, would insist he didn't remember, and stalk off.

Addy felt helpless.

She wanted to turn to Marco for help, but he spent so much time fighting with Tomiko. The two were always at each other's throats. Addy even considered confiding in Tomiko, but she had begun to suspect that the girl resented her, was jealous of Addy's friendship with Marco—a friendship far stronger than his marriage, it seemed.

Even here on this island, with the people closest to her, Addy felt alone.

CHAPTER THIRTEEN

In her dreams, the message haunted Ben-Ari.

A message from the darkness. From light-years away. A message calling for aid.

Over and over, that gravelly voice spoke, rife with tears, staticky.

I beg you. We need your help. Our children . . . They took them. They took them all. The creatures. The creatures with dark robes and masks. Please, I beg you. Help us. We—

Ben-Ari bolted up in bed, drenched in sweat, the blankets like a trap around her. She shuddered, shoved the blankets off, and lay in the darkness, trying to cool off, to breathe.

The message had come on Christmas. Just after the party, when Marino had come to visit her. The alarms had blared across the ship. An urgent Mayday.

Ben-Ari rose from her bed, shivering, suddenly cold. Barefoot, she padded toward the porthole and gazed outside into the darkness. They were close now—close to the source of the distress call.

The message had not used a wormhole, only simple radio. It was three years old already. Ben-Ari remembered the last time she had intercepted a Mayday. It had been ten years ago that she had flown to Corpus, answering an urgent call for help. It had been on Corpus that she had seen hell.

And back then, I had two hundred battle-hardened, brave soldiers, armed with advanced weaponry, the galaxy's best killers. Today I have scientists.

She lowered her head.

This was not a warship. This was not a crew of killers. And she was heading into danger.

"Am I fool?" she whispered to the stars. "Am I leading us into another hell?"

She inhaled deeply. Creatures with dark robes and masks. Could it be them? The grays?

If so, then I must face them. I must learn who they are. I must face my fears.

A message beeped on her communicator. She jumped, exhaled shakily, and cursed her nervousness. She was the captain of this ship. She could not jump at mere beeps. She read the text message.

"Where are you, Captain? It's five a.m. You backing off on a date?"

Ben-Ari rolled her eyes, some of her fear abating. She typed back.

"Your face has got a date with my fist, Marino."

She deleted the message before sending it. Too chummy. She was still his captain.

But this was good. She needed this. She needed him—Marino. A strong warrior. A man she could train with. Somebody to depend on in a fight.

She remembered how he had visited this very chamber with a bottle of champagne, how he had kissed her. Her cheeks flushed. There would certainly be no more of *that*. That had been a mistake. She cared for his muscles, not any other part of him. She nodded.

She pulled on sweatpants and a tank top, not bothering to shower; she would be sweaty again in moments. She made her way, barefoot, down the dark corridor. Only several people were awake at this hour, and they stood at attention as she walked by, recognizing her despite her lack of uniform.

When she stepped into the gym, she saw Marino there, battling a padded robot. Her security chief had perhaps retired from wrestling, but his body was still strong, beefy with muscles, and sweat glistened on him. He wore a black martial arts uniform and a black belt.

"Captain!" He turned toward her, smiling, and wiped his brow. "Glad you could make it. I look forward to teaching you a few things."

Ben-Ari gave him a small smile. "Thank you, Marino, but I haven't come here as a student. I have years of experience with Krav Maga. Maybe you'll be the one learning from me."

He bowed, hands pressed together. "I'll go easy on you."

He lunged toward her, spinning and swinging a kick. He was twice her size, but Ben-Ari was younger and faster. She ducked, dodging the leg, and tossed a blow. He blocked it. They pulled back, then lunged forward again, fists and kicks flying.

He landed the first blow, hitting her chest.

She fell back, struggling to breathe.

"You all right?" Marino asked. "Was I too harsh? I'm sorry, I—"

She screamed and leaped toward him. He blocked one of her blows. She slammed her fist into his chest, knocking the air out of him.

Marino managed to laugh. He grabbed her and tossed her over his shoulder. She fell down hard onto the rug. He was on her at once. Before she could rise, he had her pinned down, his fist held above her face.

"A good attempt," he said.

She grumbled and wrenched herself free. He helped her up.

"How did you do that?" she said. "I was moving so fast."

He nodded. "You were. But I predicted your move. I began my defense before you even began your assault. The great fighter is always thinking two moves a—" He blocked her fist, then grinned. "Now now, sneaky!"

They sparred again.

He blocked her blows again, then knocked her down.

She yowled, leaped up, and attacked wildly. He swept out her leg. She fell onto the mat with a thud.

Again and again, he thwarted her. Soon she was aching. His own attacks were not powerful, not enough to break bones, but they would leave bruises.

"You're good!" he said, blocking a kick. "You almost got my kidney."

"You're better," she grumbled. "Damn it! I thought that . . ."

"That because I'm an athlete, just a showman, I don't know what I'm doing?" When she attacked again, Marino tossed her over his back, slamming her down hard. "I assure you, I know how to fight."

She lay on the ground, winded, aching. She shoved herself up.

That does it, she thought. A sneer found her lips. She would not let this cocky wrestler strut around the *Lodestar,* thinking himself superior to her. She launched a wild attack, lashing fists and kicks, exerting all her energy. She would end this now. She would win. She—

She screamed as he grabbed her arm.

He twisted the limb behind her back.

He pulled her against him, and she yowled, her arm close to dislocating.

"This," he said, "is the Bear Trap grip."

She couldn't move. If she just shifted a centimeter, her arm would shatter. She could barely speak. "It's . . . a good one."

He loosened his grip—just a bit. Not enough for her to free herself. Just enough to release some of the agony. His body was still pressed against her, his strong hand gripping her wrist, twisting her arm behind her back.

"Do you know why it's called the Bear Trap?" he said, still not releasing her.

She tried to free herself, nearly passed out from the pain. "Enlighten me."

"The story tells of a hungry bear who stepped into a trap. It closed around his leg. The hunters would soon arrive. The only way the bear could escape was by chewing off his own leg. The only way to escape this grip, Captain, is to shatter your own arm. A sacrifice few are willing to make."

Marino released her, and she stumbled away, breathing raggedly and rubbing her aching arm. She turned back toward him. He stood still, giving her a small smile.

"Teach me this grip," she said.

His smile widened. "Not today. We must save something for another session. And the workday starts soon."

She took a step toward the showers, then froze and winced. Marino noticed. He moved toward her, placed his hands on her arm, and began to massage.

"Let go of me," she said.

"This'll help."

He kept rubbing her muscles—and he was right. It was helping. She closed her eyes, and his hands moved to her shoulders, then rubbed her back. She did not resist him. His hands were like magic, removing the kinks from her muscles, relieving the sting of the blows he had dealt her only moments ago.

Yet as Marino rubbed her body, Ben-Ari didn't like the little smirk in his eyes. He was too familiar. And she kept remembering last night, how he had kissed her. And she hated that she liked this memory. That she wanted him to kiss her again.

And why not? she thought. This was not the military. There were no laws prohibiting this. Did Earth truly expect her to go celibate? Marino desired her; she knew that. And what if she desired him too? Was that truly so wrong? He could perhaps alleviate the unbearable loneliness here in space.

I'm thirty years old, and I've never had a serious relationship, she thought. *I'm on the fast train to spinsterhood. Maybe it's time to jump off—and to let Marino catch me.*

"Better?" he finally said, removing his hands.

She nodded. "Surprisingly, yes."

He winked, then stepped into the shower.

That day on the bridge, Ben-Ari caught herself sometimes glancing his way. Marino stood at the security station, handsome in his uniform, monitoring the ship's readiness. She hated that he did not leave her mind. That when the professor was teaching her alien genetics that night, she kept thinking of Marino. Foolishness. Damn foolishness!

That night, as she knocked on his chamber door, she kept cursing herself. Marino smiled, unsurprised, as if he had been waiting for her. Ben-Ari cursed herself again, and she wanted to flee, but she stepped into his quarters.

Foolishness, foolishness! she thought as she lay in Marino's bed, as he made love to her, as his hands worked a new magic. She felt silly. Felt stupid. Yet that night, as she slept in Marino's arms, no more nightmares rose. No more grays haunted her dreams. For the first night in a long time, she felt safe.

CHAPTER FOURTEEN

He sat alone in his office.

He sat staring at *Under the Stairs.*

He had been staring at the manuscript for an hour, making no progress. Again his mind was storming. Tomiko had wept that morning, had shouted, had broken down, devastated that he had lit her favorite scented candle during a power outage, not knowing she was saving it for Christmas. Steve, who used to be good for a beer and chat, had been spending all his time outside, sawing, hammering, building more and more cabinets, speaking to nobody.

Marco had become afraid of approaching either one. Tomiko—for her volatility, liable to kiss him and smile one day, to explode the next, oscillating between angel and demon. Steve—for his dead eyes, his sunken cheeks, the hollow man he had become since his abduction.

I'm afraid to even leave my office, he thought. *Afraid to see them in the hallway.*

Finally he opened his door and peeked outside. The coast was clear. He crept down the hallway, a thief in his own house.

He made his way downstairs, step by careful step. The living room was empty too. He proceeded. He would just go to the kitchen, grab a beer—no, not a beer, he couldn't drink anymore. He'd grab a Coke, get a boost, go back to work. He tiptoed across the living room.

Walking on eggshells, he thought.

He was nearly at the kitchen when he noticed that Addy was sitting on the couch. He nearly jumped.

"Addy?"

She looked at him. She said nothing.

Marco frowned. "Addy, I didn't see you there. Normally when you're around, the TV, radio, and computer are all blaring, and you're singing, dancing, and swinging around your hockey stick and katana, one in each hand. Why so quiet? Who died?"

A tear streamed down her cheek. Still she was silent.

"Addy!" He hurried to her side. He sat beside her on the couch. "What's wrong?"

"What's wrong?" she whispered. "Everything."

"Everything is not wrong."

Addy stared out the window. Her eyes were blank. "He's different. Steve. He just works on his cabinets all day. And he screams in his sleep. I try to help him. He can't remember. He can't remember anything. I'm scared, Marco. I'm scared he'll never come back."

He looked out the window too. Steve stood outside across the yard, working on his cabinets, eyes emotionless.

Marco looked back at Addy.

"*I* came back," he said softly.

She looked at him, eyes damp. "You were gone?"

He nodded. "In Haven. For two years."

"I remember," Addy whispered, and she leaned against him.

"Steve will come back too," Marco said. "We'll give him time, and help, and love, and he'll come back."

Addy sniffed. "Hey, you know what, Poet?"

"What?"

"You're right. It's too quiet here. I need the TV on." She switched it on, and her eyes widened. She grabbed Marco's arm. "Poet, Poet!" She leaped up. "*Space Galaxy V* is starting!"

"God, Addy, you're breaking my bone." He wrenched her fingers off.

"You can't go!" She tightened her grip. "No going back to work for you. This is *Space Galaxy V*, officially the *worst* film in the *entire* franchise. And you're going to stay for the full two hours and riff it with me."

He grimaced, her hand like a vise. "Can I at least go pee first?"

"No! You'll miss the part where Captain Carter fights the lizard man! Look at that rubber suit. Now that's a prop right there!"

Marco squinted. "Scaly, big-nosed, breathes fire . . . kinda looks like you."

"Your nose will be smeared across my fist if you don't watch it." Addy gripped him tighter. "Ooh, ooh, look! Captain Carter's girlfriend, the beautiful blue alien Nala. You can see her boobs in the next scene!"

"I'll stay for that," Marco said.

She finally released him during the commercials, and he grabbed them drinks and popcorn. They sat, watching the movie. They laughed when they glimpsed the zippers on the rubber alien suits. They shed a tear when the noble Commander Mork died, sacrificing his life to save the crew. They hooted in excitement when Captain Carter blasted away his arch nemesis, the nefarious King Kapoor, in a daring space battle. When flying saucers appeared on the screen, held up by wires, Marco and Addy fell silent.

"I don't like this scene," Addy said.

"Me neither," Marco said, relieved when it was over.

Addy moved closer to him on the couch, and when a scary alien appeared on the television, she moved even closer, and their bodies touched. Instinctively, they grabbed each other's hands.

He looked at her. She turned to look at him. They stared into each other's eyes, silent, their faces only centimeters apart. They were still holding hands, and their bodies were touching. For a long moment, they just looked into each other's eyes.

Addy leaned a little closer. Marco's pulse increased. Her face was so close he could feel her breath. Their lips almost touched.

"Poet," she whispered.

"Addy," he whispered back.

"There's popcorn on your tooth." She pointed. "Right there! On the front one." She tried to grab it.

Marco pushed her hand away. "Don't poke your fingers into my mouth."

222

"But it's weirding me out!"

"So stop looking at my teeth!"

Addy rolled her eyes. "I can't help it. It's a popcorn the size of my fist!"

He cleaned it off his tooth and placed the offending kernel in a napkin.

"Don't throw that out!" Addy said. "That's good popcorn!" She made to grab it.

"Don't you eat my tooth popcorn!" he said. "That's disgusting."

"But I'm hungry!"

"There's more popcorn in the bowl!"

Addy pouted. "Only little ones."

They kept watching. Laughing. Bantering. And this was good. This was relief. This was happiness.

This is who we are, he thought. *The real us. Marco. Addy. Like we used to be. Like we were before the wars. This is the Addy that I love. This is the me that I love. This is how I want to be every day. Here with her.*

When he finally went back upstairs, leaving Addy, he felt empty. He felt deflated. He felt cold. He missed Addy already.

When he approached Tomiko that night, she wouldn't speak to him. She turned away. When he lay at her side, she turned her back to him.

"Tomiko?" he said, placing a hand on her hip.

She wriggled away from him. "Don't touch me. Go to Addy. It's her you love."

"I love *you*," Marco said.

223

"You're a liar!" Tomiko's voice shook. "You're a goddamn liar." She rolled toward him, tears in her eyes. "Don't you know how you hurt me? I know you slept with Addy. With Lailani. With a million other girls. I know you love them. And who am I? Nobody to you. You don't laugh with me like you do with Addy. You don't fly to Japan for me like you do for Lailani."

"Tomiko!" Marco tried to embrace her, but she moved away. "You're the one I chose. I'm here with *you*. I married *you*. I share my bed with *you*."

"*Your* bed?" Tomiko said. "Sleep in it alone!"

She stormed out of the room.

"*Our* bed," he muttered. "Fuck. *Our* bed."

Marco remained alone in that bed, wishing he were back downstairs. With Addy. Watching a cheesy movie and fighting over popcorn. The bed was cold and empty, and Steve was still hammering outside. Marco tossed and turned all night. The sounds of Steve sawing and hammering continued until dawn.

When the sun rose, Tomiko made him blueberry pancakes, his favorite. She smiled. She laughed with him. She walked with him along the beach.

My demon and angel, he thought, holding Tomiko's hand, and she was beautiful in the morning, a spirit of the sea. *Maybe she's like me, like my life, woven of darkness and light. May we know only light. May we banish the demon and let only the angel remain.*

* * * * *

A week later, Tomiko came into Marco's office, holding a positive pregnancy test.

And this time she was smiling. This time she hugged him.

"We'll make this right, Marco," she said. "We're going to have a baby."

Marco kissed her. "We're going to be happy."

Be happy. Fix this. Heal. Build.

Outside in the yard, Steve was still building his cabinets, cabinet after cabinet. Here inside the house, Marco was determined to build too. To build bridges between him and Tomiko. To build a family. To build a good life, one free from trauma and pain and tears and blood. To finally, after ten years in hell, build a little paradise.

They spoke little of the baby at first, perhaps still nervous after the miscarriage several months ago. But as time went by, as Tomiko's belly began to swell, their optimism swelled with it. The local doctor detected a heartbeat, the most amazing sound Marco had ever heard. He moved his office into the dining room, leaving the room upstairs to become a nursery, and Steve set aside cabinets for a day to build them a crib.

"We're going to have a baby!" Marco said every day, scarcely believing it.

It seemed surreal, yet as time went by, it became their reality. And soon they reached that magical week twelve, the second trimester. That milestone that meant the danger was past, that it was time to tell the world, that things were official. That this baby was coming.

"We're going to have a baby," Tomiko said to him, smiling as they placed the crib in the nursery.

The doctors never could explain why she started bleeding in the thirteenth week. The nurses said these things just sometimes happened. The ambulance ride was silent, solemn. The hospital room was deathly quiet. The monitor showed no heartbeat. A flat sound, an air raid siren after the danger had passed. All clear. All clear.

Quiet surgery. A quiet goodbye.

"A miscarriage," the radiologist called it.

"Stillborn," a nurse said.

The obstetrician looked respectfully mournful. He stepped outside to give them time.

Marco and Tomiko remained in the hospital room, silent.

Thirteen weeks of nerves and smiles and fear and joy. They ended here—a silent bed, a silent room. All clear.

They returned home. Their child remained behind.

CHAPTER FIFTEEN

"We can try again," Marco said, holding his wife's hands. But she only gave him a blank stare.

She went to sleep in the spare bedroom. Marco remained alone in their bed. Alone with his grief. Alone with his thoughts—racing, charging, storming through his mind, never ceasing, never dimming. A thousand chattering, singing, weeping, screaming voices in his mind.

Echoing.

Miscarriage, a doctor said.

Stillborn, said a nurse.

Thirteen weeks and a crib that moved into the shed. And a nursery that turned into a spare bedroom. Then it became Tomiko's room.

Silent breakfasts.

Steve—working in the yard, building cabinet after cabinet, a hundred cabinets piling up outside, rotting in the rain.

Addy—always patrolling the house, armed with rifles and knives, muttering of grays, vowing to fight a war she could not see.

Tomiko—locked in her room all day, staring at the wall, holding her belly, silent. Letting nobody in.

In here, between them, Marco—lost. More lonely than he had ever felt.

"Walk with me along the beach," Marco said to his wife. "We'll find some new seashells for our collection."

But Tomiko just went into her room and closed the door.

"Addy, you want to go into town?" Marco said. But she wanted to patrol the hills again, rifle in hand, hunting grays.

Marco languished in his office. He paced. He typed. He tore up paper. He sent off *Under the Stairs* to his publisher, and it sold, and money came pouring in—more money than Marco had ever seen, enough money to keep them fed for the next couple of years. But he found no joy, and if he had any fame, it was far beyond the sea, and if he had any readers, they were beyond the vast oceans of his solitude.

It was a large house, but it was cold, and it was a beautiful island, but he was trapped.

My child is dead.

"Is it a boy or a girl?" he had asked the doctor, but they hadn't known. And Marco never saw the child. Too small. Just big enough to fit in the palm. He had wanted to see it. They had not let him.

"We can try again."

And Tomiko closed her door and locked it, and Marco returned to his office. He stayed up all night, trying to write, finding no words.

He knocked on her door.

"Tomiko, would you like to walk on the beach today?"

She opened the door. She looked at him. She shook her head and withdrew into her grief.

Marco returned to his office. And he began to write. It was a sequel to *Under the Stairs*, a book he titled *Dangers Untold*. This novel was about Anabel Lee's little brother, a boy called Marillion—the same boy who had gone missing in the first book. Grown up now, Marillion had become a goblin-being, a prince of monsters, and had forgotten his humanity. He drank from the magical fountain, restoring his youth and fostering his madness. He danced in halls with creatures of stone, wood, and fire. He kidnapped children who lived in the house above the stairs, and he took a human girl to be his bride, and he named her the Goblin Bride, for he infected her with his spell. He became a beast, a cruel jester-king of dark magic, bedecked in finery, his hair grown wild, his jewels sparkling with vicious light.

The Goblin Bride feared her husband, but she loved him too, for she still saw the humanity within the prince. She began to suspect that he had once been a boy, once kidnapped from the house above the stairs, once lost and confused and very much like her. If only she could tame him! If only she could restore his memory, restore his humanity! Yet the monstrous prince was so old already, his youth but a trick of the fountain, and his mind was muddled by so much dark wonder and dangerous magic.

One day, the Goblin Bride discovered a cruel treasure under his castle. In the dungeon, Marillion kept babies imprisoned in glass cages, captives he had snatched from the world above the stairs. The Goblin Bride freed them, and the babies became birds of many colors that flew away. Upon discovering her treachery, Marillion was incensed, and he locked the Goblin Bride in a golden cage atop his tower. There she became a bird herself, forever beautiful, forever trapped. As time went by, Marillion realized that he too had become a gaudy bird, and that he wore a cloak of feathers, and that his castle had become like a golden cage to him. And he remembered that he too had once been human.

Remorseful, he freed his bride from her cage, only to discover that her transformation was complete, that she could not become human again. He placed the golden bird, once his precious Goblin Bride, in the tree that had once been Anabel Lee, his beloved sister. There they lived in symbiosis—sister and bride, tree and bird—and Marillion sat every day in his garden and wept for his loss.

Marco wrote this story for weeks.

And weeks became months.

And draft after draft piled up on his desk.

And *Dangers Untold*, the sequel to *Under the Stairs*, became his longest, most ambitious work, a single novel that was the length of the entire *Dragons of Yesteryear* trilogy.

"Marco," Tomiko said, coming into his office one day, "do you want to go back to Crete? Just for a few days? We can go back to that place where we had the fried calamari."

"Can't," he said, staring at his work. "Not until *Dangers Untold* is done."

"I thought it's done already," Tomiko said, standing at the doorway.

"The first draft is done." He glanced up at her, then back at his notebook. "The first draft is the easy part."

She took a step closer. "So when will it be done?"

"When it's done!" Marco said. "I don't know, all right? The creative process is unpredictable, but I can't just go off on vacation while I'm writing. I'm too caught up in it. Once I'm done, we'll go. Okay? Not to Crete. Somewhere new. Somewhere . . ."

Somewhere without aliens, he thought.

A week later, Tomiko approached him again.

"Marco, do you want to visit Malta this weekend?" she said. "Just for a night or two."

"Tomiko, you know that we can't," Marco said. "I'm not done writing, and Malta is expensive."

She spoke in a small voice. "I thought you're making good money now."

"I am," he said. And he was. The *Dragons of Yesteryear* and *Under the Stairs* were still selling, and royalty checks were still coming in every month. They were making enough to keep the lights on, keep food on the table, even leave some money left over to squirrel away every month.

"So . . ." Tomiko looked at her toes. "So why can't we go?"

Marco slammed his notebook shut. He turned around to look at her. "Tomiko, I was poor all my life. On Haven, I was so poor I could barely eat. Have you ever been so poor you were worried you'd starve? I was. For two years, Tomiko. For two years I was so poor I could barely afford food. Sometimes I ate nothing but plain white rice for days on end. I lived in an apartment the size of this office, with pimps and prostitutes downstairs, with junkies going through my trash bin. And if I never sell another book again? If I can't finish this one or write another? I refuse to be poor again, all right? So we have to save our money. And I have to work hard to make more money."

She dared meet his gaze. "But—"

"No buts!" Marco said. "Look, if everyone else had jobs, fine. But Steve can't sell a cabinet to save his life. And Addy just roams around the hills all day, claiming to be hunting grays. And you—"

"I don't have a job because we live on a fucking island!" Tomiko said, eyes flooding with tears. "You want me to work? Move back to Osaka with me!"

Marco groaned. "We've been over this a million times. My life is here. My house is here. This is the house I dreamed of for years, Tomiko. When I was languishing in Haven. When I sailed in a starship across the galaxy and back. What kept me going was the dream of owning a house by the beach. And you want us to move into some cramped city, to rent an apartment again, to live like that? Like I did on Haven?"

"So that I can work!" Tomiko said. "So that I can contribute too! What can I do on an island? There are no jobs here."

"God! I told you!" Marco stepped closer to her. "You don't have to work. I'll support you. But you need to support me too. You need to give me space to write, to—"

"You write seven days a week!" Tomiko said. "From early morning to past midnight! I said we can go to Crete, to Malta, to—"

"All places that cost money!" Marco said.

"Don't you raise your voice!" she said. "I'm trying to fix this. I'm trying to be happy. To be your wife."

"You're the one who retreated into the spare bedroom after . . . after what happened. You're the one who shut me out. Who slept in a separate bed. Who wouldn't talk or—"

"Because I was mourning!" Tomiko shouted, weeping now. "Because my baby died!"

"It was my baby too!" Marco roared—so loudly that Tomiko jumped. She covered her eyes and fled the room.

Marco began to chase her, then stopped. Fine. Let her run! She always ran from him. She never wanted to work out anything. And he had responsibilities. The others didn't understand. He had to feed them all. Steve and Addy ate like pigs, and he refused to move to Osaka with Tomiko, and it was all up to him. His burden! If he couldn't finish this book, they'd all starve. And what use was Crete or Malta then? They didn't understand. None of them did! They didn't understand he was doing this *for them.*

"Good, run then!" Marco shouted at the empty hallway. "That's all you do!"

He slammed his door shut.

He returned to his work.

He began to take his meals in his office. He brought in a spare bed and slept there. He finished *Dangers Untold* and began working on *The Last Birds of Summer,* the third book in the series. It was about the escaped birds, how they were lost in an endless sky, finding no place to land, growing wearier and wearier, dreaming of finding a cliff or tree, a rest for weary wings. They had to keep flying. They *had* to. All the other creatures of the sky tried to slow them down, to ride on them, to drag them into the darkness below.

He was my kid too.

His eyes burned.

He kept writing.

When he passed by Tomiko in the corridor, he did not meet her eyes. Days went by without them speaking, and he remained in his room, trapped in this cell, refusing to leave until he completed the series, and it grew longer, grew from three books to four, but there were still stories to tell. There was still food to buy. Still money to earn. Still the three of them downstairs, eating, always eating, and he had to feed them, and he had to delve into his story until it was completed. And it consumed him, a cancer inside, and he felt like he too had become a tree or perhaps a caged bird.

I won't go back to Haven, he thought.

I won't work at a call center again, he swore. *Call center. Cell center. Prison cell. Cancer cell. I won't be sick again. I won't be poor again. I won't die. I won't live in tunnels. I won't see others die again.*

He was my baby too.

He died. He died.

No more will die.

I will save them. I will save them all. I won't let them starve.

"Not now!" Marco said when Addy knocked on the door, inviting him downstairs to dinner. "I have to finish this chapter. I'll eat tomorrow."

She left food outside his door.

"No. I can't. Go without me."

So they went to the beach without him. Good. Let them have fun. Let them swim and relax. Without him. Because he had to support them. He had to feed them. They always had fun while he languished here in his prison cell. A caged bird. Another page. Another royalty check. They ate, ate, ate. They were always eating. But he would save them. He wouldn't let them starve. He wouldn't let them be poor. He would suffer for them.

He was my baby too.

He died. He died.

I won't let them die too.

Outside the window, he saw them. Addy, Steve, Tomiko. On the beach. Having fun. Thanks to him. Thanks to his work, his burden. He would save them. He promised. Nobody else would starve. Nobody else would die. It was a miscarriage or stillborn; he didn't know. It didn't matter. What mattered was writing this scene. Was earning another meal. For them. It was for them! Why couldn't they understand? Why couldn't they give him space?

He shut the blinds on the window. He didn't want to see them, to hear them. They couldn't understand the chains that bound him here. The responsibilities that he had. To them, this was a dream—a house on a beach, sunlight, beauty, peace. *He* had to suffer to make this possible. He had to bleed onto the page so they could swim and laugh. And they wouldn't leave him alone. And he had to keep flying. There was no place to land for the last birds of summer.

"I'm not hungry!"

"Poet, damn it, you—"

"Go away, Addy!" *He was my baby too.*

"Fine!" Addy slammed his food onto the floor, shattering the plate. "Eat like a dog."

"I already work like a dog to keep you fed!" Marco shouted.

Addy flipped him off and marched downstairs.

"Fucking asshole," she muttered under her breath.

Marco slammed the door shut. He was trapped in a cage. A bird. A beautiful bird of many colors, dying. A prince trapped in a tower.

My prince died.

He wrote another page. He paced the room. He ate off the floor. He vanished back into a world under the stairs, a world of feathered princes, of wandering goblins in tunnels glittering with gems, of castles in the hearts of shifting labyrinths, of strange creatures in floating forests, of dangers untold and impossible dreams.

Finally one night, after nine months in his office, he stepped downstairs.

He had finished *Phantasmagoria*, his series of dark beauty. His story of Anabel Lee and Marillion and the lost birds of stolen summer.

He was done.

His baby had died. He had created this life of ink.

All his nightmares, his dreams, his terrors, his visions, nine months of madness—all were on the page, the ink drying.

It was two in the morning. He stepped into the living room like a man freed from prison, like a man after an alien abduction, returned to the world from the strange beyond.

And he saw Tomiko sitting alone in the kitchen, staring out the window, a tear on her cheek.

"Tomiko?" he said gently. He stepped toward her. He sat at her side. "Tomiko, I'm done. The series is done. I know I've been distant lately. I know I haven't been paying you attention. But that'll change now." He took a deep breath. "It's all out of me now. It's all on the page. Everything that happened—it's there. A fresh start now. You and me. Are you willing to start over? To make this work?"

She kept staring out the window. Red rimmed her eyes. Another tear flowed.

"We were always fools," she whispered.

He nodded. "Yes. But we can still make this work. We can try to have a baby again."

Tomiko turned to look at him, eyes damp. "Marco, I'm leaving you. My bags are packed already. I'm leaving in a few hours. At dawn."

Sirens.

Sirens blared inside him.

Planets collapsed.

"You don't have to do this." He heard his voice as from a distance. "We can still fix things."

She pulled off her wedding ring. She placed it on the table between them.

"Marco," she whispered, "I met somebody else. A few weeks ago. He's picking me up in the morning. I'm sorry."

He stared, silent.

The sirens—silent.

He was my baby too.

Knives inside him. Scum claws inside him. Silence. No more waves outside. No more breath in his lungs. Silence. Endings.

He left the kitchen. He stood by his office window. At dawn, he saw the car pick her up. An older man. His hair already graying. They drove off.

Silence.

He sat down on his bed, the bed by his desk where he had spent these past nine months. His glass cage of isolation and inky dreams. He closed his eyes.

He felt no grief. No shock. No relief. He felt numb. He slept.

CHAPTER SIXTEEN

In her vision, one star of the leaping bear constellation—the tip of a claw—had shone brighter than the others, pulsing, beckoning. It was toward this star that Lailani now flew.

Finally! Lailani hopped in her seat, desperate to reach her destination. The *Ryujin* was comfortable enough. It was no larger than a school bus, but it was far roomier than any home Lailani had ever lived in. With HOBBS and Epi around, there was good company, and the board games and movies had offered entertainment. Yet over the past couple of weeks, cabin fever had begun to possess Lailani. She had found herself pacing the cabin, even going for several spacewalks just to clear her mind.

I need shore leave, she thought.

And yet, as she watched the star draw nearer, fear grew in her. What if she couldn't find the hourglass? What if the vision had been a trap, leading her into the grays' claws? Even if she did find the hourglass, she dreaded traveling back in time, dreaded facing that day again—seeing her younger self, eighteen years old and possessed, murdering her friend. Reliving that day in memory for the past decade had been bad enough. And to see it again in the flesh?

Epimetheus sensed her unease and nuzzled her. Lailani took a deep breath, steeling herself.

"This is a big system," she said. "My scanners are detecting seventeen planets around this star. Sixteen are gas giants. The last one . . ." She frowned, leaning closer to her monitor. "Humans have spotted and logged it already from a distance. It has an entry in Wikipedia Galactica." She typed on her tablet, bringing up the entry. "The planet is called Mahatek, but no human has ever set foot here, nor flown nearby. The wiki just calls it a small, Earthlike world, still unexplored. Maybe we'll expand the entry." She gave a shaky grin. "That's us, boys! Explorers."

They drew closer to Mahatek. It was a green world coated with swirls of white clouds. There were no oceans, but many rivers spread across its surface, connecting countless lakes. She detected no space stations, no starships, no satellites. There was life down there—her scanners picked up the right chemicals for it, and all that green looked like plants—but if there was intelligent life, it was not spacefaring.

She flew closer, and more details revealed themselves. Her suspicions had been correct; the green was a thick cover of trees. The rainforest coated most of the planet. Only the poles were devoid of plants. The land was rugged, full of mountains, craters, and deep valleys, suggesting a tumultuous geological era in the distant past.

She saw no cities. No farms. No sign of civilization.

Doubt filled her. Had her vision truly been a message from a friendly, mysterious force? Or just a dream? It had felt so real . . .

"It's a big planet, boys," Lailani said. "Almost as big as Earth. How do we find the hourglass here?"

Epimetheus placed his paws on the front viewport, gazed down at the planet, and sniffed. Lailani patted him.

"Yes, Epi, I bet you can sniff it out. But let's find you the best starting point."

The Doberman wagged his tail.

"Mistress," HOBBS said. "If this hourglass can bend time, it is obviously an advanced piece of technology. Perhaps it sends out an electronic signal. I suggest we orbit the planet and scan for a beacon."

"Think we can pick up any signals through the dense foliage?" Lailani said. "Even if the hourglass has some kind of wireless connection, would it really have that large a range?"

"Perhaps not," HOBBS said, "yet whoever built the hourglass might have built other technological devices. Perhaps a radio used to communicate with other worlds."

Lailani nodded. "All right. Let's begin to orbit. We'll start with the equator and spread out." She sighed. "This might take a while, boys. We might need to bring out the *Risk* board again. And this time no knocking the pieces over, Epi!"

Inwardly, however, she worried about more than boredom or cabin fever.

The grays were after her. She knew this. The face she had seen still haunted her. The voice still echoed.

You will scream for our goddess . . .

A shudder ran through her.

"Not my circus, not my monkeys," she muttered. "I'm after the hourglass."

Yet it seemed the monkeys had escaped the circus—and they were on her tail.

She scanned the planet for any electromagnetic signal. Nothing. Instead of joining the boys in the lounge, she remained in the cockpit, gazing at the green planet below. It was a beautiful world. Mountains soared, capped with snow. Jungles spread across valleys. Rivers coiled, branched out, and regrouped, forming a blue painting on a green canvas. When she magnified the view, she could even spot birds.

But no signals. No technology. No civilization.

"Whoever found a needle in a haystack had an easy job," she muttered.

Within ninety minutes, she had completed an orbit of the planet—and had found nothing. With one orbit, she had scanned only a thin strip of Mahatek. She adjusted her path, and the *Ryujin* began another orbit of the planet, this time scanning a second strip.

Another ninety minutes passed. Again, she found nothing.

"This is going to take forever," Lailani said when Epi came to visit her in the cockpit. "We have to think more strategically. Where would we find the hourglass? Obviously, somebody had built this hourglass. And that means there will be a settlement here. Where would somebody choose to live on this world?" She chewed her lip. "Not down on the surface. Too dark with all these trees. Too easy for an enemy to sneak up on you." She tapped her chin. "Think back to Earth, Epi. Jungle civilizations. Machu Picchu. They built that sucker on top of a mountain, right? So let's scan mountaintops."

Epimetheus yipped in agreement.

She took over manual control and searched for mountain ranges. Specifically, mountain ranges that would suit potential habitation: easy to defend but not impossible to access, near a source of water, and not so tall that the atmosphere would thin out. After another few orbits of the world, she found several promising candidates.

"Here we go, a few mountains in the Goldilocks zone," Lailani said. "We're gonna have to get closer. Hold on, boys! We're diving in."

She flew downward, plunging into the thick atmosphere, praying that her repairs to the hull held together. Fire raged across them. The ship shook violently. The crack on the windshield widened, and Lailani cringed and dug her fingernails into her seat. In the hold, dolls, electronics, and board games fell off shelves and rattled. Epimetheus mewled and hid under the mattress, and HOBBS fell with a thud.

A scrap of metal—which Lailani had bolted on after the battle—tore off the hull. Another scrap followed. Fire raged, blazing into the ship. Air screamed. A porthole shattered, spraying shards. Lailani screamed. A crack tore open in the hull. HOBBS had to jam himself into the opening, clinging on for dear life, holding the ship together with his metal fingers.

The fire faded.

They flew through clear sky.

Lailani slumped in her seat.

"Holy hell," she muttered. "This ship definitely needs an underwear dispenser."

She saw the mountain range below. Flying this close, more details appeared. As they descended, individual trees came into focus. Clouds swirled around them. Snow shone on mountaintops. Mist hovered in valleys and roiled alongside rivers. They flew low, scanning the landscape. Minutes stretched into hours, and more and more, Lailani felt like this quest was hopeless. Like she was chasing but a dream.

She looked away from the landscape. She looked at the photograph on the dashboard. A photograph from ten years ago. They were all so young. Marco looked serious as always. Addy was grinning and holding up rabbit ears behind his head. Ben-Ari stood at the head of the group. And Lailani herself—head shaved, smallest in the platoon—was making a silly face, cheeks puffed out, eyes crossed, her arm slung around Elvis's shoulder.

"Did I come here for nothing, Elvis?" she whispered. "I tried. I wanted to save you. To redeem myself. I want to go back to that time. To when we were young. To when we were happy."

Her eyes dampened, and she lowered her head. Yes. She had been happy then. Even with the war. Even with the hardships of military life. She had been with friends. She had found purpose. After nearly starving to death in the slums, after surviving a suicide attempt, she had found new life, new joy.

Until she had ripped out Elvis's heart.

"I'm sorry," she whispered, tears flowing down her cheeks. "I would do anything to atone. But it was a dream. Just a dream . . . I can't change the past."

Epimetheus began to bark.

"What is it, Epi?" She looked up. "Epi?"

He was leaning against the viewport, paws on the glass, barking. Lailani's heart thrashed, and she looked outside, expecting grays. Her eyes widened.

No. Not grays.

"Civilization," she whispered. She narrowed her eyes, struggling to bring them into focus. "At least, the ruins of civilization."

Fresh tears budded in her eyes, but now they were tears of hope, of relief. Now her quest seemed just a little less impossible.

She flew lower and circled the mountain. The ruins spread across the tallest mountain, crumbling, overgrown with moss. Back home in the Philippines, Lailani had a frayed photograph of Machu Picchu pinned to her fridge. These alien ruins reminded her of that photograph, but they were far larger, spreading over the mountain. There were walls, homes, temples, pyramids, archways, staircases, granaries—hundreds of structures in various states of disrepair. Tens of thousands of people must have lived here once, but aside from the birds, trees, and moss, Lailani saw no sign of life.

That wasn't necessarily surprising. The galaxy was billions of years old. Most species only existed for a million years or so, many much less. That meant that when you discovered alien civilizations, it was almost always just ruins.

"I just hope the hourglass is in better shape than the rest of this place," she said. Epimetheus yipped in agreement.

A new challenge presented itself. There was nowhere to land. The *Ryujin* was an aging, cheap ship, and it had no hover technology. It needed a runway or at least a swath of open field. There would be no landing on this mountain, not with its cliffs, sharp peaks, and jagged ruins. Lailani spent a while circling the mountain, searching for a place to land. But even at the foothills, the jungle coated the landscape. There would be no landing here either, not unless she found a vat of napalm in the back and burned down the forest. Even their cannons wouldn't clear an area wide enough, and Lailani wasn't prepared to waste ammo on a few alien trees.

She came to fly over a river several kilometers away from the mountain. Some areas of the bank were covered with thick grass, and no trees grew there. She scrunched her lips. If she could slow down over the river, just skim over the water, then veer onto the bank . . .

"Kemi would be able to do it," she said. "So let's go for it."

HOBBS looked at her. "Mistress?"

"We're going down," she said. "Hold on. This'll get bumpy. And potentially wet."

She descended, flew along the river, and lowered herself until she was only a few meters above the water. Birds fled from her advance. Furry animals hooted in the trees. Lailani slowed her flight.

"Nice and easy, nice and easy," she mumbled, gently guiding them lower. "Just . . . like . . . whoa!"

The *Ryujin*'s keel hit the river. Water splashed up, covering the windshield. Fish slapped against them. Lailani cringed and climbed a meter higher. They flew onward, trailing algae. She saw the stretch of clear bank ahead. Just a small area between the trees. She was still too fast. She slowed down some more. Her nose dipped. She cringed as she skimmed water again, pulled upward, was too high. The bank was just ahead! She veered toward it, and her wing dipped, hit the water, and ripped up algae.

"Hold on!" she screamed as she lowered the *Ryujin* onto the riverbank.

They plowed through grass.

They stormed across the riverbank, moving toward the trees. Too fast. Too fast!

She shoved down on the brakes with all her might. They plowed through grass and soil. Their nose was still too high, and she lowered it too quickly, and they hit the dirt and nearly flipped over. She tried to correct for her error, and they spun, digging grooves into the soil, kicking up patches of grass, soil, and shrubs.

They skidded toward the trees, and Lailani grimaced as they slammed into the trunks.

"Still easier than parallel parking." She hopped out from her seat, but she was suddenly struck by dizziness and grabbed her head. "Just . . . need a moment to find my land legs."

They stumbled out from the starship: a woman, a hulking robot twice her height, and a Doberman with a tail that wagged like the wind. Lailani hadn't taken many clothes: just a couple of pairs of shorts, some T-shirts, and sandals. That wouldn't do here, not with all these branches to scratch her and insects to bite her. So she wore the spacesuit she had found on the ship, sans helmet. She had done some amateur tailoring during the journey, and the old white suit—originally far too large—almost fit her now. Thankfully, spacesuits had come a long way over the past two hundred years. They were no longer the bulky, awkward suits Lailani had seen in the history books. Her outfit was light and comfortable enough, and it would protect her from the bugs. She carried her rifle over her back, her knife at her belt, but her true weapon was HOBBS; he was a one-robot army.

The planet was hot. Damn hot. The air was thick with mist and the aromas of living things. Already sweat was gathering inside Lailani's suit, and Epimetheus was panting. Lailani looked around her. The river lay a hundred meters away beyond the grooves they had plowed through the earth. The alien trees grew everywhere else, trunks twisting and knobby, branches heavy with moss and vines. Lailani couldn't even see the mountain from here.

She began to climb a tree, thankful for the many knobs on the bark. It was a long climb, and Lailani was winded by the time she reached the top. Thousands of alien insects fluttered here, beating green wings that looked like leaves, their magenta eyes shining like berries. They seemed to have evolved camouflage to blend into the rainforest canopy. Lailani waved them aside and gazed around. From up here, she could see more of the landscape. The mountain soared in the distance, the ruins upon its crest.

Damn. It was farther than she had thought. She must have misjudged the distance when landing the starship. A valley of mist, at least ten kilometers wide, separated her from the foothills, and it was another couple of kilometers of climbing steep slopes to reach the ruins. Even if she survived this journey, would the hourglass truly be there—or some clues to its location?

Lailani sighed. "It could be worse. The planet would be swarming with alien monsters like Corpus or Abaddon. I could live with these friendly little leaf insects."

That was when she heard the grumbles rise from below.

Across the forest, trees shook.

Shrieks pierced the air.

"I just had to jinx it," Lailani muttered, cringing.

She scurried down the tree. With every branch, the grumbles and shrieks grew louder. Trees shook across the forest. Birds fled. She leaped down onto the forest floor.

"Boys, we're about to meet the locals," she said. "And they sound bloody pissed off."

Epimetheus ran up to her side. HOBBS stared around, the blue lights of his eyes sharpening. He raised his right arm, and the gun unfurled from within.

The sounds grew closer: screeching, rumbling, thumping feet, bending trees. The ground shook. Even the insects fled. Lailani unslung her rifle from across her back, and Epimetheus growled at her side.

"I don't enjoy killing natives," Lailani said. "But whatever comes out of that forest—if it looks hungry, shoot!"

As a child, she had once found a turtle roaming a riverbank in Manila. She had lifted the little creature, placed him in a cardboard box, and tended to him. She had found some colored chalk in a dumpster, had decorated the turtle's box, but dust from the chalk had gotten into the turtle's nose, killing him. For three days, Lailani had kept the dead animal, only throwing it out once it began to reek. She had never forgotten that smell. The smell of dead turtle.

Now, a similar stench blasted out from the forest ahead. The trees parted, and the creatures burst out.

Lailani took a step back, raising her rifle.

Sweet mother of God.

They were massive. They were as large as the HSS *Ryujin*.

"Dinosaurs," she whispered. "Goddamn fucking dinosaurs."

The creatures were bipedal, their talons larger than swords. Their skin was scaly, and feathers grew along their backs and sprouted from their tails, bluish green and yellow, perhaps

251

evolved as camouflage. They roared, jaws large enough to swallow men whole, and their sharp teeth were obviously not meant to chew on plants. Four eyes swiveled on their heads, providing vision in every direction, and spikes thrust out from their sides like urchins.

They were not true dinosaurs, perhaps, but they were just as large and looked even deadlier.

And they came charging toward Lailani.

"Back!" Lailani shouted and fired into the air. "Back, beasts!"

The giant aliens kept charging. Lailani winced.

"Run, boys!" She spun and began racing toward the river. "To the water!"

Lailani, HOBBS, and Epimetheus ran. A dinosaur slammed his foot into the *Ryujin*, tossing the starship into the air. More of the creatures emerged from between the trees. There were several species here, some with long necks, some with stubby bodies, some covered in armored plates, others feathered, some covered with spikes. Each was massive, and each looked hungry for human flesh.

"We'll lose them underwater!" Lailani cried, arms pumping. "Into the river!"

She reached the riverbank, prepared to dive in, then skidded to a halt. Her arms windmilled.

Oh shit.

Scaly heads emerged from the water. Long necks unfurled. Jaws opened, screeching. The creatures looked like something a crocodile crossed with an electric eel would have nightmares about. Each was as large as the dinosaurs.

Lailani skidded back from the riverbank.

The land-beasts came charging toward her.

I hate killing animals, she thought. *But it's us or them.*

She fired her assault rifle in automatic, emptying a magazine into one of the dinosaurs.

The bullets hit its scaly skin, doing no more damage than pebbles tossed at rabid dogs.

The creatures stormed onward.

Great. So they're bulletproof.

"Along the riverbank—run!" Lailani cried.

They ran along the bank. Epimetheus ran at Lailani's heels, barking madly. The creatures were everywhere. They emerged from the trees. They leaped out from the water.

"HOBBS, damn it, fire on them!" Lailani cried.

The robot ran at her side. "Mistress, I am programmed not to harm any native lifeforms on unexplored worlds, and—"

"Fuck your programming, do it now, or I'm switching you off and letting you rust here!"

HOBBS nodded. He fired a missile. A dinosaur leaped toward them, a gargantuan beast coated with red feathers. The alien let out a deafening roar before the missile slammed into its neck.

Scales shattered. Blood showered. The creature fell, slamming into one of its comrades—and blocking the companions' path along the riverbank.

Lailani cursed, skidded to a halt, and turned toward the river. Once more, the long-necked creatures emerged from the water, snapping their teeth. She turned back toward the trees. An alien stormed toward her, large as a tank, covered with thick, spiky hide. Lailani fired, but her bullets did no harm. It took a missile from HOBBS to knock the creature back.

Dinosaurs ran from both sides of the riverbank. Cursing, Lailani ran into the forest. She loaded a third magazine and fired everywhere. The towering, feathered dinosaurs leaped from all directions. They uprooted trees. They kicked up soil. One of the creatures swiped a tail, slamming it into Epimetheus. The Doberman yowled as he flew through the air.

"Epi!" Lailani shouted. She ran toward him. The dog rose to his feet, took a step, wobbled, and fell.

Lailani fired. Again. Again. The creatures swarmed in. HOBBS fired a missile, slaying one of the beasts. But another dinosaur grabbed the robot between its jaws, lifted HOBBS overhead, and tossed him down. Bolts and gears spilled out, and HOBBS groaned. His arm detached yet again.

Lailani retreated until her back hit a tree. The dinosaurs loomed above her, drooling, scratching the earth. They knew they had won the battle. They knew it was time to feed.

"I'll protect you, Epi," Lailani whispered, and the dog growled at her side.

One of the dinosaurs leaned in, roaring, strings of saliva dangling like guitar strings between its teeth. It prepared to swallow Lailani, but another dinosaur knocked it back, claiming the meal for itself. A third dinosaur joined the fray. Soon the beasts were squabbling over who'd get to eat Lailani. Behind them, HOBBS tried to rise, only for a dinosaur to whip its tail, knocking the robot back down.

In moments, one of these creatures would eat her. But Lailani didn't worry about her own death. She had faced death a thousand times.

She thought of Sofia falling into the fire.

She thought of Elvis, his heart in her hand.

She thought of the living. Of Marco, Addy, and Ben-Ari, facing evil, needing her help.

The largest dinosaur, a beast coated with green feathers, emerged the victor. It grabbed Lailani with yellow talons and lifted her overhead. Its jaw opened beneath her, lined with teeth, filled with drool. The heat and stench of the gullet assailed Lailani.

No, Lailani thought. *I will not die today.* She took a deep breath, and she let the word fill her mind.

Nightwish.

Her chip shut down.

The alien inside her woke.

Awareness unfolded before her. Her consciousness expanded, branching out, filling the forest and space above.

She was Lailani. She was the hive. She was a million centipedes in the dark, spreading across the night.

She was more alive, more aware, more powerful than she had ever been.

The concept of the individual vanished. She could view the world from her own eyes. From the eyes of birds and insects. From the eyes of the aliens, of the creature holding her. She was one. She was everything.

Lower me.

Snorting, blinking, shivering, the dinosaur lowered Lailani to the forest floor. She stood before the beast, small as an ant before a raven. The alien roared. The sound shook the forest. Fury exploded through it. It leaned in, jaws wide, desperate to feed.

No!

She lashed out with her mind.

The dinosaur pulled back, shrieking, clawing the soil. Around it, the other beasts snarled, snapped, screeched. Another leaned in to bite. Lailani snapped her head toward it, staring. The dinosaur pulled back, growling, whimpering.

"Back."

They resisted. They roared.

"Back!" she said.

Their howls shook the forest. Their tails slammed into trees. Their claws dug into soil and stone.

"You will stand back!" Lailani said. She spread out her arms. Leaves rustled around her, flying into the air. She levitated a foot above the ground, and fire blazed around her head, weaving an unholy halo. "I am Lailani de la Rosa. I am human. I am alien. I am the hive. I am she who gazes from a thousand eyes. I am she who is all, who is one. And you will obey me. Stand back!"

The creatures trembled before her. They shuffled backward, snarling as if to salvage their pride. Trees cracked around them. Finally they turned. They rumbled away, leaving uprooted trees and drool in their wake.

Lailani landed on the ground.

Her eyes began rolling back.

Hunger filled her. Hunger for flesh. She looked at Epimetheus. She saw his blood pulsing. His heart, delicious, red, waiting for her fangs. She—

She screamed, a sound rising from deep inside her.

Stop this. Stop this. Stop this.

Serenity. She gasped for air. *Serenity!*

With a crackle inside her skull, the chip turned on.

Her skull sucked up her consciousness like a vacuum cleaner. She slammed back into her body.

She tilted over.

She thumped into the dry leaves, shivering, drained. She wept blood.

And Epimetheus was on her, licking her face, nuzzling her neck. She managed to wrap her arms around him.

"I sent them away," she whispered. "They can't hurt us, Epi. They are monsters. But so am I. So am I . . ."

Her eyes rolled back. She could see no more. She faded.

CHAPTER SEVENTEEN

"I got a job offer."

Steve stood in the yard between his unsold cabinets—
dozens of cabinets, some simple, others elaborate works of art, all
fading away in the sunlight.

Addy gasped. "That's great!" She stood on her tiptoes and
kissed his cheek. "I'm proud of you. My big, strong, genius go-
getter! Is it a carpentry gig?"

Steve did not smile. He had not smiled much since his
abduction a few months ago. He had regained his strength but
little of his joy. His cheeks were no longer sunken, his skin no
longer sallow, but his eyes always seemed so cold.

"Engineering," he said. "Building and maintaining
antennae. Like I did in the army."

"That's fantastic!" Addy grinned. "I know you were hoping
for your cabinet business to take off, but this is a great
opportunity. I'm so proud of you, baby. Which island is the job
on?"

"It's not on an island." Steve met her gaze. "It's off-
planet."

Addy stepped back. "Where is it?"

"Corpus."

The word hit her like a hammer.

"Corpus," she whispered.

The planet where, ten years ago, she and her friends had crashed. Where they had plunged into the mines, seeking an azoth crystal. Where they had faced the scum and their deformed hybrids. Where she had lost so many friends—Diaz, Singh, Beast, and many others. Where she had seen Coleen Petty rise from the dead, twisted into a centipede with a human face. Where Addy had shed so much blood. Where they had nuked the mines from above, creating the nuclear ooze where the marauders had mutated, forged of scum and human DNA.

Corpus. The world of all her terrors. Lailani had called it Hell. She had been right.

"Hell," Addy whispered.

Steve stared at her. "It's still humanity's greatest deposit of azoth. Only azoth can bend spacetime, enabling warp speed. To rebuild humanity's fleet, we must return to Corpus. We must mine the crystals. That's where the job offer is. That's where I'm needed, where I can make a difference, where I can prove my worth. And that's where I'm going." He clenched a fist. "Because I am worth something." His voice softened. "And I want you to come with me, Addy."

"What?" She guffawed, though it felt more like a sob. "You want me to go to fucking Corpus? You know what happened there. You know what happened to me. You know I still wake up with nightmares about that place. You can't go there!"

His eyes hardened. "I can, and I will."

"Steve!"

"Listen to me, Addy." Steve grabbed her arms. "Listen to me. I . . ." His body tensed. "I remember. More and more. Every day, I remember more of what happened to me." He seemed ready to cry, then tightened his jaw and breathed heavily. "I remember who they were. What they looked like. Gray creatures. Aliens with cruel eyes. They're going to come back, Addy. They were here to research us. To study our defenses. To find our weaknesses. And one of these days, they're going to attack in earnest. And I need to do what I can to stop that. And that means getting that mine in Corpus up and running again, so that we can rebuild our fleet."

Addy exhaled slowly, her anger flowing away with her breath. "Oh, baby." She touched his cheek. "We fought our wars already. Can't we let somebody else pick up the torch? You've fought enough. Stay here. With me on this island. Others will be there to do the work."

"Yes." His jaw tightened. "Others will work. Marco will work. Miners will work. Soldiers will work. And I'll stay here, building cabinets that nobody buys. Just spending all day in the middle of nowhere, useless, haunted with memories, building these goddamn, fucking cabinets."

"You'll find work here!" Addy said. "You—"

"There is no work here!" Steve roared. "This is a retirement island, Addy. And nobody asked me if I wanted to retire! I had work to do in Toronto—to rebuild, to help people.

But you dragged me here! I have work now to do in Corpus. And you want me to stay! I'm twenty-nine. I'm only twenty-nine, and you want me to retire already, to let Marco support me, but I'm not useless. I'm not weak!"

"I never said you were!" Addy said, eyes moist.

"You say it every day!" he shouted. "I see it in your eyes! You spend all day talking to Marco. About his work. About how much money he makes. About how he supports us all. And I'm just here in the yard, building these fucking, piece-of-shit cabinets."

He stepped toward one cabinet, an elaborate piece engraved with rearing horses and worked with semiprecious stones. He grabbed it, raised it overhead, then slammed it against the ground. It shattered.

"Steve!" Addy cried.

"I'm sick of building these things that nobody wants!" He grabbed another cabinet, this one made of expensive cherrywood, worked with mirrors. He hurled it against the ground, and the mirrors shattered, and the wood snapped.

"Stop it!" Addy said, tears on her cheeks.

But Steve ignored her. He kept moving across the yard, smashing his creations, shattering dozens of cabinets—a year's worth of labor and artistry. He became a beast in his rage, and Addy could only stand in shock, staring, scared.

"Steve!" She grabbed his arm. "Steve, please. I know. I know what happened. I know you're hurt. I know that they hurt you. But I can help you. You have to let me—"

He shoved her back. "I don't have to do anything you say, Addy. Don't you understand? I've always followed you like a dog on a leash. Throughout the war against the marauders. Here on this island. I was always just there, just dragging behind you. I'm done. I need to do this. To be . . . useful."

Tears flowed from her eyes. She touched his cheek. "You're useful to me."

He stared into her eyes. "That's not good enough."

"Steve. Baby." She clasped his hand. "I can't go with you."

"I'm going," Steve said. "For once, I'm making a choice. I'm choosing my own path. My ship leaves in two days. Follow like I've followed you all this time. Or stay."

He turned away. He walked into the house, leaving her outside in a yard full of smashed cabinets.

Two days later, Addy stood in the same yard, the smashed cabinets still around her, and watched the rocket rise from an island on the horizon. She watched the trail of smoke stretch upward. She stood, watching, until the rocket was gone. Until Steve was gone. She stood alone.

Finally she knelt. She picked up a small, decorative tile, shimmering blue. Steve had glued it onto a cabinet, a piece from a larger mosaic. Addy tucked it into her pocket, a last memento from him. From somebody she lost. She lowered her head, and she stayed there in the yard until the sun set, and her world was dark.

CHAPTER EIGHTEEN

The bridge of the *Lodestar* bustled, officers moving back and forth between glowing workstations. Viewports coated the walls, ceiling, and floor of the round room, connected to cameras outside the ship, revealing a full view of space wrapping around them. Ben-Ari felt as if she floated in open space. She sat in the center of the hubbub in the captain's seat, a cup of chamomile tea growing cold in her hands.

Aurora swiveled around in her seat to face her. The pilot's eight tendrils were busy gripping controls and tapping an array of monitors. Her body flashed green, yellow, and blue, and her optic translator spoke in a fluid, female voice.

"We should be at Yarrow within the hatching of a limpet podling, mistress of dark waters."

"Convert 'podling hatching' to Earth time units and add to dictionary," Ben-Ari said, speaking more to the small, round translation device than to Aurora. "Try again."

Aurora flashed through colors again. "We should be there within an hour, mistress of dark waters."

"Convert 'mistress of dark waters' to 'Captain' and add to dictionary," Ben-Ari said.

The alien octopus seemed to smile—as much as a mouthless creature that digested its food through organic tubes could smile. "Aye aye, Captain."

Ben-Ari nodded. "Good. Better. You'll be speaking fluent English in no time."

An hour. Only an hour until they arrived at their new destination, answering the Mayday call.

Ben-Ari sighed.

Petty let me command the Lodestar *to discover new life, form new alliances. Now we're embroiled in violence again.*

She pulled up her tablet and replayed the message.

An elderly man, his beard long and white, appeared on the monitor. He sat in what looked like a farmhouse, and he wore a straw hat. Corn swayed outside the window, a familiar crop. Yet this was clearly an alien world. Sienna clouds swirled across a yellow sky, and indigo mountains soared on the horizon, taller than any mountains on Earth. The farmer spoke, voice filled with grief.

"To anyone who might receive this message. I am Obadiah, Head Father of Yarrow Colony. I beg you." His voice cracked. "We need your help. Our children . . . They took them. They took them all." He wiped his eyes with a handkerchief. "My three grandchildren were among them. The creatures. The creatures with dark robes and masks stole them. If anyone receives this message, I beg you—help us. We—"

Suddenly the old man gasped. He looked behind him. Shadows stirred.

The message ended.

Ben-Ari suppressed a shudder. Yarrow Colony was formed five years ago, home to a couple hundred families. Despite its jarring yellow-and-blue colorings, the planet was remarkably Earthlike, the most clement of all planets humanity had discovered so far. The air was breathable. The soil was lush. There were alien plants and gentle wildlife. Yarrow was a little piece of heaven. The only problem was the location. Even the fastest starships required months to travel between Earth and Yarrow. Most colonists preferred closer colonies—at Mars, even at Alpha Centauri, which lay weeks away from Earth. Yet a few hearty farmers had taken to colonizing distant Yarrow, as cut off from Earth as the Mayflower colonists from Europe. They were an honest people, guided by faith, who yearned for simpler times. They lived a rustic life, using little technology, only a handful of transmitters to be used in emergencies.

As far as Ben-Ari knew, this was Yarrow's first emergency.

"Well, well!" The voice rose behind her. "And what nonscientific, highly-dangerous mission does our captain have us taking today?"

Her heart sank. She turned to see Fish step onto the bridge. For once, the exobiologist wore his uniform. A day in the brig had, perhaps, instilled that bit of discipline. Yet he still wore his crocodile-tooth necklace against regulation, and his long blond hair cascaded across his shoulders rather than being pulled into a ponytail.

And worst of all, he was questioning her orders again. Was he begging for another day—or even a week—in the brig?

"Watch it, Fish," Marino grumbled. The hulking wrestler moved toward the Alien Hunter.

"Back off, drongo," Fish said. The Australian was not, perhaps, a professional fighter, but he was a tall, broad man, almost as large as Marino, and had spent years wrestling aliens on TV. He stood his ground. "To remind you, I outrank you, Marino. And part of my duty is to question our fearless leader if she's leading us into muddy swamps." He turned toward Ben-Ari. "If I may remind you, sheila, our job is to head to the Epsilon sector, not go swimming after random crocs."

Ben-Ari wondered if she should shout, should discipline, should exert her dominance. That was how she would act in the army. She would scold. She would have her sergeant manhandle recalcitrant troops away. That was how things worked in the military.

But this is not the military. I have to remember that. These are not my soldiers. And if I treat them like soldiers, they'll keep rebelling. She took a deep breath. *Perhaps I'm the one who needs to change. To soften.*

She tried another approach. She turned toward Fish and smiled gently.

"Of course, Fish. I want you to always bring your concerns to my attention. I appreciate it. You're the ship's expert on aliens. I mean that." She kept smiling gently. "But isn't one of our missions to reach out to those in need? We're the only ship within light-years of Yarrow. I think that we can tolerate a slight delay to help." She remembered that Fish enjoyed surfing and added a personal touch. "After all, even a surfer riding the mightiest wave will swim aside to save a drowning man. Am I wrong?"

And amazingly, it worked.

Fish's anger flowed away.

He was an exobiologist. A celebrity. A billionaire. But deep in his heart, he was still that old adventurer, a kid exploring new worlds.

"Yes, of course, you're right." Fish cleared his throat, suddenly seeming sheepish. "In fact, my businesses back on Earth donate quite a lot to charity this time of year. I'm all about helping mates in need." He gave Ben-Ari a smile—an actual warm smile. "Good on ya, Captain. It's a fair dinkum. I'll be down at the biolab if you need me."

As Fish left the bridge, Professor Isaac approached Ben-Ari, an eyebrow raised.

"It seems like you have a new fan," the professor said.

And it seems like I'm still learning, Ben-Ari thought. *And not just science.*

They entered orbit about Yarrow, a clement world orbiting a small star. Grassy plains coated several continents, and silvery lakes sparkled under deep blue mountains. Dawn rose over Yarrow's horizon, casting shimmering rays across its golden atmosphere. Here was a virgin planet, untouched by industrialization, pollution, or devastating wars.

In thirty years, I wouldn't mind retiring here, Ben-Ari thought.

The *Lodestar* was incapable of entering an atmosphere; she had been built in space, and in space she would remain for the rest of her service. Following their battle with the saucers, they had only one shuttle left. Ben-Ari entered the craft, choosing Isaac and two security guards to join her. They flew down, plunging into the yellow sky of Yarrow.

They flew toward the colony. A hundred houses rose on a grassy hill, surrounded by farmlands. Cows, sheep, and horses grazed in the fields. Orchards swayed in the breeze. The spaceport was just a dusty field with a handful of old, rusting shuttles, probably not used since the colonists had moved here twenty years ago. Wagons—actual wooden wagons—stood among the old spacecrafts.

Ben-Ari landed her shuttle, and the crew emerged into the sunny field. The air was hot but pleasant, scented of growing things. Crickets chirped and a dog wagged his tail. If not for the tan sky and indigo mountains, this could have been a peaceful village back home.

A man came riding a horse toward the crew, and Ben-Ari recognized Obadiah, the man from the Mayday call. He wore a wide-brimmed hat, black trousers, and a vest over a white buttoned shirt. He sported a long white beard, though his upper lip was cleanly shaved. He dismounted before Ben-Ari and her crew and shook their hands.

"Thank you! Thank you for coming! Welcome to our community. I am Obadiah, Head Father of Yarrow. I'm proud to welcome you in our colony. I . . . I . . ." Suddenly his eyes filled with tears, and he trembled.

Ben-Ari wrapped her arms around the old man. "It's all right, Father. We're here to help. Is there a place we can sit and talk?"

They made their way along a dirt trail and into the village. Looking around, Ben-Ari saw a playground, a few discarded bicycles, and dusty toys. But no children. The few adults she saw peeked from the windows of their homes, daring not approach. It seemed like a village from a lost era. No cars, no electricity, just simple living. And yet there was also fear. There was grief. It hung in the air.

Obadiah led them into his home, a country-style farmhouse. They settled down in the library. Obadiah had an impressive collection of books, many of them leather bound. The furniture looked like real oak, and artwork hung on the walls; they looked like actual paintings, done by humans on canvas, not generated by computers. In an era of plastic, ebooks, and robotic artwork, seeing wooden chairs, paper books, and oil paintings was like stepping back in time.

With shaky hands, Obadiah poured them drinks—thick milk, pumped from the cow that morning. He mumbled something about fetching sweet biscuits his wife had baked, but he broke down again, tears flowing. Ben-Ari had to gently guide him into a chair, assure him that the crew had already eaten, and coax him into telling his story.

"It began three years ago," Obadiah said, dabbing at his eyes with a kerchief. "That's when the first child disappeared. A sweet lass named Emmy. One day she went to the hatchery to see the new chicks. Her dog was with her. We've never had any trouble here. The local wildlife never approached. Never had a need for fences or guards. Sweet Emmy . . . She never came out." The old man's voice cracked. "We found her dog by the hatchery. He had been decapitated. What kind of monster would do such a thing?"

Ben-Ari had to pat the old man's back until he calmed down. She spoke softly. "And the other children—they vanished too?"

Obadiah nodded. "One by one. Sometimes two or three a day. We forbade them from leaving the village. We guarded them. Finally we saw their kidnappers. Men. Men from another world. Men with black robes and hoods. When we tried to fight them, they killed our fighters. We are simple folk. We have no weapons. They butchered all those who resisted them. But they didn't want the adults. Only the young ones. By now the children are all gone."

Ben-Ari frowned. She held the old man's hand. "Could they have been aliens, Obadiah? Maybe tall aliens with large heads, with oval eyes?"

"Aliens?" He blinked his damp eyes. "No. No. Only men. I saw them myself. Cruel men. Men from . . ." He shuddered and spoke in a low voice. "From the desert world."

"The desert world?" Ben-Ari shared a glance with her crew.

Obadiah shivered. "We don't like speaking of it. There are two planets orbiting this star. Two colonies. One is Yarrow—this peaceful world of plenty, of sunlight, water, and life. The second planet is called Isfet—a desolate desert world, hot and dry, too close to the sun. The men there are cruel. Wicked. Heathens. They practice dark arts and twisted science. For most of our time here in Yarrow, they had left us alone. But it's them that took our children." He clenched a shaky fist. "I recognized their faces. Please help us, Captain! You are strong, mighty, and brave. You have weapons. You must bring our children back! Please. Please bring our children back . . ."

He could say no more, only bowed his head and wept softly.

The crew flew back to the *Lodestar*, somber.

The starship flew across the star system, heading toward the dry neighboring planet.

They flew in silence.

They did not engage their warp engines, not here within a solar system. With their conventional engines, it was a five-hour flight to Isfet. Ben-Ari knew that she should sleep. She had barely slept in days, consumed with worries. Instead, she headed to the lounge, where a few last Christmas decorations still hung. The hour was late. She stood alone by the window, watching the stars stream outside.

"Trouble sleeping?" rose a voice behind her.

She turned to see the professor enter the lounge.

She gave him a wan smile. "I've never been a good sleeper."

"What I find," said the professor, "is that when my mind is troubled, a little hot chocolate goes a long way." He approached the bar, where he ordered two hot chocolates from the drink dispenser. He approached Ben-Ari at the window, holding two mugs. "I added extra whipped cream."

She gave a little laugh. She remembered, with a sudden awkward pang, how Marino had come to her chamber with a bottle of champagne and two glasses. Her cheeks flushed to remember how she had slept with Marino, a memory that both warmed and embarrassed her—especially the latter, now with the professor here. She accepted one of the hot chocolate mugs. She sipped.

"It's good," she said.

"You know, it's often customary to tell your bartender your troubles," the professor said. "I think that by bringing you this drink, I might qualify. I'm always happy to teach you science. But also to provide a listening ear."

She sighed. She stared out into space. "Soldiers rarely talk of their troubles. Rarely share their pain. We're trained to kill, not feel. Sometimes it seems like all I know is killing." She looked at him. "I accepted this mission because President Petty asked me to. Because he believed in me. Yet it seems that all I can do here is fight. Fight the grays. Fight these new enemies we approach. We are officers of HOPE. A program of exploration. A program meant to inspire humanity. Of optimism, of wisdom. We're meant to reach out to the stars in friendship and curiosity, paving a path to the future. Is Fish right? Am I wrong to keep engaging in scuffles? Am I still acting like a soldier, and a scientist should lead us?"

The professor gazed out at the stars with her. "I can tell you everything there is to know about this hot chocolate. The chemical composition of the milk and cocoa. The engineering and programming inside the machine that prepared it. The biological functions that let us taste the chocolate, digest it, even the chemicals in our brain that bring us enjoyment of it. Yet knowledge is one thing. Experience—quite another." He took a sip. "Wisdom, Einav, is both knowledge and a deep understanding of what it means to be human."

"Then I'm not very wise," she said.

He looked at her. "I would argue that you are the wisest member aboard this ship. Einav, the world's best scientists fly here with us. Geniuses. All of them. We have expert biologists, engineers, computer programmers, astronomers, physicists, geologists . . . Yet we have brought no poets. No philosophers. No dreamers. Petty did not choose you for this mission because you're a soldier, Einav. There are millions of soldiers. He chose you because you're decent. Because you're ethical. Because you're wise. Because you're *human*."

She looked at his kind face, and tears filled her eyes. She spoke in a whisper. "So why do I feel so broken?"

Her hands trembled. The mug shook. The professor placed his hands around hers, steadying her grip. His hands were so warm, enveloping. Soft hands—not the callused hands of a warrior—but there was strength to them. There was comfort.

He stared into her eyes and spoke softly. "The wisest are often broken, for by shattering, by hurting, by grieving, we acquire our wisdom, our humanity. The cosmos is vast, filled with billions and billions of stars, planets, and nebulae to explore. But what is rare is humanity, kindness, and love. In this vast darkness, in all this emptiness, it is love that gives us hope. Love that makes this journey worthwhile. There will always be more stardust to explore, to analyze, to learn from. Science can take a nap today. Right now we have a more important mission: helping fellow humans. A mission of kindness. You knew this. You understood this deep in your bones, even if you struggled to know why. And that is why Petty chose you. That is why you represent humanity here in the darkness. And that is why we will follow you. Always. Not only because of your mind, and a brilliant mind it is. But because of something far more important. Your heart."

Her tears flowed.

"Thank you," she whispered. "You still teach me so much."

She slept for an hour. She was showered, caffeinated, and uniformed when they arrived at Isfet.

She stood on the bridge, watching the planet come closer.

Isfet, she thought. *The Ancient Egyptian word for evil and chaos. Who would give such a name to their world?*

274

She watched it approach. Dry. Hellish. Too close to its sun. A planet of missing children.

Ben-Ari shuddered.

CHAPTER NINETEEN

Abyzou walked through Gehenna, the Dark City, his necklace of hearts beating and dripping against his chest.

This city was filled with delights—captives from a thousand lands, all waiting to be dissected, their organs savored, their screams like music. The Sanctified Sons had captured thousands of the apes from Old Earth, bringing them here for slavery, for pleasure.

There were dens of human slaves where, for only a few coins, one could cut open the flesh, claim a heart, keep it beating, a memento of eternal pain. Abyzou had taken many such hearts, forming his beating necklace, his pulsing bed, his living meals, hot and wet and rife with his victims' agony.

There were other dens where, for even cheaper, one could take the apes into a bed, could thrust into them with a different sort of blade, could discover a different sort of pleasure in their flesh. Abyzou had copulated with many of the female apes. Only yesterday, he had filled one with his seed. One, years ago, he had taken as his wife, creating inside her hybrids of holiness.

Yes, there were many pleasures in Gehenna, this city of shadows. Pleasures of hearts. Of sex. Of taking and creating life. Even here, in this dead world of ash and black stones, a world where no grass could grow, there were great delights, hot and sticky and intoxicating. Those pleasures beckoned.

But tonight Abyzou resisted their lure.

Tonight he had a greater task.

Tonight he came to see his queen, his goddess, his mother.

Tonight, after a million years of waiting, the Sanctified Sons would rise to eternal glory.

He walked down the city's main boulevard. Along the roadsides rose statues of ancient gods, hybrids that stared with obsidian eyes. In their mighty hands, they held braziers filled with burning prisoners, the wretched souls kept alive, forever blazing, never dying, eternally lighting the night. Their screams rose like sweet music. Between these statues, Abyzou could see the rest of Gehenna sprawling across this desert world. Temples. Towers. Massive faces that stared from deepest shadows.

It was a city of might, of holiness.

Yet it was but a shell of what awaited the Sanctified Sons, the glory they would soon claim. After so long here in darkness, they would finally seize their prize.

The Temple of Nefitis soared ahead, a mighty pyramid, and upon its crest blazed a great eye. There, high above the city, she reigned. There she ever watched.

Nefitis.

Our goddess, Abyzou thought. *My mother.*

He reached the base of Golgalath, the pyramid of the goddess. Two guardians rose here, many times his height, ancient beings risen from the earth, humanoid and rancid, whipped, flayed, draped with bandages that dangled and festered. None remembered their names, for they were of the lost race of giants, deformed in the nuclear holocaust, mummified and rotting. Their arms were raised, their hands meeting above the pathway, forming a wretched archway. Their hands had fused together long ago, flesh melting into flesh, bone growing into bone. They gazed at Abyzou with empty eye sockets, caverns large enough for vultures to nest in.

"Who comes to see the goddess?" they rumbled.

Abyzou stood before the guardians, back straight, and raised his staff. The wind blew his cloak, and his necklace of hearts dripped.

"It is I, Abyzou, Born of Nefitis, Lord of Pain, Baptized in Blood, Head of Legions! Your prince!"

The mummified guardians stepped back, their footsteps shaking the earth.

"Pass, son of Nefitis, and praise her."

He climbed the stairs that ran up the pyramid's facade. Guardians stood here, noble warriors, the finest of their race. Grays, the humans called them. A meaningless name. They were the Sanctified Sons, the blessed seed of the night. The humans were primitive, mere apes, hairy and foul, their skulls so small, their minds so limited. The Sanctified—their heads so large, their wisdom infinite—were the most evolved race in the galaxy. The humans would learn this.

Abyzou's lips peeled back, and he sucked air between his needlelike teeth. Yes. Soon he would be there. On Earth. Soon he would torment billions. Soon all would scream under his claws!

Finally, he reached the top of the pyramid. The great Eye of Horus shone here upon the pyramid's crest, gazing upon the city. Below the eye, an obsidian platform thrust out like a tongue.

Here, upon this outcrop, she sat on her throne of rotting flesh.

Nefitis. His mother.

She was tall and cadaverous, her wrinkly gray skin clinging to her bones. Her fingers were long, tipped with claws that gripped her seat. Her breasts were bare, thin and long, dripping bloodied milk. Abyzou still had fond memories of sucking from those wilted nipples. Metal shards had been nailed into the goddess's brow, forming a crown that ever bled, its wounds ever screaming, for pain gave Nefitis her strength.

She raised her heavy head, bloated and splotched, and she opened her eyes—eyes blacker than the space between the stars, all-seeing. They stared at him. They stared into him. They peeled back every layer of him, as surely as his hooks peeled the skin off his victims.

Abyzou couldn't help but shudder. So many times in his childhood, Nefitis had grabbed him, sunk her claws into him, pulled out his organs and infested them with maggots, then shoved them back in, diseased, twisting with pain. Punishments to harden him. To break and rebuild him. He still bore the scars. The fear. The worship of her.

I crawled out of her womb the most blessed of the Sanctified Sons, he thought. *And cursed with a yoke of agony. For her, I suffer. And someday I will sit upon her throne!*

"Mother." Abyzou prostrated himself, and his necklace of hearts bled, forming a pool around him.

She spoke, voice creaky, ancient beyond measure, a voice that could drive lesser minds mad.

"Rise, my son."

He rose before her. He had crushed the hearts when prostrating himself. They dripped, trailing blood down his chest.

"Mother, the hour draws near," he said. "We faced Ben-Ari in the darkness. She approaches the desert world where the apes worship you. Very soon now, she will meet our servants."

The goddess leaned forward in her seat. "And upon her ship?"

Abyzou nodded. "One of our servants, Mother, posing as a member of her crew. Ben-Ari does not suspect."

Nefitis's mouth formed a thin, sickly smile, the lips peeling back to reveal black gums.

"The pieces are moving," the goddess said. "We arrange our assault. All falls into place, and the Ape Captain plays her part. Soon, my son. Soon we will be ready. Soon our assault will commence. How fares the fleet?"

Abyzou raised his chin. "The fleet is mighty, Mother! It is ready to fight."

He turned. He gazed with her.

They hovered over the city. Thousands of them. Disk-shaped battleships, forged of dark metal, engraved with runes. Flying saucers, the humans called them. The chariots of the Sanctified Sons.

Abyzou turned back toward the goddess.

"Soon, Mother, Earth will be ours!"

He inhaled deeply, as if he could already taste the victims. Earth. The promised land. The world they had craved for so long. Soon it would be theirs. Soon the apes would scream in their chains, bowing before them!

"Dine with me tonight, my son," the goddess said.

Abyzou gasped. This was an unexpected delight. The goddess rarely dined with others.

"Yes, Mother!"

The servants brought forth the meal—a human woman, gravid with child. She wept and struggled, but the Sanctified Sons held her tightly. Her belly was obscenely swollen, and Abyzou could see the spawn squirming inside.

Sudden terror flashed through him. For an instant, Abyzou was sure it was his wife. That it was Mila, the female he had chosen from Old Earth, had brought back here in chains, had impregnated many times. Nefitis had already consumed one of Mila's children—punishment for a battle Abyzou had lost on a distant jungle world.

But no. This woman was not Mila. She looked like her—long golden hair, rounded hips, weepy eyes. But it was not his beloved, the mother of his children. Just another ape. Just one among the thousands the Sanctified Sons had brought here to dissect, to impregnate, and on some nights—like tonight—to eat.

But you will never be eaten, Mila, Abyzou thought. *You are pure. You are mine. You have given me children with the intelligence of Sanctified Sons and the hardiness of apes, perfect children to colonize your world. You will be the wife of a god, and all will cherish you. Your children will someday reign!*

A bloodstained altar rose on the platform, a place of sacrifice for the goddess. They placed the pregnant woman upon it, and they bound her limbs to the stone with serpents. She screamed. She wept. She begged.

"Prepare her for the feast," Nefitis said.

Abyzou nodded. "Yes, Mother."

His claws were sharp, and the human's skin was thin. Abyzou needed no tools. He cut her open, and he pulled out her child—wriggling, squealing, coated with blood. He carried the baby toward his mother, the cord still attached. It was not a hybrid. It had a small head, small eyes, small brain. The father had been a mere human. This spawn was fit to consume.

"Mother," Abyzou said, holding out the babe.

Nefitis took the child in her hands. She stroked the bloody cheek. "So precious. So frail. So . . . succulent."

As Nefitis fed, Abyzou returned to the bound mother. Her meat was not as tender; it would be his portion. The woman was still screaming. She stopped when Abyzou cut out her living heart, when he added it to his collection. It pulsed on his necklace, a soothing rhythm. With his knowledge and skill, he could keep it alive for many days.

He leaned over the carcass, and he fed. He ate his fill. And as he fed upon the corpse, he imagined feeding upon Earth itself, sucking it dry, and savoring its screams.

Soon, Ben-Ari, he thought, *you will scream here too. You will bear me many children before your heart hangs around my neck. I'm coming back for you, Einav Ben-Ari. Soon you will be mine.*

CHAPTER TWENTY

The lawyer leaned back in his seat, shirt opened to reveal a golden chain gleaming against his hairy chest.

"Sorry, kid." He swatted away a mosquito, his knockoff Rolex jangling. "I sympathize. Truly I do." He pulled out a box of cigarettes. "Smoke?"

Marco just stared at him blankly.

The lawyer shrugged. "Mind if I have one then?" Not waiting for an answer, he lit a cigarette.

The office was small and cluttered, and a construction crew was busy installing a new toilet down the hall. Curses and dust filled the air.

Marco blinked, struggling to steady himself.

"But we can fight this, right? Go to court? See a judge? Plead our case?"

The lawyer took a long drag on his cigarette. "Sure, kid. If you wanna pay for it. You know what I charge per hour, and a court battle might take a few years. I'm happy to take on the case. But I'll be honest with ya, kid. You'll lose." He blew out a smoke ring. "I tell you this 'cause I'm ethical. Most lawyers would take the case without a blink, and I'll still take it, if you insist. But if we walk into court, you'll walk out a lot poorer, and I'll walk out a lot richer."

Marco couldn't comprehend it. It seemed surreal. It wasn't sinking in.

"Let me get this straight," he said. "So Tomiko keeps my house—*my* house, the house that I paid for, that I built before we even got married. And she gets all my money. And she gets half my book royalties going forward."

The lawyer took another long drag on his cigarette. "Technically, she only gets half your money. The other half goes to the government. See, you run a small corporation for your income. Tax efficient. But to pay Tomiko, you gotta withdraw that money and pay those taxes. Government gets half, Tomiko gets half. You get nothing." He stubbed out his cigarette. "Sorry, kid."

Marco tugged his hair. "A year ago, you told me incorporating would save me money!"

"And it did," said the lawyer. "So long as you remained married. Sorry, kid. Divorces are tough. I see it all the time. You ain't the first guy who sat in this chair to hear the sad news."

Marco slumped back in his chair. "So everything I have— gone. Tomiko gets to live in my house with her new boyfriend. I give them all my money. And I pay them half my earnings going forward—for the rest of my life."

"Or her life," the lawyer said. "She might die first."

"I'm eight years older!" Marco said.

The lawyer nodded sympathetically. "It's hard. I know. I see it all the time, and every time, it's a tragedy." He lit another cigarette. "I had a guy in yesterday. Fifty-five years old. Five kids. Be lucky you're only paying Tomiko half. He's paying most of his salary to his wife and her new husband. She kicked him out of the house. He lives in a trailer now. Still has a great job, mind you. A doctor. Makes a lot of money. Just has to hand over his paycheck every month." The lawyer pointed his cigarette at Marco. "You got off lucky."

Marco leaped to his feet. "Lucky! But . . . Tomiko is the one who left *me*! She cheated on me! Can't we tell a judge that? Can't we—"

"Kid, there are only two divorce courts left in the country. The judges don't have time to listen to who did what, who's to blame, who cheated on who. They got to process a bunch of these divorces every day. They ain't gonna listen to your sob story. I will, because I'm paid per hour. They won't." He held out his box of cigarettes. "You sure you don't want one?"

Marco stared at the lawyer in numb shock. "So where am I supposed to live?"

The lawyer sighed. "Some of the younger guys go back to their parents. Some move into homeless shelters. They crash in friends' houses. A couple of guys set up a nice little tent under a bridge. As I said, I see it all the time." He jutted his thumb at the hallway. "My buddy there who's installing my new toilet? He just went through it himself six months ago."

A sweaty construction worker's head appeared around the corner. He gave Marco a grin and thumbs-up.

"I sleep in a bathtub!" he said.

Marco left the office.

Addy was waiting outside, sitting on the curb. She wore a tank top, revealing the tattoos on her arms, and was smoking a cigarette. She offered him the box. "Cig?"

"Why does everyone think I want to start smoking?" Marco said.

Addy shrugged. "Hey, I'd offer you a couple billion bucks, but I lost them all at the dog track while you were inside. So how did it go? Does Tomiko own all your limbs now or just the legs?"

They walked through the smoggy Greek city, dodging mopeds and bicycles. Marco spent a while describing the situation. With every word, Addy's face grew more dour. By the time they reached the port, her shoulders were slumped, and she was on her last cigarette.

"I'm ruined, Addy," Marco said in a hoarse voice. "Our house. Our savings. Half our future earnings. Gone. We're homeless and broke."

Addy spat. "Shit's fucked up."

Marco's eyes burned. He took a shuddering breath. He could still barely comprehend this reality. "Addy, I—"

"Wait." She put a finger on his lips. "Not yet. Come."

She dragged him along the boardwalk, and they found a little taverna overlooking the water. They sat, and Addy ordered two fried tilapia fish, a plate piled high with fries, and two glasses of beer. Marco didn't mind paying for the meal. In a few days, he would be destitute. Let him enjoy one last meal on the waterfront.

"All right." Addy pointed at the pint of beer. "Get to nursing this, then talk."

Marco took a sip. And he talked. The world seemed to crumble around him, and he spoke between sips, voice shaking.

"Addy." He clasped her hand across the table. "For years, we dreamed of this. When we were in the army. When we fought the scum. For two years in Haven, living in that shithole of an apartment. Throughout our war with the marauders. We dreamed of owning a house on a beach. Of having a good life. Of me writing my books, becoming a successful writer. And it happened. It happened, Addy! Somehow we did it. We achieved this dream. Somehow after all the shit, we found paradise. And now, after only a year, to lose it all . . ." His voice shook, his eyes dampened, and the beer was bitter. "We lost it all. We're homeless now. We're broke. I don't even know if I can write another book. How can I be motivated, knowing that half the royalties will go to Tomiko's new boyfriend? I don't know what to do. I'm sorry, Addy. I'm so sorry."

Addy gave her last cigarette a puff. "Fuck, man."

Marco gave her a wry smile. "Remember, we defeated the scum and marauders, but we couldn't defeat the evil Tomiko." He sighed. "Sorry. I should stop telling that joke. I know Tomiko isn't evil. I know I'm partly to blame. I'm angry. I'm hurt. I really thought it was meant to be. When I met her on the beach a year ago, just after we had built our house, I felt as if the cosmos itself had sent her to me. A gift. She approached me herself, telling me she was a fan of *The Dragons of Yesteryear.* And her name was Tomiko. Tomiko! Like the heroine in *Le Kill,* my unpublished novel." He looked down at his hands. "It seemed so perfect. A sign that she was meant for me. How did this all go wrong?"

Addy gave him a strange look. "Dude, I thought Tomiko was just a nickname we gave her. You know, after the character in *Le Kill.*"

He shook his head. "No! Her real name is Tomiko. That's why I was so amazed when I met her, why—"

"Dude." Addy tilted her head. "Her real name is Kiko. I saw it on her passport."

"What?" Marco snorted. "Addy, I think I know my wife's name. Besides, she introduced herself to me as Tomiko. When we first met! Nobody but you knew about *Le Kill,* about the character in my unpublished book."

Addy slumped in her seat and exhaled slowly. "Uhm, Poet? You didn't know that I met Tomiko a couple of weeks before you did? We talked on the beach for like an hour. She told me that she had seen you from afar, that she liked you, but was too shy to approach. She asked me questions about you. So I told her. About how you're a famous writer. About how you wrote *The Dragons of Yesteryear* and it's a huge hit. About how you also wrote *Loggerhead* and *Le Kill* but nobody else read those ones. She told me that she doesn't read books, that she can barely read English, but that you're cute, and . . ." She gave him a soft look. "She never told you any of this, did she?"

Marco could not speak for long moments. Finally he could only manage, "No." He shuddered. "Addy, did you tell her about the character in *Le Kill*? About the fictional Tomiko?"

Addy winced. "I don't remember. Maybe." She bit her lip. "Yes."

"She lied," Marco whispered. "She lied to me. About being a fan of my books. About her name. About everything. She was an orphan girl, poor, homeless. And she duped me. She lied and she took everything from me." He looked at Addy in horror. "I stepped into the trap. I loved her. I . . . Oh God."

Addy tossed her fish bones to a stray cat. "That is some fucked up shit, dude."

And the world began to spin around Marco. He could barely breathe. The images flashed before him: Tomiko approaching him on the beach, beautiful and shy, sweet lies on her lips. Tomiko bleeding. Tomiko in a hospital bed. Two babies dead. Grief. Tears and shouts. Tomiko getting into a car with another man, old, hair white.

I saw a lie, he thought. *I saw a fantasy. I saw what I wanted to see.*

His eyes burned. He was shaking.

"Addy," he whispered, and tears filled his eyes. "Addy, she lied to me. She broke me. Addy, I'm broken now. After everything I faced—the scum, the marauders, Haven—after everything, she broke me. I have nothing now. I'm dead. I can't do this. I can't fight another war. I can't catch my breath. I can't breathe. I—"

"Enough." Addy glared at him. "Enough, Marco!"

"I—" he began.

Addy rose to her feet, frowning at him. "Shut up! Just shut up, Marco! Stop this. Stop pretending you're some blameless victim. Stop feeling sorry for yourself. Stop acting like a *child.*"

"I'm not—"

"You are!" Addy said. "You think you're completely blameless? So, she told a couple of lies. Big fucking deal. How many times have you bullshitted girls to get into their pants?" She snorted. "Look, you have some of my pity. So don't add your own self-pity to it. Self-pity is disgusting, and right now, you're dripping with it. And don't sit here, telling me how Tomiko is the devil, when you spent the past year neglecting her, drowning in your work to deal with your grief. For fuck's sake, you fought alien bugs. I'm not going to sit here, listening to you mope about a girl. Man up."

Marco couldn't believe he was hearing this. "Addy, I just got dumped, I just learned that everything I fought for is being taken away, that everything was a lie. I'm miserable, and—"

She reached across the table, grabbed his shoulders, and tugged them up. "Sit up straight! Stop slumping. Stop *whining,* for Chrissake. Yes, dude, it sucks. It fucking sucks. You got your ass kicked. So you can sit around whining like a boy, or you can take it like a man. All right? I lost my partner too. I lost the house too. And thanks, by the way, for putting that house down under your name instead of *our* names. That really helps us now. We're both equally fucked here. But you don't see me whining. Stop being a *fucking baby*."

For a moment, Marco could only stare at Addy, scarcely believing what he was hearing. He wanted sympathy from her. A hug. A kind word. Not this harshness. Everyone betrayed him. Everyone was hurting him. Everyone—

No.

He forced a deep breath.

Addy was harsh, but she was right.

Slowly, his anger faded. He nodded.

"You're right," he said. "I acted like a child. A moment of weakness. We'll figure this out together. Like we always do. We'll keep fighting." He sighed and looked around him at the boardwalk. "But it still hurts. Not just the house. Not just the money. Everything else too. Everything that happened. With the miscarriages, and . . ."

Addy's eyes softened. She held his hand across the table. She looked into his eyes.

"I know," she whispered.

"I wanted to finally be happy," he said, holding her hand. "I thought we could be, you and I. That we deserved happiness. But then the baby died. And then we lost Tomiko and Steve. And now we lost the house and money. And . . . I thought we earned all of that. After everything, that it was our time for joy."

She stubbed out her last cigarette. She gazed at ships sailing across the water. "Marco, I learned something long ago. Back when I was a kid, when my mom beat me, when my dad was in jail. I learned that the universe don't owe us jack shit. You can win the lottery one day, get cancer in your dick the next day. It's all random. It's fucking random, and we're just leaves caught in the storm. Oh, we flutter around sometimes. We pretend that we can fly. But we're just leaves in the wind."

"Very poetic." Marco slumped in his chair, remembered Addy's warning, and sat back up straight. "Did you come up with that yourself?"

Addy shook her head. "Nah. Learned it from a book."

He cocked an eyebrow. "You? Read a book? Did you cut out the backs of a bunch of cereal boxes?"

"Ha ha, very funny, asshole." Addy reached into her pack, pulled out a book, and slammed it on the table. "*The Way of Deep Being* by Guru Baba Mahanisha. It's good shit."

Marco lifted the book and examined it. The front cover displayed an intricate mandala. The back cover showed a photo of the author: an alien of a species Marco didn't recognize. Baba Mahanisha sat on a mountaintop, clad in orange robes, deep in meditation. He was vaguely humanoid, but he had two trunks like those of an elephant, and his skin was wrinkly and brown.

"I never pegged you as a spiritual woman," Marco said, returning the book to Addy.

"I'm not," she said. "But dude, look at the author. Elephant Man! Like my favorite movie. That's fucking metal. I bought it just because of his photo."

He sighed. "Addy, it's a book about spirituality and meditation, not a freak show."

She pointed at the book again. "Did you not see him, dude? Two trunks!"

Marco sighed. "Let's go home. And let's pack our things. Before Tomiko gets to own all our clothes and books too— including your Elephant Man book!"

Addy gasped and clasped the book to her chest.

They took the ferry back to their island.

They packed their things into suitcases, leaving what didn't fit.

They walked along the beach, dragging their suitcases along the wet sand. At sundown, they reached crumbling columns that rose along the water, the remnants of some ancient temple. Here they lay down on the sand and looked up at the stars. The night was warm, the sky clear, and the waves washed over their toes.

Addy stretched. "Well, Poet, old boy, here we are again. You and me, alone against the world. Oh! And Elephant Man!" She grinned, pointing at the book.

Marco moved a little closer to her. Their fingertips brushed, and he took her hand in his. A star fell above. The world had crumbled. He had lost everything he had dreamed of, everything he had built.

But no. Not everything.

Addy is still with me.

He turned his head to look at her. She gazed up at the stars, a soft smile on her face. Addy was worth more than his house, his money, his books. In a world of storms, ever raging, ever changing, a world of random tragedies, Addy was a constant in his life—the shining light in his darkness.

"I'm glad you're with me, Addy," he said softly.

She kissed his cheek. "Always."

CHAPTER TWENTY-ONE

"So, HOBBS, you seem . . . rather breakable." Lailani wiped sweat off her forehead and glanced at the robot. "No offense, but hasn't your arm fallen off three times by now?"

They were hiking through the jungle of Mahatek, heading toward the mountain and ruins upon it. Mist hung in the air, insects buzzed, and plants kept poking them with hooked tendrils. Lailani kept slashing her knife ahead of her, cutting a way through the brush. They couldn't have landed more than twenty kilometers away—normally, that would only take half a day to walk. But in this jungle, each kilometer felt like a marathon.

My kingdom, my kingdom for a machete!

HOBBS rattled and clanked with each step. The big robot was several times her size, dented, rusty, clattering, and falling apart. He was still deadly—she had seen him tear through his enemies—but sometimes Lailani worried that if a dragonfly landed on him, HOBBS would finally fall apart.

"Yes, mistress," the robot said. "I do not have the necessary tools here to repair myself properly. It was Dr. Elliot Schroder who made me, mistress, the galaxy's premier expert on robotics. Only he can properly fix me. He lives in hiding on a lonely world orbiting Bernard's Star." HOBBS's eyes dimmed. "I should not have said that, mistress. Master Schroder has ordered me to keep his location secret." He tilted his head. "When you purchased me, your new ownership must have overridden my security algorithms."

Lailani frowned. "I thought you were made by the military."

"Oh, no, mistress!" the robot said. "Chrysopoeia Corporation builds the military robots, and they are far more lifelike, indistinguishable from real humans. You have met an Osiris model, have you not?" A sigh clattered through HOBBS. "Sometimes I wish I were an android. Then people would not fear me."

Lailani placed a hand on him. "I don't fear you. I think you're beautiful."

His blue eyes brightened. "Truly, mistress? But I am all dented and rusty, and my arm keeps falling off. I am afraid I am showing my age. I am already twelve years old."

She barked a laugh. "If you're old, then I'm ancient!" She was almost twenty-nine and had begun to dread her creeping age. Officially, she was twenty for the ninth time in a row.

"You are still young for a human, mistress. But robots rarely see service past ten years. That must be how I ended up in JEX's Starship and Robotics Emporium. My previous master must have sold me once I became too old. I do not remember."

"That's horrible." Lailani chopped at a dangling vine. A six-legged frog leaped off the vine, squeaked angrily, then scurried away.

"I would not know, mistress," HOBBS said. "JEX wiped my memory. I have no recollection of who owned me, of what service I performed. Though I imagine that it was brutal and violent. I remember JEX complaining about dry blood in my sockets and gears. And I was, after all, built for war."

"But you remember the man who built you?" she said, swatting away a mosquito. "That Schroder dude?"

"Oh, yes, mistress! That memory is hardcoded and forever precious to me. Master Schroder is a very wise creator and a kind man. Once our mission is completed, I would very much like to visit him. He could repair me properly. Perhaps then I will not break as much, and I will be a better servant to you."

Lailani bit her lip. She stood on her tiptoes, pulled down HOBBS's head, and kissed his metal cheek.

"HOBBS, I'm sorry," she said. "I was an asshole. When I said you're breakable, I didn't mean to imply that you're creaky or old. I think you're beautiful. And wonderful. And amazing. And after our quest, we'll get you all polished up, change your oil, and you'll be good as new. I promise you, HOBBS. I won't abandon you like your old masters. I'll take care of you. Forever."

His eyes seemed to soften, if that was possible in a robot. He stroked her short black hair, his large metal fingers surprisingly gentle.

"And I will take care of you, mistress. Sometimes losing your memories is a blessing. Sometimes having memories can be a burden. I know that you suffer this burden. I cannot carry it for you. But I will always be here at your side, helping you march on, fighting to keep you safe. There is still some fight in me yet."

She picked a flower and slung the stalk through a groove in his armored plates. "I think you are far wiser, and far kinder, than any fancy android, sir."

As they traveled onward, signs of an ancient civilization appeared. At first, they found only small artifacts: a cloven helmet, the copper engraved with rearing serpents; a spearhead shaped like a bird, the shaft long gone; and shattered pottery, roots growing through the clay, the shards still showing painted hunters. Blessedly, they even found a road. It was formed of cobblestones, and many weeds and even trees were growing from it. No feet had walked here in years, it seemed, and the forest was slowly reclaiming the road. But it allowed them to walk faster, and Lailani finally sheathed her knife and stopped dreaming of machetes.

As they moved closer to the mountain, they found more and more ancient treasures, everything from coins to crowns. In the afternoon, they rested in the shade of a towering statue carved into a cliff. It could have dwarfed the Statue of Liberty. The statue was vaguely apelike, with six limbs, two tails, and an impressive jaw with sharp fangs. Lailani didn't know if this was how the locals had looked, or whether this was simply an imaginary god.

A couple of hours later, she found an answer. A tomb plunged into a hillside, and when she peeked inside, she found skeletons. They matched the statue though they were much smaller, no larger than her. The skeletons were draped with beautiful jewels: bracelets, necklaces, crowns, and rings, all worked with gemstones. She spent some time in the tomb, seeking an hourglass, but came up empty.

She continued her journey along the old road. She saw no living members of this species. It seemed they had gone extinct eras ago. That evening, Lailani spotted a different species: a turkey-sized animal with green fur, golden horns, and rows of eyes across its abdomen. It didn't look remotely intelligent, but it did look tasty. A shot from Lailani's rifle felled the animal.

By nightfall, they reached the foothills. Lailani built a campfire and roasted her catch. She bit into the tender meat.

"Tastes like chicken," she said.

She shared the meal with Epimetheus, giving him the lion's share.

She made a bed of leaves and vines, and she slept by the fire, Epimetheus curled up atop her feet. HOBBS remained up, guarding the camp. Before she drifted off, Lailani gazed at the robot. He sat with his back to her, watching the night. The firelight painted him orange, and fireflies glowed around him.

Who are you, HOBBS? She wondered. *What did you do in the past? You say you don't remember. But I see that it haunts you. We need each other, don't we? Us broken things, not fully human. We were both built as weapons. We both just want an end to war.*

At dawn, they began climbing the mountain. The native Mahatekis had carved a narrow path along the mountainside, just wide enough for Lailani to place one foot before the other. HOBBS barely fit. As they climbed, alien birds plagued them, large as eagles and black as ravens. One of the bastards scratched

Lailani, and another bird nearly knocked Epimetheus down the mountainside. Lailani had to shoot three of the buggers before the rest fled.

As they climbed higher, they discovered artwork engraved into the mountainsides. Native Mahatekis were portrayed here—thousands of stone warriors, clad in feathers, fighting with spears and bows and arrows. Other engravings showed the gods, splendid creatures that towered above the mortals, and Lailani saw flecks of gold where gilt had once covered the engravings. In some engravings, the natives rode the feathered dinosaurs Lailani had encountered below. At least those gargantuan aliens had survived, even if their masters had not.

Runes were etched into the stone, an ancient language she could not read. She had her tablet with her, and she took photographs of these engravings on the mountainsides.

Perhaps no other human will visit here for thousands of years, she thought. *Perhaps this is all that remains of this civilization. Let me preserve what I can.*

She chewed her lip. "Boys, I don't see any sign of technology. The aliens in the engravings are using spears and bows. How could they have built the hourglass—a time machine? Are we in the wrong place?"

Epimetheus and HOBBS were silent, perhaps sharing her concerns.

They slept on the mountainside. The wind blasted them throughout the night, rain fell, and the wood they found was too wet to burn. Dawn rose sticky and hot, and Lailani found that insects had bitten her during the night, had laid eggs in her skin. She grimaced in disgust, bit a stick, and carved them out with her knife. She disinfected and bandaged her wounds, cursing herself for sleeping outside her spacesuit. When she put on that spacesuit, she cursed again and quickly tore it off. A scorpion fled, leaving a red, swollen bite on her leg.

At noon, they reached the mountaintop. Lailani paused to gather her strength. From here upon the mountaintop, they could see for kilometers around. Several other peaks rose around them, draped with greenery. Clouds floated between them. Below, the jungle spread into the horizons, giving way only where rivers cut through it.

Gazing upon the landscape, Lailani gasped, and her eyes widened

"Look!" She pointed. "More dinosaurs! They're flying!"

The creatures were huge—as large as the *Ryujin*. She could see that even from here. Their wings sprouted blue, green, and golden feathers. Their jaws opened wide, shrieking. They flew between the mountains, dived into the misty valleys, and rose again. They circled the sky. One flew so close to Lailani that the shadow fell over her, and the beat of its wings blasted back her hair.

"The natives used to ride them," she whispered in awe. "Like we saw in the engravings. No. They're not dinosaurs." She smiled shakily. "They're dragons."

She stood for a long while, watching these magnificent creatures fly, until finally they headed into the distance and vanished into the mist, beasts forgotten by time.

Perhaps I will burn my photographs, Lailani thought. *Perhaps I don't want anyone to ever find this place, ever tame these wonderful creatures.*

She turned away from the view. She gazed at the mountaintop. She had reached her destination.

Ahead loomed the city gates. Not much remained. The city walls were crumbling, sprouting weeds, and twisting trees grew from them, grabbing the craggy bricks with their roots. Stone guardians flanked an archway, a hundred feet tall, still clutching stone spears. Countless years of wind and rain had withered their faces. All that remained were empty eye sockets filled with weeds and birds' nests.

A cobbled road led through the city. Lailani walked at the lead, rifle slung across her back. HOBBS and Epimetheus walked behind her. Terraces were cut into the mountain here, forming hundreds of ledges, and brick walls held them up. They reminded Lailani of the rice paddies back home. Perhaps crops had once grown here, but today only weeds and trees grew from the terraces. Past these farmlands rose hundreds of stone buildings, most barely standing. Their roofs had fallen. Trees grew from them, roots clutching the crumbling walls. Thousands of people must have lived here, but Lailani saw no skeletons, no sign of the natives, only old statues along the roadsides.

Deeper into the city, she saw larger buildings. Temples. Palaces. Towers. Creepers, trees, and moss coated them all, slowly tugging them back into the jungle. Within another few centuries, only scattered stones would remain. Largest among them all loomed a round building, windowless, its walls engraved with stars.

"It's an observatory," Lailani said, eyes wide.

She walked toward the round building, leaving the crumbling temples and palaces behind. The observatory towered, as large as a castle. When she stepped around a copse of trees, Lailani found a weedy courtyard leading toward the observatory's arched entrance. A statue of a native Mahateki, green with moss, rose in the courtyard. The alien stood with his head lowered, holding a stone hourglass.

Lailani gasped.

"It's here," she whispered.

She raced toward the statue. She reached up, hand shaky, and touched the stone hourglass. Was this the artifact she sought? No. Merely a stone hourglass, part of the statue, mossy and cracked.

"The true hourglass must be inside," she said, looking up at the observatory.

"Mistress, this was a preindustrial society," said HOBBS. "Whatever hourglass we find here will merely tell time, not change time."

"I must trust my vision," Lailani said. "It brought me this far."

Back on the *Ryujin*, she had a framed photograph of herself with her platoon. She kept a copy in her pocket. She pulled it out now. She gazed at that teenage girl, a survivor of the slums, her head shaved, her wrists scarred, her arms around Elvis. She tucked the photo back into her pocket.

"I believe," she whispered.

Epimetheus barked in agreement.

She approached the observatory's entrance, a towering stone archway. The keystone was shaped like a wise face, eyes closed. The companions stepped inside to find a vast hall, weeds pushing through the floor tiles. Moss covered the walls, and when Lailani brushed it aside, she revealed faded murals of stargazing natives. This confirmed what she had suspected—this was indeed an observatory.

She frowned and approached a wall. "HOBBS, look at this."

The robot joined her. They pulled vines off the wall, revealing an engraving. Paint had once covered it, the colors now faded and flaking. But Lailani could still make out the images. The artwork was life-sized, showing a group of Mahatekis staring attentively at a gray.

"The grays were here!" Lailani drew her gun, snarling. "Those fuckers! They beat us to this place!"

"Long ago, Mistress," said HOBBS. "This engraving seems centuries old."

She holstered her gun, cursing her nervousness. She took another look at the engraving. Were the Mahatekis worshiping the gray? She cleared off more moss. No. They were learning from him. The gray's stone hands were expressive, as if he were explaining something difficult. Mathematical formulas and charts were engraved around him.

She brushed off more moss. And there, beside the stone gray—an engraved hourglass.

Lailani gasped. "Look, HOBBS! The gray in the engraving! He taught the natives how to build the hourglass!"

HOBBS nodded. "That makes sense, mistress. Time travel involves complex physics, beyond what most species—even humans—are capable of. The Mahatekis were clearly highly intelligent, judging by the complexity of their architecture and artwork, but preindustrial. They needed help with this technology."

Lailani frowned. "Why would the grays share such rare technology?"

"I do not know, Mistress," HOBBS said. "I cannot speculate. Let us keep searching. Perhaps we will find answers."

She nodded and they kept exploring the observatory. Doorways and staircases led to the rest of the complex. Lailani chose a staircase at random and climbed. Epimetheus followed. HOBBS, who weighed more than both combined, stayed below, preferring not to disturb the ancient construction. Lailani was winded by the time she reached the top floor. A dome rose here, large as a planetarium, with several small openings in the roof.

"Look, Epi." Lailani pointed. "See those holes in the roof? They were carved intentionally. They form a constellation. To let the starlight in, I bet."

She brushed moss off the floor, and she saw silver stars worked into the stone, forming a map of the heavens. A great stone dial rose in the center, carved with runes. She did not understand the purpose of this chamber. Was it used for science? For worship? For a mix of both?

She spent a while searching, but she found no hourglass. She did, however, find hidden chambers in the walls, and inside were ancient scrolls. She unrolled several parchments, revealing beautiful illustrations of orbits, constellations, solar systems, and many diagrams she did not understand. Letters in a foreign language looked like mathematical formulas.

"They were scientists, Epi," she said. "They didn't have technology like us, maybe. But they understood science. They were stargazers."

She stepped back downstairs.

"Sorry, HOBBS, no hourglass in this building," she said. "Maybe in the temple?"

They explored the temple next, moving chamber by chamber, encountering statues, scrolls, and nesting animals—but no hourglass. The palace took even longer to explore, but besides several skeletons draped in jewels, it revealed nothing. They spent the night outside, sleeping by a campfire, hungry and pestered by insects. This time Lailani slept in her spacesuit.

"I can't believe it," Lailani said when dawn rose. "Fuck! I was sure the hourglass would be in the observatory." She pointed. "I mean, there's a statue outside and it's holding an hourglass. God! Maybe somebody else got here first. Took the hourglass."

She shuddered. "The grays said they were seeking it too. Those wrinkly ass fuckers!"

She grabbed fistfuls of her hair—it had just grown long enough—and tugged in frustration. Was all this—fleeing Earth, battling the grays, surviving this jungle—for nothing?

Her eyes watered. *Damn it. Damn it!*

"I just wanted to save them," she whispered. "To save Sofia. To save Elvis. To save my own soul. To redeem myself." Her tears flowed. "To change the past. But maybe that's impossible. Maybe I can't change who I am. No chip in my brain can change that. No hourglass can undo my sin."

She sat on the ground and lowered her head. Epimetheus curled up at her side, and she wrapped her arms around him, but even he could not comfort her today.

She felt a large, hard hand on her shoulder. She looked up to see HOBBS standing above her.

"I am sorry, mistress," he said. "I know what it is like to fail. To feel lost." He raised his hands and looked at them. "Sometimes I can still see the blood, dark and dry between my moving parts. I do not know who I killed. I have no memory of the killings. Only of the dried blood. I can still feel it. Sometimes I still feel buried under the weight of guilt." He patted Lailani. "I know how you feel. I am sorry."

Buried. Lailani nodded. Yes, buried under guilt. That was how it felt. To be crushed under stones, in a dark underground, in—

She leaped up.

"Buried," she whispered.

HOBBS tilted his head. "Mistress?"

"HOBBS, come on!" She grabbed his hand. "Hurry!"

They raced back into the observatory, and Lailani began exploring the floor, tapping with a stick. Finally, in the center of the room—there. A large flagstone the size of a manhole cover. When she tapped it—a hollow sound.

"A basement," she whispered.

She grabbed the flagstone and strained. It wouldn't budge. She stumbled back, panting.

"HOBBS, my darling?"

The bulky robot nodded. "Allow me, mistress." He grabbed the round stone, strained for a moment, then managed to pry it free. He placed the thick stone disk aside. It probably weighed more than Lailani.

Where the stone had been—a staircase led underground.

Lailani's fingers trembled. She lit her flashlight and climbed down.

The passageway was narrow. HOBBS barely fit. The air was hot and musty. Cobwebs hung everywhere, and roots crawled across the walls. Insects scurried underfoot, white and eyeless. Lailani wondered if they had lived here underground for centuries, sealed in the darkness. Stone faces gazed from the walls, mocking, laughing, snarling, perhaps the faces of ancient gods.

She reached the bottom of the staircase. A round door stood here, twice her height, and carved of stone. A star system was engraved onto the door. The sun and planets were formed of jewels, and silver grooves marked their orbits. Lailani leaned against the door, but it wouldn't budge. Even HOBBS, with all his might, could not push the door open.

"Damn it!" Lailani said. "What do we do? Blast the door open with missiles? The ceiling is likely to cave in."

"Perhaps this is not a door at all, mistress," HOBBS said. "Perhaps this is merely a round stone wall, and this is the extent of the underground."

Lailani stared at the massive stone disk. At the jeweled sun in the center. At the gemstone planets along the silver orbits. A map. A map of this solar system. And around the door, she saw smaller jewels, pale and glimmering, representing the stars.

"It's an orrery," she said. "A starmap. And a riddle."

She closed her eyes, bringing back to memory the dome high above, the round windows allowing a view of the stars, the map of the planets and sundial on the floor. She opened her eyes. She grabbed one of the gemstone planets embedded into the door. She nudged it. The planet slid along the silver groove, its orbit around the gemstone sun, like a toy train along a track.

Lailani grinned.

"HOBBS, I need you to do some math," she said. "We need to arrange these planets to match the view of the sky we saw engraved in the dome above."

HOBBS nodded. "Yes, mistress. There are sixteen gemstones on this doorway, matching the sixteen planets in this star system. To the ancient Mahatekis, the planets would have appeared like wandering stars, forming fluid constellations."

"One planet formation must have been holy to the Mahatekis," she said. "So they carved holes into the dome above. When the planets reached the right positions, the light would shine through, lighting the altar we saw above. Perhaps it denoted a holy day, and they needed to track it accurately for worship." She nodded. "Let's try arranging that shape here. Can you help?"

They worked together, moving the planets. It was easy to recognize Mahatek on the doorway; it was the only green gemstone, matching the green world. The other gem colors matched this system's other planets. Finally they arranged the last planet, a red gas giant formed of rubies, into position.

"This should be a match, mistress," HOBBS said. "This configuration would give a viewer from Mahatek the lights to shine through the dome above."

"And maybe reveal some secrets," Lailani said, leaning against the door.

It slid open with barely any resistance.

Lailani glanced at her companions.

"Ready, boys?"

"Ready," HOBBS said.

Epimetheus barked once. *Ready.*

They stepped through the doorway.

Lailani shone her flashlight around. HOBBS turned up the brightness on his eyes, adding two beams of light. The glow illuminated a chamber coated with moss, mold, dust, and cobwebs. A mural was still visible on the walls, depicting native Mahatekis bowing before a king. The monarch, drawn larger than the commoners, stood on a dais, a scepter with a crystal head in hand. His fur was gilded, his head raised high, and his eyes were two diamonds.

"Look!" Lailani pointed at the mural. "The hourglass!"

The device appeared in the mural too! The king was holding it in one of his four hands!

Excitement growing in her, Lailani walked deeper into the chamber. Her light revealed a group of stone statues. They stood twice Lailani's height, even taller than HOBBS. They were formed of boulders piled together, only vaguely humanoid, gruff stone monsters. Their rocky faces were long and stern; they reminded Lailani of the Easter Island heads. Gems shone in their eyes. The statues formed a ring, protecting something behind them.

Lailani pointed her flashlight, and her eyes widened.

"Look, boys!" she whispered.

Beyond the statues rose an altar. And upon the altar he rested. The man from the mural. The King of Mahatek.

He was no longer handsome or noble. His tawny fur had withered away; only patches remained. His skin clung to his bones. His cheeks were sunken, his eyes closed. They had mummified him, and he was more than a skeleton, but not *much* more. In one of his hands, he still held the scepter from the mural, the one with the crystal head.

In another hand, he held the hourglass.

"It's real," Lailani whispered, eyes damp. "I knew it."

It was a beautiful artifact, adorned with gold and jewels, filled with purple sand. But Lailani didn't care for its beauty or treasures.

It can bend time, she thought. *It can send me back. To undo everything.* She wiped her eyes. *To bring back the lost.*

She raised her chin, struggled to keep her lips from trembling, and took a step toward the king in his tomb.

The statues moved to block her way.

Lailani froze, and her jaw unhinged.

She took a step back.

"Did you just see that?" she whispered over her shoulder.

She looked back at the statues. They stared at her, crystal eyes shining. They were blocky things, merely stones stacked together like Inuit inukshuks. Their fists were larger than Lailani's head.

Lailani took another step toward them.

Again the statues moved, shedding dust.

And then the statues spoke.

Their voices boomed, echoing in the chamber, impossibly deep, the bass rippling through Lailani's chest. They spoke in a foreign tongue, but they sounded angry. Their massive stone hands rose, and their eyes blazed.

Lailani gulped and took another step back.

"How can this be?" she whispered. "Is this magic?"

Epimetheus growled at the statues. HOBBS stared at them, and humming rose from his internal circuits.

"Technology, mistress," he said. "Advanced technology unlike any humanity has developed. Giving life to stone, thoughts to crystals . . . Fascinating."

"Sounds like magic to me," said Lailani.

HOBBS nodded. "That which we do not understand always seems like magic. One man's scientist is another man's wizard."

"Well, I ain't no man, and I'm getting that hourglass," Lailani said.

She had a translating app on her tablet, enabling her to speak to a hundred alien species, but she doubted these statues knew any common tongues. So she spoke in English, hoping they understood her tone if not her words.

"Stand back, stone guardians! I don't want to harm you or your king. I seek the hourglass to undo an evil from the past. Will you let me have it?"

She took another step toward them, testing her limits.

The statues' crystal eyes flared, blinding her. The guardians' patience had run out. They lunged toward her, stone fists swinging.

Lailani leaped back, but she was too slow. A stone fist grazed her arm. She yowled as it drew blood; any closer and it would have crushed her bone. Another statue lurched toward her, arm swinging. She ducked, dodging the fist.

"That does it!" She raised her rifle and fired.

Bullets slammed into the statues—and shattered.

Hot metal shards bounced back toward her.

One bullet's shard sliced her calf, taking off more skin. More shrapnel hit HOBBS, and Epimetheus whimpered, ducking. Fuck! So much for using bullets. She tried to back away, to retreat, but more statues emerged from behind, blocking the exit.

"I will handle them, mistress!" HOBBS said.

The robot stepped forward. He was a large machine, but smaller than these guardians. With a rumble, HOBBS began to fight.

He shoved one stone guardian, knocking the beast against the wall. Another statue punched the robot, denting the steel plating. HOBBS swung his own fist, knocking back another guardian. More stone fists slammed into him, denting, cracking, bending. HOBBS fell to one knee.

"HOBBS!" Lailani cried.

The robot bellowed, shoved himself up, and drove his shoulder into a stone guardian. He spun around, punching, hitting another golem. Creaking and shedding rust, HOBBS grabbed one of the stone soldiers. Armor bending, HOBBS managed to lift the massive creature overhead, then toss him into two more statues, knocking them down.

Lailani wanted to help. But she saw her opening. She knew her task. She ran between the fallen guardians.

One reached out toward her. Lailani leaped, escaping its hands. She landed behind the automatons and raced toward the mummified king.

The stone guardians bellowed behind her. They rose and reached toward her. HOBBS knocked one back down. Another guardian nearly reached Lailani. HOBBS grabbed its head, yanked it back. The guardians mobbed him, pounding him, bending his armor. Half his face was crushed. Epimetheus was barking in fury, biting and scratching at the stone creatures.

"Mistress, grab the hourglass!" HOBBS cried, voice slurred.

She stared down at the mummified king. He lay before her, wreathed in jewels. The hourglass rested under his skeletal hand—right there, within her reach.

More fists flew into HOBBS. The robot cried out wordlessly. Screws rolled.

Lailani turned away from the hourglass. She reached down, grabbed the king's jeweled scepter, and wrenched it free.

She spun toward the guardians, raising the scepter. The crystal on its head beamed with light.

"Stop!" she cried.

The guardians stared at her with their crystal eyes—eyes that matched the crystal on the scepter. They froze. HOBBS stood between them, cracked and sparking.

Lailani took a step forward, waving the scepter like a brand.

"Back!" she said.

The guardians stepped back.

"Up against the walls!"

She swung the scepter from side to side. Its crystal shone. She herded the stone guardians against the walls.

"You were right," she said to HOBBS, a smile trembling on her lips. "Technology." She hefted the scepter. "Remote control."

HOBBS looked at her, creaking. Then he fell to his knees.

"HOBBS!" Lailani ran toward him. Epimetheus joined her, licking the robot in concern.

"I am fine, mistress," HOBBS said, his voice staticky, his jaw bent. "Just a little winded. You saved my life, mistress."

"Only because you distracted them long enough. We'll get you patched up, buddy. I promise. And hey, look on the bright side. Your arm didn't fall off this time!"

HOBBS nodded. "I favored the other arm, mistress." He groaned and struggled to his feet. "I am fine, mistress. I will perhaps not be waltzing anytime soon, but I am otherwise functioning."

Her eyes widened. "You made a funny! That's the first time I heard you crack a joke. They must have hit you hard on the head." She couldn't reach that head, not with him standing up, but she kissed his chest. "I'm glad you're still with us, Hobster." When Epimetheus whined, she mussed his ears. "Now don't you get jealous, Epi! You just got a little scratch."

Reassured that her boys were all right, she returned to the mummified king. She pried the hourglass from his hands. It was smaller than she had thought at first, small enough to fit in a coffee mug, and filled with purple sand. She tilted it from side to side, but the sand did not stir. On closer inspection, she saw a network of gears, tiny moving gemstones, and buttons worked into the hourglass's flat edges.

"It's definitely some kind of machine," she said. "But how does it work?"

Epimetheus barked and ran ahead, moving deeper into the tomb. The dog turned back toward Lailani, gave a pointed whine, then turned back toward the shadows.

Lailani glared at the stone guardians. She pointed her scepter at them. "Stay!"

She turned and followed Epimetheus. HOBBS joined them. At the back of the tomb, they discovered a towering wall, several times Lailani's height. The wall was covered with inscriptions—thousands, maybe millions of tiny symbols carved into the stone. Along with the alien language, she saw several drawings of the hourglass's mechanics, graphs, and mathematical formulas.

"So," Lailani said, "we found the user manual." She sighed. "It couldn't have come in a little booklet, could it?"

"Do not worry, mistress," HOBBS said. "I have a photographic memory. I've already stored this image in my memory banks."

"Do you understand it?" Lailani said.

"I think so, mistress. It is mostly machine code, I think. A computer program. I believe that I can code an interface for it, translate it into a language I can run." He nodded, clanking noises emerging from his skull. "Yes. Yes, this is amazing, mistress! It describes how the hourglass can manipulate spacetime. The sand in the hourglass, mistress! It is powdered azoth."

She gasped. "Like the crystals that let us bend spacetime to go faster than light."

"Yes, mistress. Azoth has a unique property. The way other crystals can refract light, azoth crystals can refract spacetime itself, the fabric of the cosmos. Humans use it to bend spacetime like a tablecloth, shortening the distance starships must travel between two points. The Mahatekis discovered another property of azoth. They could use it to bend the fourth dimension—time." HOBBS's eyes shone. "It is truly astounding, mistress. The instructions describe exactly how many grains of sand to spill, and at what angle, adjusting to the local gravitational forces and velocity, to calculate the date you travel to."

Lailani winced. "You mean I'd need to spill an exact number of sand grains?"

HOBBS nodded. "Yes, mistress. A task impossible for human hands. You would invariably spill too few or too many grains, ending up many years off the mark. But I remind you, mistress. I am a robot. My hands are steady. My eyes can capture the exact number of grains spilled. I will help you travel to your destination."

Lailani patted the robot. "Hobster, my boy, I do believe that finding you was the best thing that ever happened to me." When Epimetheus whined, she groaned and patted him. "That is, right after finding you, my jealous little Epi. Now come on, boys. It's time to go home. Let's blow this joint."

"I thought you did not want us to blow up anything, mistress," HOBBS said.

"Blow, not blow up," Lailani said. "It's—forget it. Let's amscray."

They passed between the stone guardians, Lailani holding them back with her scepter, and climbed the stairs. For so long now, Lailani had felt hopeless. Had felt herself fraying at the seams, crushed with guilt. For years now, she had suffered with the shame of who she was. A monster. A demon hybrid. A creature that had slain a friend. Tears filled her eyes as she climbed the stairs, moving back toward the light.

But it'll be over soon, she thought. *I'll cleanse my soul soon. And this nightmare—this nightmare that has been my life—will be over.* She dabbed her wet eyes. *And we'll all be together again. Me. Elvis. Sofia. Marco and Addy and Ben-Ari. I can bring Kemi back too. I can save everyone.*

As she climbed back toward the light, she thought it like a metaphor. She was leaving the shadows of her life—a life of poverty, despair, depression, a life surviving suicide attempts and war and loss. She was heading toward the light. Toward friends and love. Toward finally finding peace.

She reached the hidden doorway, and she climbed onto the main floor of the observatory.

She froze.

She screamed.

She raised her rifle and fired.

They had been waiting for her. Hundreds of them. Filling the chamber.

The grays.

CHAPTER TWENTY-TWO

The *Lodestar* entered orbit about Isfet, a hellish desert world.

Ben-Ari stood on the bridge, staring down at this searing planet. She clenched her fists.

Isfet flew too close to the sun for comfort. Its surface was searing hot, dry, lifeless. Their telescopes revealed sand, dunes, canyons, craters, and rocky mountains. There was only a thin atmosphere, and the radiation was immense. It made the Sahara seem hospitable.

If anyone wanted to hide, here was the place. Nobody in their right mind would land on such a world.

Men in dark robes, she thought. *What are you doing here?*

"Captain," said Professor Isaac, "we're detecting an unusual structure. It's accompanied by distinctive radiation. Perhaps just a geyser."

He brought it up on a monitor. The image was still distant, but as the *Lodestar* flew closer, it came into view.

"A pyramid," Ben-Ari whispered.

"Perhaps just a mountain," said the professor.

She shook her head. "No. This is a manmade structure. These are our guys."

The pyramid rose from the desert, casting a long shadow. They saw no other structures around it. No spaceport, no homes, no farms, not even roads. Just that pyramid rising from the desert. It had been built from local sandstone, blending into the surroundings. The surface was tanned and polished, reflecting the sunlight.

Isaac worked at his monitor. "According to our scans, the pyramid stands three hundred meters tall." The professor turned to look at Ben-Ari. "That's twice the height of the pyramid of Giza."

"Whoever lives here wanted to hide," Ben-Ari said, "but obviously not *too* badly." She turned toward her pilot. "Aurora, bring us to an orbit above the pyramid. Keep us five hundred kilometers above the planet surface." Next she faced her security officer. "Marino, full power to front shields."

"Think we've got a fight on our hands?" Marino said, cracking his knuckles.

Ben-Ari thought for a moment. "Yes," she finally said.

Marino's eyes flashed—a mixture of excitement and fear. He nodded. "Full power to shields."

They entered orbit around Isfet. Their scanners showed a thin yet breathable atmosphere. Ben-Ari saw no water. If any existed here, it was underground. Mostly, this world was just rock, sand, blinding light, and intolerable heat.

"Surface temperature estimated at fifty-two degrees Celsius," Professor Isaac said. "It's a hot one."

Ben-Ari cringed. That was ten degrees hotter than the hottest day she had experienced at Fort Djemila back in an Earth desert.

Fish walked up toward them, his tanned face crinkling as he gazed out the viewport at the desert world.

"Crikey!" the Alien Hunter said. "Why would any bludger live on this dry, bodgey rock when Yarrow, an ace planet, is nearby?"

"For the isolation," Ben-Ari said. "A coward commits his evil in hiding. We'll find the missing children here."

Fish placed a hand on Ben-Ari's shoulder. "We'll find those ratbags who kidnapped them too, and they'll be sorrier than a fly in cobwebs. Nobody kidnaps little kids when the *Lodestar*'s around."

She turned to look at the tall Australian. He looked down at her with a small smile and nod.

They blasted down in the shuttle: Ben-Ari, Professor Isaac, Fish, Marino, and three security guards. In the small shuttle, it was a tight squeeze; the three guards had to stand between the seats. They all wore spacesuits. They all carried weapons: a plasma rifle for Ben-Ari, assault rifles for Marino and his boys, and pistols for the professor and Alien Hunter.

As they flew, Ben-Ari felt that old fear.

One of my people betrayed us. Somebody led the grays to us.

No. It was nonsense. She had dismissed that notion as mere paranoia weeks ago. And yet it would not leave her. Was the traitor back on the ship? Or even here in her shuttle, one of her inner circle?

Keep your eyes open, Einav, she told herself. *Trust nobody.*

They touched down on the sand by the pyramid. The structure soared above them, blinding in the sunlight. Ben-Ari was used to thinking of pyramids as craggy and crumbling, like the ones in Egypt, but these walls were smooth and polished. This was no ruin.

She emerged from the shuttle. The gravity was lighter on Isfet. Ben-Ari weighed only half as much here, allowing her to bounce across the sand with ease. The heat bathed her at once, and sweat dampened her uniform. The sunlight blasted against her with almost a physical force. The others followed, hopping across the sand, approaching the pyramid. They all still wore their spacesuits and helmets; the atmosphere here would be punishing, rough on the lungs, cruel on the skin. They saw no life. Not even insects or scrub. The only sign that anyone had ever lived here was the pyramid.

As she drew closer to the pyramid, Ben-Ari gasped.

She had not seen it before, not with the glaring sunlight. But it loomed above her now—a massive engraving, hundreds of meters tall. It sprawled across the surface of the pyramid.

"It's her," Ben-Ari whispered. "Nefitis."

She remembered the alien queen from her vision. A gray, but taller than the others, cadaverous, naked, a crown nailed into her head. That queen stood before her now, five hundred meters tall, carved into the pyramid's facade. The creature's stone eyes seemed to stare down at her.

In her hand, the engraved goddess held an ankh—a cross with a handle. Ben-Ari knew the symbol. It was the Ancient Egyptian symbol for immortality. In Egyptian art, the gods were often portrayed holding ankhs. Why was this alien queen holding one, a symbol from ancient Earth?

"Fuck me dead!" Fish exclaimed, coming to stand beside her. "Who the hell is that sheila?"

Communicators were embedded into their helmets, transmitting their words to one another.

"Her name is Nefitis," Ben-Ari said softly.

"I thought Obadiah said there were no damn aliens here," Fish said. "Only men in dark robes. What the hell is going on?"

"I don't know," Ben-Ari said. "But we're going to find out. Does anyone see a door?"

They walked around the pyramid, bouncing over the sand, dwarfed by the monolith. They moved out from the sunlit side into the pyramid's shadow. Here, finally, they saw what appeared to be a doorway. It was triangular, barely large enough to allow passage. Inside, they saw only shadows.

"Does anyone see a doorbell?" Fish asked. "Do we just walk in?"

Ben-Ari raised her plasma gun. "I'll go first. Guards, follow me. Fish, Professor, you walk behind. Marino, bring up the rear." She took a step toward the doorway, paused, and turned to stare at her crew. "If you're threatened, do not hesitate to fire, to kill. You are now soldiers. Understood?"

"Yes, Captain!" they said together.

Ben-Ari nodded. At that moment, she missed her friends more than ever. Missed her brave soldiers. Missed Addy, Marco, Lailani, and the rest of them. They had not only trained to fight. They were dear friends.

But Ben-Ari had a new crew here. New followers. Maybe even new friends. She would lead them well.

She stepped through the narrow opening, entering the pyramid.

It was like entering a tomb. The temperature plummeted. A dark corridor stretched ahead, the walls covered with murals.

Ben-Ari cursed.

"Grays," she muttered, staring at the artwork.

The murals were done in Ancient Egyptian style, but they depicted different themes. Some murals showed saucers flying in the sky. Others showed gray aliens descending to the world, and many humans—painted to look much smaller—bowed before them. Some murals showed gray aliens standing over piles of human skeletons.

"What the hell is this?" Marino muttered from the back of the line.

"Keep your guns raised," Ben-Ari said. "Keep close to me. We're going to find some answers."

As they kept walking, the sunlight faded behind them. Only the flashlights mounted onto their helmets lit the hallway.

Ben-Ari had once taken a virtual reality tour of Egypt's pyramids, had explored the tunnels that coiled inside the structures. This place reminded her of that old tour, but the stones here were not craggy, the murals not faded. This pyramid was new.

The tunnel eventually opened up into a tomb.

The stone chamber was the size of the *Lodestar*'s bridge. Most of the room was empty. In the center, a ring of candles shone, surrounding a glass display case. Inside the case stood a gray alien.

Ben-Ari gasped, prepared to fire. But this gray was dead— long dead, by the looks of it. She stepped closer, eyes-narrowed. The alien's eyes were closed, and his arms were folded against his chest, holding a golden ankh. The creature was mummified, skin brown and wrinkly, wrapped in shreds of linen.

"A mummy," she whispered. "An alien mummy."

She leaned closer, staring at the creature. The slits where the nose should be. The massive head. The frowning mouth. The long, twisting fingers, still tipped with claws.

"Who are you?" she whispered.

The creature almost seemed to be breathing, a movement so subtle she must have imagined it. The visions from her dream returned to her: a distant world, dark, storming, a rotting queen on a throne . . .

"Greetings, greetings!"

The voice boomed and echoed through the tomb, so loud that Ben-Ari started and raised her gun.

A man entered the chamber, clad in a black robe and hood, his open hands held out before him.

"Do not fear me!" the man said. "I am a mere servant of Nefitis." He bowed, then straightened and pulled back his hood.

Ben-Ari inhaled sharply. Around her, her companions hissed too, and Marino raised his gun.

A gray! she thought at first, staring at the robed figure. But no. This was a mere man. Yet he was hideously deformed. His nose had been sliced off, leaving only two holes for nostrils. His head was bald like a gray's, but normal human size, and his eyes were small and blue.

"Do not be startled by my appearance," the man said. "All adherents of Nefitis seek to be closer to the goddess—in spirit as well as body. When I joined our order, I cut off my own nose, then burned the flesh upon the altar of Nefitis. Thus I proved my devotion to her, seeking to mimic her appearance as best as my frail mortal body can."

Sick bastards, Ben-Ari thought, staring at the deformity. His ears too, she saw, had been sliced off, leaving only holes. His little fingers too were gone, mimicking the way grays had only four fingers per hand. She knew that some religions practiced body modification—circumcision leaped to mind—but she had never seen a faith distort its adherents so extensively.

"My name is—" she began.

"Einav Ben-Ari," the man completed for her. "Yes, we know who you are. We've been watching your ship for a while now." He gave a little nod. "I am Harsiese, son of Baphmet, cleric of Nefitis. Welcome to our humble home! We do not entertain guests often, but we'll be glad to serve you some refreshments, and—"

"What is that creature?" It was Ben-Ari's turn to interrupt. She pointed at the mummy. "Is that Nefitis?"

The man gave a hearty laugh. "No, of course not! That is merely one of her ancient servants. We call him the Scribe. We do not know his true name, only that he descended with Queen Nefitis down onto Earth five thousand years ago. It was a day we call the Golden Dawn." His eyes became glazed, and his voice dropped to an awed whisper. "It was a day most glorious. The day the goddess herself delivered her wisdom to humanity. If only I could have been there to see Nefitis in person! To hear her holy words!" He pulled a scroll from his robes. "Here is the Holy Writ, the words of Nefitis herself, but only a few sentences from a great saga. It is our mission to seek the full text of her wisdom. So much has been lost to history . . ." He shook his head wildly, as if clearing it of thoughts, and smiled. "But come now. I prattle on while you are weary from your journey. Come, come, I will serve you some sweet water from our wells."

The robed man walked toward a door at the back. Ben-Ari glanced at her crew and nodded. They lowered their weapons and followed.

The man took them down a corridor lined with more display cases, and inside stood mummies of more grays. Dim orange lights shone overhead. Archways led to other corridors, and Ben-Ari saw more robed figures moving to and fro, all in black robes and hoods. When the light shone in their hoods, Ben-Ari saw more deformed faces: the noses and ears sliced off.

Fish inched up toward her, leaned down, and whispered into her ear.

"I don't like these shonky ratbags," he whispered. "You think they're the ones who kidna—"

"Hush," she whispered. "Keep your eyes open and your fingers near your triggers."

Robes rustling, Harsiese led them into a chamber the size of a movie theater. Columns surrounded the room, and dozens of men stood between them, robed in black. Torches crackled, and where the light shone into hoods, Ben-Ari saw missing noses.

A statue dominated the chamber, twice a man's height—a statue of Nefitis. The alien queen was carved from sandstone, and she held out one arm, holding a stone scroll. A glass pane appeared on the statue's base. The glass protected scraps of parchment—a real scroll. The parchment was badly damaged, only several words visible, written in Egyptian hieroglyphics.

"The Holy Writ," Harsiese whispered. "The original copy. The true scroll of Nefitis, written five thousand years ago. It's all that remains of her words. And someday, we will find the rest of the scroll. Someday the wisdom of Nefitis will be complete!" His eyes shone with fervor. "And that day, the cosmos will tremble before her glory!"

Ben-Ari cleared her throat. "Harsiese, your faith is admirable. But we've not come here to worship. We come seeking missing children. We will search this pyramid. You will help us.

Once we've searched every corridor and chamber in this place, we'll leave."

Harsiese turned toward her. For an instant, rage suffused his mutilated face. His eyes narrowed. His lips pulled back in a sneer. But then the moment was gone.

"Of course, of course!" Harsiese said. "We have no secrets here. We would be glad to show you around. But are you sure that first, you wouldn't care for those refreshments? My servants would be glad to serve you water, and—"

With a sudden jerk, Harsiese pulled a baton from under his robes. He thrust it, and a ball of electricity flew toward the crew. The bolt hit one of the *Lodestar*'s security guards, and the man fell, a hole in his chest. Across the chamber, the robed clerics leaped forth, drawing swords and maces.

"Fire!" Ben-Ari shouted, pulling her rifle's trigger. A bolt of plasma blasted forth.

She hit a cleric, but the man kept charging. As his cloak billowed and burned, she saw armor underneath. The man lashed his sword, and Ben-Ari screamed and swung her rifle, parrying with the muzzle.

"Kill them!" she cried, swinging her rifle in a semicircle. The stock cracked against the cleric's head, knocking the man back.

She spared a brief glance around the chamber. Damn! Dozens of clerics were fighting here, and dozens more came racing from the corridors. She had only five crewmen left, none of whom—aside from Marino—had ever fought a battle before.

One of her security guards fired her gun, hit one cleric, but another robed figure tossed a throwing star. The steel slammed into the guard's throat, and the woman fell, gurgling on blood. A second security guard slew three clerics before a robed man lashed his sword, cutting out the guard's legs. Another blow from the sword finished the job.

Ben-Ari sneered. She fired her gun. She hit a cleric. She fired again, again, knocking down two more attackers. Throwing stars flew toward her. She cursed, fired, and hit one of the projectiles in the air. She ducked and rolled, dodging several more stars. One of the weapons sliced across her side, tearing through her uniform and skin, and she cried out. She leaped up, firing again.

From the *Lodestar*'s crew, they were down to only four. Fish and the professor stood back to back, firing their guns. Marino had grabbed a sword from a fallen cleric, was swinging it madly; he was perhaps out of bullets.

And more clerics came rushing in.

There was no way they could win this battle.

For an instant, terror filled Ben-Ari. Not for herself. But for her crew. For her new friends who would die here.

Then she gritted her teeth, the old soldiers' instinct kicking in.

She fired two blasts, knocking back two clerics. She ran.

She ducked under a swinging sword. She leaped up and thrust her rifle, shattering a man's teeth. She landed, rolled, rose firing, and ran again.

Past puddles of blood, she reached the statue of Nefitis. She stood before the display case at its base. Behind the glass, she saw it—the holy scroll.

She swung the stock of her rifle into the glass. Again. Again.

Finally the hardened glass shattered.

"No!" rose a cry. Harsiese stared in horror, hands raised. "Stop her!"

Ben-Ari pointed her plasma rifle at the scroll. "Stop!" she shouted. "Stop or I burn it!"

The clerics—there must have been a hundred of them here—all froze.

They stared, eyes simmering with hatred . . . and with fear.

"Drop your weapons!" Ben-Ari cried. "Do it—now! Or I burn the scroll!"

"Do as she says!" Harsiese shouted, panic entering his voice. "Drop your weapons!"

With clatters, a hundred clerics dropped batons, swords, maces, and throwing stars. Several corpses lay on the ground—a handful of clerics and three of Ben-Ari's own people. Fish and the professor stood back to back, panting. Marino had suffered a wound to his side, but he was smiling and standing tall. The martial artist gave Ben-Ari an approving nod.

"Up against the wall!" Ben-Ari shouted. She kept her rifle pointed at the scroll. "All of you other than Harsiese—against the wall! Robes off! Now, now!"

At a nod from Harsiese, the clerics obeyed, disrobing and standing naked against the wall. A few had hidden extra weapons under their robes; Marino relieved them of the blades, adding them to a pile in the corner.

As the clerics stripped naked, Ben-Ari grimaced. The men had emasculated themselves, she saw. They had not only cut off their noses to look like the grays; they had removed their genitals as well.

She reached into the shattered case and pulled out the scraps of parchment.

Harsiese winced. "Captain, this scroll is five thousand years old. The touch of unsterilized hands, even just the unfiltered air, can—"

"Shut up or I'll cut out your tongue to match your nose," Ben-Ari snapped. She tightened her grip on the scroll. "You want me to be gentle with this?" She sneered, rage flowing across her. "You murdered three of my crew. I would gladly rip this parchment to shreds and burn what remains with my gun. But I'm in a good mood today. I'm willing to return this scroll to you—if you play nice. You're going to give me a tour of this little museum of yours. When we're done, you can have your paper back. Do we have a deal, Harsiese?"

He bared his teeth at her, face red. His eyes blazed with unadulterated hatred. When he took a step closer to Ben-Ari, reaching out his hands, she tightened her grip on the scroll. The ancient parchment gave an uncomfortable crunch, and a wisp of dust glided down. Harsiese froze, blanching.

"We have a deal," the cleric hissed. "Now be careful with that!"

"Marino, grab him," Ben-Ari said to her hulking Chief of Security.

The wrestler grinned. "Gladly, Captain." He stepped toward the mutilated cleric and grabbed his arms.

Ben-Ari stared at the naked clerics who stood against the wall. "You lot are staying here. My officers are going to guard you. Professor, Fish—keep your guns on them. If any one of them so much as moves to scratch a phantom nose, you fire to kill. Understood?"

Both men looked queasy. Neither one had seen this side of her before.

It's not a quality I was born with, Ben-Ari thought. *It was forged in fire and tempered in ice.*

"Yes, Captain!" they both said, and she was happy to hear determination in their voices. They were scared, both of them. But they would do their jobs.

I'll make soldiers of them yet, Ben-Ari thought with a wry smile.

"All right, Harsiese," Ben-Ari said. "Give us the grand tour."

They stepped through an archway, leaving the chamber with the statue—and leaving the professor and Fish to guard the others.

They continued to explore the pyramid. Harsiese led them down a corridor lined with doors. Through the doorways they saw the clerics' living chambers—austere rooms without beds, only sand on the floor, and metal ankhs on the walls.

Another corridor branched off into command centers, and here Ben-Ari finally saw modern technology: monitors, hieroglyphic keyboards, and computers that oversaw the planet and the stars beyond. Several monitors displayed satellite views of the Yarrow village.

"These bastards only pretend to be ancient monks," Ben-Ari muttered. "They have the latest tech."

They kept exploring. They climbed down staircases, plunging underground. They reached a massive hangar, and inside they saw several starships. Most were no larger than buses, probably used for travel within this star system. One larger ship was installed with warp engines. This was the clerics' interstellar starship, probably the one that had brought them here from Earth.

"How long have you been here?" Ben-Ari said. "I don't recognize this model of starship."

"Thirteen years now," Harsiese hissed. He was still trapped in Marino's grip. "Our work has only begun."

"What work are you doing here?" she said. "Tell me!"

"I told you, Captain," the cleric said. "We seek the entire scroll. Not just the scraps you hold, as holy as they are. But the entire Holy Writ, the commandments Nefitis delivered to the Ancient Egyptians five thousand years ago."

"So why are you searching here?" Ben-Ari said. "Why not search Egypt? Why this desert planet a hundred light-years away?"

"Oh, the original scroll was destroyed long ago," Harsiese said. "It burned with the Library of Alexandria. Only those scraps you profane have remained. There is no use seeking the scroll now." The cleric's eyes lit up. "But if we can return five thousand years into the past . . ."

Ben-Ari frowned. "Time travel? It's impossible. Scientists have been trying to crack that nut for centuries. It can't be done."

Harsiese's eyes burned with a strange light. "Oh but we believe it *can* be done, Captain. That is our purpose here. That is what we are building. Let me show you. Follow me."

The cleric led them out of the hangar, and they left the starships behind. They walked down a corridor, climbed down another staircase, and entered a large laboratory, nearly as large as the starship hangar. The room was filled with cables, monitors, and computers. Several robed clerics were working here, gloved and masked. They started, eyes widening with shock to see the visitors.

"Return to your work, friends!" Harsiese said. "Do not worry. I'm merely showing our dear visitors around."

Ben-Ari looked across the chamber. In its center, upon a stage, stood a towering orrery. It was formed of many metal hoops that circled a chair like planetary orbits around a sun. Lavender crystals were embedded into the rings. Ben-Ari recognized them—azoth crystals. The stones mined in Corpus. The stones used to bend spacetime.

"Our time machine." Harsiese gestured at the metallic rings. "At least, our early prototype. Unfortunately, it doesn't quite work yet."

"You're mad," Ben-Ari said. "All this, just to go back for an old scroll?" She shook her head sadly. "All this effort, the resources you must have spent here, for a pipe dream, for—"

"Papa?" A high-pitched voice rose from ahead. "Papa, who is the pretty lady?"

The smallest, oldest man Ben-Ari had ever seen limped toward her, leaning on a cane. He couldn't have stood more than four feet tall. His fingers were twisting with arthritis. His limbs were stick thin, draped with wrinkled skin. His head was bald, the skin so papery Ben-Ari could see the veins, and no teeth remained in his mouth. Like the robed clerics, his nose and ears had been surgically removed. Ben-Ari thought that he must have been over a hundred. She was surprised he still lived.

Harsiese turned toward the diminutive elder. "Now, now, Timmy. What did I tell you? No leaving the playroom."

"But I wanted to see the lady!" squeaked the old man. "Is my mommy going to come here too?" He looked at Ben-Ari. "Are you somebody's mommy?"

Ben-Ari blinked. She realized that the old man wore children's clothes.

Shock pulsed through her.

She walked around the time machine. She saw a glass wall. Behind it—a dusty room, mold on the walls, with a few mattresses and toys scattered across the floor.

The room was filled with tiny old people. None looked younger than ninety. They were all so thin, so frail, bent and white with age. Some could only move with canes. None was taller than a child. All wore children's clothing.

All their noses and ears had been sliced off.

Harsiese came to stand beside Ben-Ari. He sighed.

"It happens to them all," he said. "It has been happening since the beginning. We place a child in the machine—a child at the prime of health and innocence. We try to send him back in time—sometimes several centuries, sometimes just a few days. No matter what we try, it fails. The child remains here. And then . . ." Harsiese shook his head sadly. "Somehow, we confuse their inner clocks. We break their flow of time. They begin to age rapidly. Within only months, they grow old. None live for longer than a couple of years." He stroked young Timmy's wrinkled, liver-spotted head. "Timmy here is only eight years old. And yet biologically, he's already a hundred. Within a few more weeks, he'll be gone, and we'll need more children. But soon, Ben-Ari! Soon we'll crack the secret! Soon our machine will work! Soon we—"

Ben-Ari struck him.

She struck him so hard that he fell to the floor.

"You sick bastard," she whispered, voice shaking, tears in her eyes. "You twisted monster."

Harsiese lay on the floor, his lip bloodied. He stared up at Ben-Ari, and he began to laugh.

"What do you know of monsters, girl?" He bared bloodied teeth. "What do you know of twisted terror? Do you think you know evil, child, because you faced some backward insects in battle? You know nothing of true might, true terror, true pain— pain far greater than death. You have seen only the ravages of the flesh; you have never seen the shattering of the eternal soul. But my goddess will show you. Yes, child." He laughed, gurgling on blood. "Nefitis knows your name. She speaks of you in her scroll, the very one you hold. When my goddess rises again into the world, your screams will fill the endless void!"

For a moment, Ben-Ari could only stare at the man in horror.

In her mind, she saw it again. The vision she had experienced on the grays' starship. A dark, storming world. A vast, black city. A dark pyramid, an eye upon its crest. An alien queen upon a throne. Eyes that promised endless torture. She felt her consciousness detaching from her body again, as it had back on the saucer. She felt herself slipping into that world, that plane of fear, saw the queen reach out her claws . . .

She forced herself back to the present. She snapped back into her body.

"It's over for you," Ben-Ari said, able to speak no louder than a hoarse whisper. "It's over, Harsiese. This little sick operation of yours. This twisted cult. This evil. It's over." She looked through the window at the children—their bodies so old, their souls so young. "They're finally going home."

They began ferrying the children up to the *Lodestar*.

They used the shuttle for the first batch, gently escorting several children into the small vessel. Then—despite objections from Harsiese—used the clerics' own spacecraft to transport the other children. Within a few hours, they had rescued seventy-three of Yarrow's children.

Hundreds had gone missing from Yarrow. These seventy-three were all who remained.

"Most have another couple of years of life," the *Lodestar*'s doctor told Ben-Ari, eyes soft. "Some maybe only months. They're still aging rapidly. Some might reach age thirteen, maybe fourteen if they're lucky. They will need medical care throughout their lives. Their medical challenges will be daunting, more than Yarrow's two doctors can handle."

"Would you agree to stay on Yarrow with the children?" Ben-Ari asked. "At least until we can send for another medical team from Earth."

The doctor, a silver-haired man with half-moon glasses, nodded. "I would be honored, Captain."

As the *Lodestar* still orbited the desert world of Isfet, and as the rescued children rested in the medical bay, Ben-Ari met with her lieutenants on the bridge.

"We will not leave the Nefitians unpunished," she said. "We will not leave them to keep terrorizing Yarrow, their neighboring world, or any other worlds they can reach."

Fish's eyes widened. He stared out a viewport at the desert world below. "You're not suggesting we nuke them from orbit, are you?" He frowned. "I know they're nasty buggers, but that seems harsh. Even for us."

Ben-Ari shook her head. "No. I won't sentence them to death. Nor will I carry them to Earth to face trial there; they have committed their crimes beyond Earth's jurisdiction. But I *will* punish them." She gazed out at the dry, yellow planet. A wasteland. Scorching hot and desolate. "Life in prison would suit them well. And they have built a prison for themselves. Marino, summon your entire security force. And come with me. We're going back down there."

They worked for long hours in the pyramid, destroying every last bit of Nefitian technology. The time machine. The computer systems. The communicators, the radars, the transmitters. Finally they blasted the Nefitian starships, leaving nothing but charred remains. A few of the clerics tried to resist; the *Lodestar*'s security officers held them back.

"You will never more terrorize your neighbors," Ben-Ari said, standing outside in the sand, speaking to the captive clerics. "You have no more starships to reach Yarrow with. You have no more communicators to call for aid. All your technology is gone. Your world lies far beyond the reach of Earth. Nobody knows you're here. Nobody but me. You will spend the rest of eternity here in this desert."

Harsiese broke forward from the group of clerics. The robed man hissed at her. "You are dooming us to death! This world is dry and lifeless! Without our starships, without being able to visit Yarrow, we have no access to food, to water, to—"

"Your life here will be hard," Ben-Ari said. "I agree. Yet there is water deep underground, far below this desert. We have left you drills. You can reach it. There's not much food here. You'll have to build terrariums. To farm. It will be a hard life. But that is your punishment. This pyramid, where you've imprisoned Yarrow's children, will become your own prison."

Harsiese shoved aside security guards.

"You're sentencing us to slow death!" he shouted, saliva spraying. "Curse you, Einav Ben-Ari. Curse you forever! You will scream in the halls of our goddess! Curse you!"

She turned away from them.

She tightened her jaw.

She walked back toward her shuttle.

"Come," Ben-Ari said to her crew. "We're leaving this place."

The *Lodestar* flew out of the star system. They left behind two planets. A green world of plenty, its children returned to live out their final days with their families. And a dry, desert world, hot and blinding, left helpless in the glare of its sun.

Ben-Ari stood on the bridge, watching those two worlds grow distant, then vanish into the darkness.

She closed her eyes, remembering the terror she had seen on the saucer. The grays performing ritualistic surgery on waking victims. The vision of the dark queen. The ankhs engraved into their walls.

Who are you? she thought. *What is your connection to the clerics we fought? What are you planning, Nefitis?*

There was something linking this all—the clerics below, the gray saucers, the abductions, the time-travel device . . . Some connection she could almost grasp, yet the puzzle kept falling apart in her mind.

She was tired. Bone-tired. She did not remember the last time she had slept. She would return to her chambers, shower, not even bother with a book—just collapse into bed for eight hours of uninterrupted sleep. In the morning, her mind would be clearer, and—

Professor Isaac burst onto the bridge, hair in disarray, uniform wrinkled.

Ben-Ari rushed toward him. "Professor! Are you all right?"

"I just got back from the biolab," he said, unable to hide the tremble in his voice. "My team has completed the DNA analysis on our captive gray. Captain . . . you better come with me. Now."

He rushed off the bridge, and she followed.

CHAPTER TWENTY-THREE

She entered the *Lodestar*'s biolab, a room full of tubes, vials, vats, and scientists. Aquariums held the various species the *Lodestar* had discovered on its journey so far. Furry little creatures hung on branches. Insect-like aliens scuttled back and forth, feeding on crickets. Alien plants swayed and reached out tendrils and snapped their jaws. In other tanks lived more exotic aliens: some made of liquid, others gaseous, other aliens made of rock and crystal.

Professor Noah Isaac, Chief Science Officer, led Ben-Ari through the lab. At the back, a vial of blood floated over a workstation.

"This," the professor said, "is the blood we drew from Specimen A001. The gray sleeping on our ship."

She nodded. "What did you find?"

The professor hit some buttons on a control panel. A hologram appeared, showing a double helix. A strand of DNA.

"This is A001's DNA," the professor said. "Do you see anything unusual?"

She looked at him. "Noah, now is not the time for a science lesson. What—"

"Just look, Einav," he said softly. "Remember what I taught you."

She returned to the hologram. She stared at the DNA strand, frowning. What did he expect her to see here? She was not a scientist! He had been teaching her a little about DNA, of course. She could recognize base pairs. When she zoomed onto sections, she could recognize genes. When she zoomed out, she counted forty-six chromosomes. He had been teaching her all this. She knew the basics. She . . .

She spun her head toward the professor.

"I can understand this," she whispered. She looked back at the double helix. "But . . . how? Alien DNA is different from ours. Always is! Not even formed of double helices sometimes. Not always organized into chromosomes. Often complete alien structures. And yet this is . . ."

"Human," the professor said.

She titled her head and raised an eyebrow. "Surely you have the wrong blood here. Or you contaminated it."

The professor shook his head. "We ran the test several times, each time with a fresh vial of blood drawn directly from our guest. Specimen A001, the comatose gray aboard our starship, is human."

"Impossible!" Ben-Ari said. "The giant head. The four fingers on each hand. The alien features."

The professor nodded. "I didn't say he's *Homo sapiens*. He is not. But he belongs to the genus *Homo*. Same as us. Same as the Neanderthal, *Homo erectus*, *Homo habilis*, and other species of human, all of them extinct. But while those species are earlier on our evolutionary branch, the grays are further along. What we are looking at, Captain, is the DNA of a highly evolved human. Here is what our descendants might look like in a million years."

She inhaled sharply. "Are you telling me that . . ."

"When I was down on the surface of Isfet, I took blood samples from the Nefitian clerics. I had my suspicions, even then. The gray's DNA shows remarkable similarities to the Nefitians' DNA. Yet when I compare the gray to the DNA of other humans—to myself, to others in my staff—that similarity eludes us. The grays, Captain, are not just highly evolved humans. Specifically, they're highly evolved Nefitian clerics. They evolved to survive on a cruel desert world with low gravity—their bodies slender, lightweight, dry, able to withstand terrible radiation and drought. They evolved from the clerics we left abandoned below."

Ben-Ari stumbled toward a chair. She had to sit down. She stared at the professor, shock pulsing through her.

"Does this really mean what I think it does?" she whispered.

Professor Isaac nodded. "I'm afraid so, Captain. The Nefitian clerics eventually rebuilt their time machine. It took them a million years, and they looked quite different by the end, but they rebuilt it. And now they've come back in time to haunt us."

Ben-Ari stared for a moment in shock.

Then she clenched her jaw.

She began marching through the lab.

"Captain!" The professor hurried after her. "Where are you going?"

She kept walking, not turning around to look at him. "To the brig. To Specimen A001. I'm going to finally wake him up."

* * * * *

She stepped into the brig, teeth bared, fury blazing through her.

Because fury was better than fear. And right now, deep down, Einav Ben-Ari was terrified.

The gray, Specimen A001, lay on a cot, still comatose. Tubes and an oxygen mask were keeping the alien alive.

No, not an alien, Ben-Ari reminded herself. *A human.*

She began ripping off tubes, pulling them out of the creature's veins.

"Captain!" Isaac raced into the room after her. "I must object. You might kill him. You—"

"Leave us," she said.

The professor stiffened. "Einav. I—"

"*Leave us.*" She turned to stare at him. "That is an order, Commander."

The professor stared at her. He seemed almost ready to argue again. But then he nodded and left the brig.

Ben-Ari closed the door, remaining alone with the unconscious gray.

She stared down at the creature on the cot. He was taller than her but probably not much heavier, being so lanky, his wrinkled gray skin clinging to his bones. His heart pulsed under his ribs, its glow faintly visible like the heart of a baby fish. The cranium dwarfed the small, pinched face.

Ben-Ari drew the vial of adrenaline from her pocket.

She slammed it down, piercing the creature's chest.

The gray jolted up, ripping his straps, screaming.

Ben-Ari stepped back, drew her pistol, and aimed it at the creature.

"One wrong move, buddy, and I spray your brains against the opposite wall."

The gray stared at her. For a long moment, he was silent, blinking, adjusting to the light.

Then he began to laugh.

It was a laugh that sounded like cracking teeth. Like burning starships. A demonic laugh that oozed cruelty.

"Finally you understand," the gray hissed. "Yes, Einav. The hour has come and passed. The Wakening, we call it. You have been to Isfet. You have stranded the clerics. Our evolution has begun." He grinned wickedly. "And so has your pain."

Ben-Ari sneered. She grabbed the creature by the throat, shoved him back onto the bed, and squeezed.

"So you're Nefitian." She growled. "Is that right? You're the descendant of those monks I exiled."

The creature cackled. "Your brain is so small. Your mind is so slow. It took you so long to grasp, and even now you are unsure. Yes, ape. In my veins flows the blood of the elders. Of Harsiese, the great cleric of old."

"They were neutered!" she said.

"Not all," said the creature. "Not my elder. Not Harsiese. We are him. All of us. The millions of my kind—the Sanctified Sons, descendants of Harsiese. For a million years, we suffered, abandoned where you left us. No more. No more!"

"Why are you here?" she said. "What do you want?"

The gray stared into her eyes and licked his slit of a mouth.

"Earth," the creature hissed. "We want Earth."

She tightened her grip on his throat. He wheezed, but the cruel smile never left his face.

"So go back to *your* Earth!" she said. "Earth in your timeline. A million years from now."

The creature cackled. "You destroyed it. You petty apes! You polluted our world. Filled it with smog, with trash, with poison. Do you truly think it lasted a million years? It does not survive a thousand years from this day!" He sneered. "For a million years, we suffered, lost, exiled, Earthless. But we dreamed of Earth! Of that world of old, in a time when it still harbored life. It will be ours again, ape. It will belong to the Sanctified Sons, and the apes shall perish."

Those words rattled her. Earth—the world she had fought for, had killed for, had suffered so much for—only lasting another thousand years? Her head spun. She had to force herself to inhale. She sneered at the gray.

"What makes you think I won't go back to Isfet right now?" she said. "I'll nuke the damn pyramid from orbit. I'll kill Harsiese and his people. You'll never evolve if I slay your ancestors."

The gray hissed at her, his grin widening. "It is too late, Einav. Too late to change the timeline. I am already here on your ship. My kind has already visited Earth. We abducted many humans. We landed in Roswell. We landed in Area 51. We landed at ten thousand places. Nefitis, my queen, has even landed in Ancient Egypt, delivering holy words to the humans—the humans who formed her religion, who moved to Isfet, who evolved into us. The circle is complete. We are woven throughout your past, throughout the fabric of human civilization. If you slay the Nefitians now, you will create a paradox in time." He cackled. "You. Your people. Earth itself. All will vanish."

Ben-Ari released the creature. She stepped to the back of the room. A tremble ran through her.

She thought back to the physics lessons the professor had taught her. Could it be true? The Nefitian clerics were still down on Isfet! Only hours away! She could kill them now! She could stop these monsters from evolving!

And then the monster on her ship would vanish. Then the history of Earth itself would change. All those abductions. The carvings in Ancient Egypt. Countless movies about UFOs and little green men. The Nefitians' very existence on Isfet—an order that only came to being because the goddess Nefitis had traveled back in time to Egypt . . .

All would be paradoxes.

The change could unravel spacetime itself, could destroy the world.

"Yes, finally your tiny brain understands," the gray said. "You cannot change the past. Your dear professor should have taught you that."

"Then you cannot change Earth!" she blurted out. "You can't conquer my world! It's too late for you. You would be changing *your* past!"

The gray grinned. "Oh, but we did not evolve on Earth. When you destroyed our starships, you made sure of that. After we conquer your Earth, our ancestors' evolution on Isfet will continue, undisturbed." The creature rose from the bed. He stepped toward her, ignoring her pistol. He loomed, two feet taller, staring down at her. "Earth will be ours. The clerics came from Earth. It is our birthright. Our promised land. And we shall return—with glory, with might! Earth shall be reborn, greater than before. Nefitis and her children are coming."

Red lights flashed.

Alarms blared across the ship.

A voice boomed from the speakers.

Red alert! Red alert!

Ben-Ari stared at the gray for an instant longer. He stared back, smiling thinly.

Then Ben-Ari raced out of the brig and slammed the door behind her, sealing the gray inside. She ran down corridors and onto the bridge.

Officers were bustling across the bridge. Alarms blared. Lights flashed.

"What's going on?" Ben-Ari shouted. "Why are we on Red Alert? Why—"

And then she saw it.

They appeared on the top viewports.

There were thousands.

"God," she whispered.

Saucers. Thousands of saucers flying through space. All of them engraved with ankhs.

And they were heading toward Earth.

For only three breaths, Ben-Ari allowed the horror to overwhelm her.

I did this.

One breath.

I created the grays.

A second breath.

All of Earth will fall.

A third breath.

I will fight this. I will fix this.

"Aurora, set a course to Earth!" Ben-Ari said. "Top warp speed. As fast as we can go. We must beat these creatures. We must reach Earth before them and raise the alarm. And where the hell is Marino? I want us battle ready and—"

The lights across the bridge dimmed.

The engines gave a horrible hum, then shut down.

The monitors all went dark.

The *Lodestar* floated through darkness, idle and silent.

The saucers streamed overhead, still distant, but a few detached from the group. They came flying toward the *Lodestar*.

"Computer, status!" Ben-Ari barked.

A female robotic voice emerged from the ship's speakers.

"All engines shut down. All shields shut down. All weapon systems shut down. Nine minutes and fifty-nine seconds to enemy fleet's arrival. Nine minutes and fifty-eight seconds . . ."

"Captain, we're dead in the water!" the professor cried. "They'll destroy us."

"Captain, all our controls are dead!" Fish shouted. "I can't do a thing from up here. We're like a shag on a rock. Somebody must have taken over the ship from the engine room."

Ben-Ari looked at the empty security station.

Fuck.

She ran.

CHAPTER TWENTY-FOUR

Lailani screamed, spinning in a circle, firing her assault rifle.

"HOBBS, Epi, run!" she shouted.

But there was nowhere to run. She knew that. The grays filled the ancient observatory. They towered above her, skeletal, their hard gray skin resisting her bullets. Their massive black eyes glared, boring into her. Their mouths opened in sneers, revealing teeth like needles. The observatory was ancient, crumbling, its walls filled with weeds and cracks, and through holes Lailani saw more grays outside, saw their saucers hovering.

She kept firing until her gun clicked. Epimetheus growled at her side. HOBBS stood with them, dented and cracked from his battle with the stone guardians below, barely able to stay standing.

They were surrounded.

"What the fuck do you assholes want?" Lailani shouted at the grays.

One of the grays stepped forward, a sneering creature, deep grooves framing his thin mouth. A blood-splattered cloak hung around his shoulders. His neck was long and gangly, holding a necklace of bleeding, beating hearts.

Lailani recognized him. He had pursued her in the asteroid field.

356

She spat out his name. "Abyzou. So you survived that asteroid field. Or *did* you? You look like roadkill scraped off a space rock."

The gray sneered. "Lailani de la Rosa." His thin nostrils flared. "I smell the stench of the centipede upon you."

"He who smelt it, dealt it," Lailani said. "I'm warning you, Abyzou. I'm very, very good at killing aliens. I've killed about a billion of them so far. Look me up in Wikipedia Galactica. But this is your lucky day. I'm retiring from the business. So you better get out of my way, or I might just come out of retirement especially for you."

Abyzou began to laugh. It was a horrible sound, a sound like shattering teeth.

"Aliens?" he said. The hearts on his chain beat faster, dripping blood across his chest. "Still you do not understand, do you? No. We are not aliens. We are you." He leaned closer, sneering. "We are humans. Evolved. Perfected. To us, you are but an ape."

Lailani frowned. A chill washed her. Epimetheus mewled and moved closer to her.

"Humans?" she whispered. "But how?"

But she understood.

Of course.

These grays were far too humanoid to be aliens. Lailani thought back to the famous chart she had seen as a child, showing a monkey evolving into an ape, an ape into a caveman, a caveman into a modern human. If you extended that diagram to the right, you'd eventually end up with creatures that looked like this—like the grays.

"You're evolved humans," Lailani whispered. "You came back in time." She clutched the hourglass to her chest. "So why do you need my hourglass?"

The grays moved in closer. They reached out their long, knobby hands, four-fingered, the smallest finger lost in their evolution.

"Nobody but our goddess, the blessed Nefitis, may alter time," Abyzou hissed. "With your small, weak mind, you cannot imagine this power! You cannot imagine the responsibility. You would undo the fabric of spacetime. Only we, the children of Nefitis, may have this power. For your pride, ape, you will die."

Lailani glared at him. She laughed mirthlessly. "It was one of your own who taught the Mahatekis how to build the hourglass! I saw the engraving. There is a traitor among you!"

Abyzou lashed his claws toward her.

Lailani screamed and swung her rifle.

The gray's claws tore through the barrel, shattering the metal.

Lailani scampered back, drawing her knife. Epimetheus leaped forward, barking madly, and closed his jaws around Abyzou's leg. It was a mighty bite, a bite that could have killed a man, but Abyzou tore the Doberman off like a Band-Aid. He tossed Epi into the air, and another gray caught him, began to cut him.

"Epi!" Lailani shouted. "HOBBS, fight them! Kill them!"

The robot's guns emerged from his forearms. He sprayed bullets, knocking down several grays. His missile launcher emerged from his shoulder, and he fired a shell, tearing through other grays. Lailani allowed herself a moment of hope—but then the grays swooped in.

Their claws knocked Lailani down.

They drew metal rods, aimed, and fired pulses of energy. Bolts slammed into HOBBS. The mighty robot fell.

Lailani struggled to rise. She limped toward HOBBS. Claws lashed at her, and she swiped her knife, cutting them. The grays kept firing, pounding HOBBS again and again. The robot kept trying to rise. More blasts knocked him down.

"HOBBS!" Lailani cried, tears in her eyes. The grays grabbed her. Claws dug into her skin. They pulled her away from her robot.

HOBBS knelt on the floor. His armor was cracked open. His arm had detached again. A gash spread across his abdomen. She could see his innards, a jumble of circuits and cables like entrails. They were spilling out.

"Mistress . . ." he whispered. "I . . . am . . . so—"

Abyzou walked toward the robot, raised his hands, and blasted out blue lightning.

The bolts slammed into HOBBS, shattering his body, knocking him down.

"HOBBS!" she screamed, thrashing in the grip of several grays. "Damn it, Abyzou! You son of a bitch!"

The cloaked gray turned toward her, laughing.

"Now, Lailani . . ." Abyzou stepped closer, raising his claws. "Now you die."

She closed her eyes.

She thought the word she dreaded. The word that had almost killed her. The word that meant everything.

Nightwish.

She did not need to open her eyes. She saw. She was everything. She was one.

"You should leave," she whispered.

The grays surrounded her, a writhing mass of them, of dark eyes, of such power. She saw their power. She saw their minds. So much vaster than the minds of humans. They spoke inside her.

You will scream for us. Your little tricks cannot stop us. You are weak.

She spread out her arms. She hovered over the floor, eyes closed, wind blowing back her hair.

"Perhaps," she whispered. "But my friends are not."

She reached out her mind, for she was everywhere. She was inside every tree. Every insect that flew. And inside *them.*

She summoned them.

And they answered her call.

They flew from the mountaintops. From the misty valleys. From their nests in the forests. Dozens of them, then hundreds—massive, fast as falcons, coated with feathers. Roaring with fury, they arrived—the dragons of Mahatek.

The beasts slammed into the walls of the observatory. They clawed at the windows. One squeezed through the archway, reared in the chamber, and howled, voice shaking the mountain.

The grays turned toward the creatures, firing.

And the dragons fought back.

The dragons' massive claws, longer than swords, tore into the grays. Their jaws grabbed them, tore them apart. A wall fell. More of the dragons stormed in, shrieking, attacking, ripping into the grays. They kept arriving, more and more of them, descending from the sky, slamming into the observatory. The roof crumbled and bricks rained, crushing grays. Another wall shattered. Dust flew. Grays died. And still the dragons kept arriving.

"Time to get the fuck out of here!" Lailani shouted, leaping through the rubble.

A chunk of ceiling slammed down ahead of her. She scurried back. Another stone slammed down beside her.

"Epimetheus!" she cried. "Epi!"

The Doberman came racing toward her, leaping between the falling bricks. He jumped into the air, and she grabbed him.

"Come on, Epi, help me find HOBBS!"

They ran through the devastation. A gray reared before them, claws reaching out. An instant later, a dragon grabbed the creature, lifted him, and tore him apart. Lailani and Epimetheus kept running.

They found HOBBS in the center of the collapsing observatory. His eyes were dim, but they still shone. His armored plates were torn open, and cables spilled out from him, sparking.

He seemed to be bleeding, but of course that was impossible; it must have been the blood of the grays.

Lailani knelt by him. "HOBBS!" She shook him. "Hobster, you still with me, buddy?"

He managed a whisper. "Mistress . . . "

She tried to lift him. She could not. Even with her chip turned off, with her alien power, she was too weak.

She closed her eyes. She inhaled deeply.

Come to me. Help me.

One of the dragons, the largest one, landed before them. He was a mighty blue beast, the tips of his feathers green, his eyes golden. He lowered his scaly head.

Lailani climbed onto his back. The dragon beat his wings, hovering. He lifted Epimetheus with one talon, HOBBS with the other.

As the roof crumbled around them, the dragon took flight. They rose from the collapsing observatory and into the sky.

Below them, Lailani saw the observatory collapse inward, burying the grays. The rest of the dragons rose around them, crying out in triumph.

So much for preserving ancient cultures, Lailani thought. She placed a hand on her pocket, feeling the hourglass there.

Lailani stroked the dragon's neck. His scales were smooth, shimmering like mother of pearl. She spoke into his mind.

Can you take us to the river? To our starship?

She could observe his thoughts.

Yes, my friend.

The dragon dived low, passing through mist, heading toward the valley. They glided over the forest, flew along the river, and finally reached the grassy clearing where the starship *Ryujin* waited.

Gently, the dragon placed Epimetheus and HOBBS on the grass, then extended down a wing like a ramp. Lailani climbed down, and she placed a hand on the mighty creature's snout. The dragon nickered and gave a low, happy grumble, and his golden eyes shone.

"Goodbye, my friend," Lailani whispered.

The dragon took flight, circled above once, then headed toward the mountains.

Lailani took a deep breath.

Serenity.

Her chip turned on. She returned into her mind. She was just Lailani again.

She knelt by HOBBS. The robot lay in the grass by the *Ryujin*, his armor plating hanging loose, several pieces missing. Half his head was crushed. His left arm was missing, the stump spraying sparks. His eyes still shone, but they were so dim, flickering. His fingers twitched.

And he was still bleeding.

Lailani frowned. At first, she had mistook it for grays' blood on his armor. But she saw that fresh blood was seeping from the cracks on his body. How could this be?

"Mistress," HOBBS whispered. "My . . . armor . . . Help me . . . remove it."

With a trembling hand, HOBBS reached to the steel plate across his chest. Lailani helped him, and the plate swung open like the door of a cast iron stove.

Inside, she saw a heart.

A human heart.

Her eyes dampened.

"HOBBS," she whispered. "How can this be? You're alive. You're alive, HOBBS!"

The heart was still beating. Arteries ran from it into the machinery. But the heart was weak. Losing blood. Trembling like a bird caught in a hand. Lailani grabbed her medical kit from her pack, but how could she heal this? She found the leaking artery. Delicately, struggling to calm her trembling fingers, she wrapped a thin band of gauze around the cut, then applied tape. She found a leaking vein closer to the shoulder. She sealed it too. The bleeding finally seemed to stop.

The heart kept beating. Weak. Fluttering. But still alive.

"You're a cyborg, HOBBS," she whispered, looking up at him. Tears flowed down her cheeks. "Part human."

"So it would seem, mistress," he said, voice labored. "I . . . did not know. Who . . . am I? Who . . . was I?"

His eyes blinked. His heart rate quickened. He struggled to rise but fell to his knees.

"Come, let's get you into the ship."

She guided him into the *Ryujin*. HOBBS managed to take only several steps, to climb into the hold, and there he collapsed.

"HOBBS!"

"I . . . am losing power, mistress." His voice was weak. "I am dying."

"No!" She knelt above him, shaking him. Epimetheus licked the cyborg's metal cheek. "I don't let you die. Not here. Not ever. Stay alive, HOBBS!" Her tears flowed. "That is an order!"

"I . . . was honored . . . to serve . . ."

His eyes went dark.

"No." Lailani shook him. "Damn it, HOBBS!" She sobbed. "Live!"

She swung open his chest. His heart was still.

Lailani grabbed it in her hand.

Ten years ago, she had ripped out Elvis's heart, had held the dripping muscle in her hand.

Today she held HOBBS's heart. And she squeezed. Again. Again.

"Live," she whispered. "Live, damn you. Live!"

She pumped the heart in her fist. Again. Again. She wept. Again.

His heart remained still.

Lailani closed her eyes, tears flowing. She remembered herself as a child, a homeless toddler in the slums of Manila, huddling under tarp and corrugated steel for shelter from the hurricanes, eating from landfills to survive. She remembered one day being so sick after eating from the trash, vomiting, maybe dying. She remembered her mother—only a teenager—holding her, rocking her, singing a soft song. Lailani had never forgotten

that song. She sang it now to HOBBS, weeping and holding his
heart.

"How many miles to Babylon?
Three score and ten.
Can I get there by candlelight?
Yes, and back again.
If your heels are nimble and light,
You may get there by candlelight."

Her voice faded, and tears hung on her lips.

And in her hands, the heart gave a weak flutter.

Lailani let out a sob.

"Live," she whispered, squeezing the heart.

And it pumped again. And again. And when Lailani
removed her hands, it kept pumping.

She sobbed with relief. HOBBS lay still, unconscious, his
eyes dim—but his heart still pumped.

"He's alive, Epi, but he's hurt," Lailani whispered. "He's
hurt bad. Because of me."

She rose to her feet, hands covered with his blood. She
would not see another friend die for her. She had caused too
much death. She needed HOBBS; his memory banks still held the
hourglass code, and only he knew how to use it. But it was more
than that. HOBBS was her friend. And Lailani had vowed to save
her friends, to never let more death weigh upon her.

She made her way into the cockpit. Epimetheus joined her. She flipped switches, and the *Ryujin*'s engines roared to life.

"All right, Epster," she said, reaching out to pat the Doberman. "Before we can use the hourglass, we need to save our friend. And there's only one man in the universe who can fix him." She pushed down on the throttle, and the *Ryujin* raced across the grass. "Dr. Elliot Schroder. His maker. We're flying to Bernard's Star, Epi. We're flying to find him."

The *Ryujin* skimmed the water. They rose higher, the creatures in the river snapping their jaws below. They soared through the sky, traveling upward in a straight line, and breached the atmosphere.

Dented, nearly falling apart, the *Ryujin* glided through the darkness. They left the green world of Mahatek behind. As Lailani sat in the cockpit, clutching the controls, she stared into space with narrowed eyes, her lips a thin line.

I will keep fighting, she vowed. *I will fight the grays. I will fight the demons inside me. I will never surrender.* She gazed at the photograph on her dashboard, showing her and her friends, then back at the unconscious cyborg behind her. *I will save you all. I swear it.*

They flew onward, a speck of light and life in the infinite emptiness.

CHAPTER TWENTY-FIVE

Ben-Ari raced through the dark starship, arms pumping.

The robotic voice emerged from the speakers, frustratingly calm.

"Nine minutes to enemy fleet's arrival. Eight minutes and fifty-nine seconds to enemy fleet's arrival. Eight minutes and . . ."

She tuned it out. She barged into the engine room.

It was a vast, shadowy chamber filled with pipes, turbines, massive gears, and towering machinery.

At once, Ben-Ari saw them: several dead engineers, lying at her feet.

The engines were cold.

The robotic voice kept intoning, counting down to the saucers' arrival. To the *Lodestar*'s destruction.

The ship had no shields.

No engines.

No guns.

Eight minutes until the enemy arrived.

Ben-Ari raised her pistol. She took a step deeper into the engine room. Shadows. Nothing but shadows.

She had eight minutes. Eight minutes to save her ship. To get their power back on before the saucers arrived. Eight minutes or they were all doomed.

"Marino!" she shouted. "I know you're in here. Show yourself!"

From the shadows—a deep laughter. It echoed. She could not pinpoint its location.

Ben-Ari sneered. She took another step forward. A bridge stretched out ahead, spanning a pit filled with turbines. The laughter seemed to have come from across the bridge. She took a step onto the crossing.

"Captain!" Fish's voice came from behind her. She spun to see the Australian racing down the corridor toward the engine room, several security guards with him. "Captain, the power generator across the bridge! We have to—"

The heavy metal door slammed shut and locked.

On the other side, she heard Fish slamming against the door, cursing, calling to her. Soon she heard gunfire—the security guards firing at the door's lock, unable to break it.

"Hello, Einav!"

Another voice—from deeper in the engine room.

She spun around.

She saw him there—across the bridge.

"Marino," she spat.

He took a step onto the bridge, holding a remote control; he must have used it to slam the door shut. Turbines below the bridge were moving, churning, snapping, raising a metallic din.

These turbines only powered the ship's life support system, delivering oxygen and heat across the ship. They would not help the *Lodestar* fight or flee the grays. The shields, the engines, the cannons—they got power from other turbines. Those turbines, across the bridge, were cold and still.

"Hello, Captain!" Marino said. "The power generator Fish talked about? It's behind me. You'll have to get by me first."

She raised her pistol, aimed, and—

Marino hit another button on his remote control.

A massive magnet on the ceiling—it was the size of a tabletop—came to life.

It yanked the pistol from Ben-Ari's hand. The weapon slammed against the magnet. She screamed and yanked off her wristwatch before the magnet could rip off her hand. Her buttons, her belt—they tore free and flew upward. The bridge itself thrummed and creaked as the magnet tugged it.

She howled and raced across the bridge.

"Good!" Marino said. "Come to me, Einav! My goddess wants you alive. I will take you to her!"

Below the bridge, the turbines chugged away, slamming into one another. Marino stood ahead, waiting, smiling at her. He had removed his HOPE uniform. Instead, he wore a black martial arts uniform. His shirt was opened, revealing a golden ankh around his chest.

Ben-Ari leaped toward him, fist flying.

He blocked her attack and laughed.

His fist flew her way, and she ducked, swayed, and nearly fell off the bridge.

"Why, Marino?" she shouted. "Why do you serve them?"

He kicked. She tried to block the blow, but he was too strong. His foot hit her chest with terrifying force. She fell back. She gasped for air, but her lungs would not work. She saw stars.

"I have seen her glory!" Marino said, standing on the bridge before her. "I have seen the goddess Nefitis. Soon you will see her too." His voice dropped to a hushed whisper. "You don't know her power. You don't know her might, her evil. But you will. You will not die today, Einav. You will live! I will bring you to her. That is her wish. I will hear you scream!"

She screamed now. She lunged herself toward him. She tossed fists and kicks, but he blocked every blow. She could see the power generator—just behind him! She had to reach it. To turn the engines back on. To let the *Lodestar* fight. The voice kept emerging from the speakers.

Five minutes to enemy fleet arrival.

"You'll never make it out!" Ben-Ari shouted. "You'll die here with us!"

"No, Einav," Marino said. "We won't die today. The grays intend to board this ship. To torture everyone aboard. The others will be granted death after a few days. But not you, Einav. Not the one who marooned the clerics. My goddess knows how to extend your life. You will suffer for a million years under her claws! Your species will be but an ancient memory before you're granted the mercy of death."

She swung her fist again. He blocked. She managed to land a blow on his side, but he didn't seem to feel the pain. He slammed a fist into her head. She stumbled back, swaying, and slumped against the side of the bridge. She tasted blood.

The speakers intoned their warning.

Four minutes to enemy fleet arrival.

"Why, Marino?" Ben-Ari whispered, stumbling back toward him. "Why did you help us? You fought the grays with me! You helped me capture one! You helped me fight the clerics! Why, if you're a Nefitian too?"

He blocked more of her blows. He swung another fist, hitting her jaw. She could barely stay standing.

"That was my task," he said. "To make sure the circle of time continued. To make sure you indeed marooned the Nefitians. That they could evolve on a desolate, desert world, cut off from the rest of humanity. That they would become the Sanctified Sons, the master race. You have performed admirably. I was just there to oversee your work. For that, my masters will reward me greatly. When they conquer Earth, I will serve in their palace, while the rest of humanity bleeds. You created my masters, Einav. Now you will scream for them!"

He reached out, grabbed her arm, and twisted it behind her back.

She howled in pain.

He held her in the Bear Trap grip—the one he had shown her in the gym.

"Yes, Einav. You know this grip, don't you?" He laughed. "A grip impossible to break free from. I must only keep you here for a few more moments. Soon, Einav." Bending her arm, he kissed the top of her head. "Soon my goddess will be here for you."

The pain was terrifying. She couldn't breathe. She could barely see. Her arm felt ready to dislocate.

Her eyes began to roll back. Her blood trickled from her mouth.

With his free hand, Marino stroked her hair.

"So sweet," he whispered. "So fair. I will enjoy seeing your torture. I will enjoy hearing you beg." He kissed her ear. "I enjoyed fucking you in my bed. I'll enjoy far more when you're in chains."

She couldn't see. She couldn't breathe. Her arm began to dislocate. Her legs were weak. One minute to arrival. Fifty-nine seconds. Fifty-eight seconds.

In the darkness, she saw the goddess's eyes.

She saw cruelty, death, despair. Her ship in ruin. Her homeworld lost.

And in the haze, she saw the professor smile.

She saw Marco and Addy, her dearest friends.

She saw her sweet little Lailani.

She saw Kemi, forever in her memory.

I will not let them down.

She lunged and twisted, and her arm snapped.

She screamed as the shattered bone ripped her skin.

She tore free from Marino's grip, howled, and kicked him in the face.

He stumbled and hit the edge of the bridge.

She kicked again, hitting his chest, and he teetered over the ledge. Their eyes met. She saw his horror.

Then she kicked a third time, and Marino tumbled down into the pit. His body slammed against the turbines, and the great machinery caught him at once, crushing him, ripping him apart, scattering him across the gears.

Her left arm hung at an odd angle, bone protruding. The pain was terrifying. But Ben-Ari stumbled across the bridge, moving toward the power generator at the back. *Thirty seconds. Twenty-nine. Twenty-eight.*

She fell, coughing.

She began to pass out.

Almost blind with pain, she rose to her knees, then to her feet.

Nine seconds.

Eight.

Seven.

She reached the control box. The power generator was cold.

Six.

Five.

Four.

Through a porthole, she saw them. Right outside. Thousands of saucers. She saw the grays inside, staring at her across the distance.

Three.

Two.

She cranked a lever.

One.

Power raced back into the engines.

The saucers fired.

Ben-Ari hit her communicator. "Aurora, get us out of here!" she cried.

The ship shook as lasers slammed into the shields—just as those shields came back to life.

The engines roared, bathing her with heat, as the *Lodestar* blazed across space, moving at many times the speed of light.

Through a porthole, she saw the saucers growing smaller, then vanishing in the distance.

She limped back across the bridge, gasping for every breath. She unlocked the door.

Fish was there. He grabbed her as she stumbled. He lifted her into his arms.

"I got ya, sheila," he said softly. "You're safe."

"I . . . I'm sorry, Fish," she whispered. "I thought you were the traitor. I thought you hated me. It was Marino . . . Marino . . ." She smiled at him, barely able to keep her eyes open. "I fixed our engines."

Her eyes rolled back, and darkness washed over her. She heard the engines humming, but they faded into the sound of waves, and she was back on the beach at Greece, back with her friends, the water tickling her feet.

* * * * *

For a long time, she floated in darkness.

For a long time, she was lost in memory, in dreams, in shadows.

When finally her eyes fluttered open, Ben-Ari found herself lying in an infirmary bed. Her jaw was numb with pain, and her arm was in a cast.

She bolted upright into a sitting position.

"The saucers!" she blurted out. "The grays! They're chasing. Where's my communicator? Nurse! Doctor!"

A warm hand touched her shoulder. "It's all right, Einav. It's all right. Aurora took us out of their range."

She turned to see the professor sitting beside her. His face was soft with concern, his eyes warm like his hand.

Ben-Ari took a shuddering breath, trying to calm her racing heart.

"How long was I out? Tell me everything."

"A few hours," the professor said. "The saucers are still chasing. There are many of them. But we're keeping a good distance between us. We can't yet open a wormhole to Earth. Not while flying at warp speed. Once we've put enough distance between us and the saucers, we'll let Earth know." His face hardened. "And we'll join the fight. Science will have to wait."

She gave him a wan smile. "Spoken like a true soldier."

"You taught me a few things, Captain," Isaac said softly. "When you first came aboard, I confess: I thought you too young, too inexperienced, wrong for this job. Perhaps that was my pride; perhaps I wanted your position for myself." He shook his head sadly. "I was a fool. I would have failed. You've led us well, Captain. I'm proud to serve you. And I'm proud of you. Deeply."

Tears filled her eyes. Yes, perhaps he was proud of her. Perhaps her soldiers back in the HDF had looked up to her. Perhaps Petty admired her. And yet a deep pain, shameful and hidden, gnawed on her. Perhaps it was the painkillers she was on. Perhaps it was the blood loss. But the words slipped out from her mouth, unbidden.

"Marino never wanted me," she whispered. "I thought that . . . that maybe finally a man . . ." She lowered her head. "But he lied."

The professor's eyes hardened. "Marino was a traitor, a fanatic, and a fool." His eyes softened, and he placed his hand atop hers. "You are more than a captain, a soldier, and a heroine. You are also a kind, intelligent woman. You are wonderful, and someday, you'll meet the man who sees the woman and not just the legend."

Tears filled her eyes. She touched his cheek. "My dear professor." Suddenly her tears were streaming down her cheeks. "I was scared. I was so scared."

These were words she never would have uttered to Marco, to Addy, to any of her soldiers. Feelings an officer, a captain, should never confess. But she couldn't forget those burning eyes. That vision. The terror of the grays. And worst of all, the knowledge that she had done this. That she, in her wrath, had created them.

Professor Isaac pulled her into his arms. He was not a soldier. He was not physically strong. He had never charged into battle, guns firing. But he felt like the wisest, strongest man she had ever known. Like the father she had always wanted. No, that was wrong—not like a father. Perhaps not even like a mentor. Like something she had never felt before. She laid her head against his shoulder.

A fleet of saucers was heading toward Earth. A dark queen was rising. Earth—even if Ben-Ari could save it from the grays— was doomed to die in only a thousand years, drowned in pollution. All the cosmos, it seemed, was tearing apart.

But for one moment, let me be safe. For one moment, let me remain in his arms.

The *Lodestar* flew onward—her ship, the flagship of humanity, a single light in the infinite darkness. They had gone into space for curiosity, for discovery, for adventure. They flew now for hope, for life, and for a distant blue dot called Earth.

CHAPTER TWENTY-SIX

"Well, Addy, old friend, once more we're homeless."

She placed her hands on her hips. "I'm not old. I'm twenty-eight." She frowned. "Or twenty-nine? What date is it? Definitely not yet thirty. I think." She glared Marco. "Shut up."

Marco rolled his eyes. "Fine, Addy, my young and innocent friend. Once more we're homeless." He sighed and looked around him. "At least it's on a beautiful Mediterranean beach this time, not the smog of Haven."

Addy reached over and patted his crotch. "It's this little guy's fault. If you thought with your brain, instead of your pants, we wouldn't be in this mess." She nodded. "Once more, your dick leads us straight up shit's creek."

It was his turn to glare. "Don't call my guy little."

They stared at each other, glowering, fists clenched, teeth bared . . . then burst into laughter.

They laughed for a long time.

We laugh because otherwise we'd be crying, Marco thought. *And we've cried enough.*

"Come on, Ads," he said. "Let's find a place to sleep tonight. We'll figure out a plan tomorrow."

They walked along the beach, carrying their backpacks. Marco looked back only once. He gazed at his house—at what had once been his house, that was. It stood there on the beach. The place he had fought for, dreamed of for years in the war. The house he had built with his best friend. With Addy. The house where Tomiko now lived with her new boyfriend. The house he had lost.

But it doesn't matter, he thought. *Because it's just a thing. Just an object. Just a place.* He looked at Addy. *What matters is her.*

She noticed his stare. "What are you lookin' at, butthead?"

He punched her shoulder. "You're the butthead."

"Then why don't you kiss me, since you can kiss my ass."

"Well, maybe I will!" Marco said.

"Good!" said Addy.

"Good!" said Marco.

They stared at each other in silence again. Addy bit her lip. Then they kept walking, silent, staring forward.

The house vanished behind them.

They reached a cliff that thrust into the sea like a breakwater, blocking their way along the beach. It was too tall to climb, a wall of white stone. The water was shallow and warm, however. They waded through the sea, the water rising to their knees, then their waists, finally up to their shoulders. They held their backpacks overhead. Like this, walking in the water, they circled the cliff.

Past the stony barrier, they found a peaceful, sandy cove. The cliffs formed a horseshoe, protecting a bay of shallow water and a sandy beach. The only way here was through the water. They walked through the shallows, heading toward the beach. On the golden sand rested an old shipwreck, its wood cracked and crumbling in the sun. It seemed like a good place to spend the night.

They placed their backpacks on the sand near the shipwreck. The sun set into the water, casting golden rays. Marco and Addy sat side by side in the sand, leaning against each other, watching until the sun vanished beyond the sea, until the stars emerged.

"It's beautiful here," Marco said. "It's so beautiful."

"We should stay here forever," Addy said softly.

"And fish for a living?"

She nodded. "Why not?"

Marco hesitated, then reached out and held her hand. "Addy, I lost everything. My house. My money. My career. I have nothing left. You lost everything too. I know. But we have something. We have each other, like we always did." His eyes stung. "We found each other at age eleven, when we lost so much in the war. We've been together since. So long as we're together, we'll be all right. Marco and Addy, together against the world."

She pulled him close. She knuckled his head. "You're such a poet, you know that?"

Then Addy yawned. It was contagious. A yawn stretched across Marco too, and Addy yawned again. They rolled out a blanket and lay down, their toes by the water.

It was almost winter, and the breeze was cold. Addy wriggled closer to Marco, and he wrapped his arms around her. They pressed together, keeping each other warm. They did not sleep. The moon glowed above, and he looked into her eyes. She gazed back, face peaceful, the smallest of smiles on her lips.

Addy, he thought, just savoring that word. Her name. *Addy.*

He remembered that day long ago. The day her parents had died. The day he had lost his mother. The day their fates had forever entwined. He remembered surviving awkward, painful youth at her side. He remembered enlisting with her, suffering through boot camp with her. She had been with him in Corpus, when the nightmares had risen. She had fought with him on Abaddon, the homeworld of the scum. She had been his anchor on Haven, and she had fought with him against the marauders. Eighteen years of pain. Eighteen years of friendship. Of love. Eighteen years with the most important person in his world.

She was still gazing into his eyes, lying with him on the beach, her arms around him. He stroked her hair. And then he kissed her. And she kissed him back. For a long time, they lay side by side in the sand, kissing under the moonlight.

They pulled apart.

They stared at each other.

Again, they burst out laughing.

"You did it!" Addy grinned. "You kissed my butt!"

"So you *are* a butthead?"

Her grin grew. She nodded. "Yes! I mean—" She frowned. "Hey! You tricked me." She punched him. "No fair."

They stared at each other a moment longer. Marco leaned in to kiss her again. But Addy turned her head away.

Marco pulled back, feeling empty, feeling awkward.

"Addy?" he said softly.

"I don't want us to do that again," she whispered.

Her words stabbed him. He pulled his hand back from her hair. "Okay."

She looked at him. She placed her hand on his cheek. "You don't understand. Not because of how I feel. I love you, Marco. I love you so much. But I'm scared."

"Of what?" His voice was barely a whisper.

She stood up. She walked several paces away. She stood in the darkness, facing the water, the moonlight shining on her hair. Marco stood up too, and he came to stand beside her.

"Of you hurting me," she finally said.

"Addy, I won't." He reached out to take her hand, but she pulled away from him.

"Marco," she said, "I'm not interested in a one-night stand. I'm not interested in just being a rebound. In just helping you forget Tomiko. I'm not that kind of girl."

"I know you're not." Marco walked around her so that he faced her, could look into her eyes. He held her hands, and this time she let him. "Addy, I love you. I love you so much. You've always known this. And . . . maybe this can work. Us. We've been together for so long, and we're already best friends, and—"

"Marco." Tears filled Addy's eyes. "You and I—a couple? I'm like your sister."

He shook his head. "But you're not my sister. And that was many years ago."

"Yes. Many years ago." She looked away from him, her tears reflecting the moonlight. "Marco, I'm almost thirty. I found a white hair a few days ago. I plucked it out. My body is scarred. I smoke like a chimney. I'm ten pounds overweight and—"

"Only ten?" he said.

She glared, raising a fist. "Watch it, Poet!" She sighed. "Marco, I know who I am. And maybe you want me now, in your pain and loss. And maybe you truly love me. But what happens in a month or a year? When you meet another petite little Asian girl, another Lailani or Tomiko? She'll be nineteen, and half my size, and have perfect skin without any scars, and a perfect soul without any pain. She'll adore you—you, the famous author, the war hero, the intellectual who can show her the galaxy. She'll make you feel like a protector, a knight who can save a damsel, and all men want to feel that way. She'll be a delicate rose, and beside her, I'll just seem like a clumsy old ox with a donkey's laugh and an elephant's ass. She'll understand books, artwork, science, all those things you can talk about with Ben-Ari but which I don't understand. She'll be smart, and I'll seem so stupid. And then I'll be like Anisha. Like all the others, dozens of your girls that I've seen come and go over the years. Just another used sock for you to toss away. And I can't be that girl, Marco. I can't." She looked down. "Because it would hurt too much."

"Addy." He placed a finger under her chin and gently raised her head. "Addy, listen to me. I don't care if you're two hundred pounds overweight. I don't care if your hairs all turn white. I don't care that you have scars. Do you know why? Because just a few minutes ago, kissing you—that felt better than any time I spent with Tomiko. That felt more right, more wonderful, than anything I've ever felt with anyone." Now his eyes were damp too. "Because I've always loved you more than anyone. You've always been the most important person to me. You're the love of my life. It took years for me to admit it, but I always knew it. It took being with all those other girls. With getting married. With getting divorced. I had to take that path to find that it leads to you. Deep down inside, I always knew it would. I always knew that it's you. Addy, I'm not interested in you because of your age, weight, whether you have scars, or anything else. You are beautiful. *I love you.* Do you hear me? You're my soul mate. You're my other half. And I want to grow old with you."

She bit her lip, fresh tears falling, then smiled shakily. "So I can eat hot dogs until I gain two hundred pounds?"

His jaw unhinged, but then he nodded. "Yes."

"Now you're talkin'! That's all you had to say. Fuck love. Woo me with hot dogs!" She bit her lip and reached for his crotch again. "Especially one little hot dog."

He frowned. "Hey!"

She hugged him, closed her eyes, and pressed her cheek to his. "I love you too, Marco. I love you so much. I'm just happy we're together. And whatever happens, happens, all right?" She caressed his hair. "So long as we're together."

He nodded. "We'll always be together."

She looked around at the cove. The moonlight shone on the water, the seashells in the sand, and the shipwreck. The white cliffs soared around them, protective walls, and the stars shone above. A secret, hidden place. A beautiful bit of heaven.

"Poet, no matter what happens, we'll always have this place," Addy said. "Even if we leave. Even if the grays attack and there's another war. Even if we're far away from here, and scared, and suffering, and cold. We'll always remember this place. It'll be *our* place. Shipwreck Cove. And no matter what happens, no matter where we end up, we can always remember. We can always hold each other and pretend that we're back here."

He kissed her cheek. "This will always be our place. Shipwreck Cove. A secret place for just you and me, nobody else allowed."

They lay back down, and they made love on their blanket under the stars. Ten years ago, after the nightmare of Corpus, they had made love—a night of terrified passion, seeking comfort in each other's arms while the cosmos unraveled. This was different. They were older now. Their bodies had changed. Their souls were harder, yet also filled with more cracks. And this night, they were not scared. They were not just seeking comfort in sex. This night they were in love. They slept holding each other until dawn.

My crazy Addy, he thought when he woke up, when he found her still in his embrace. *Marco and Addy against the world.*

"Poet," she said that morning as they walked along the shore, the water up to their ankles. "I thought of something."

He raised an eyebrow. "Well, that's a first."

"Ha ha, very funny." She rolled her eyes. "Remember how we left Earth together once? When we went to Haven?"

"Of course."

"Well . . ." She chewed her lip. "That was a mistake. We should never have gone to Haven. But there's another place I want to go with you. Another world. To a world called Durmia. Where this book is from."

She raised her book—a copy of *The Way of Deep Being* by Guru Baba Mahanisha. Marco had seen her reading and rereading it over the past year. He looked again at the image of the author— an elephantine alien, clad in robes, with two trunks.

Marco cocked an eyebrow. "Why? Need to get the book autographed?"

Addy nodded. "Yes. I want to meet Baba Mahanisha. His book helped me, Poet. It really did. It taught me meditation. How to deal with my pain, my past. How to find peace. And I think Baba can help you too." She held his hand. "I know how you suffered, Marco. What you lived through—what we both lived through. I saw you break down in Haven. I saw it happen again here in Greece. And I need you to do this with me. To learn Deep Being. To find peace."

He lowered his head. He nodded. Yes, she was right. In Haven, he had fallen apart, had nearly lost himself. Here on Earth, after Tomiko's second miscarriage, he had nearly lost himself again. There were too many memories. Too many scars. Addy spoke truth; he needed to find peace.

"I'll read the book," he said.

"That's a great start," Addy said. "But not enough. Baba Mahanisha also teaches Deep Being in person. He doesn't accept many pupils. But I hope he'll accept us. Travel with me to see him, Marco. He's wise. He'll help us. I want this to work. *Us* to work." She wiped her eyes. "But before we can be one, we must be whole with ourselves."

Marco looked around him. The beach was beautiful. But this was no longer their home. And here too lurked dark memories. He thought for long moments in silence, and the only sound was the waves. Finally he spoke again.

"Addy, I worry that another war is looming." He gazed at the sea. "That the creatures who kidnapped Steve will be back. Not just to abduct a few people. But to launch war like the scum and marauders before them. Maybe even a worse war. Can we truly abandon Earth now? What if Earth needs us to fight again?"

"Then we'll return to battle healed," Addy said. "Stronger, braver than before. Baba Mahanisha is wise. He'll teach us this strength. All Durmian warriors study Deep Being. Perhaps the baba knows more about the grays too. He knows many things. He's centuries old. If anyone can teach us about the grays—who they are, how to defeat them—he can."

"So he'll teach us both peace and war?"

Addy nodded. "Peace and war are like light and darkness, like love and hate, like good and evil. One cannot exist without the other."

"You're speaking like a Deep Being expert already," Marco said.

"You're goddamn right," Addy said.

He gave her a thoughtful look. She still cursed like a sailor. She still tended to shout and punch. She was still fire and fury. But there was a new softness to Addy. A new wisdom. Perhaps these teachings were a way for her to grow, to leave the broken, angry girl behind, to become a woman at peace with herself, perhaps the woman she could have been had she not grown up in hell, had not fought through fire.

She needs this just as much as I do, he thought.

He nodded. "All right, Ads. Let's do this. We have a bit of money—whatever Tomiko left us. Enough to buy an old beater of a ship, even if it's just a rusty fridge with a rocket attached. To Durmia! To wisdom. To peace."

And hopefully not to war, he thought, though her words lingered. *War and peace. One cannot exist without the other.*

As it turned out, they could afford a ship slightly larger than a fridge, though not by much. It was a Volkswagen, ten years old, the size of an RV. The previous owner had painted flowers on the hull, psychedelic blobs on the roof, and peace symbols on the wings. Marco half-expected to see Scooby Doo leap out of the back.

"It's . . . a hippie van," Marco said, standing in the used-starship lot. "Are we going to fly to Durmia, or are we flying to a Grateful Dead concert?"

"I like it," Addy said. "It's colorful."

"It's giving me seizures," Marco said.

"Then don't look directly at it!" she said. "Pretend it's the sun."

"It's brighter than the sun," Marco muttered.

Addy rolled her eyes. "We'll paint it black later, so it suits your gloomy mood. Besides, it's all we can afford." She thought for a moment. "I'm going to name her *Shippy McShipface*."

"Addy!" Marco groaned. "We'll give the ship a proper name."

"*Shippy McShipface* is proper as fuck." She patted the ship. "I'm going to be happy in this old girl. She's a fighter."

"A fighter?" Marco eyed the flowery ship dubiously. "I just hope we don't have to fight aliens in it. It'll be embarrassing. The guns on the front probably fire flowers."

"Excellent!" Addy climbed into the ship. "You can finally get me some flowers."

"I did get you flowers once," Marco said, struggling with their suitcases. "You sliced through them with your katana, remember?"

Addy peeked out from the airlock. "Oh yeah. That reminds me, did you pack my katana?"

He groaned, swaying under his burden. "Yes, Addy, it's in the long suitcase. Now can you help me carry something?"

"No time. Got to explore *Shippy*." She vanished into the hold, then peeked back out. "Now hurry up, slowpoke! Bring me my sword! I've got some practice to do while you unpack."

Grumbling, Marco climbed in after her. He let the suitcases drop to the dusty floor.

"Great," he muttered. "I get to spend the next few weeks trapped in a hippie van with an insane samurai wielding a katana. Can't see what might go wrong."

Addy hopped toward him, mussed his hair, and kissed his cheek. "That's the spirit!"

They entered the cockpit, which contained two seats, the upholstery tattered but comfortable. They took flight from the used-starship lot. They soared. Soon they saw all of Greece below, then all the Mediterranean, then all the planet, a blue marble hovering in space. Marco had seen Earth from space many times before, but it always astounded him.

That's all we are, he thought. *Our entire world. Just a marble in the vast emptiness.*

As they flew onward, leaving Earth behind, Addy placed her bare feet on the dashboard and lit a cigarette. She shoved a memory key into a slot. The music of Bootstrap and the Shoeshine Kid, an old blues duo from just after the Cataclysm, filled the cabin.

"Poet, old boy, this is the life, I tell ya. Two vagabonds, a ship full of gas, and good music." She cracked open a beer. "All we need is to build a little hockey rink in the back."

Marco patted her thigh. He left his hand there. It felt good. He looked at Addy, and she looked back, joy in her eyes. And for the first time in many months, perhaps in years, Marco was happy. This felt right. She felt right.

My path took me to many places, he thought. *To many houses that were not my own. But my path always led to you, Addy. It led me home.*

He looked back out into space. There was still danger ahead. There were still battles to fight, enemies to defeat, demons to wrestle. His war was not over. Perhaps it would not end for many years.

But I'm fighting at your side, Addy. So long as we're together, we have hope.

He remembered how he had driven her away in Haven. How the marauders had kidnapped her. How he had nearly lost her. He vowed to never lose her again.

Addy sang along to the music, playing air drums. Finally she curled up in her seat and slept, her head against his shoulder. Marco stayed awake, flying the ship onward, seeking a world of wisdom, of knowledge, and of peace.

CHAPTER TWENTY-SEVEN

Abyzou stood on the bridge of his flagship, leading his fleet of ten thousand saucers. They stormed forth, roaring for war.

His thin lips peeled back in a grin. His clawed fingers curled into fists. In the dark viewport before him, Abyzou saw his reflection against the stars. The massive cranium, coated with wrinkly gray skin. The oval eyes, darker than space, hungry for victory. The chain of hearts, ripped from the chests of his victims, bleeding down his bare torso. The reflection of a prince. A conqueror.

"Soon, apes," Abyzou hissed. "Soon you will all suffer."

The small female ape—the one named Lailani—had nearly killed him. She had summoned the beasts of Mahatek, had toppled the observatory upon Abyzou. Many of his fellow Sanctified Sons had died under the rubble. But Abyzou had climbed out, bones shattered, lungs flooding with blood. He could still feel that agony. The bolts that held his bones together grinded inside him. Good. His grin widened. Pain gave him fury. And fury gave him strength.

The bridge of his flagship was dark, the walls forged of black iron and inlaid with golden hieroglyphs. Other Sanctified Sons worked here at holographic stations, the light glimmering on their bloated heads and black eyes. Deeper in the saucer, thousands of warriors stood in armor, holy warriors of Nefitis, armed with electric spears and chariots of fire. Behind the flagship, the ten thousand saucers flew, all filled with more warriors, with enough might to topple civilizations.

"You will fall, apes." Abyzou licked his lips. "Earth will be ours." He raised a fist. "From Earth we came, and to Earth we return!"

Across the bridge, his warriors raised their own fists, repeating the holy words. "From Earth we came, and to Earth we return!"

Abyzou stared through the front viewport. He saw it ahead, so close he could almost reach out and grab it.

The *Lodestar.*

Ben-Ari's starship.

Ben-Ari. The one who had marooned his ancestors. Who had created his race.

The one who would scream so beautifully.

Abyzou turned to look behind him. The ankhs were already there, ten feet tall, carved from wood. There were four. Four torture instruments for the four heroes of humanity. An ankh for Einav Ben-Ari. For Lailani de la Rosa. For Marco Emery. For Addy Linden. Humanity worshiped these four sniveling simians. And so they would scream! Very soon now, Abyzou himself would crucify them. He would savor their pain. He would take them to his mother. And Nefitis would feed upon them!

That day—very soon now—humanity would shatter. And the Sanctified would rise.

"Soon, Mother, I will prove my worth to you," Abyzou said. "I will prove that I am no worm."

Sudden pain stabbed him. The memories flashed through him. Memories from his childhood. Of Nefitis beating him. Breaking his bones, healing them, breaking them again. Pulling out his organs. Infecting them. Shoving them back in. Making him cry. Making him strong. Turning him from worm into warrior.

That pain would be over soon. It would belong only to the apes.

Abyzou took a shuddering breath and looked ahead. He stared at the *Lodestar*. The human starship was fleeing, and it was fast, but it could not escape the fleet of saucers for long. And there, beyond the *Lodestar*—a distant white light. A star.

The sun.

Abyzou magnified the view. He squinted. He saw it now, and his heart swelled. Around his neck, the hearts on his chain beat faster.

From here, it was just a speck. It glimmered in the darkness, pale blue. His destination. His promised land.

Abyzou grabbed a throttle and shoved it forward. His saucer increased speed. Behind him, the ten thousand others matched his pace. They stormed toward that distant world. Toward conquest and glory. Toward Earth.

—

The story continues in . . .

Earth Honor (*Earthrise* Book 8)

DanielArenson.com/EarthReborn

NOVELS BY DANIEL ARENSON

Earthrise:
Earth Alone
Earth Lost
Earth Rising
Earth Fire
Earth Shadows
Earth Valor
Earth Reborn
Earth Honor
Earth Eternal

Alien Hunters:
Alien Hunters
Alien Sky
Alien Shadows

The Moth Saga:
Moth
Empires of Moth
Secrets of Moth
Daughter of Moth
Shadows of Moth
Legacy of Moth

Dawn of Dragons:

Requiem's Song
Requiem's Hope
Requiem's Prayer

Song of Dragons:

Blood of Requiem
Tears of Requiem
Light of Requiem

Dragonlore:

A Dawn of Dragonfire
A Day of Dragon Blood
A Night of Dragon Wings

The Dragon War:

A Legacy of Light
A Birthright of Blood
A Memory of Fire

Requiem for Dragons:

Dragons Lost
Dragons Reborn
Dragons Rising

Flame of Requiem:

Forged in Dragonfire
Crown of Dragonfire
Pillars of Dragonfire

Misfit Heroes:

Eye of the Wizard
Wand of the Witch

Kingdoms of Sand:
Kings of Ruin
Crowns of Rust
Thrones of Ash
Temples of Dust
Halls of Shadow
Echoes of Light

Standalones:
Firefly Island
The Gods of Dream
Flaming Dove

KEEP IN TOUCH

www.DanielArenson.com
Daniel@DanielArenson.com
Facebook.com/DanielArenson
Twitter.com/DanielArenson

60250730R00241

Made in the USA
Middletown, DE
28 December 2017